TAKEN

THE TAKEN SERIES
BOOK ONE

E. C. RODERICK

Sandy Pier Press

ALSO BY E. C. RODERICK

TAKEN — Book 1

Hummingbirds Know Where to Fly — Book 2

The Pulse of My Heart — Book 3

For all inquiries about this book contact:
E. C. Roderick
P.O. Box 453035
Los Angeles, CA 90045
www.ecroderick.com

Cover Design: Mary Ann Smith

Editor: Tiffany Tyer

Library of Congress Control Number: 2021913445

ISBN 978-1-7374357-1-6 (paperback)

ISBN 978-1-7374357-0-9 (ebook)

ISBN 978-1-7374357-2-3 (hardback)

Publisher: Sandy Pier Press
Los Angeles, California

PIRACY NOTICE

For Thel, Erika, and Alan

TAKEN

Time is an illusion

—Albert Einstein

PROLOGUE

I love the ocean. But it's dangerous. It's tempestuous and tranquil at the same time. It's expansive, and it seems the earth suddenly ceases to exist at the brink of the horizon, where nothing else can be seen as water turns into sky.

The light cobalt-blue sky begins from the water and spreads like a canopy high overhead as the bright sun beams down on me. It's the end of April, and the hot, dry summer is not yet upon us. It's midday, and there's a light breeze that stirs my pink polka-dot ribboned straw hat. I glance at the pier to my right, seeing the large Ferris wheel rotating above, and then return my gaze to the front, watching them play together in the sand at the edge of the folding aquamarine waves as they crash and lap up to their little feet. I decide to pace closer toward the shoreline and sit on my beach towel beneath the sun umbrella, just watching.

My small son turns from the bucket of sand he has just emptied over his damp feet as his wet, gilded head glistens under the sun and waves at me while I watch him and his sister together from a slight distance. I wave back, happy to see them playing, when my daughter, the same age as he, rushes toward the incoming wave to catch the ocean in her sand pail. Her damp locks reflect the sunlight and shine like polished onyx.

I look past them as the waves surround their ankles, and my vision ceases at the edge of the horizon where the earth ends. I remember what it is like to be at the edge of the world. Where everything seems to suspend in zero gravity right before the plummet. All that I know vanishes right before my eyes as I'm falling helplessly into a black chasm. Falling... falling... falling... There's no control. I frenetically struggle to grasp onto something to stop from tumbling downward. But there is nothing to hold on to as the earth has opened and is swallowing me whole. There's no hope. There's only stark fear. It is free fall into the unknown right before imminent death.

I pray to God to save me.
Then He does as I open my eyes.
A man whom I have never met appears.
He calls me Ceisdein and Leannan.
He says he will find me.
So, I will tell you how he and I begin...

PART I
THE BEGINNING

CHRISTMAS

2017

CHAPTER 1

L os Angeles International Airport

"Now don't forget to call when you get there," Mom said as we got out of the car in front of the airline terminal.

"Yeah, Mom," I said.

"Your grandfather will be waiting for you in Cheyenne when you get there, as you know, so don't forget to call us once you're at the ranch."

"I know. I won't forget," I said. Dad rushed to get my luggage out of the trunk of his Audi sedan.

"And don't forget to call when you arrive in New York at your Aunt Aidia's," Dad said, coming around the car toward me.

"Sure," I said. He passed my luggage to me. I took it and released the handle so I could easily roll the bag.

"Give your dad a kiss, Sweet Pea," he requested naturally. It didn't matter to my parents that I was a full-fledged adult woman with a medical career. To them, I was still their sixteen-year-old girl. I didn't mind it, really. We were a close-knit family and cared about each other. He gave me a kiss on the side of my head and then tapped my nose.

"All right, Mom," I said as I turned toward her. We exchanged hugs and kisses.

"Here, you'll want this, I'm sure." She reached inside the car and gave me my messenger bag.

"Oh yeah, thanks," I said, grateful that she remembered it.

"Tell Kyle to give us a call too before we leave for our trip. Your brother is always missing for far too long. I can never get a hold of him these days."

"All right, I'll tell him," I said.

"Good. Give him and Dakota hugs and kisses from us, and wish them a Merry Christmas from us too," Mom said.

"I will," I agreed.

"We're going to miss you kids for the holidays this year," Dad said.

"Don't worry about us. You and Mom just go ahead and have a nice time in Hawaii. You haven't had a vacation together since I don't know when. It's long overdue."

"I'm still concerned, you know. Are you sure you don't want to come with us instead?" Mom asked.

"No, definitely not. Stop worrying about me. I'm fine," I insisted. Mom sighed, looking at me with some skepticism.

"You're sure?" she pressed.

"Yeah, I'm sure." She didn't believe me. She knew a lie when she heard one; being a former prosecutor, she could unravel anyone—especially her kids. But she didn't press anymore and seemed to let her troubled thought go.

My mom, Bernadette Seveine Engle Esperanza, was a woman with a pleasant disposition. Especially when she decided to quit her longtime career as a federal attorney to instead become a law professor at UCLA.

My dad, Leonardo Miguel Cielo Esperanza, had a relatively friendly, easygoing disposition—particularly for being an army veteran. He served three tours in Vietnam as a field trauma surgeon before I was born and did a stint in the First and Second Gulf Wars until he ultimately settled as a burn specialist at the VA hospital here in LA. Now my parents have settled comfortably as a retired couple, living in the same house they have had for five decades in Santa Monica.

"She'll be just fine, Bernadette," Dad encouraged, assuaging Mom. But he knew otherwise too. "You better get going, Sweet Pea—don't want to miss your flight."

I glanced at my phone and caught the time. The plane would be boarding soon, and I could see through the terminal windows that the line through security was already long. It was going to take a while to get through it before I reached my departure gate.

"Okay, yeah, I better go," I said, tucking my phone inside my coat pocket. I gave my parents one more hug and kiss before leaving them, then darted through the automatic glass doors and inside the terminal.

After scanning my e-ticket and easily checking myself into my flight, which helped me bypass the long line at the airline counter, I staked out my place at the end of the security line. I anxiously waited in line with everyone else who was departing before I finally entered the security checkpoint. Passing through the metal detector, I shoved my toes back inside my red pumps and grabbed my carry-on luggage. I trotted toward the correct airline gate just in time to board my flight headed to Cheyenne. I was making a pit stop in Wyoming to visit my grandfather and his wife before arriving at my final destination in New York City.

After pushing my suitcase inside the overhead compartment on board the airplane, I was happy to finally take my seat. I tucked my messenger bag beneath the seat in front of me and retrieved my phone from my coat pocket to check my messages. While waiting for everyone to board the plane, I sent out a couple of emails to my close colleagues at the pediatric medical practice we shared. I also texted my brother, Kyle, who lived in

Manhattan with his wife, Dakota. I was very much looking forward to the visit, since we hadn't seen each other in a little over a year. After texting, I browsed the Web to further pass the time before the plane was ready to depart.

Noticing that it was going to be a full flight as passengers continued streaming into the cabin, I knew that I wasn't going to have the luxury of an open seat next to me as I glanced at the crowded aisle. A pleasant middle-aged, beachy couple moved awkwardly down the aisle with their young son, their hands full between the young child they were minding and the carry-on luggage they were holding. Their child appeared to be approximately four years old, and he was cute as a button with plump pink cheeks, big brown eyes, and slightly long, wavy auburn hair nearly touching his shoulders. His parents seemed to have their hands curiously full with him as they passed by my seat. The toddler boy was quite expressive and communicative while he asked his father all sorts of questions about flying on an airplane. It seemed that it was the boy's first flight. He was evidently amazed by his surroundings, and between his tiny tightly gripping fingers was a pin of airline wings that the captain had given him the minute the family had boarded.

Watching the family pass by made me think about my own circumstances. My child probably would have been a few months younger than this cute little boy walking by me now if the accident hadn't occurred. It had been three and a half years since it happened, and not a day went by that I didn't lament and dwell on it. The sadness at times was unbearable. So when I could, I forced the memory of my unexpected tragic loss out of my mind, not wanting to be reminded of it.

"Hi," a young man said, appearing to be about my age, as he lifted his carry-on baggage up into the overhead compartment.

"Hi," I replied modestly, interrupted in my thoughts as I observed him close the compartment door. He proceeded to sit in the aisle seat next to me. He was noticeably attractive, with a slightly chiseled face, dark-brown hair, and blue eyes.

"Thought I was going to miss my flight. I should've just shown up in boxers—would've made it through security a lot quicker, I'm sure," he joked.

"Yeah, I guess so." I laughed a little. "But you might have been arrested for indecency, and then you really would've missed your flight."

"Yeah," he chuckled. "Enjoying the friendly skies is long gone, unfortunately."

"Yeah."

"Oh well," he said, shrugging his shoulders. "Such a long time ago, it seems."

"It does seem long ago. And we aren't that old."

"I know." He lightly chuckled as he fastened his seat belt, ready to go. "But I always sound old, though, whenever I fly."

"Oh." I smiled.

"I liked it better when I was a kid."

"Yeah?"

"Yeah. Everything was easier, straightforward and fun. Not like it is today with so many obstacles in the way. I'm wondering when they'll start asking me for my ID to buy a cup of coffee," he said ironically.

"Hopefully not before we land," I said.

"Yeah, no kidding," he responded with a grin.

The door at the front of the plane had been latched shut, and one of the flight attendants began speaking over the intercom. While the flight attendant was giving instructions, the plane jarred a little as it started backing away from the terminal and taxied out onto the tarmac. My neighbor retrieved his phone from his pocket and checked the time. He then placed his phone on his lap, and I gazed out the window as we rode down the runway. There were several planes ahead of us waiting to move, so we waited for a little while before taking off. The flight attendants had already taken their seats, and the cabin was quiet from further announcements, leaving passengers to speak quietly among themselves.

"So, are you from Wyoming?" my neighbor asked.

"No," I said. "I'm from LA. I'm visiting my grandfather and his new wife there."

"Oh, I see. Should've known," he said.

"Why?" I asked curiously.

"You're too pretty a girl to be from there," he said.

"What?" I asked awkwardly. "Well, I'm sure there are plenty of pretty girls there too."

"None like you, I can tell ya," he said confidently as he shook his head a bit.

"Yeah? How do you know?"

"I'm from there."

"Are you?" I responded surprisedly.

"Yeah. I was born there. Lived there my whole life until I went to college."

"Really?"

"Yeah."

"So, where did you go to college?"

"I went to Cal Tech and studied computer engineering. I work for Sony now as a programmer," he said.

"Do you work at the studio in Culver City?"

"Yep."

"Oh," I said, impressed.

"How about you?"

"I'm a pediatrician. I share a practice in Santa Monica with some colleagues of mine from medical school."

"That's great. Where did you go to med school?" he inquired.

"Harvard," I said.

"Harvard?"

"Yeah."

"Wow, nice," he said. "I'm Jim, by the way." He introduced himself and stretched out a large hand for me to shake.

"I'm Sylvina," I said, shaking his smooth hand.

"That's a beautiful name," he remarked.

"Thank you," I said.

"Well, it's nice to meet you," he said.

"Nice to meet you too," I replied politely.

"Oh," he said, hesitating briefly. "I should've known."

"Known what?"

"Your husband's a lucky man." He noticed the sparkling platinum bands on my wedding ring finger. His eyes locked on to the flawless two-carat, cushion-cut pink diamond glittering in the sunlight coming through the window beside me.

"Thank you," I said demurely. I didn't reveal the fact that I was a widow. Instead, I chose to leave the impression as it was because in my heart I was still married, and I wanted it to remain that way. Coping with the loss of my husband was something that remained at the forefront of my consciousness every day, and I didn't know if I could ever move beyond the void it had created in my life.

My travel companion didn't have much else to say after he observed the ring on my finger, except for a few humorous comments here and there that we both got a chuckle out of. I spent most of the time in flight listening to music on my phone, working a little on my laptop, and napping. Overall, the flight was comfortable, except for a bout of light turbulence, which bounced and rocked the plane a bit like a small roller coaster. The jarring didn't last for long, though, and the rest of the flight was smooth.

After several hours, we landed easily, and I disembarked, wishing my traveling companion a nice farewell.

When I arrived at my grandfather Ed's sprawling Wyoming ranch, I was happy to be reunited with him and his new wife, Julie. They placed me in a nice guest bedroom for my brief visit, where I could glance out the windows and view the Grand Tetons in the background. The snowcapped mountains were toned in hues of cool gray and lavender against a cloudless light Prussian blue sky, and the earth seemed calm but formidable. The scene was captivating, and it inspired me to wonder about my true place in the world. I often thought about it when I was alone since I had lost my husband and infant to an untimely death. But I thought about what had happened to me even more so now, since the awe-inspiring environment surrounding me was still and quiet, removed from the noise of everyday distractions consuming my mind back at home.

I wasn't sure how I was going to get through this holiday season, as I turned away from the windows feeling bereft of happiness.

~

Today. New York City.

It was biting cold outside. I scurried in from the winter air as I rushed inside Dean & DeLuca Café in the Village. Dakota and I had planned to meet here for lunch, since it was close to the bookshop she owned. I glanced around the café for a table and spotted a couple of free seats in front of a large window. Dakota hadn't arrived yet, so I quickly grabbed the vacant seats and made myself comfortable.

Shortly, a waitress came up to me and took my order for hot cocoa and a peanut butter cookie. She was young and pretty, and seemed nice. She appeared to be about twenty years old, and was most likely a NYU student, I gathered. But, I thought to myself, why on earth would she have cut her blonde hair so short, spiked it up like a pineapple top, and dip-dyed it bright carmine? And what on earth possessed her to have pierced her nose and bottom lip with noticeable, small silver studs? I just didn't understand it. I also wondered about the black nail polish on her dainty fingers and the strange interlacing Celtic tattoo around her wrist. It never failed to baffle me why some girls her age would tarnish their attractive looks that way.

I shrugged mentally. Live and let live, I supposed.

"Okay," said the waitress as she took my order with a pleasant smile, then left me by the window.

The café was becoming packed with people. The lunch crowd had arrived. I sensed it was going to be a moment before the waitress would return with my order, so I picked up the stray *Newsweek* magazine laying on the empty chair next to me and started flipping through the pages. Before I started reading too far into one of the news articles, I pulled my phone out of my pocket to check the time: 12:10 p.m.

"Hey, sorry I'm late," Dakota said suddenly as she swept through the place and slid into the seat beside me.

"No problem. How are you?" I asked.

"Great, except frozen. I need a coffee or hot cocoa," she said.

"I've got hot cocoa coming."

"Sounds good. I think I'll order the same." She quickly flagged the waitress and ordered. "Did you also order lunch already?"

"Just a cookie," I said as our waitress left us.

"A cookie? Is that all?" she asked.

"I know that's bad, but I'm not too hungry."

"Still, you could have a salad or something."

"I know," I said.

"All right," Dakota said, and snatched the café menu from the middle of the table to look at it. "Okay, I've decided," she said, making a hasty decision. She just as swiftly returned the menu to the center of the table and proceeded to order for both of us when our waitress returned.

It was nice seeing Dakota again, and it was pleasant having lunch together like we often did when we were in college. She and I were best friends in school. I was thrilled when she told me that we were going to be sisters once my brother had proposed to her. I really enjoyed her company because she had a unique sense of humor, was carefree, and we had a lot in common. Her wry, mocking sense of humor always caught me off guard with laughter. She could always shed light on a grim situation and made me consider a less serious side to life. But the most important thing about Dakota was that she was extremely supportive of me when my husband died, and for that, I would always be grateful to her. She was my best friend, and she was my sister.

"So tell me. How are you doing?" she asked me as the waitress set piping hot cups of hot cocoa before us along with my cookie.

"All right, I suppose," I answered.

"That's a load of crap. I can tell just by looking at you," she said. "You look awful." One thing about Dakota was that she could always be depended on for her frankness. "What? Well, you do," she said, clearly observing the annoyance on my face.

"Thanks," I replied, rolling my eyes.

"Seriously, are you eating?"

"Am I eating? You mean am I going to eat here with you? Uh, obviously, yes," I said. Dakota frowned at me.

"Well, you're too thin. Nobody is gaunt on purpose," she said sarcastically.

"Do I look that thin?" I asked with a little concern.

"Maybe not that thin. But any thinner, you would," she answered honestly.

"I haven't been that hungry lately," I admitted. Dakota nodded contemplatively.

"Don't misunderstand me, Sylvie. You've always been beautifully thin. People would die to have your natural ballerina figure, but right now you're too thin. You need to eat—regularly."

"I do eat regularly. Now can we just leave it alone?"

"Fine, for now." We both took a sip of our hot cocoa. "So, are you dating anybody?" she asked as she set her mug on the glass tabletop.

"No."

"You're still not ready," she commented. Her tone was one of understanding rather than nosy persistence.

"No. I'm not," I replied honestly. She shrugged a little with a compassionate look.

"Maybe in time," she responded thoughtfully.

"I don't think so," I said certainly.

"I understand. But don't be so sure, because you never know how life will turn out."

"I know what you're saying. I hear you, but I just don't feel it."

"I'm not pushing you."

"No… I know."

Our waitress finally returned to our table with our order and carefully placed our food in front of us. She inquired if we needed anything else. Dakota and I were both satisfied, so our waitress retreated and we were left alone again.

"Did you visit your Aunt Aidia?" Dakota asked as she bit into her panini.

"Yeah."

"How is she?"

"Great. She gave me the recipe for her chocolate lava cake. I can't wait to try it out," I replied as I scooped up a bit of Chinese chicken salad onto my fork.

"Mmm… sounds good. Are you going to eat any of it once you make it?" Dakota asked. I gave her a quirky grin.

"Maybe," I said.

"Well, make sure you give me some when you make it."

"For sure."

"Promise me you'll make it when we get to my parents' house."

"Yeah, sure," I said, smiling.

"My parents are really excited to have all of us this year for Christmas."

"It should be nice," I agreed. "Is your sister and her family coming too?"

"Mm-hmm, they're arriving today from DC," she informed me. "Desiree is big as a house with her third child. They're driving. The plane was off-limits for her because of all the restrictions. It's a pain—especially with two- and three-year-old toddler boys."

"Yeah, I guess it would be," I said.

"I think they're having a boy again this time."

"Oh, that's nice."

"Yeah, well, we'll see. She's kinda got her hands full with two right now."

"I'm sure she'll be all right."

"She was hoping for a girl, though, to kinda offset the boys' energy." Dakota and I both laughed a little. "She and her husband have agreed that three is the limit."

"So they're not going to try for any more afterward for sure?" I inquired.

"No, they've made up their minds."

"Oh."

"Seriously. Isn't it amazing, though, how there are plenty of others who keep trying and trying until they get what they want?"

"I know."

"I assure you, that would never be me."

"Nor me," I agreed. Dakota lifted a knowing eyebrow and subtly nodded her head. "So, I take it you and my brother still don't see yourselves having kids?" I asked casually. Dakota stuffed her mouth full of her panini again and began chewing.

"Well," she started with a mouth full of her sandwich, "I'm not ready for that. But Kyle wants one."

"Does he?" I asked interestedly.

"Yeah. But I don't know."

"Why not?"

"I don't know..." she said as she chewed. "I like owning my own business. There's just so much to my bookshop that I really enjoy. Plus, I haven't gotten to the point yet where I can hire a good manager to look out for it when I'm not around," Dakota explained after she swallowed the food in her mouth.

"Oh." I understood. "So, you mean if you got to the point where your business allowed you more freedom, then you'd be ready for a child?"

"Well… I don't know. The thought of being solely responsible for an innocent human being kinda freaks me out a little. Besides, I still just like being able to hang out with our friends—go to a play or movie every once in a while, whenever I want to. I couldn't do that with a kid," Dakota said honestly.

"There are babysitters, you know?" I suggested.

"Sure there are. But how would you—" she interrupted herself.

"It's okay," I reassured.

"Well, I was just going to say, you're even busier than I am. I mean, you're a physician. How were you going to handle being a mom and a professional at the same time?" she asked.

"Our plan was that I was going to take some time off with the baby, then I'd go back to work," I answered.

"So, were you going to hire a nanny once you returned to work?" she inquired.

"No. We were going to leave the baby with my parents."

"Oh."

"Besides, I was also going to shorten my work week by a day, since I could do that with my practice."

"Oh," she said thoughtfully. "That sounds like a workable situation." I nodded a little. "You know, Kyle told me that men are at the mercy of women when it comes to having children."

"What do you mean?" I asked.

"That it's really women who decide when men can have children. Essentially, if we don't want to, then it's not happening—but if we do, then all of a sudden, there is a baby," she said.

"Hmm… That's interesting."

"It's true, isn't it?"

"Well, Matt and I both really wanted to."

"Yeah, but if *you* didn't want to, then would it have happened?" she asked, lifting her brow in question. I thought about it.

"I see your point," I replied.

"Exactly," she said. "Hey?"

"Hmm?" I took another bite of my salad.

"Not to abruptly change the subject, but have you packed yet? Because we're leaving tomorrow."

"I just have a few things left to put in my suitcase. I'm pretty much done."

"That's good, because I still need to pack everything before Kyle comes home. I need to close the shop early today to do that."

"What time does he want to leave tomorrow?" I inquired.

"Early. He wants to be out of town by seven at the latest, since we've got an all-day drive," she said.

"Okay," I said.

"Wanna hang out with me while I close up the shop? Keep me company while I pack?" she requested as her glance fell onto my figure skates resting by the window. "Oh, you went skating?"

"I was going to," I replied.

"Oh, okay, then go," she said instead.

"Well, sure, I can keep you company," I responded.

"No, no, it's okay, just go and have fun," she encouraged.

"Are you sure? Cause it's no big deal."

"Yeah, no, go skate. It'll be good for you."

"Okay."

"Which rink are you going to?"

"The Pond."

"Oh, it's nice there."

"Yeah. I'm only going for a couple hours. So I can still help you pack if you'd like."

"Yeah, that'd be great."

"Hey, do you think we could stop off at Amherst on the way and go to Atkins to get some of those cider doughnuts?" I asked eagerly.

"Mmm, of course! How could we not? I wouldn't think of driving through without stopping," Dakota said excitedly.

"I wish we had enough time to visit our campus. It would be so nice to walk around," I said, reminiscing.

"I know, like old times."

"Yeah."

"I loved Mount Holyoke."

"Me too. It seems like I was just there yesterday."

"Please don't remind me," I said ironically.

"Spare me. You look like a kid still," Dakota scoffed. "So, yes, we'll definitely stop for those doughnuts."

"Yum."

On the heels of our conversation, we agreed that I would meet her back at her home at four o'clock.

CHAPTER 2

I liked skating at the Pond in Bryant Park. It was less crowded, and the rink wasn't too small. I was listening to a suite by Bizet on my phone and lost myself in the spontaneous choreography amid a camel layback combination spin. I made several combination jumps comprising of a triple axel, double flip, and double lutz, followed by a double toe loop. When the section of the Carmen suite I was listening to ended, I decided to warm down with practicing my edges around the rink. As I curved my blades, edge by edge into the ice, I thought I heard someone calling my name, and I stopped for a moment.

"Sylvie?" said a tall, slender, effeminate middle-aged man skating toward me. He had a shortly trimmed mustache and beard. He was vigorously waving at me as he approached.

"Yeah?" I said cautiously as I watched him approaching me, taking note of his black turtleneck and matching athletic pants. He was also accompanied by a much shorter man who stood at the height of his shoulder.

"Sylvie? Is that you?" the tall man called out to me again. I stood still, caught off guard as I stared at him. "Oh my God! It *is* you!" he expressed excitedly, grabbing and pulling me into his arms with a big embrace.

"Keith?" I said, stunned, as I stood looking again at him once he released me from his friendly hug.

"Yeah!"

"Oh my God! I can't believe it!" I replied, shocked. I recognized him from a long time ago when we were friends.

"I know!" he exclaimed breathlessly as he placed his gloved hand over his heart.

"What are you doing here?" I asked confusedly, equally glad to see him.

"Well, I could ask *you* the same thing!" he replied.

"I know—well, I'm here for Christmas. I'm visiting my brother and sister-in-law. We're actually driving up to the Berkshires tomorrow to celebrate Christmas with my sister-in-law's family," I explained.

"Oh, how *sweet*," he said. "Isn't that sweet, Ricky?" Keith turned to his friend, who was dressed in dark denim jeans and a black peacoat with the collar turned up over the burgundy cashmere scarf tucked around his neck.

"Sounds nice," his friend said amiably.

"Oh, this is Rick, my better half. Rick, this is Sylvina. We were friends way back when," Keith said, introducing us.

"Nice to meet you," I said.

"Nice to meet you too," Rick said, holding out his hand for me to shake. "You never told me that you had such gorgeous friends."

"I know, she could be a model. I used to tell her that all the time. So, did you listen to me?" Keith replied cheerfully.

"I'm afraid not," I said.

"No wonder I haven't seen you on the cover of *Vogue*," he joked.

"So, how do you two know each other?" Rick asked.

"We used to skate at the same rink back in LA," Keith said.

"Yeah," I said.

"Oh?" Rick said.

"Let's see, how long ago was that?" Keith asked.

"Oh gosh, it has to be about thirteen years ago—at least," I answered.

"God, has it been that long?" Keith responded dramatically.

"Yeah, it has."

"How crazy is that? Where did the time go?" he asked.

"I don't know," I replied.

"Did you compete too?" Rick inquired.

"No," I said.

"Well, she should have," Keith countered. "She was *extremely* good."

"I don't know about that," I said self-consciously.

"*Stop!* Yes, you were too," Keith insisted.

"Well, you're the one who won three national championships, right?" I replied.

"Well, what can I say," Keith teased.

"There you go," I kidded back.

"How 'bout that," he replied, grinning.

"So, how did you guys meet?" I asked.

"We met in South Beach through an acquaintance. I moved there and didn't have a friend in the *world*. I thought I wanted to live there, but I really missed LA. I was going to move back, except I met Ricky. It was love at first sight," Keith explained.

"That's nice," I said. "So, are you guys on vacation or something—for the holidays?"

"Oh, no. You see, Ricky here is in fashion, and he acquired this new position as a buyer for Saks," Keith informed me.

"Wow," I said, impressed.

"I know! Isn't that great?" Keith said.

"So you live here now," I said.

"We do."

"How do you like it?"

"I didn't think I would, but I *love* it."

"That's nice," I replied.

It was interesting seeing him again after so many years. He had lost a large portion of his hair and was bald at the top of his head. A ring of shortly cropped salt-and-pepper gray auburn hair encircled the sides of his head. He had a closely trimmed mustache and beard matching his cropped hair. He appeared somewhat heavier due to age, and his cheeks had filled out a little around his facial hair, making him look slightly like a walrus. A couple of wrinkles on his brow and crow's feet around his hazel eyes had replaced the snappy, spry urban skating whiz kid I remembered as an adolescent.

"So, what about you?" Keith asked.

"I'm a pediatrician," I said.

"No way! You're a doctor?" he asked, waving a hand over his mouth in surprise.

"Yes, I am," I responded.

"Check this girl out! You're amazing. Isn't she amazing?"

"Amazing," Rick agreed simply.

"You have to have a lot of brains for that. You can't be stupid," Keith said frankly.

"No, you can't be stupid," Rick agreed, causing me to smile a little.

"You are such a smart girl, Sylvie," Keith said thoughtfully.

"Thanks," I said humbly.

"Well, that's great. It's just wonderful. Caring for children is such an important contribution to our world. Isn't she a good girl?" Keith asked.

"It appears she would be a good girl," Rick echoed.

"She is, let me tell you—heart of gold. I know from experience," Keith said, scrunching his nose up in a grin.

"Well, thanks," I replied modestly.

"Hey, why don't you join us for some coffee? We were just about to get some," he said.

"Okay," I accepted gladly.

"Great, now we can *really* catch up," Keith said enthusiastically. So, we skated off the ice, with Rick less skillfully following behind us. There was a local café located just outside Bryant Park, which we ducked into, leaving the winter chill outside. We sat easily together for a while around a small coffee table, catching up on our lives over the past thirteen years. Keith told me all about his traveling adventures as a professional ice-skater. He also revealed how he recently quit the exhaustive tours for the serenity and simple pleasure of coaching young champion hopefuls. Compared to him, my life seemed less adventurous when I told him about my long academic career to become a pediatrician.

"But I thought you were in an aspiring rock band at one point," Keith said.

"Right," I replied, reluctant to recount the memory only because it was a silly idea when I was in high school.

"You were in a band?" Rick inquired, impressed.

"Yeah, she was," Keith answered for me.

"It was my brother's band," I clarified.

"But you were the lead singer, weren't you?" Keith asked.

"And I played guitar," I said.

"That's right! And the fiddle! Now I remember," Keith said.

"Really?" Rick inquired interestedly.

"Yeah," I said, amused by their reactions.

"Wait, what was the band called again?" Keith asked, trying to remember.

"Blushing Bride," I recalled.

"Oh my God! That's right!" Keith laughed.

"You weren't an all-girl band, then?" Rick asked, entertained.

"No, I was the only girl in the band," I said.

"Clever," Rick replied, grinning widely. "So, how old were you when you were rocking out?"

"I was fifteen," I replied, taking a sip of my hot pumpkin spice coffee.

"I can't believe it's been that long since we last saw each other," Keith said.

"I know," I agreed. "I left the band when I got into college. But my brother stuck with it for a lot longer. They got another girl singer and worked the LA scene for a while until my brother graduated college, decided to get married, and quit. Now he's a stock analyst on Wall Street."

"A stock analyst? That's a bit of a difference, wouldn't you say?"

"Yeah, I know. His friend's dad got him the job."

"Interesting. Is he still doing that?"

"Mm-hmm. Fortunately for him, he was able to get another job after the market crashed, but a lot of his coworkers were laid off."

"Lucky for him."

"Yeah, I guess it helps knowing someone."

"Seems to be the case with everything." Rick sighed.

"Hmm," Keith responded. "So where are you living in LA?"

"Um, Santa Monica," I replied.

"Nice," Keith said.

"It's conveniently close to work," I said as I removed my gloves to grip my coffee cup better while I sipped from it.

"What a gorgeous ring!" Rick expressed, his eyes instantly seizing onto my wedding band.

"You didn't tell me you got *married*!" Keith interjected, fully captivated.

"Check out that rock! Holy cow!" Rick admired. "I'd recognize a Tiffany's ring anywhere. May I?"

"Sure," I said, letting him take my hand to see the ring. It was a flawless two-carat purplish-pink cushion-cut diamond set uniquely in a white diamond-studded platinum engagement band. The platinum wedding ring itself was a shared setting with a full circle of alternating diamonds and pink sapphires. Matt had completely surprised me with his proposal when he gave me this ring. I remembered every aspect of that happy, brilliant day when he asked me to marry him as if it had been only a minute ago. My heart warmed wistfully, and I felt my face relax a little with a distant grin as I thought about how joyful he was when I said yes to him.

"Isn't that simply divine?" Rick commented, highly impressed, as he gently turned the ring around my finger with his well-manicured, smooth, small fingers. "Your husband must do well."

"Hmm," I muttered, retrieving my hand from his light clasp as I forlornly glanced at my ring. Actually, my late husband wasn't as wealthy as the ring might have portrayed. He'd made a decent living as an anthropology professor at UCLA and had a newly published book listed on *The New York Times* best-seller list a month before he died. So, whenever I glanced now at my wedding band, it had immeasurable value to me; I vowed the day he died that I would never remove it from my finger—just as I had done the day we got married.

"So, when did you get married?" Keith inquired curiously.

"Four and a half years ago."

"Really?"

"Mm-hmm."

"Well, why didn't you say anything?" he asked. I inadvertently changed the mood of our conversation as I hesitated answering him.

"You know what? It's okay," Rick interrupted understandingly, and gave Keith an uncertain glance.

"What?" Keith protested.

"Well, it's obvious she's suffered a loss. I'm sorry, I hope you don't mind my observation," Rick said to me sympathetically.

"It's all right," I said.

"I'm so sorry. I didn't know," Keith said regretfully.

"It's okay," I said.

"Rick is clairvoyant. I bet you didn't know that," Keith said. I grimaced doubtfully. "It's true," he assured me. "It just gets on my nerves sometimes—that's all."

"What?" I said confusedly, turning to Rick. "Is that really true?"

"I just have a sense about things, that's all," he said dismissively.

"What do you mean?" I asked.

"It's just that sometimes—I don't know… I just get an overwhelming sense about things," he replied simply.

"Like, you can see things? Like ghosts or the future?" I inquired skeptically, although I kept my pleasant demeanor.

"No, nothing like that—necessarily," Rick responded.

"Then like what?" I asked.

"It's more like a strong feeling," he said.

"Oh… Are you ever right about your feelings?" I inquired.

"Oh, yeah, he's good," Keith interjected positively.

"Can you give me an example?" I asked.

"Okay." He considered carefully. "Well, you seem to me to be a naturally good-hearted, spirited individual."

"Okay, that's an easy supposition," I agreed, regarding myself.

"Except right now, I can see that you're really sad. You've experienced something enormous in your life that has landed you in a spiritually depressed place," he continued. "I don't know what it is, specifically, that put you there, but that's the condition of your aura at this moment in your life, that I see," he explained.

"Oh…" was all I could think of to say as I remained nearly unresponsive and silently stunned by his perception.

"Is that true?" Keith asked me seriously, reading my obvious expression.

"Um—I lost my husband three and a half years ago. This time of year is just a hard time for me to deal with being without him," I said.

"Oh my God," Keith replied sympathetically.

"He died—unexpectedly. It was a car accident. We were only

married a year before it happened. The driver was drunk when he hit my husband and fled the scene. The police eventually caught the guy though." I didn't want to explain any further, because there was no point. I didn't manage grief very well, and I didn't wish to revisit the trauma that had landed me in this position of feeling alone and despondent with missing the man I loved. "But my patients need me, so work keeps me busy. I don't know what I'd do without it. I'm sure I'd be a wreck otherwise."

"Oh, honey, I'm so, so sorry. I had no idea," Keith said compassionately. He gently covered my hand with his.

"I'm sorry for your loss too," Rick responded carefully as well. A silent, cumbersome pause ensued for a moment. "Would you mind if I looked at your hands for a minute?" Rick began again cautiously, appearing contemplative.

"Um—okay," I replied awkwardly, feeling skeptical. He reached for my hands, turning my palms faceup, and delicately pulled them toward himself. He quietly gazed at them as he glanced back and forth between my two hands, taking his time to study my palms. The minutes seemed to drag by as he quietly examined my hands. I wondered when he was going to finish scrutinizing them, as his occasional grimaces were beginning to make me feel uncomfortable. At one point, he appeared very puzzled, but there were a few instances where he lifted his brow, seeming pleased.

"So?" I interrupted finally. "What do you see?"

"Well, for starters," Rick began, "from what I can tell, you're going to lead a very full life."

"Okay," I responded, inwardly unimpressed as I truly doubted him.

"There are definitely children in your life that are your own. Three of them, I'm sure," Rick discerned, carefully looking and feeling my hands between his soft fingers.

"That's impossible," I countered.

"Don't give up," he replied, lifting his dark-brown eyes back to me. Then, he seemed to have a second thought enter his mind when he returned his examining gaze to my palms. "But it's really weird."

"What?" Keith chimed in curiously.

"Well, looking at everything is confusing. It's all jumbled up," Rick observed with a puzzled look on his face.

"What do you mean?" I asked.

"The lines say one thing in one area, and then they are contradicting in another area. I'm reading that you're extremely adventurous," Rick noted.

"Adventurous?" I remarked dubiously.

"Mm-hmm," Rick said confidently.

"I'm hardly that," I said.

"That's no surprise, because then I'm reading the opposite. I also see that there are two marriages in your life," he observed.

"Two?" I questioned.

"Well, why not? Anything's possible, if you're open to it, right?" Keith interjected. I glanced at him wordlessly, thinking how skeptical I was of this palm-reading business.

"I don't get it. It's like it's saying that you were born, and then you weren't born, then you were born again," Rick explained, frowning a bit.

"Like what? She was reincarnated or something? Or had a near-death experience?" Keith asked Rick. My heart suddenly skipped a couple of beats at this supposition, because in fact I *had* been close to death at one point in my life as a consequence of the car accident.

"Well, look. Look at this," Rick said, pointing to my right palm. His index finger followed along the longest line at the center of my palm. "This is the life line right here."

"Uh-huh," Keith replied, looking closely.

"Okay, now, hers, you see here where it starts?" Rick pointed it out on my hand.

"Yeah," Keith said.

"It goes down like usual, but about a third of the way down, it stops—and then it picks up again after this gap here." Rick examined my hand thoroughly.

"Uh-huh," Keith muttered, engrossed.

"So, if you continue to follow it down her hand another third of the way down, it breaks again. You see there's a second gap before it continues to the end at the top of her wrist," Rick observed.

"What does that mean?" Keith inquired curiously.

"I'm not sure," Rick replied thoughtfully. "Now, if you look at her left hand, the line is nearly identical to her right one."

"So what does that mean?" I decided to ask.

"Well, it's unusual to see both hands so closely resembling each other," Rick stated.

"Really?"

"Yeah, because most of the time, there are differences in both hands, which provide for some change in your life as it goes on. But yours is expressing that your life is fated," Rick explained.

"*Fated?*" I asked, frowning somewhat, since I entirely disagreed with the notion of predestination.

"That's right," Rick replied certainly.

"I hope not bad?" Keith said uneasily.

"Yeah," I agreed.

"No, I don't get anything bad from it—actually, the opposite. There's a lover," Rick said.

"Ooh, really? A lover, huh?" Keith asked.

"Okay," I said unbelievingly as I retrieved my hands from Rick. "There's no lover," I assured them. Keith and Rick exchanged glances when my phone suddenly rang.

"I'm sorry, I didn't mean to offend you," Rick said.

"No, no—it's okay," I replied easily. "Please excuse me while I answer this." I was secretly relieved as I grabbed my ringing phone from my coat pocket.

"No problem," Keith said. I quickly answered my phone, and it was Dakota calling me to find out where I was, wondering if I was still going to help her pack, since the day was getting late.

"I'm sorry, I've lost track of time," I said after I hung up my phone and tucked it away in my coat. "I regret that I have to go."

"Do you?" Keith asked, appearing disappointed.

"Yeah, I've gotta meet my sister-in-law now."

"Sure, I understand," Keith said, and then he asked to put his contact information in my phone. So I gave him my phone, and we mutually exchanged contact information then returned our phones to each other.

"It was nice meeting you," Rick said courteously to me as I gathered my belongings.

"Yes, it was nice meeting you too," I replied.

"Take care, Sylvie," Keith said, standing up from his chair to give me a hug. "Don't be a stranger."

"Okay," I agreed. "You take care too."

"I will."

"Have a safe trip," Rick said.

"Thanks," I responded before turning to go.

"Merry Christmas," Keith said.

"Merry Christmas," I replied. I ducked out of the warm coffee shop back into the windy, cold air and quickly hailed a taxi. I hopped into the inviting warmth of the cab, anticipating my arrival at my brother and Dakota's apartment. I removed my gloves from my hands as I instructed the cabdriver to head to Midtown to Madison and Eighty-Third Street. The driver proceeded to skillfully maneuver through bumper-to-bumper street traffic at the height of rush hour.

I glanced at my right hand resting on my knee and turned it over, thinking how ridiculous Rick's palm reading was. The idea of clairvoyance was illogical and improbable to me. But as I recalled the conversation, an unusual feeling came over me because there were a couple of things he had said with confidence that were true. He was keen in his insightful assessment of my normally cheerful disposition and the present depression I was experiencing. It was also ironic how Keith articulated Rick's suggestion of my near-death experience. I wondered how much of his palm reading was coincidental, and if any of it by some fluke could be true.

The taxi hit a pothole, making me jump in my seat a little and jarring me from my thoughts. I raised my eyes from my hands and peered out the window. People were fashionably bundled up in their black winter coats walking along the congested sidewalk. I spotted a young woman wearing a bright red empire-waist, knee-length peacoat and admired her coat while quickly putting Rick's silly palm reading into perspective, dismissing it for good.

WE LEFT the city the next morning a little later than our planned seven o'clock on the dot. It was the day before Christmas Eve, and the feeling of the festive season was palpable. Holiday decorations lined the streets, along with merrily embellished storefront windows all over Manhattan as we drove through the city and maneuvered our way to get onto Interstate 95 going north.

My brother was very nice to indulge my desire to stop off in Amherst to go to Atkins to get some of their delicious cider doughnuts. The journey through Western Massachusetts toward Amherst would take us a bit out of the way toward Williamstown. In this case, we were looking at eight hours drive time rather than if we drove up the New Jersey Turnpike and got on the Garden State Parkway going north, which would have been faster. Still, it was a good day for a drive, and we were going to enjoy the long ride—particularly once we exited the city. But getting to that point was grueling—we became stuck in gridlock traffic for a good three hours just to get out of the city. Both lanes going north moved slower than molasses in January due to the rush of Christmas travelers hurrying to leave town.

The traffic going southbound had grown congested, too, with last-minute holiday shoppers and commuters trying to get into town.

Still sleepy from getting up so early this morning, I decided to close my eyes as Kyle started the song *"High"* by The Cure on the stereo.

When I awakened, I realized that we had long since cleared the city and were now swiftly moving up Interstate Highway 91. I noticed that Dakota seemed to have fallen asleep also when I asked Kyle for our current location. He informed me that we were passing through Connecticut, and we were close to making a pit stop off the highway as he proceeded to take an exit ramp. Unfortunately, there was not much available for fine dining on a road trip, but the sight of fast food coming around the bend was always a welcomed sight when starving.

WE HAD DRIVEN THROUGH HARTFORD, Connecticut, and were well on our way north as we sped along the highway, making good time. In a few hours, we would arrive at our first destination, when at last we exited the highway into Northampton and took Bay Road just past Hampshire College toward Atkins. When we arrived at the unique country health-food store, Dakota and I eagerly rushed inside to pick up the long-awaited doughnuts along with some other flavorful snacks and treats.

Afterward, we set out on the road again, and once we were on Route 2 toward Williamstown, we were only a couple of hours away from our final destination. It had grown quiet inside the vehicle after the rush of sweets passed, and the smooth swaying of the ride lulled Dakota into another nap while I made myself comfortable again in the back seat admiring the changing woodland scenery. All the maple and birch trees were dormant with their barren branches reaching toward the cloudy sky. The evergreens remained thick with their viridian needles as they stood like winter guards scattered around the landscape.

When we entered the Berkshires, the terrain became more rugged as exposed basalt mountain faces trailed irregularly alongside the highway. As the land leveled out somewhat, we passed by a number of orchards and dairy farms. I had always liked the countryside; there was something I couldn't explain that was very serene and pleasant about it.

The sky had clouded over, and the weather was more frost-prone. It certainly appeared chilly, but it didn't seem like there was any wind outside. Kyle was listening to the region's Christmas forecast on satellite radio. According to the broadcast, the region had been experiencing several days' worth of gloomy cloud coverage with no precipitation. The cloudy overcast was projected to pass into crisp, partly sunny skies by Christmas day, with a temperature high of forty degrees Fahrenheit and a low of twenty degrees. I was glad to hear that the gray clouds would clear, and we were also lucky not to have any precipitation. However, I did reconsider that some light snow for Christmas would have been really nice too.

Route 2 took us right into the heart of town, and we soon passed through where Williams College was located. As we followed the route west taking us over several tributary streams from the Hoosic River, we passed a nice community of houses and the town's oldest church and cemetery. We continued driving up an incline, and within minutes we were driving alongside a stream up into the wooded mountains.

As we drove up the gradient due west, we entered into a sudden patch of fog where the road changed. The day had grown late, and the fog was unexpectedly thick, making it very difficult to see. We carefully crept through the mist, and within minutes we had safely cleared the fog bank.

The dashboard clock read four fifteen p.m., and the sun had just about gone down completely as twilight set in. Kyle kept his headlights on, and the road became invisible again at one point as we cleared another curtain of very thick fog. The landscape was now full of shadows with barren trees framing the highway.

After a few minutes, we turned off the main highway. Momentarily, the road let us out into a circular, stone-laid driveway facing the front of a nice, large, typical New England Colonial-era house with titanium white-painted clapboard siding and lampblack shutters. The lights were on inside, and white icicle Christmas lights hung from the edge of the multi-gable roof around the entire front of the large house. Kyle gently awakened Dakota from her snooze, and we eagerly stepped out of the SUV. We were glad to finally stretch our cramped limbs and happy to have arrived at our final destination.

The frosty air outside smelled smoky from the chimney mixed with pine and enhanced the cheery feeling of the season. Dakota took the key hidden beneath the big flower pot on the stone porch beneath the portico between the fluted ionic columns and proceeded to open the wreath-covered front door. An instant rush of warmth combined with the smell of pot roast, garlic mashed potatoes, seasoned mixed vegetables, and apple pie came from the kitchen. Suddenly, a gust of excited voices rang out from various locations within the house followed by plenty of happy family faces headed toward us. Dakota's whole family was there to greet us with abundant warmth and affection.

She came from an emotional family never short of affection. Her mother, Rita, was an average height, slender woman. She was an eccentric redhead Irish gypsy abstract-expressionist artist, who avidly delved into holistic health. Mrs. Rita Rockport even had a specially made Zen room designed for herself where she could privately practice yoga and meditate three times a day. An attractive older woman who had exotic mannerisms, she appeared fun-spirited, but reminded me of a haphazard witch with her shoulder-length curly hair mussed every which way around her head. Also, the loud geometric pattern on the long, flowing silk house robe she was wearing added to her theatrical effect, and strongly reminded me of Dakota both in appearance and personality.

Dakota's father, on the contrary, was quite the antithesis. There wasn't much to say about him. Mr. Eric Rockport, unlike his wife, was serious and dry but had a witty sense of humor. His dark-brown eyes were warm and inviting, particularly when he smiled or laughed. He was a serious economic professor at the local college, standing tall and lanky at six feet, two inches, with a narrow face and short, thick snow-white hair that came close to grazing his ears.

Desiree, Dakota's one and only sibling, resembled their father with her light, straight sandy hair, coffee-brown eyes, fair complexion, and long face. She was a couple of years older than Dakota and shared their mother's offbeat, hilarious sense of humor. But she also had her father's logical, dry, and good-natured wit.

Desiree's husband, Miles, was nice and curious looking. He was a tall, thin, young forty-year-old man with short dark-brown hair cropped close to his head, parted on the left side, and it appeared lacquered like the character Alfred E. Neuman on the front cover of *Mad* magazine—freckles and all. The former FBI agent had recently turned over a new leaf to become his own boss as a carpenter designing fun and whimsical furniture for children's rooms. Desiree, who was a very eight-months-pregnant woman, seemed not quite relaxed with her husband's new business decision, since his income would no longer come from a stable source. But he yearned to work for himself and insisted it was the perfect time to start a business instead.

Finally, Desiree and Miles's two boys, Luke who was five years old and Cameron who was three years old, were rambunctious, free-spirited, happy little boys—especially given the evidence of chocolate frosting currently on their faces. Apparently, to their grandmother's theatrical dismay, during the excitement of our arrival, the boys had snuck into the cake in the kitchen and caused a comical stir around the house.

The Rockports were a warm and welcoming family and easily made me feel right at home. They gave me the guest bedroom on the second floor at the back end of the house next to the boys' room. At first, I wondered warily how it was going to be being placed in a room in close proximity to the young boys; I was sure to hear their continuous goofing around and clamoring next door as I began settling pleasantly into my room.

After an enjoyable dinner with the family, it was nice to finally relax in my room with some peace and quiet for the night once the children were tucked into bed.

CHAPTER 3

The next day was Christmas Eve, and it was going to be another active, full day. The family spent the entire day preparing for their annual Christmas party. Mrs. Rockport and her daughters slaved all morning and afternoon in the kitchen cooking delicious food they were going to add to the catered buffet. The boys and I gladly trimmed the tree and decorated the rest of the house, while Kyle, Miles, and Mr. Rockport chopped wood outside in the cold and shot the breeze with some quality beer.

After all the time-consuming preparations had been put into place, I could hear guests arriving from upstairs in my room while I was changing into my cocktail dress. Dakota's parents were known for throwing extravagant Christmas parties, where the entire college faculty had been invited along with their families.

After I had finished dressing for the party, I snuck through the back corridor toward the kitchen and unwittingly entered into an ongoing conversation between Dakota and her mom, to my discomfiture.

"*Mom!* Come on! Will you *just* stop already? You're driving me crazy!" Dakota exclaimed as I entered the kitchen.

"Oh, hi, Sylvie," Mrs. Rockport said nonchalantly as she suddenly noticed me entering the room.

"Hi," I replied awkwardly, watching Mrs. Rockport place a large crystal bowl on the island in front of Dakota, who was stirring the liquid contents of a sizable pitcher.

"Will you please tell my daughter here that it is time for her to stop being so selfish and give her mother some grandchildren?" Mrs. Rockport said, placing the nutmeg to the right of Dakota's pitcher. I frankly didn't know how to respond, so I didn't say anything.

"Mom!" Dakota said, irritated. "Not everyone wants what you want. Besides, you already have two obnoxious grandsons, with another bouncing whatever on the way. So stop with the pushing."

"Who's pushing? All I'm saying is that the clock doesn't last forever. You could hit menopause early, you know—as early as your forties. Did you know that? It happens, I should know," Mrs. Rockport said glibly. Dakota's eyes widened at the new information about her mother, and she appeared stunned.

"Well, I'll just do IVF if that should happen to me, and *if* I decide that I'm ready then," Dakota countered, using her mother's dismissive mannerism.

"Don't kid yourself, darling. That stuff is painful and has a low percentage for success," Mrs. Rockport criticized. Mrs. Rockport suddenly turned to me and clasped her heart. "Look at this girl," she said admiringly, then waved a maternal finger at me. "Now, don't you let yourself go to waste either, dear. You're too young and simply too gorgeous for that to happen—"

"Mom," Dakota interrupted.

"Look at this *face*," Mrs. Rockport continued, ignoring her daughter. "You have a rich and full life ahead of you, my dear

Sylvie. Keep an open mind and an open heart. I should do your chart."

"My chart?" I inquired, puzzled.

"Your astrological chart," Mrs. Rockport answered. "It's to help you gain a better understanding of yourself in terms of the stars."

"Oh," I replied cluelessly.

"Okay, Mom, enough already. Jeez!" Dakota interjected, annoyed, rolling her eyes as well. "It's one thing to harass your own daughter, but do you have to do it to my beloved sister-in-law too? C'mon, spare us! *Please*," Dakota pleaded. Mrs. Rockport sighed a little at her daughter, then she smiled at me.

"Lovely dress, dear," Mrs. Rockport said to me instead with an admiring expression.

"Yes, it is," Dakota agreed favorably. "You look amazing!"

"Thank you," I replied. "You both look very nice too."

"Oh, thank you, dear," Mrs. Rockport said. Mrs. Rockport did indeed look really well put together in her short cream silk embroidered jacquard, fitted kimono jacket, and matching smooth silk taffeta knee-length skirt. She looked considerably different from the night before when we first arrived. Her present appearance concealed the liberal, laissez-faire woman that she was and portrayed a more restrained, conservative woman suitable for a serious businessman's wife. She had straightened the wild curls on her head and pulled her hair back into an attractive bun. Her makeup was light and unassuming, which kept her appearance warm and accessible.

Dakota was always good-looking and even more so this evening dressed in a beautiful cotton-candy-pink silk organza cocktail dress. Her dress was pleated in tiers from the scoop neck tank-style top and flowed into a nice billowy skirt above the knee. The dress was lovely on her small, pretty figure. She said it had been her favorite dress from Carmen Marc Valvo's couture collection. And with her short red hair flipped up at the ends in layers at chin level and parted on the right just over pixie bangs that were clasped by a straight rhinestone barrette, she appeared vogue perfect.

"You know, my nephew, Nole—well, I've told him so much about you, and he has been wanting to meet you for a while," Mrs. Rockport told me elatedly.

"Mom, don't you even dare entertain the thought," Dakota quickly scolded her mother.

"Oh, *Dakota*," Mrs. Rockport chided back. "Now, you listen to me, Sylvie, he's very nice. I think you two might have a lot in common. He's a physician as well."

"I see," I replied, bewildered.

"He's a neurosurgeon at Columbia," Mrs. Rockport informed me optimistically.

"That's nice," I responded, dazed. I suddenly felt ambushed.

"Yes, and he loves to go to rock concerts," she said matter-of-factly.

"Oh," I replied.

"Actually, he said something about liking John Mayer or something like that," she said.

"Oh," I said.

"Mother, for crying out loud. I can't believe you're trying to set them up. In case you've forgotten, she's a grieving widow. Won't you show some respect?" Dakota interrupted, seeming quite annoyed and embarrassed by her mother.

"Yes, she's a widow. But *she's* not the one who died, is she? The world, in fact, *does* still go on," Mrs. Rockport replied bluntly.

"Yes, but you didn't ask her how she might feel about it," Dakota said, reaching for the bottle of bourbon in front of her to pour into her special eggnog mixture.

"Well, speak of the *devil*," Mrs. Rockport said abruptly, noticing her nephew entering through the doorway.

"Ask her about what?" he inquired sociably as he came toward us. Nole strode comfortably into the kitchen with both hands in his charcoal-gray trouser pockets. He seemed like a fairly nice guy. He was not significantly tall, but stood above average height at about six feet and had a reasonably handsome face. He was young, and I gathered he must be around the same age as Dakota and me. Although, his medium brown hair was already dusted with specks of gray along his hairline. His pale blue eyes sparkled as he smiled openly at all of us.

"*Nothing*, Nole," Dakota said to him as he stood near us.

"Ooh, it appears I've interrupted girl talk," he said light-heartedly.

"It's okay, forget it," Dakota replied, unbothered, and started pouring some bourbon into the large pitcher.

"Well, I'm going to leave you kids alone while I look for your dad, Dakota," Mrs. Rockport said, and swiftly left the kitchen.

"Shit." Dakota scowled suddenly.

"What's wrong?" I asked.

"There's no more bourbon," she said.

"There's no more anywhere in the house?" Nole asked.

"Yeah, there's no more. This was the last bottle. I had to steal it from Dad's office. I didn't pay attention to the amount left inside. I just grabbed it thinking I had enough," Dakota explained, dismayed.

"Well, maybe you can just buy a bottle from the bar," Nole suggested.

"No, it's not the same kind. I've seen what they have. I knew I should've gone to the store when I had the chance earlier today," Dakota said, frustrated.

"Well, I could go for you. It's no big deal," I offered.

"No, I couldn't ask you to do that," she replied.

"Really, I don't mind. I know how to get to Stop and Shop from here. North Adams is what? Only ten, fifteen minutes at the most away from here?" I replied.

"But it's dark out, and it could flurry, which will wind up taking you longer to get there and back," Dakota said.

"Well, she wouldn't go alone. I could go with her," Nole said. I suddenly glanced at him, and he smiled at me. I smiled at him in return. "I don't think we've been properly introduced. I'm Nole, by the way. Dakota's cousin."

"Right," I said, smiling awkwardly.

"And you're Sylvie," he said confidently.

"That would be me," I joked.

"It's nice to finally meet you. My aunt has told me some really nice things about you," he said.

"It's really nice to meet you also," I said politely in spite of feeling uncertain.

"Well, now that you two are acquainted, never mind you guys going to the store, it's okay. I'll just get Kyle to go. He won't mind. He knows the area well," Dakota said.

"Are you sure?" Nole asked.

"Yeah, it's okay. Thanks for offering. I appreciate it," she replied.

"Well, I'll go find Kyle, then," I said, volunteering.

"Oh, thanks," Dakota said, distracted by the special eggnog she was anxiously trying to make.

"Sure. Excuse me," I replied, and turned toward the threshold. I could feel her cousin watching me as I left the kitchen. I was relieved to make this escape, since I had not anticipated Mrs. Rockport's scheme to play matchmaker with me and her nephew.

I searched all over for my brother. When I finally found him, he was in the slightly crowded pool room with a large cigar in his mouth shooting pool balls across the table with three other male guests. I stood in the corner of the room watching him put several balls in the pockets as I waited for the best opportunity to seek him out among the slight crowd. When he finally sent the white ball into the back left corner pocket, I caught his attention with a wave. He proceeded to make his way toward me.

"Hey, what's up?" he asked when he approached.

"Can I borrow the keys to your car?" I heard myself ask spontaneously.

"What for?" he inquired.

"Dakota's out of bourbon for her eggnog, and I said I'd go to the store to get some more," I lied.

"Well, I'll go. You don't have to go," he said.

"I don't mind," I said honestly.

"Yeah, but it's dark and freezing out, and you could take a wrong turn or something," he said.

"You have GPS in your car, and I've also got it on my phone. So I can find my way. All I have to do is take the road back down the mountain to Main Street and stay on it. It'll take me right through town straight into North Adams. We passed Stop and Shop along the way as we were coming into Williamstown. I remember where it is," I informed him self-assuredly. Kyle looked at me unconvinced. "I won't ding your car. I promise," I added lightly. He narrowed his eyes and considered for a moment.

"All right," he replied reluctantly.

"Great," I said.

"You should be back within an hour—just in time for dinner," he said, calculating quickly.

"Don't worry. I'll be back in time to eat," I assured him.

"Be careful, it's snowing now," he warned.

"It is?"

"Yeah, the forecast changed. A couple of inches or so was forecasted tonight. So be careful driving."

"New England weather is so fickle," I commented.

"I know. So be careful on the road," he repeated.

"Okay," I said.

"Oh, and watch out for shopping carts—and don't park next to any junk cars," he insisted.

"Don't worry." I sighed.

"Seriously," he insisted again.

"Seriously," I agreed.

"All right. The keys are upstairs in our room in Dakota's knickknack dish on her vanity table," he informed me.

"Okay."

"If you're a second late, I'm calling the cops."

"Don't be ridiculous."

"I'm not kidding."

"I know you're not."

"Okay. The clock is ticking."

"Ticktock," I replied sarcastically. Kyle lowered his chin and gave me a scowling look.

"Just hurry up," he said impatiently.

"Well, stop talking to me and I will," I responded. I abruptly turned on the ball of my foot, heading out of the room back down the hallway for the back staircase.

I RETRIEVED my knee-length cream-colored empire-waist Rockwell wool coat from my room. After I found the car keys in Dakota's room, I snuck out of the house in a rush. My brother's vehicle reflected the driveway lights like an illuminated black stealth vehicle. I triggered the remote entry lock and hurried into the car, instantly turning on the engine. It didn't take long for the cabin to warm. I idled in the brand-new vehicle for a moment, assessing where everything important was located on the dashboard, and found the headlight switch. After setting the GPS for my destination to Stop and Shop, I put the SUV in drive and pulled out of the driveway into the winter night flurries.

The narrow driveway wound down the hill for a bit before it intersected the main two-lane road, which wound farther through the mountain passageway. My instincts matched the GPS map—I took a left onto the main road and proceeded to follow it down the gradient. This road would eventually merge onto Main Street and take me through Williamstown, then west on Route 2 eventually into North Adams. According to the map, my driving time to the store was approximately twenty minutes.

As I was enjoying listening to the Christmas melodies sung by Nat King Cole over the car speakers, I felt some relief now that I was alone away from the party. Socializing was uncomfortable for me, especially in big gatherings, and the pressure to be fun and outgoing was a bit too much for me to handle right now.

Before I knew it, I could see Stop and Shop just off the road. I turned into the lamplit parking lot, arriving just in time before the store closed. There were some last-minute shoppers exiting the store as I pulled into a prime parking spot right next to a handicap space in front of the store entrance. I hurried into the grocery store and quickly scanned around for the alcohol aisle. Once I found it, I skimmed the lane for bourbon. After a minute, I located the brand Dakota was using in her recipe and swiftly turned out of the aisle, headed for the shortest checkout line.

Soon, I returned to driving up the highway through the falling snow, headed east back through town. Driving along Main Street, I glanced at the clock in the car and took note of the time —5:40 p.m. I'd be arriving in time for dinner. Except the falling snow had started to grow heavy, and I was forced to reduce my speed to carefully drive up the mountain pass. I hoped that I wouldn't be too late for dinner now.

When I rounded the bend in the road due west, my visibility was significantly reduced. The road was slick, and the snowflakes were thick and heavy. Snowflakes stuck to the windshield wipers as they crossed the windshield. I slowed the vehicle to a snail's pace and clicked the headlights on high for a moment, but it made visibility worse. I dimmed the lights again and switched on the fog lamps instead. It didn't really seem to help either, but the lamps didn't make seeing any worse. So I continued to carefully crawl around the mountain bend through the snow.

Suddenly, a figure appeared without warning on the road several yards directly in front of the vehicle, and I instantly slammed on my brakes. Swerving off to the side of the road to avoid hitting what I believed was a man, I landed in shrubs, very closely facing a tree trunk inches away from the hood of the SUV.

I paused, completely flabbergasted. After calming myself down for a second, I unthinkingly got out of the car in the middle of my confusion and paced toward the front of the vehicle. Scarily, I saw just how close I had come to completely crashing into the tree trunk directly in front of me off the road.

My brother was going to *kill* me, I knew, when I suddenly noticed the large scrapes on the front bumper of his beloved brand-new luxury vehicle.

Recalling the figure in the road, I abruptly swung around and suddenly felt more worried. I glanced down the highway, but could only see a few yards ahead. It was bitter cold outside, and the snow had started coming down thickly.

I didn't see a single soul anywhere. The silence in the air around me was deafening. The bad feeling I had was growing and sunk fast into the pit of my stomach. So, I quickly hopped back into the car and turned on the ignition, then backed the SUV out of the embankment and onto the road. The headlights pointed ahead, and my breath escaped me as a shiver of frigid foreboding went down my spine when my eyes landed on where the man had originally appeared in the road. But he was still nowhere to be seen through the car windows.

I hesitated with my foot on the brake pedal for a second, not fully knowing why. But when my foot shifted over to the gas pedal, the vehicle unexpectedly stalled. When I pushed down on the gas again, the vehicle oddly didn't seem to want to budge, like in the case of a blown transmission.

Then, the electricity automatically began flickering inside the car until all the lights abruptly went out and the vehicle engine shut off. The thought of instantly being stranded on a desolate highway, in the middle of the wooded mountains at night in the snow, greatly unsettled me. I whipped out my phone, only to discover that to my added disconcertion, my fully charged cell phone also appeared to be dead in my hand.

"What?" I said to myself, extremely confused.

In a moment, all the lights in the car suddenly came back on, and my phone glowed again. I turned the key in the ignition; however, the car remained unresponsive. I instantly decided to call 911, but the call strangely wouldn't go through. Yanking the phone away from my ear, I saw that the cell signal was nonexistent. So I changed my location within the car to try to get a cell signal, but to no avail.

I was hesitant to step outside of the car again. Still, what other choice did I really have? I had to search for a phone signal. I remembered first before stepping out of the vehicle to reach for the dashboard and activate the GPS distress signal. As I waited for a response through the dead air, suddenly white noise came through the speakers. I turned off the radio, but the noise kept coming through as the electronics in the car went haywire again. Suddenly, all of the car lights went out once more.

I took a deep, apprehensive breath, and released the car door. It popped open, letting in freezing air. Stepping out into the icy chill, I stayed relatively close to the automobile. I shifted toward the front of the car in search of a connection for my phone. As I was approaching the front driver's side headlight, the lights turned on again and beamed ahead in the whiteout. *Thank God!* My phone simultaneously gained full signal strength! Great relief washed over me.

However, my alleviation immediately disintegrated when I eerily felt someone unseen on the whiteout road watching me. Then all of a sudden, a firm hand distinctly slid over my left shoulder. I gasped from sheer fright, simultaneously whipping around to see that not a soul was near. My heart stopped, and suddenly I was stone-cold to the bone. A soft whisper came forth through the freezing atmosphere, uttering, "Sylvie." It was a man's voice that came against the back of my neck. I also sensed my loose hair being physically moved away from my neck over my shoulder by an invisible hand.

I immediately took flight back toward the open car door and hopped in, securing myself inside in complete panic, utterly terrified.

Oh my God! Oh my God! I repeated frantically to myself, gasping, completely frightened. My heart was pounding as though it would leap from my chest. *That wasn't real,* I told myself, finding it really difficult to breathe. I believed I was beginning to have a breakdown. Perhaps I had finally reached my breaking point, and I was *truly* losing my mind. Tears started emerging helplessly from my eyes. I didn't know what to do. I was entirely beside myself when I nearly jumped out of my skin as a sudden, tremendous bang sounded out loud like a sonic boom, except at extremely close range. My heart skipped, and my ears began ringing. The vehicle started rocking. I thought someone was trying to break into the car, but there was no one to be seen, and I realized that the ground was strangely quaking instead as the tremor grew stronger.

The quaking seemed to last a good minute and was strong enough to bounce the car around like a toy on a trampoline. Screaming, I was being mercilessly jostled around like a rag doll inside the automobile. The tremor finally ceased when a low-pitched rumbling sound unexpectedly erupted out of the air, sounding like jet engines as the throttle is decreased when an airplane comes in for a landing. Except the sound was immeasurably louder than any landing jetliner. The noise grew more intense, causing severe pain in my ears and nearly causing me to faint.

Without warning, the atmosphere was set aglow in an opaque luminescence.

"Oh my God," I whispered to myself in quintessential amazement at the unimaginable sight before me. The atmosphere was

alight, and I could miraculously see up close, magnified to the approximate size of a quarter, the detail of every single falling snowflake in all of its splendid, ordered design. The titanium-white crystalline flakes hovered and floated downward on eddy currents in hyper suspension. Each crystalline flake danced in overextended motion as it refracted like a glass prism in the light. The snowflakes slowly ebbed and flowed toward and away from each other as they bounced and glided downward toward the frozen earth. I glanced up toward the glowing sky to locate the source of the radiance. But the luminescence was vast and seemed to span a wide area over the mountainous land with no distinct point of origin. Then, within what seemed to be a nanosecond, the snowflakes resumed falling faster than the eye could capture, and the light vanished.

I sat in the car for a moment entirely staggered.

When I realized my inaction, without hesitation I turned the car ignition, and to my utter relief, the vehicle started again. Immediately pressing the gas pedal, I zoomed away on the road. Except I had not gone too far when the car suddenly impacted something undetected in the middle of the highway with such force that the airbags deployed. The wind was instantly knocked out of me, and I heaved and gasped for air. My face stung from the sudden, powerful, burning burst of the airbag in the steering wheel hitting me. Thrown into a daze, it took me a suspended moment to finally regain my breath, and when I did, I lifted my gaze to see what I had crashed into. But there was absolutely nothing visible on the highway ahead of me.

Bewildered and incomprehensibly perplexed, after some consideration, I stepped dazedly outside of the vehicle to see the damage. The damage was extensive, as I had anticipated. I remained at a complete loss when I saw the entire front of the SUV had been smashed, crumpled like a soda can. I gazed ahead of the vehicle and saw that the road was clear of obstacles.

What the...?

I didn't understand what I could have possibly collided with in order to have received such unparalleled damage to the car. It was as if I had hit some kind of invisible barrier.

My head was in enormous pain. I moaned as I rubbed my closed eyes. The pain was consuming me more than any migraine I had ever experienced as I began to feel mounting pressure on my body, like gravity forces holding me still in a centrifuge. It felt like a sharp dagger had entered my brain, and I collapsed onto the icy, damp paved road when the gravity force suddenly ceased. The temperature in the air had abruptly dropped to a subzero degree, and the atmosphere became muted. My vision distorted. Then, the world vanished.

hen I regained my awareness, I wondered how long I had been unconscious, since it was now daylight. My head was foggy and achy. Not being particularly keen on ingesting alcohol, I had never experienced a true hangover, although presently I felt as though I had the worst one ever imaginable. It took me a moment to become oriented as I rubbed my eyes and head, wishing for the pain to go away.

After several minutes had passed, when my senses finally coalesced, I was alarmed to discover myself lying outside. I found myself in a thicket of bloodroot blossoms by a basalt outcrop within the forest off the road. There was no one else around but me as far as I could determine. I picked myself up and dusted the dirt from my cream-colored wool coat. My body felt stiff and noticeably sore, like the way arthritis might feel once it has settled deep in the bones. I was extremely achy and tired, as if I had been bluntly beaten and internally bruised. I looked myself over, and as far as I could tell, there were no visible signs of physical injury.

I glanced around my surroundings and began wandering through the trees out onto the road, looking for my brother's vehicle. But it was nowhere in sight. I thought that was odd and disturbing. No evidence of the car around anywhere, it seemed, as I searched the road. I frantically gazed around, wondering, *Where in God's name has the car gone?*

I started walking down the road in hopes of encountering the SUV. I pulled my phone from my coat pocket. I pressed the on button, and to my utmost relief, it started up. The screen glowed again, but I noticed the date and time didn't register—and it read, "Service Unavailable." Disappointed and frustrated, I shoved the phone back into my coat pocket.

I continued pacing along the road, feeling that I should have already reached the vehicle by now. Taking in more of my surroundings, I started growing more confused and very concerned. I wondered if someone might have actually stolen my brother's SUV. In which case I was certain to receive a double dose of haranguing from him. I took out my phone again, checking for cell reception—nothing.

I noticed that it was strangely warm outside. The weather had completely changed. Instead, it was hot and very humid.

Where did all the snow go?

The sun was shining brightly, and there wasn't a single cloud in the sky. I had not ever recalled seeing such an amazingly bright, deep cerulean-blue sky in all my life.

As I gazed confusedly at my whereabouts, it dawned on me that the season had completely changed. The trees were in full bloom instead of dormant. Wild violets, pink columbine, buttercups, and lily of the valley flowers carpeted the forest floor, and the sound of hundreds of birds chirping among the trees resonated throughout. A monarch butterfly suddenly flew right past my face. I glanced up, following its flight path high among the trees, and oddly, I sighted a bald eagle soaring above in the sky. I had never seen that species of bird freely flying around, because of its endangered status. Profoundly perplexed, I wondered how the season could now obviously be summer when it was supposed to be winter.

As I continued walking, it occurred to me that the road was composed of grass and dirt in two parallel paths fit for slim wheels, which forged through cleared vegetation over the ground. I wondered where the paved road had gone as I noticed that the path itself was much narrower than before. I glanced to the right and left of me, noticing that the trees bordering the road were significantly larger—enormously larger. In fact, the trees were at least as large as the ancient redwoods and sequoias on the West Coast. The forest was old—it seemed ancient, actually. The woods weren't made up at all of the young, slender evergreens, birches, dogwoods, and maples that I remembered foresting the New England seaboard.

I stopped in the road for a moment, pondering the oddity of my surroundings. How could I have missed months of my life without having ever known it? I knelt, grabbing a bit of dirt from the ground and releasing it between my fingers back to the earth, realizing this experience was real. I glanced down at my clothing. My cocktail dress corresponded with my last memory of being on my way to returning to the Christmas party from the grocery store. How could I explain my circumstances? This was completely bizarre—and extremely frightening.

I knelt again and snatched up a piece of shrubbery in the path and gazed at it. I could clearly see that the plant life I now held in my hand was real, and it quickly reconfirmed that I was not dreaming. The soft dirt I was walking on, the rich smell of the forest filling the air, the hot sun beaming on my face, and the faint breeze moving my hair were all real—telling me without a doubt that I was not in a state of some form of mental stasis.

As I was mulling over my unusual circumstances, the approaching sound of a marching snare drum was coming forth from around the bend in the dirt road. In a moment, a number of strangely dressed men in cardinal-red eighteenth-century British military uniforms began appearing at a distance, marching six abreast per row. There appeared to be anywhere from one hundred to one hundred and fifty men, and they were headed right toward me.

These men must be fanatic American history enthusiasts and belong to some kind of historical reenactment society. As strange as I thought they were for being grown men playing pretend like kids, I was glad to see others on the road beside myself. The road was quite narrow, and I thought I would have to move off to the side in order for them to pass. But as we began encountering one another, the men proceeded to adjust their ranks, allowing room for me to pass instead.

A peculiar feeling came over me as I began making my way past them. I noticed the men overtly looking at me with weird expressions on their faces. They sized me up from head to toe, and ogled my uncovered legs as if they had never seen a woman's knees in all their lives until now. I stared right back at them, thinking they were a bunch of oddballs.

"Whoo, 'ers pre'y!" I heard one of the men say to another in a strange English accent.

"Very well pre'y," jeered another man in the same dialect.

"*Look! 'Ers* got no frock!" observed another man, pointing at my clothes. He was looking at me as if I were as good as naked. I stared at him, thinking how ridiculous he was.

"Bonnie legs!" Another man lasciviously pointed to my feet as he walked by me.

"Never you mind! I'd lay claim ter those legs around me anytime!" joked a different man with a pockmarked face as he gawked lewdly at me.

"Ooh, how I would like tae taste that quim," snickered someone else in the same smutty manner, and a number of taunting male voices laughed outright.

I was suddenly extremely offended. I had never in all my life heard such surly, gruff, disrespectful, sneering, snickering, misogynistic jokes made in my presence. These men took their role-playing too far, I believed. I began picking up my walking pace in order to get quickly past them. A few of the men stumbled into each other while staring raunchily at me as I went by. I wondered how many more pigs were going to make idiotic remarks as I moved alongside their ranks.

"March on!" ordered a commander on horseback approaching from behind the men. His stern eyes immediately locked on to me as he came nearer. He slowed his horse out of file in front of the trailing carriage. He was drawing closer to me. He appeared to be in his late forties or early fifties with salt-and-pepper hair tied back beneath his gold-trimmed black tricorn hat. Given the gold epaulets on his shoulders, the gold gorget suspended from his neck, and the crimson silk sash wrapped around his waist, he wore an officer's uniform. I was uncertain about his rank, however. He had a rugged face, a square shaven jaw, and a broad brow. He looked threatening as he sat seriously and high above me on his tall horse. When he came close enough, he pulled his horse to the side next to me. I stopped in my tracks, looking up at him. His hard blue eyes thoroughly rolled over me, and he glared at me suspiciously. The carriage following behind had also stopped, along with a number of other surrounding officers, all looking curiously at me. A wigged officer inside the carriage peered out, appearing in his early fifties also.

"What is the matter?" asked the wigged officer from inside the carriage as he gazed out the window. His accent, I noticed, was well-spoken English from England.

"A loan lass, sir," answered a different bronze-haired officer with a deep Scottish brogue. He appeared fairly younger than the other two officers. I supposed he was approximately in his late thirties. He was also raised high on his horse, looking strangely at me. In fact, I noticed several more officers mounted on horses who had stopped and were eyeing me questioningly. The wigged officer in the carriage glared at me oddly also as he distinctly looked me over from head to toe.

"Is she hurt?" the gray-wigged man asked.

"Are ye hurt, lass?" asked the younger bronze-haired officer.

"No," I said, glancing back at them strangely. There was one other officer, I had noticed, who remained close and strictly observant. The shade from his tricorn hat obscured his face while he sat high on his horse, so I couldn't estimate his age or see exactly what he looked like.

"She appears unharmed, General," the shaded officer observed in the same Scottish accent.

"Well, indeed that is most fortunate. Allow me to introduce ourselves—I am General Abram, and this is General Cairns, here at your service," the Englishman said politely as he continued to peer out of the window of his carriage.

"Nice to meet you," I responded automatically.

"Indeed, a pleasure, Miss," General Abram said courteously.

"Are ye stranded, lass?" General Cairns inquired in his Scottish brogue as the sun caught his older appearance.

"Yeah, actually, I was just in a car accident up the road, and I need to call for some assistance. Except, oddly enough, I can't seem to find my car anywhere—it's like it's vanished or something. I tried calling for help on my phone, but the reception is dead around here. So, I just decided to walk back to town," I explained. The officers glowered at me for some strange reason. They were looking at me as if I were speaking a foreign language. General Abram suddenly reached into his coat sleeve and pulled out a lace handkerchief. He held it out to me. I simply looked at it with puzzlement.

"Your nose, Miss," he said, waving the handkerchief for me to take.

"What?" I replied confusedly.

"Thaur's bluid comin' from yer nose, lass," General Cairns informed me.

"*Blood?*" I replied strangely. I took the kerchief doubtfully and put it to my nose. I wasn't anemic and never in my life had experienced a bloody nose. Yet when I pulled the handkerchief away after wiping my nose and saw in fact that there was blood coming from it, I was shocked.

"Are ye fit?" General Cairns asked.

"Yes, are you well?" General Abram inquired.

"Yeah—I'm okay, thank you," I replied, concerned.

"Are ye alone?" General Cairns inquired curiously. *That is an odd question. Why would he want to know that?* "It isnae safe fur a lass such as yerself tae be alone in the wilderness," he stated forthrightly as he glared at me in a disapproving manner.

"Yes, it most certainly is not safe for you to be unescorted," General Abram agreed.

"Excuse me?" I inquired confusedly.

"Where are yer kin?" General Cairns asked sharply. My *kin?* I hadn't heard that term used since—ever. *Why does he want to know where my family is?* That was the second personal question he had asked me, and I was beginning to have my doubts about them all.

"I don't have any," I lied spontaneously.

"Are you alone, then?" General Abram asked, appearing significantly astonished.

"Yes," I replied, deciding it was none of their business to know anything more about me. General Cairns furrowed his brow a bit, scrutinizing me with his blue eyes.

"Tae waur did ye say ye waur traveling?" he asked.

"To town," I said obviously.

"What town would that be, Miss?" General Abram asked, clearly looking out from the window of his carriage.

"Williamstown, of course," I said, looking at them like they were a collection of nitwits.

"*Williamstown?*" General Abram echoed.

"Yes—where else?" I replied. "You know, if you don't mind letting me pass, I'll just continue on my way," I responded courteously. I was finished with them and in no mood to be drawn into their silly game. General Abram's fine brow lifted somewhat on his straight face, appearing surprised, or incensed to some degree.

"She's feisty," remarked the lower-ranked bronze-haired Scottish officer, listening to the conversation. General Abram's eyes slightly narrowed on me as one side of his thin lips wryly tilted upward.

"Well, I say—come now, Miss, there is no need for rudeness. Mayhap I may offer to you some assistance in your time of distress," General Abram suggested gallantly.

"Whit is yer name, lass?" General Cairns asked abruptly.

"I don't see how that's any of your business," I replied defensively. General Cairns's brow lifted high on his head in astonishment.

"Well, I dare say!" General Abram expressed with a questionable eye on me.

"Aye," General Cairns agreed stoutly. I had quickly grown tired of answering their ridiculous questions.

"Well, thanks for the handkerchief," I said politely regardless, patting my nose again. I started around the mounted men. But the Scottish general suddenly blocked my path with his horse.

"Nae, lass, yoo're not goin' anywhaur. Yoo're coming with us," he said resolutely.

"Wait a minute. I'm not going *anywhere* with you," I responded, feeling even more uncertain about my situation.

"Aye, ye are. Let's go," General Cairns replied unyieldingly.

"No, I'm not," I objected tersely, quickly feeling panic rise within me. The frightening thought entered my mind that I had stumbled upon a rogue group of lawless men who found their kicks by bizarrely dressing up in eighteenth-century British army attire and kidnapping women. God only knew what else they did with their defenseless hostages.

"You mustn't remain here vulnerable to beasts and savages—

unclothed as you are," General Abram commanded, glaring scandalously at me.

"Come along, lass," General Cairns ordered.

"No!" I protested quickly.

"Then we shall take ye by force. Seize her!" the Scotsman commanded of one of the nearby foot soldiers waiting around. I was suddenly taken by the upper arm.

"No!" I shouted, snatching my arm free from the twentysomething-year-old foot soldier. The soldier swiftly reattached his clasp around my arm, and held me tighter. "Let go of me! You haven't the right to just take me! *Let—me—go!* This is illegal!" I responded frantically as I squirmed fiercely to break loose from the soldier's strong grip.

"She's here feisty, General," the young foot soldier said worriedly.

"Aye, bind her wrists," General Cairns ordered.

"You can't do this! Get your goddamn hands off me!" I said, opposing strongly. Shocked gasps came from surrounding accomplices as I swore in my determination to break free from the young soldier's grip. I was determined not to be removed from my present location; I had no idea what would become of me if I relented to their aggression.

"Silence yerself, lass, or I'll gag ye!" the Scottish general warned. For a split second, I considered complying in order not to further upset my captors. On second thought, however, I knew I had to fight for my life, or I would never see my family and friends again. I screamed and tussled as I felt a rope quickly being tied around my wrists.

"General Cairns!" shouted another officer from a distance ahead of us in the ranks. He made a signal to his commanders.

"What is it, Captain Meyers?" General Abram inquired aloud with annoyance from inside his carriage. Suddenly, General Cairns ceased speaking and keenly glanced around the area after noticing the captain's signal. He gazed around their surroundings for a second, then made his own signal back to the captain.

"Halt!" cried the captain, and the troops ahead promptly stopped marching on the path. Suddenly, they all fell quiet and stood still. The company seemed to be alerted to something unseen. The men were quietly glancing around themselves, keeping their eyes on the silent woods.

An isolated, high-pitched cry abruptly sounded out among the trees. Subsequently, an unexpected chorus of high-pitched wailing began. The sounds echoed noisily throughout the encompassing woods. All of a sudden, a single, nearly naked man dressed like an Indian brave darted from the trees, wildly screaming with a raised tomahawk in hand. He ran toward an unassuming soldier and forcefully swung his weapon, hitting the young soldier hard in the head, spilling what realistically looked like his blood. The soldier instantly dropped to the ground, and I thought that these men were really serious about acting out their roles and perhaps they should go to Hollywood. The man who played the Indian brave looked thoroughly authentic as he also appeared to fit the proper ethnicity of the culture he was portraying.

"Assume yer positions!" General Cairns ardently hollered out, and the men promptly took their stances. "Company—*FIRE!*"

Suddenly, shots rang out and gun smoke started filling the air. Countless warring Native Americans swiftly emerged from the woods, shrieking like crazed, possessed savages. Tomahawks swung everywhere. Swords were clinking. Guns fired back and forth between the soldiers and natives. The fighting quickly merged into a large blur of animated, twisted, mangled limbs. I stood there dumfounded in the thick of the skirmish, again thinking to myself how incredibly authentic the scene appeared, and that these men were really good actors.

The officer that had been obscured from the sunlight by his tricorn hat had his sword drawn, fighting with an Indian near me while still mounted on his horse. He was suddenly shot in the leg with an arrow and keeled over, falling off his saddle. He hit the ground with a *thump*, acting like he was in pain. I mentally congratulated him on his acting efforts, because his misfortune looked authentic. I remained standing there entirely bamboozled while staring down at the injured man.

Remembering the rope around my wrists, which had not been fully secured before this surreal event started taking place, I proceeded to promptly remove it. Without warning, I felt someone sharply grab hold of my forearm and yank me off the road into the woods. I was tripping and stumbling over the brush as I was mercilessly pulled through the vegetation. I unsteadily caught a glimpse of my next captor and realized I was now being kidnapped by a young man playing the part of an Indian brave.

"Hey! What are you doing?" I protested. I was surprised by my unexpected ability to suddenly yank my arm free from his firm grip. He abruptly stopped galloping and turned, looking at me. He was painted in very frightening black war paint all over his face and bare shoulders, and was dressed in a loincloth. His head was entirely shaved, and he glared at me with wild eyes. "Leave me alone!" I told him. He stared at me for a second, quickly assessing me. He then uttered words in a language completely unknown to me.

"What?" I questioned.

He grabbed my arm sharply again, continuing to speak in his native language, and proceeded to forcibly pull me farther into the forest up along the slope. He wrenched his grasp firmly around my wrist so that I couldn't escape him. His musket was slung over his shoulder, and I noticed the tomahawk swinging in his other hand. Fresh red stains were dripping from the blade. The sight of it was unreal to me.

As he continued mercilessly yanking me up the slope through the trees and low growth vegetation, I glanced over my shoulder and saw at a distance from our vantage point the vigorous skirmish taking place below on the path. My captor called my attention back to him as he hostilely yelled at me again in his native language. It seemed he was chastising me for not paying attention or something to that effect. I frowned at him, wondering why he wouldn't just speak in plain English. I belatedly realized that he was trying to get me to step over a large boulder, which was outcropped from the silt soil on the hillside. As I clumsily maneuvered my feet over the rock, I noticed to my regret that my favorite smoky-rose leather buckle peep-toe Salvatore Ferragamo high-heeled shoes were becoming ruined. With one last heave, he jarred me over the boulder and rashly continued tugging me up the forested hill.

Everything was happening too quickly, to the point where it was difficult for me to catch my breath and merely understand what was occurring. I kept pleading with my captor to release me. I promised him that I wouldn't call the police, and that he needn't have to worry about being apprehended by the law. He didn't respond and continued jerking me farther along into the forest. The aggressive sounds from the fighting down below were quickly falling behind, and I was *very* concerned for my well-being.

The moment we arrived at the crest, an unexpected gunshot went off at extremely close range, startling the *crap* out of me! My ears rang, and everything became muted for an instant. My captor immediately dropped backward, pulling me down to the ground beside him. Bells were ringing loudly everywhere. I rolled over, swiftly snatching my arm away from him, and caught a shocking glimpse of his face. I was absolutely stunned frozen as I stared at the grisly sight before me. What I was currently witnessing did not properly register in my mind as the sight of blood gushing from the man's head.

The vision was *unreal.* These individuals had gone way too far with their theatrical role-playing! Unbeknownst to me, I had apparently encountered a group of men who were, in fact, unscrupulous, dangerous individuals. I stared at the injured man at my knees in front of me, wondering, *How can anyone be so stupid as to play with live ammunition?* I gasped in horror, never having seen a thing like it in my life. His face had been blown off!

"Come along, lass!" a man voiced abruptly as he unexpectedly came from behind a tree, facing me. The pistol in his hand was smoking. He suddenly hoisted me up to my feet, but I couldn't take my eyes off the devastated man now lying as a corpse in the soil.

"That man—" I gasped in utter shock.

"He's dead," confirmed my newest captor, who spoke with a deep Scottish brogue.

"Dead?" My eyes remained transfixed on the limp body.

"Aye. Let's go!" he directed impatiently, and began tugging me away with him.

"No!" I immediately jerked my hand out of his grip as I finally looked up to see who *this* particular man was now trying to steal me away instead.

"Are ye injured?" he inquired with an edgy look on his face. I was trembling. My legs were like gelatin, and I nearly collapsed. He suddenly strengthened his grip around my upper arm. "Bear up, lass," he said at once. A tense expression swept across his face as he gazed at me. He was anxious and quickly wanted us to move. But I wasn't willing to go anywhere with him.

"Who are you?" I demanded nervously, sounding frightened even to my own ears.

"Come," he urged quickly, again wanting us to leave the area.

"No!" I stammered, swallowing dryly. "Who the hell are you?" The unfamiliar man raised his eyebrows at my demanding question.

"I am a man trying tae save our skins. Now we must go!" he ordered. "Can ye steady yerself or must I carry ye?"

"Let go of me!" I stared at him with considerable alarm. He released me, and I steadied my wobbling legs.

Paying close attention to the strange way he was dressed, I skimmed over the bright scarlet coat he was wearing. It was long with tails that hit at the back of his knees, and there was no collar at the neck. A gold breastplate hung around his neck, catching the sunlight and glinting in my eye. The long lapels of his coat were folded back over the fabric at the front, revealing fine gold braided trim down the front. The cuffs were thick and were folded back about five or six inches along the forearm. His coat was open and exposed a tan waistcoat with many brass buttons going down the front. A fine white linen flounce shirt with a matching stock encircled his neck.

I immediately started backing away from him. He suddenly snagged my arm, tightly holding my wrist and pulling me back toward him.

"I shan't let ye go," he said, determined.

"Who are you?" I asked him again, on the brink of being utterly beside myself.

"Ye must come with me," he insisted urgently.

"I don't know you," I said as goose bumps came over my skin.

"Aye, ye dinnae ken me," he agreed while standing strangely before me in eighteenth-century British military dress. His uniform looked like an officer's, of which rank I did not know.

"But I—" I started, extremely bewildered and frightened as he appeared like an uncanny ghost. All muddled from the car accident last night, to having awakened on the road alone with the car missing, to witnessing the skirmish, to presently seeing this strange man before me, I did not know what to think.

"At yer back, lad!" another man abruptly shouted from the left, hastily closing in at short range and heading toward us. In a red blur, this man was running vigorously through the trees dressed in the same military fashion. My new captor swiftly swung around with his basket broadsword drawn and was suddenly engaged in a fight with a different battling Indian painted in black from head to toe, as my new captor's redcoat companion quickly raced forward.

I nervously watched the new clash. My new captor and the Indian fought in the dirt for perilous moments, rolling over each other in a blur of dusty red and black. Blades were drawn as each man was trying to gain the upper hand in order to stab the other to death with their drawn weapons. Suddenly, my new captor lost his advantage and was thrown onto his back, overtaken by his Native American aggressor. The Native American now had a knife at my new captor's throat, ready to slice him wide open at the jugular.

"No!" I screeched uncontrollably. The brave abruptly looked up in my direction and spotted me hiding between the giant ferns. He glared malevolently at me, conveying his intent to make me his next victim. Suddenly, a bayonet drove right through the Indian's back and exited his lower stomach through the liver. He howled excruciatingly and dropped like a lead weight over my captor. I stared, flabbergasted, as the second redcoat yanked his musket and freed the bloodied bayonet from the mortally wounded Indian.

"Are ye alrecht, lad?" his rescuer inquired as he carelessly shoved the motionless Indian off his friend with the heel of his boot.

"Alive," answered my captor when he shifted out from under his lifeless attacker's body and began to get to his feet with the aid of his friend.

"Guid," his friend replied satisfactorily. My captor noticed me hiding in the ferns between the trees. His friend noticed and followed his line of sight, discovering me too. I was terrified to come out, and moved farther back inside the thicket as I perceived the men coming determinedly toward me. The fern patch was dense and full of scratching needles, inhibiting me from making a clean escape. My captor charged through the vegetation and pulled me out into the open among the trees again with his friend standing directly in front of me.

"Whit have ye found, eh?" his friend inquired curiously.

"A lass," my captor responded.

"Aye. Who is she?"

"I dinnae ken."

"She's from the road."

"Aye."

They both scrutinized me for a minute, grimacing as they scanned me from head to toe. They gawked at me strangely as if I were an extraterrestrial.

"She speaks English, but 'tis a curious accent. It disnae soond like anything from these parts in the colonies," my captor observed.

"I huvnae heard of it either."

"Aye."

His friend narrowed his eyes on me, examining me further with a suspicious look on his face.

"She's half dressed," his friend said, observing me with a critical eye. "Her coat and shoes are very fine."

"Aye, I've noticed that also," my captor replied, appearing somewhat flushed. Suddenly, I was feeling tremendously self-conscious, as if they were viewing me through X-ray glasses and could see my nakedness in spite of my clothes.

"I'm not half dressed," I disagreed strongly, looking at them like the perverts I thought they were. They both exchanged ironic glances.

"Give us yer name, then, lass," the friend demanded. My captor prudently glanced at his friend while replacing his pistol inside his holster belted around his waist. The weapon appeared menacing, I thought, as I watched him tuck it away. My heart continued racing wildly in my chest, and my blood ran cold as I stood between these two strange men. "Weel, give us yer name," the friend insisted again, leaning slightly toward my face with his hand resting on top of the pummel of his sword hanging from his belt.

"It's Sylvina," I stammered, chilled to the bone.

"Sylvina," he echoed with a questioning stare.

"That's a bonnie name," my captor said.

"Dinnae be foolish, brother," his friend warned with a deriding glance.

"So, who the hell are you guys?" I heard myself demand despite my fear. The strangers both raised their brows at my question.

"I'll do the asking haur, lass," the friend said intolerantly.

"I reckon she's frightened, Finley," my captor observed. Finley fleetingly glared at his companion. I briefly speculated that they might, in fact, be related, since there was some resemblance between them.

"Give me yer full name, lass," Finley demanded, appearing rather threatening.

"Why?" I asked distrustfully.

"She's a tart," Finley said.

"I absolutely am not!" I said, outraged. I attempted to move away from them, but Finley solidly clasped my arm, fixing me in place before them.

"Who is yer employer?" he questioned.

"My employer?" I looked at him confusingly.

"Aye. 'Tis been a long time since we have come across a fine whore as yerself, and I reckon ye must have fled yer employer," he said.

"Are you insane? I'm not a whore!" I protested with great offense. The two men glanced at each other. "Now you let me go this instant!" I demanded, finding my determination.

"I cannae do that," he said caustically.

"Let me go!" I jerked my arm around, trying to shake off his grip. It didn't work.

"I must ken who ye are. I have little patience, lass. If ye regard yer life, tell me yer full name," he ordered, looming with intimidation. My throat went dry, and I swallowed hard. I realized there was no other choice but to tell them.

"It's Arboles. My last name is Arboles," I said, revealing my married name.

"Ye speak Spanish?" he questioned, now appearing suspicious.

"So what if I do?" I said flippantly. "And French, for that matter. I speak it very well too, in fact. What's the difference?"

The two men looked at each other again. I nervously swept several long stray ringlets away from my face and tucked them behind my ear. Their eyes bugged as they noticed the two-carat pink diamond brilliantly glittering above my glistening platinum wedding band.

"Christ!" my captor expressed with surprise. "Look at that!"

"Aye," Finley agreed.

"That's an exquisite ring," my captor observed, very impressed.

"Aye," Finley said.

"Whaur is yer husband, lass?" my captor asked.

"Aye, whaur is yer husband?" Finley echoed.

"I don't have a husband," I responded as I looked at them with distrust.

"Nae husband?" Finley asked suspiciously.

"No. I'm widowed," I confirmed. He said something in Scots to my captor.

"Aye," replied my captor.

"She wears fine earrings too—and the necklace. Do ye see it?" Finley asked.

"Aye," my captor replied. Finley whisked out a hand and snagged a few locks of my hair, examining it. He rubbed the texture between his fingers. He leaned in close and took a sniff.

"She disnae carry the scent of one recognizable," Finley said. His companion also took a whiff.

"I dinnae recognize it either, yet it is a fine scent," my captor determined.

"Quite fine," Finley agreed. "Have ye any kin?"

"No," I lied. I didn't want to jeopardize anyone I cared about. I didn't know who these people were, or what kind of deceitful antics they were up to.

Finley looked at his companion, saying something in Scottish. I assumed he was obviously talking about me in a tone that sounded skeptical. His companion responded in a curious manner and ventured to speak further. It seemed the conversation might have been a sort of disagreement, since they both went back and forth with differing body language that mimicked the inflection in their voices. They frequently took glimpses of my ring while speaking. As I watched their discussion, it made me feel incredibly uncomfortable that they had discovered it on my finger. I slipped both hands inside my coat pockets, hiding the piece of jewelry as they kept scrutinizing eyes on me.

They examined my pink tourmaline and diamond dangling earrings, my graduated diamond and pink sapphire pendant necklace, and my sterling silver Paloma Picasso Marrakesh bangle. They scoped out the fine decorative brocade and gray velvet sash on my knee-length, empire-waist, cream-colored woolen winter coat. They leered at my bare legs and observed my lovely smoky-rose crystal-encrusted leather peep-toe shoes. As a result, I distinctly felt like a dissected piece of packaged goods. I couldn't help but feel a certain level of offense and was unnerved by what they were probably considering.

"Very weel then, Seamus. Let's go. We huvnae more time tae waste," Finley grumbled, appearing noticeably dissatisfied with the outcome of their discussion.

"Aye," my captor, Seamus, agreed, seeming satisfied.

"Come along, lass," Finley ordered abruptly, and tugged me along as they both started walking.

"Wait! No!" I expressed, alarmed. I dug my heels into the dirt, extremely reluctant to proceed. Finley glared sharply at me. I tried shaking his grip off me.

"Quit!" He scowled, jerking me around a little. "Yoo're comin' with us and 'tis final!"

"No!" I exclaimed with fright. I started thrashing around to free myself from his iron clasp. "Let go of me!" I shouted while wildly flailing around. My heart palpitated loudly in my ears. I threw all my energy into it and commenced a struggle—brief as it was. Finley was a tall, well-over-six-foot, formidable man with solid strength. He quickly bound both my hands with one of his, forcefully squeezing my wrists together. I winced as it felt like the bones in my wrists would crack.

"Quit! Or I'll knock ye and put ye out!" He scowled irately. I stared astoundingly at him, definitely believing he would follow through on his threat. So, I thought it wiser to stop my wrenching around. "Much better," he said with a glower. He turned a doubtful eye to Seamus. "She's saucy," he said disapprovingly. Seamus shrugged and gave his companion an incorrigible look as my nervous eyes bounced between them.

"Why are you taking me?" I asked breathlessly. Neither one of them responded.

"Let's go," Finley said, yanking me along as they both started moving again.

"Where are you taking me?" I asked, filled with fear.

"Yoo're comin' with us tae Albany," Finley answered.

"Albany?" I echoed, stunned.

"That's whit I said," he responded in a hard, no-nonsense manner as he continued tugging me through the forest.

"Why?" I asked anxiously.

"We'll sort it all out when we're thaur," he said. I glanced over at Seamus, who was pacing on the other side next to me.

"Please—you don't have to let him do this," I appealed to Seamus, completely alarmed. "You can't just let him kidnap me like this—it's not right!" Without so much as a glimpse at me,

Seamus didn't respond. Instead, he kept his gaze straight ahead and walked along with his companion, Finley, who brutishly possessed my arm as he led me through the woods.

WE TREKKED for a period of time through the wilderness, moving past the brush. I got caught on several low branches, scratching my calves and snagging the delicate threads on my coat as we meandered through the forest. The vegetation was dense, and the air was warm, heavy with humidity. Our natural surroundings did not resemble the thin, new-growth forests typically inhabiting the Eastern seaboard, I continued to discern. Instead, these woods were massive and primitive, like some of the ancient forests that still remained across the Rockies and the Pacific Northwest.

The earth was noticeably moist, indicating that rainfall had recently occurred. My heels occasionally sank into the mud as we continued on unpredictable ground. After hiking for approximately an hour, we entered an expansive thicket of unusually gigantic ferns. I started wondering with some concern where, in fact, our location really was; none of this seemed familiar to me at all.

We finally arrived at a rushing creek where the two men decided to break for a moment. They took the opportunity to fill their wooden canteens and to take a break from hiking. I was overheated in my wool coat, but refused to take it off given the way they kept staring at my knees. It was as if they had never seen a woman's legs before. So, I decided to modestly kneel at the edge of the creek and refreshed myself by dabbing a bit of cool water on my glistening face.

As I was drawing water to my lips, I secretly studied my captors closely surrounding me. The one named Finley had a brilliant head of copper hair that he wore long just past the shoulders and tied at the back with a black silk ribbon. Judging by his military uniform, he also appeared to be role-playing as a ranking British officer. He surely seemed to have studied his part well, I thought, given the amazing detail of his uniform and his usurping, domineering disposition. He was handsome and extremely tall, standing over six feet with broad shoulders and a square jaw that was set firmly on his face.

His companion, Seamus, shared similarly handsome features. I had never seen anyone possess such rich golden-yellow hair as he had. His thick, straight hair appeared soft and silky. He also wore it long slightly past his shoulders and tied behind his head with a similar black silk ribbon. Tall like Finley, he also had broad shoulders. As I studied him, I noticed the slight cleft in his square chin and his razor-straight nose that set him slightly apart from his brother.

Feeling momentarily refreshed from the water at the creek, I heard the men having a discussion back and forth in Scots. They seemed fairly preoccupied, by the serious tone of their conversation. I discreetly glanced around my surroundings as I still knelt at the edge of the water, pretending to continue to collect water in my hand to sip. They seemed less attentively guarding me right now. I hesitated, wondering if this would be my best opportunity to try to escape. I decided it was. I all of a sudden darted away, dashing from the stream into the woods back in the direction from where we had come.

"Crap! She's fleeing!" Finley exclaimed.

I sprinted madly between the surrounding towering trees. I was whipped in the face by underbrush as I frantically moved, stumbling over everything in my path with my heart fiercely pounding in my chest. In a desperate effort to ditch them, I actually had no idea where I was headed and promptly realized that we had come too far into the forest for me to know where I was. Nevertheless, I blindly kept running. I swung myself over a fallen log, ran through poison ivy, and tripped over stones along the way.

Not too long into my flight, the sound of chasing feet crunching over dead foliage was heard at a closing distance behind me. I clumsily traversed the muddy, irregular terrain in my heels, frenziedly hoping to lose my pursuer. Suddenly, my loose ringlets were yanked from behind, and I was abruptly thrown backward. I uncontrollably tumbled to the earth with my pursuer stumbling over me.

"*Oof!*" he grunted as he landed forcefully on top of me. I tussled to extract myself from him. He powerfully whipped me around, facing him, and caged me beneath him with the full weight of his muscular frame resting upon mine. Both of us excessively panting, I looked up into Seamus's striking blue eyes as he shackled my wrists, pressing them into the soil slightly above my head with a firm clasp. I scrambled, attempting to wrench free, but he was too overpowering and had me locked beneath him. Holding me bound, he waited until I finally gave up thrashing. Completely out of breath, I grew tired and had no more strength to move.

"Dinnae do that again," he panted over me. I could feel his muscular thigh between mine, pinning me down. His tone didn't sound particularly threatening, but I could tell that he meant it. If I did run off again and failed, I didn't feel so certain that he would be as generous with me the next time.

"What do you want from me?" I asked nervously, gasping for air.

"Dinnae flee from me again," he repeated in the same calm tone. "Do ye understand?" His breath was still excited from the chase, but the look on his face was moderate. Not knowing for certain if he or Finley might ultimately hurt me, I was extremely reluctant to trust him. "Do ye understand?" he reiterated with the faint scent of rum coming off his breath.

It swiftly entered my mind that I had no choice. Considering the ease with which both men had at fatally discarding people, I nodded my head faintly.

"Guid," he said.

"Please, just let me go," I appealed to him once more, filled with panic.

"I shan't do that," he said. I sensed his breathing settle over me as I nervously examined his face at close range.

"Why?" I asked breathlessly. "Why won't you let me go?" He stared at me for a moment without answering as he intently studied me.

"Guid. Yoo've caught her," Finley observed, panting as he appeared behind Seamus through the trees.

"Aye, brother," Seamus said. "She's quick as a rabbit." He shifted off me, returning to his feet and towering over me.

"A guid thing fur the fox, then, eh? Let's go, then, brother," Finley insisted impatiently. I was suddenly grabbed by the upper arm and hoisted to my feet with Seamus attentively clutching me close beside him.

Startled and deeply confused, I struggled to make sense of all this as I was forced to accompany them again when we resumed walking through the enveloping woods. I was conscious of Seamus's large hand firmly clasped around my upper arm as he guided me across uneven ground, wondering what they were going to do to me.

CHAPTER 5

We hiked deep into the woods for what seemed to be approximately another hour. The heat was awful and oppressive. I still, however, refused to remove my coat. I thought that I'd rather die of heat exhaustion than have them gawk at me even more without it.

I wondered, with continued apprehension, where we were going. However, it seemed that the strangers had some idea where they were headed. I was somewhat surprised that they could navigate through the woods using just an antique compass instead of a map or GPS. In fact, as I continued to notice, neither man appeared to be carrying any sort of equipment that a typical hiker would have at their disposal for self-reliance and safety purposes. This furthermore struck me as worrisome, and it did not bode well within me.

The terrain was rigorous at times. It was undulating and demanding with no mercy. We were high up in the Berkshires, I at least recognized. The ground was rocky, with basalt cliffs buttressing the mountainsides as we rounded the edges. We passed beneath schist overhangs, which outcropped from the hillsides. The earth turned into silt and clay as we finally began descending the terrain, and soon the sound of a rushing, bubbling stream was heard in the near distance.

The hot, steamy air felt like an inescapable sauna and became too much for me to bear any longer. I changed my mind and started unbuttoning the large 1960s-style buttons down the front of my knee-length cream-and-gray embroidered Rockwell wool coat. I folded the coat over my arm and wiped the perspiration from the back of my neck with my fingers. We were now approaching a refreshing, effervescent brook trickling over rocks at the edge of the stream.

Apparently, my captors had been boldly staring at me with certain questionable looks of impropriety. I was compelled to assess myself and glanced down at my strapless 1950s-style knee-length A-line pleated silk taffeta dress. Excusing my ruined shoes and scraped knees, my smoky-pink dress remained unsoiled and intact. So, I reasonably considered myself decently dressed. Even the wide crimson silk sash tied in a bow at the side around my waist remained undisturbed. But it seemed by the way they were gaping at my strapless shoulders, that I might as well have appeared nude to them.

Intending to squelch their attention, I turned my back to them and faced the stream. I unthinkingly twisted my long hair off my back up into an unstable bun, then I crouched by the brook and drew water to my lips. The men remained speechless until one of the brothers shifted behind me. I glanced up from sipping water from my cupped palm and noticed Finley waving down somebody not too far off upstream. Then, a band of redcoats began emerging from the bordering woods along the water. About eight men mounted on horseback were approaching. I stood as they drew close, cautiously aware of more strange men.

"We found yer horses, lads," one of the men said as he finally got close. He brought his horse to a stop before the brothers.

"Och, guid, Bearnard. Yoo've saved us from trekkin' anymore in this goddamn heat," Finley said.

"Aye," Seamus agreed, reaching for the reins to his horse. All eyes from the new company of men were staring obviously at me now. Their expressions were full of curiosity and discernible leers.

"Guid tae see the lot of ye have yer scalps intact," Finley remarked as he grabbed the reins to his horse.

"Aye, yers also," another soiled-looking man agreed from the group.

"Ye lads have found yerselves a lass, eh?" the hairy wolf-man Bearnard said as he lifted his caterpillar brows while dismounting his horse. The others ensued, coming down from their horses as they kept their wandering, leering eyes on me.

"My brother discovered her," Finley informed them, appearing more at ease now that he was reunited with his horse and had rejoined with the other men.

In order to stem my growing self-consciousness, I made an effort to override it and daringly stared back at the gaping onlookers now encircling me. They were a band of weathered men full of stench. They reeked of rancid male body odor and sweat, and it seemed as though they had never known a shower.

Someone felt my hair from behind. My ringlets unraveled past my shoulders from the loose bun I had tied. I instantly swung my gaze around and locked eyes with a skinny, pockmarked man, fairly certain that he was the one who had touched me.

"She's quite a bonnie one," said a man standing next to the skinny, pockmarked one as he caught my chin between his grimy fingers. The odor of his hand was fishy, and his dark-brown straight hair was noticeably greasy. It appeared that his hair had not been shampooed in months. His thumb pulled my bottom lip down, and he caught a glimpse of my teeth as the rest of the men closely huddled around me.

"Don't touch me!" I snapped, abruptly slapping his hand off my face.

"I was fixin' tae tell ye not tae git too close tae the lass, lads. She micht just as weel clip yer fingers off," Seamus warned.

"Ooh! She's a saucy one," said the man with surprise as he suddenly retracted his fingers from my chin. Some chuckling went around.

"Who possesses her?" asked a man no taller than I who had slightly strange facial features that for some reason reminded me of an Oompa-Loompa from the movie *Willy Wonka & the Chocolate Factory.*

"Says she has nae husband. She claims that she disnae belong tae anyone," Finley said plainly.

"Nae one?" Oompa-Loompa replied questioningly.

"Aye—claims that she's widowed," Finley informed them while tending to the buckles on his horse.

"I dinnae ken of any *lady* who wanders about in a state of undress," said Oompa-Loompa.

"I neither ken of any *husband* who would allow his wife in public appearing like that," Bearnard said with discernible skepticism on his face.

"Mayhap she's a whore," presumed another really hairy man. I detected some anticipation in his eyes, and I glowered repugnantly at him.

"I am certainly *not* a whore!" I claimed defiantly.

"The *lady* says that she isnae a whore, lads," Oompa-Lumpa expressed with a certain amount of sarcasm. Laughter sputtered out around me from the encircling men.

"Weel, now I can let ye lads ken whether that is true or not," the hairy man said as he stepped toward me, unbuttoning his breeches. Shot with steep fear, I abruptly scurried backward, bumping into some unseen men at my back.

"Don't you dare touch me!" I warned.

"Hold back, Lachlan. I dinnae agree with rape, as ye ken," Finley said promptly.

"Aye! Hands off the lassie! Nae one tooches her! Do ye hear?" Seamus ordered. Lachlan pursed his lips at me and blew a kiss, jokingly gesturing regret. I was relieved that Finley and Seamus at least had some moral sense, and that they seemed to have authority over their gang. Acutely aware of all the lascivious stares, I couldn't help but remain on edge. I had no idea what these sketchy goons were plotting. But one thing was for sure, as it rang loud and clear: these men were dangerous.

"She certainly is fine, however. Never seen one quite like her. She's swarthy, not like the Indian lasses," Oompa-Loompa said. "Has the lass told ye her name?"

"Sylvina Arboles, she says," Finley said suspiciously. Brows lifted all around, and the group stirred with surprise.

"She's a Spaniard?" one questioned with astonishment.

"She disnae carry a Spanish accent. However, she says that she knows the tongue," Finley disclosed. "Although, she also claims tae speak French." This time, the gang practically rumbled at the additional information.

"Her English is strange," another man said.

"Aye. Whaur did ye find her?" Bearnard asked curiously.

"In the wood along the road," Seamus answered. I caught a glimpse of him seated upon a rock, preoccupied with something over his thigh.

"Och, aye, I recall her from the road," said another man among the group.

"Why would a lone lass be out in the wood?" someone curiously inquired.

"I'm certain she's a courtesan," Lachlan insisted. "I've seen enough of them, I assure ye."

"Yoo're nothin' but crap, Lachlan," Bearnard said, and whacked Lachlan on the back of his head. "Ye merely bed any wench as they will take any bit of silver from the likes of ye. The cheap bastard that ye are."

"I dinnae reckon that she is a courtesan," Seamus interjected.

"And how are ye so certain, Seamus?" Oompa-Loompa inquired sarcastically, whose name turned out to be Cole.

"The lad knows King Louis's court, and should have some idea about it," said the greasy-looking man.

"Aye, he would know about it," someone teased. Chuckles scattered among the group.

"She's tae come with us tae Albany, as we cannae merely leave her haur alone," Seamus said, disregarding his teasing companions. "We'll sort it out once we're arrived."

All of a sudden, a dense *thudding* sound hit the ground, followed by a painful groan. Heads turned. I peered through the stinking band of men and noticed a man lying limp on the ground next to horse hooves.

"Och! Fearghus has fallen off his horse," said the greasy man, whose name I learned was Angus. He rushed over to the limp man and assisted Finley to lift him.

"Is he alrecht?" the hairy one inquired as he quickly moved toward him.

"Whit happened tae him?" Finley asked as both of them carried the injured guy away from the horse and placed him on the ground against a tree.

"He took a musket ball in the arm," Angus said.

"He's bleeding quite a bit," Finley observed as he took a blade from his boot and carefully cut away the filthy, bloodstained shirt the injured young man was wearing. Finley tore the sleeve from the man's arm. I stood watching like the other men. Blood was pouring from the wound. From what I could tell, the injured man seemed quite young. He appeared to be the youngest in the bunch and was probably in his early twenties.

"Whit do ye reckon?" Angus asked Finley with concern.

"Thaur is nothin' we can properly do fur him. Poor lad. Let him have a bit of rum. Hold on, Fearghus," Finley said anxiously.

I stood idly by, intently watching, and was astounded that it seemed they were not going to attempt to do anything to help him. *At least they could disregard their stupid role-playing game and ride him on a horse to the nearest hospital*, I thought. The injured man was groaning in obvious pain. His face was covered in sweat, and his eyelids looked heavy. Still, all they were doing for him was giving him booze to choke on. It was clear that the young man could barely swallow it down. As a physician, in spite of my fear and reservation, I decidedly edged my way through the congregated men toward the injured man who looked nearly lifeless on the ground.

"If someone would bring a first aid kit over here, I'm sure I could probably stabilize him until you can get him to the nearest trauma center," I said to both Finley and Angus.

"Whit did she say?" someone asked.

"Dinnae ken," another one replied in a confused tone.

"Whit do ye mean?" Angus said sharply with a dubious look on his face.

"Well, I'm a physician," I revealed. All ears were on the conversation, and someone laughed out loud.

"Whit are ye gettin' at, lass? Ye dinnae appear the least bit a physic," Finley snapped, blatantly irritated.

"I'm a pediatrician," I said.

"A whit?" Bearnard questioned curiously, appearing obviously puzzled.

"If someone would get a first aid kit. That will help a bit," I repeated. Odd stares flanked me as no one budged to obtain a kit. "Doesn't anyone have a first aid kit with them?" My tone was no longer one of uncertainty, but one of urgent professionalism.

"Whit is a first aid kit?" one of the men inquired of Cole, who was standing next to him.

"Dinnae ken," Cole answered with a shrug.

"No one?" I questioned unbelievably, and moved close to the ailing man. My professional gumption took over, and I looked directly at Finley. "If you'll allow me, I can try to at least save his life." He glowered at me. He didn't seem inclined to let me assist. "Or, if you'd rather, you could just let him die out here." Finley clenched his jaw and narrowed his eyes, thinking for a minute.

"Go on, then," Finley permitted finally, glaring skeptically at me. I turned and knelt beside the young man's injured arm while he remained in pain on the ground. I felt his brow using the underside of my wrist. His skin was clammy, but it didn't seem that he had a fever. I turned my eyes to the wound to take a good look at the damage. There was a hole all right, and blood kept spewing from it. I took the sleeve that Finley had ripped from the rest of the man's shirt and tied a tourniquet around the arm above the wound.

"I need antiseptic," I said, turning my glance up to the staring faces hovering around me.

"Whit micht that be?" Lachlan asked, scrunching his face.

"You know—a compound that sterilizes and inhibits microbial growth, which infects healthy tissue and damages it, causing infection." I saw nothing but blank stares.

"I reckon it is an elixir, she means," one of the men presumed, attempting to sound knowledgeable.

"No, not an elixir. It's an antibiotic," I clarified. They gave me puzzled looks. "Like a simple bottle of hydrogen peroxide," I suggested, observing no level of comprehension on the faces surrounding me. "What about saline solution?" I asked. "Okay, how about some booze, then?" Bingo! Registered looks of understanding. Multiple hands holding wooden canteens were shoved toward my face. I reached for one, oblivious to whom it belonged, and took it. I was aware that there were some places in the country that still had pockets of archaic communities in spite of this modern age, but I never would have anticipated a generally well-educated population like in Massachusetts to be one of those places. I mean, this was utterly ridiculous. I poured some alcohol over the wound, and the young man they called Fearghus winced. I gently spread the flesh to get a better look. "Does anyone happen to have a Swiss Army knife available?" I inquired while still studying the gaping injury.

"How does she ken whit sort of knife the Swiss army hold?" Lachlan inquired. "I'll tell ye just how—a courtesan would ken. That's how."

"Or a spy," Bearnard said.

"Just give me a knife from someone. Any damn knife will do, I suppose, thank you very much," I said, trying to remain levelheaded.

"Whit's the knife fur?" Finley questioned gruffly, narrowing his eyes while his large frame hovered, closely watching.

"I need to make a slight incision to widen the wound in order to get the bullet out," I explained. He seemed to consider it for a second, then whipped out a long, menacing blade that he kept in his boot and had used to shred Fearghus's sleeve away. He slapped the pummel of the knife into my hand. "Thanks," I said gruffly. I then dampened the hem of my dress with a bit of alcohol and rubbed the blade down with it, hoping to clean it well enough. Afterward, I leaned over and made a small, concentrated incision. Fearghus's mouth twitched, but he refused to indicate pain and instead gritted his teeth.

I inserted my finger and carefully fished inside the warm, soft flesh. The musket ball had traveled deep into the tissue, lodging itself against the humerus bone. The men had grown completely silent as they all watched me. After a moment, I was able to retrieve the large lead ball and dropped it to the ground.

"I don't suppose any of you might have a needle and thread at hand?" I asked hopefully.

"Och, I've got that in my pack," Angus said, expressing eagerness to help.

"Very good," I said, somewhat impressed. He quickly left and hastily returned with a leather pouch. He retrieved a small tin from it. He passed the tin to me, and I opened it, finding exactly what I needed. I cleaned the needle and dampened the thread with alcohol, then proceeded to stitch the wound. When I had completed the suturing, I poured a bit more alcohol on the closed wound. I glanced around the men and determined that they had nothing clean enough to be used for the next phase. So, I resourcefully tore off my far cleaner wide silk sash from around my waist and sliced it in half with the blade to use to bandage the injury.

Though the remaining sleeve on his unharmed arm appeared soiled from sweat and dust, I believed the linen material was sturdy enough to hold his injured arm. So, with a bit of a forced effort, I successfully tore off the second sleeve and fashioned a sling for him to fit his arm through.

"There," I said, satisfied by the work I had done. Having completed the task, I poured the remaining alcohol in the flask over my bloodstained hands. "You should take him back to North Adams and see to it that he gets to an ER right away. Since the bullet was impaled against the bone, I'm sure a trauma physician there will want to X-ray his arm to see if the bone was badly damaged, and if there are any bone fragments in the surrounding tissue. Also, they'll want to replace the sutures for sterile ones. He'll also need to be prescribed antibiotics to stave off infection."

There was nothing but clueless stares on the surrounding faces after I explained my instructions. It then, of course, dawned on me that these men probably did not want to visit the hospital, since it could raise questions they would most likely not want to answer.

"Where is North Adams?" one of the men asked oddly.

"The town about a couple of hours or so back a ways, adjacent to Williamstown," I said obviously as they gaped at me.

"We huvnae seen a town since we left Greenfield," Angus said, crimping his brow.

"Crap! Seamus haur fussin' by himself over an arrowhead stuck in his leg that none of us lads waur awaur of," Cole said, sounding concerned.

"Whit's he doing?" Finley asked.

"He's tryin' tae git it out himself, and I dinnae reckon he can manage," Cole said.

"I'm alrecht," Seamus said, grunting a bit. I peered through some surrounding legs as the men stood around, and noticed Seamus picking at his thigh with a dagger. Finley moved from Fearghus's side and walked toward his brother. He took a quick look at the problem in Seamus's leg.

"Bring the lass this way," Finley ordered. The one they called Liam grabbed my arm, yanked me to my feet, and directed me in front of the brothers. I glanced down at Seamus sitting on a boulder and saw his breeches torn away from his upper thigh, exposing a similar wound as Fearghus's.

"'Tis an arrowhead that caught my leg," Seamus grumbled.

I stared at his injury, surprised that he had been wounded. He had hiked for so long without expressing any sign of being hurt. Given the type of injury, I would have expected him to have indicated some extent of discomfort or pain. Still, his breeches had been saturated with earth stains, and it would have been difficult for anyone to have detected blood on them.

"I cannae git it out. 'Tis in too deep," he groaned with his knife in hand.

Unbelievable... *Who are these people?* I wondered.

Seeing that I had no choice, I knelt before his large muscular thigh and proceeded to prepare to extract the foreign object as I had similarly done with the last patient.

"That's guid rum yoo're wasting," Seamus said as I poured some over the open injury, causing his lip to twitch. I simply glowered at him, ignoring his objection, and followed through with the surgery.

When I completed extracting the menacingly jagged arrowhead from his thigh, I finished suturing and bandaging the wound, wanting to find the nearest exit out of this whole scenario.

"Weel now, I reckon that's about the nicest needlework I've seen," someone said. An impressive look of satisfaction crossed Finley's face. The rest of the onlooking men appeared the same way.

"Now, you're going to have to find some way to stay off that leg, you know. You could easily rupture the sutures and cause bleeding all over again if you exert the leg too much," I said. I was sweating from the heat outside and from the pressure to help these strange men. I wiped my brow with the back of my hand as I straightened to my feet again. "Your muscles are going to be tender for a few days too, because of some swelling that will occur as it heals. You could probably take some Motrin or acetaminophen like Tylenol for the pain, if you're uncomfortable. Ibuprofen is good to take, because it actually helps relieve swelling. But you'll need to keep the wound sterilized. Hydrogen peroxide should work just fine for that. There will also be some clotting that'll take place, so just treat it with alternating warm and cool compresses. But you'll ultimately need to visit your regular physician to have him or her check out how well the wound is healing—you know, to make sure that bacteria hasn't set in to cause an infection. Your doctor will also want to see if there has been any tissue damage as a result of the injury."

In the middle of giving him all of this advice, I realized that while he appeared to be listening intently to what I was saying, the other men were eyeballing me with varying looks that ranged from amazement to downright distrust.

"It's also my professional opinion," I continued defensively, "that next time you guys consider not using live ammunition and instead use something like blanks, so that no one gets seriously hurt. You'll prevent a lot of hazardous accidents." I steadied a determined eye on the party participants. "I mean, really—you shouldn't be in such a location playing war games without a handy first aid kit. It's a bit irresponsible of you, don't you think? You should have a phone at your disposal and a GPS on you at all times in case of emergencies like this. And, considering the remoteness of your location, getting to the nearest trauma center will unfortunately prove to be a real-life challenge. It's not as though you can easily be medevaced from this place. So, it's probably something you all should actually bear in mind from now on for the sake of being safe."

"Whit the *devil* is she talkin' about?" Liam said abruptly, with an incomprehensible look on his face.

"I'm not quite certain," Finley said as he closely eyed me.

"It appears that she does, in fact, have the gift of the gab," Cole said.

"Aye, but the lassie seems knowledgeable about healin', whitever the devil she speaks," Angus assessed.

"Aye." Finley's eyes stayed on me as he faintly nodded in accordance with Angus's evaluation. He patted Seamus's back. "Weel now, brother, it appears thaur micht be some value tae the lass efter all," he said gruffly with an ironic look. He took a good look at my handiwork and seemed satisfied. "Work weel done, lass." I stared back at the slipshod, crooked reenactors, wondering what was going to happen to me next. "Alrecht, lads, now that both men have their wounds dressed, 'tis time we git on before nichtfall," Finley said. He took my arm, and I instinctively grabbed my coat still on the ground before he steered me over to one of the horses with Seamus slowly limping behind us. "The lass is tae ride with ye, Seamus," Finley said as his brother came around to the horse.

"Aye," Seamus replied. He grimaced slightly as he fitted his boot into the stirrup, but easily hoisted himself high over the saddle despite his injured leg. I just stood there like an idiot looking at the animal in front of me. First of all, I didn't ride horses. Second of all, I was in a cocktail dress and wondered how

I was supposed to mount this very large animal without flashing the lustful eyes watching me.

"Weel, git yerself up thaur, lass," Finley hissed, and I suddenly noticed his impatience. Briefly determining which foot went where first, I thought it safer to first remove my muddied high heels, and I slid my bare red-painted toes into the stirrup. I swung my leg over as modestly as I could while Finley boosted me up. Seamus pulled my arm, situating me in front of him on the saddle, and drew me close against his muscular frame.

My position on the horse was very awkward, since he now had me snug against him as his thighs rubbed against mine. I could feel his broad chest at my back, and I caught the wind of his breath over my head. I supposed that he didn't believe in showering or deodorant either, because he densely reeked of male body odor, sour sweat, campfire, tobacco, whiskey, and blood. I wondered how much farther down the rabbit hole would I wind up going—and where would I finally land? I had not the faintest idea. At this point, all I could do was just hope and pray to remain unscathed.

CHAPTER 6

Seamus latched his arm around my waist as he held me close so that we could both fit on his horse, and secured me to him so that I wouldn't fall off. I held on to the pommel just to keep myself balanced. However, I was convinced that any sudden movement would unquestionably land me smack on the ground with a bad sprain or broken limb.

"Tick, tick." He clucked the inside of his cheek and lightly tapped his spurs into his horse, urging it ahead of the group until we edged abreast of Finley out onto the path in the woods. The two men calmly commenced conversing in their native language. All the while, I kept wishing for this to be a bad dream. I wondered when I was going to wake up and find myself back at home in my normal life with family and friends where I was supposed to be. Except being kidnapped right now shattered that possibility and introduced a hard, indisputable reality. My inner thighs were growing tender and bothered me as they rubbed against the saddle. I tried to ignore my discomfort and let my mind wander as I wondered how I was going to escape.

I found it really odd that a bunch of filthy, lawless Scottish rogues, who were obviously not extras in a Hollywood feature film, would take interest in acting out a facet of American history. I was born and raised in Los Angeles and was accustomed to filming crews stationed around the city creating their films. No matter what the film's budget, it was always a production, with lights, cameras, actors, stagehands, tech crews, cops, trucks, and trailers blocking off areas in neighborhoods or surface streets, which tied up traffic for hours around the city. But there was no indication of any kind of production like that happening around here.

Then it occurred to me—maybe these weird men were part of some kind of extreme historical society that was also transcontinental, and they had traveled from the UK to participate. But that didn't explain the deaths I had witnessed, or the injuries I had attended to.

We started through a wide, shallow stream. Water sloshed around and kicked up in large drops, which landed on the side of my legs as we passed through. When we reached the other side of the stream, my legs and the skirt of my dress were soaking wet, and I sensed the journey was going to be rougher than I had originally conceived.

We continued riding along the side of the stream until we meandered our way out onto a small path through the mountains. Deep in the Berkshires, I couldn't discern our exact whereabouts and hoped for a discreet opportunity to gather my as yet undetected phone from my coat pocket to activate the GPS. I hoped at that point that I would be able to text my brother with information about my circumstances and location. Unfortunately, that opportunity never presented itself, since the men persevered onward without ever breaking to rest.

It was humid, and the sun was bright and strong. Even in the late afternoon, the heat persisted. We finally arrived at a small meadow near a pond, where the men decided to break and camp for the night. I wasn't the least bit comfortable about the prospect of being forced to sleep among these men. I didn't trust any of them, but I was starved for food and water, since I hadn't had any nourishment all day. Smelling the enticing wild turkeys they had caught on the fire desperately made my stomach growl, and all I wanted to do was eat.

I quietly stepped toward the shore of the pond, aware of Seamus's sidelong stare on me as he sat slightly out of the circle of his joking and chatting friends around the campfire. I knelt to wash the dried blood and dirt off my hands and from beneath my nails as best as I could without the availability of soap. It was a difficult task, but I scrubbed hard until I was relatively satisfied.

Just as I was about to pull my hands from the water, a humungous, noisy flying insect that I had never seen before landed on the dry part of my upper forearm. I suddenly shot to my toes, screeching bloody murder, wildly waving my arm, and spinning on my heels, fleeing like a maniac. In the processes of escaping the large insect, I recklessly bumped into Seamus, unaware of him having closely approached me from behind.

"Oh!" I exclaimed unexpectedly as he caught me, crashing clumsily into his broad chest. I thoughtlessly scurried around him for protection. He calmly turned, facing me with a strange look on his face. I discerned a partial grin on his lips. "What the hell sort of Jurassic insect was that?"

"I beg yer pardon?" He lifted his golden eyebrows and gazed at me with what seemed to be a combination of cautious amusement and surprise.

"A really huge, ugly-looking bug landed on me a second ago," I explained excitedly, aware that I should probably compose myself.

"Do ye mean the heat fly that merely flew away now?" he asked, unfazed.

"I guess," I said.

"Och, ye neednae fret over it, lass. It wulnae hurt ye," he assured. I had never seen a gigantic cicada like that before, and it more than frightened me with its large stinger, red eyes, and all.

"Thaur now, Seamus! Must ye cause fricht tae the lass so?" Angus called back from the group, looking over his shoulder at us, along with the full attention of the rest of the men.

"It was a heat fly instead of I that frightened her," Seamus replied to the men.

"'Tis one and the same I reckon, as a fly is drawn tae honey! Now keep quiet fur us thaur! Micht ye?" Bearnard said, and the men chuckled.

"Aye! It isnae reit that ye dip intae the sweet pot and not share amongst us," Lachlan teased. More laughter came from the men.

"Alrecht, lads, that'll be enough," Seamus insisted. He sternly looked at his buddies, then returned his eyes to me again. "Forgive them. They huvnae seen, eh, a bonnie lass in many weeks… And, eh, yoo're particularly one of unique beauty… and so the lads are merely taken, that is all." He gave me a harmless look, and maybe a faintly flirtatious grin. But I hardly took them for being harmless and continued gazing doubtfully at him. "Haur," he said, holding out his canteen to me. "Take some. 'Twill help ease the hunger whilst we await tae eat." My stomach growled loudly again, and it was hard to ignore the strong pangs. It felt like my stomach had started eating itself. I reluctantly took the canteen and a distrustful sniff from the opening. It was essentially the most potently scented alcohol I had ever smelled in my life.

"What is it?" I inquired skeptically.

"Rum," he said obviously. "Ye closely wasted it on me tendin' my leg. Do ye not recall?" I had never known rum to smell like this before. If it was as strong as it seemed, then it was as good as jet fuel, and I didn't feel safe drinking it. Nevertheless, parched and starved as I was, I put the rim to my lips and sipped a small amount. I choked, coughing as it burned like fire going down my throat and into the pit of my stomach. "Take care," he said considerately, retrieving the canteen from me.

"The proof in it is much too high to be safely ingested. Don't you think?" It had left my voice hoarse and scratchy, but the hunger pangs all of a sudden began giving way to kindling warmth burning inside from the alcohol instead.

"Do ye mean that ye find it a bit strong?"

"Yes—very."

"Och, I reckon that I find it quite suitable," he disagreed. "I assure ye, however, that it will keep ye from keeling tae the ground from hunger." He pushed the cork into the canteen and limped slightly to sit over a large log at the edge of the water. He kept staring at me, and it was making me very uncomfortable. I nervously pushed my wayward ringlets out of my face and behind my ears. The long curls had fallen from the crystal clips on the side of my head into a mess over my shoulders. The light breeze kept moving strands of hair into my face, and I realized that I had become obviously uncertain.

"May I have a look at your wound to see how it is doing?" I asked impulsively.

"Aye, ye may." He seemed slightly reticent in spite of his permission. I stepped toward him, and he stiffened as I placed my fingers carefully over his muscular thigh to gently remove the soiled dressing. The stitches luckily remained intact, and while the wound was visibly inflamed, it had stopped bleeding and clotting had occurred.

"It's really important to keep the injury clean so that it doesn't become infected," I advised while still examining the wound.

"Whit is meant by 'infected'?"

"You know, in cases when the skin is broken and becomes badly swollen—red or discolored sometimes beyond the localized injured area—filled with puss, and a possible fever could ensue."

"Och." He understood, nodding his head.

"Except I need a clean piece of material to use for a bandage," I said, observing the dark bloodied cloth I was holding between my fingertips. He shifted a little, reaching inside his waistcoat pocket.

"Will this do?" He pulled out a bright white fine linen handkerchief monogrammed with the letters *LS* and held it out to me. I placed the filthy dressing on the marshy grass, and my fingers accidentally grazed his as I took the fresh material from his hand. Ignoring the sensation of our touching fingers, I instead examined the size of the handkerchief.

"This should work for now," I said approvingly, and started redressing the wound after applying a couple of cleansing swabs of rum again over the stitches. When I had finished securing the bandage around his thigh, I carefully took up the soiled dressing laying on the grass, thinking it could possibly be washed and reused under the circumstances. He reached for the bloodied material and balled it up into his breeches pocket. "I was going to wash it in the pond for later use," I suggested.

"'Tis alrecht. I shall keep it," he said. I noticed his ears had turned pink when he tilted his head as he put the dirty cloth in his pocket. "I shall prefer that ye sit with me instead." He was polite, I noticed. Still, seeing that I really had no choice but to oblige him, I hesitantly moved to sit beside him. He sat without speaking for a moment, and an awkward silence followed as he kept his eyes ahead, looking out over the dark water.

"So, who are you?" I finally decided to ask. He returned to looking directly at me with his deep ultramarine eyes, and I was able to clearly observe his appearance. He was handsome for sure, despite the grime on his face. The cleft in his bewhiskered square chin chiseled his square jaw and faintly reminded me of my late husband. But that was the extent of any similarities. My late husband had been handsome too, with his chestnut hair, a faint dimple in his chin, and gray eyes. Seamus's head was golden blonde, and he had a perfectly straight nose, high cheekbones, and deep blue eyes. In fact, he appeared to be just about my own age, unlike my late husband, who was several years older than I.

"Forgive my discourtesy, I wisnae quite myself upon my meetin' ye in the wood back thaur, as it was raither unexpected," he said. I nodded subtly, excusing him. "I am His Grace, Duke of Monteith, major in His Royal Majesty King George the Second of Great Britain's Army, at yer aid."

I silently looked at him in utter disbelief, flabbergasted at the title he just gave me. He was obviously convinced about who he was, and apparently so was everyone else around him.

"Really?" I replied politely, although skeptical of him.

"Aye," he said.

"Nice to meet you," I responded modestly nevertheless.

"A pleasure tae make yer acquaintance indeed," he said considerately. He seemed genuine with good manners in spite of kidnapping me.

"And your brother? Who is he?" I asked cautiously.

"He is His Lordship, Earl of Kneep. Also major in His Majesty's Army."

"Oh… And everyone else?" I asked, feeling silently suspended.

"Angus, Roy, Bearnard are cousins—and they are captains. Young Fearghus ranks lieutenant, as do Cole, Lachlan, and Liam, who are also kin."

"Oh…"

Are they all delusional? Or is it just me who is totally confused?

Seamus turned a discerning eye on me. "I shall like tae pose a question tae ye, Mistress Arboles."

"Yes?" I responded hesitantly.

"I shall like tae ken how ye came tae be in the wood, quite removed from any town, alone without an escort?"

"Well… I'm not—" I started while rubbing my brow, feeling very discombobulated. The headache that I had incurred from lack of proper fluid intake and prolonged hunger was bothering me. I wasn't likely to tell him everything about myself, as he seemed to want to know. Except he did seem authentically concerned. It struck me as strange and inconsistent to everything that was occurring. "My car was stolen from me," I said, looking at him.

"Yer car?" He gave me an odd look, as if he didn't know what I meant.

"My vehicle… My transportation was taken from me, and I was left stranded off the road." His golden eyebrows lifted somewhat. His deep blue eyes remained intently steady on me. If I could somehow convince him to take me back to the location where I was kidnapped, then maybe I could find my way back home. I looked at him, thinking of how I might try inspiring sympathy from him. "You know, it seems like you could be a conscionable person." Whether that was true or not, it was as good as rolling dice. I was just going to give it a try. "And this might be considered a complete misunderstanding… If you would just please let me go—take me back to where I was abducted… Look, I just want to go home, that's all. Perhaps you might understand?" His eyes seemed to politely scrutinize me while he silently stared at me without responding.

"Tell us, then, are ye a spy?" Finley suddenly asked as he was abruptly discovered standing behind us. I wasn't sure how long he had been standing there listening to our conversation. If anyone was a spy, presumably it could have been him, I thought.

"No," I said absurdly, looking at them both. "Why would I be? That's ridiculous… Who would I be spying for, for instance?"

"Do ye ken anything about the war?" Finley inquired shortly.

"The war? Why would I know anything special about what's going on in Afghanistan? What does that have to do with anything?"

"Afghanistan?" Seamus echoed, appearing puzzled. The brothers briefly looked at each other with question marks on their faces.

"Such a place is not knoon tae us. Therefore, whaur micht that be?" Finley inquired. To my surprise, he seemed quite serious.

"The region neighbors Pakistan," I replied, looking obviously at both of them. Still, they appeared shockingly uninformed. "Do you know where the country India is?" The two men exchanged glances.

"Aye," Seamus said.

"Well, it's essentially right there in that region of the globe," I said. Finley said something incomprehensible in Scots to his brother. Seamus replied with a few sentences before returning his attention to me again.

"Are ye awaur that the Crown is also presently at war in India?" he asked.

"No, the British are in Afghanistan fighting the Taliban along with Amer—" I started correcting, but suddenly broke off, realizing an unexplained, deeply ominous feeling had come over me. I thought I ought not divulge any more information than I might mistakenly have already. From the queer looks on their faces, I clearly saw that we were not all currently comprehending each other—for whatever reason.

"Whit would the Taliban be?" Finley asked, slightly narrowing his eyes.

"They're terrorists," I said, sounding worried even to my own ears. I felt this interrogation was quickly going the wrong way, as I supposed I wasn't correctly playing their game.

Finley's copper brows rose slightly. "I reckon yoo're referrin' tae Indians. But which ones?" He then shifted a critical eye on me, and my throat went dry. "If ye regard yer life with any importance, lass, ye will tell us everything ye ken about the French. Do ye understand?"

His voice sounded threatening, and I instinctively knew that he was not a man to cross. Remaining calm, I racked my brain, quickly thinking of what kind of concocted story I could give them that might be convincing according to their perspective.

"It's as I said—I don't know anything. I'm not any kind of sleeper agent or covert operator. I don't know anything about the

French. All I know is that I am a widowed gentlewoman from Pennsylvania," I lied, deciding to play their stupid game. I couldn't very well say that I was from California, now could I? Given that it appeared these men were consistently acting like they were from 1776. "I was traveling with my chauffeur and my maid to Boston in order to set sail to New Orleans, where I am to live with distant relatives." Louisiana seemed like a good enough faraway place to safely say, I guessed. "We were unexpectedly ambushed by a wild band of men on the road. They jumped my chauffeur as he attempted to ward them off, but I believe he was killed as he was dragged into the woods by one of the attackers. They stole my team of horses and carriage as well… and made off with my maid, never to be seen again." Listening to myself, I couldn't believe that I was coming up with such a tall tale. But I kept improvising as my anxiety ran with my imagination. "I fortunately managed to escape the thieves somehow as I went running terribly frightened into the forest. They successfully took all that was left of my property… So, I was forced to wander through the woods until I discovered the road again, at which time your troops were approaching, only to be besieged again by assailing gunfire, followed by my abduction. To which I believe you know the current outcome, since here I am with you."

There. How was that for nonsense? I only wondered if they would be persuaded. Perhaps I recognized that it was probably to my best advantage to play their eccentric game.

There was no expression on Finley's face as he simply paid me the courtesy of his attention.

"Thus explains the reason fur yer wandering about in the midst of nowhere in the wood attired merely in undergarments," Finley surmised with an eyebrow arching high over one eye coupled with the sarcastic smirk on his face, making him appear blatantly doubtful.

I glanced down at my currently ruined high-fashion party dress, realizing that I had forgotten that small detail. Comparatively, relative to their manner of dress and behavior, I supposed my appearance might conceivably have been perceived as risqué. I had no excuse for my appearance, so I simply remained quiet. Finley glared at me and said something in Scots to Seamus.

"Do ye recall how yer attackers appeared?" Seamus inquired, breaking his observant silence.

"Um, well… it's hard to tell—because it all happened so quickly," I answered.

"Can ye say how many thaur waur?" Finley questioned.

"I guess I'd assume probably at least three. But, like I said, I couldn't really get a clear description of them, since everything was happening so fast—and because I was extremely panicked," I explained, fully aware of their absorbed expressions as they were paying close attention to me.

"Tell us again whit ye meant by the Crown and Afghanistan, was it?" Finley pressed.

"Well." I paused for a second. "I overheard a woman mentioning it to a friend of hers in a shop where I was purchasing items. She explained to her friend that her husband's brother had returned home wounded from serving in a war that was taking place in that region of the world." That part of the story was relatively true. "I suppose I didn't realize she was probably referring to a location in India where the war is taking place." I took a flying guess presuming other fractious international affairs were occurring around the globe during the supposed imperial period they were dramatizing. Finley's chin dipped faintly as he nodded pensively.

"I see," Finley said finally.

Seamus turned to Finley and said something in Scots. The inflection in his tone sounded reasonable. Finley's response did not seem to agree with Seamus's statement, but Seamus's reply sounded measured as he maintained an even tone. The two sincerely went back and forth debating with each other for a moment. I sensed that they were likely considering options for what to do with me.

"Aye, so be it, then. It awaits tae be discovered till we learn who the lass is in truth—and it best be sooner raither than later," Finley finally said in English, appearing reluctant and not in full accord with the end of their conversation.

"Agreed," Seamus said satisfactorily.

Finley gave him a cynical look. "Weel, then… 'Tis time tae eat. The meat is ready cooked," he said.

"Aye," Seamus acknowledged. He stood and shifted his weight over his good leg. "Come along, lass. We're done sittin' haur fur now. 'Tis time yoo've had some nourishment." He wrapped a palm around my elbow, urging me to my feet, and suggested I proceed before him. I started pacing behind Finley as he began walking toward the rest of the men, who were already eating around the fire. I could feel Seamus's eyes on me as he followed me toward the campfire.

SUNLIGHT WAS QUICKLY FADING, and I decided to use what was left of the light to check Fearghus's wound. I ensured that the wound remained clean and the bandages were stable around his arm. When I was satisfied with his examination, and after I was allowed to slip into the nearby bushes to relieve myself, Seamus determined where I was to sleep for the night. He had set out a large wool blanket over the grass among the group. It became apparent that he intended to share the blanket with me. It would be a close fit to share it, and I wasn't sure about sleeping so close. I didn't feel certain about succumbing to the vulnerability of sleeping in near proximity to all these strange men.

"'Tis alrecht, lass. Ye may be assured that nae one haur will harm ye whilst ye rest," Seamus said, observing me. He looked sincere about it. But I hesitated. "Come now," he urged unconcernedly, nodding once to the space on the blanket. "Ye neednae be concerned of brigands or Indian attackers fur that matter either. The lads are guid watchmen and quick tae arms, and I'm quick with a dirk and pistol if anyone will try tae take ye. Now come lie and sleep. We've a long journey set upon us fur the morrow."

He waited until I budged slightly to take my spot on the blanket. Not knowing whether I could truly trust him, I cautiously moved with some apprehension toward the blanket and found a place on it near the edge. He followed and placed himself close beside me. I turned on my side, facing away from him. The moonlit sky was heavily sprinkled with stars peering through the towering, shadowy black trees. A sigh came from him, and I sensed him relaxing beside me as the rhythm of his breathing drew long and regular.

The night air remained humid and balmy. Fireflies sparked like millions of flashing points of light suspended in the air before my eyes. They seemed to mirror the abundant stars hovering high above. I was very impressed to see so many brightly shining stars that my breath was stolen from me. I didn't ever recall seeing the sky so dense with celestial bodies in all my life. The view was incomparable to the times I'd gone camping in Big Bear. Even Yosemite couldn't escape pollution sometimes. Right now there were no city lights or other sources of pollution to obstruct the night sky. Tonight, right here, as my eyes stared out into black space, the stars reigned with incontestable authority and commanded the endless universe above.

The crickets were loud all around and reminded me of an overwhelming infestation. All sorts of sounds came out at night that normally would have kept me awake, like the owls hooting invisibly up in the dark trees. The frogs in the pond croaked audibly, and the sound of cicadas hummed everywhere. A few mosquitoes bit me, but at the moment, I was filled with such exhaustion and worry that I didn't care. I helplessly closed my eyes and found myself beginning to drift asleep to the harmonies of the night in spite of my deep consternation and misgivings.

THE NEXT MORNING, we awakened at the break of dawn and set out traveling on horseback. I was paired with Seamus like the day before. The sky was overcast with dark clouds. It appeared as if it would rain. The air was warm and clammy, perfectly suiting an abundance of pestering mosquitoes, gnats, June bugs, dragonflies, and all sorts of other flying insects I was not quite used to. Journeying was rough as we traveled over what essentially amounted to a foot path. We continued over uneven ground as we meticulously wound our way through the Berkshire Mountains.

Compared to the conventional standards of dense metropolitan living, this unwelcome experience was proving to be unpredictably hectic. The men were in a hurry to get to their next destination. The last time I had ridden a horse was when I was five years old on a pony ride at a farmers market in Santa Monica. So, riding on horseback with a strange man through the wilderness, accompanied by a bunch of odd Scotsmen dressed to perfection, in spite of their dirt-encrusted appearances, in eighteenth-century British military garb, armed to the max, was far from mundane. It was simultaneously bizarre and frightening.

At one point, a roaming mountain lion was spotted through the trees along the way. It had been tracking us. Bearnard sniped it off, and I unexpectedly jumped at the sound of his pistol as it discharged.

It started drizzling, and the men pushed harder through the undulating terrain. As they conversed in their native language, I began taking into account that I was considerably lucky—so far —since this time we had not been dangerously confronted by besieging men swinging tomahawks or shooting guns at each other. Plus, the fact that I had remained unharmed was also fortunate.

The men pushed hard all day, with few breaks in between to relieve ourselves. Rain continued falling, heavily soaking us. By dusk we had arrived at a large field of cleared property. Candlelight flickered in the windows as we approached a log cabin in the distance. When we came closer to the cabin, a man emerged from the front door armed with a musket. He pointed it right at us. Seamus reined in, stopping us, on his horse as the others followed suit.

"Who goes there?" shouted the man at the front door from a distance.

"It is I, Earl of Kneep, Johann Anderson!" Finley replied audibly.

"His Lordship, Earl of Kneep, did you say?" The German accent was strong in Mr. Anderson's speech, I noticed.

"Aye!" Finley dismounted his horse, as did the rest of the men. Mr. Anderson dropped the long barrel of his musket that had been aimed directly at us and leaned it against the threshold of the cabin. He picked up the candlelit lantern flickering at his feet. He started walking quickly toward us with the lantern in hand. It swung back and forth in his grip upon his approach as Seamus took me by the waist and eased me off his horse to my feet. He removed his drenched redcoat from his shoulders and draped it over my bare wet shoulders, completely covering me down to my ankles.

"Ah, *gut, gut*," Mr. Anderson said, recognizing the men. "A pleasure to see you again, Your Lordship, Your Grace, sirs." He politely bowed his head to the men.

"Nice tae see ye as weel, Master Anderson," Finley replied. I was surprised to see Finley's courteous demeanor. A far cry from the disgruntled disposition that I had witnessed from him earlier.

"*Danke*, Your Lordship," Mr. Anderson said modestly.

"Is all weel with ye, Master Anderson?" Seamus inquired politely.

"*Ja,* all is quite well, *danke,* Your Grace," Mr. Anderson said. "Come, come, please, out of the wet air. We have deer pottage on the fire that I shall bring to you, and *gut* Hessian ale, which you favor well."

"That seems fitting indeed, thank ye, Master Anderson," Finley agreed.

"*Gut, gut.* This way, my lords, sirs," Mr. Anderson said, and started to guide us toward his homestead.

"One moment, please, Master Anderson," Seamus said. Mr. Anderson stopped short and turned, facing Seamus.

"*Ja,* Your Grace?"

"We, however, have Mistress Arboles with us on this account," Seamus informed him. Mr. Anderson's skinny silhouette seemed to notice me just then.

"Ah, of course. I beg your pardon, Mistress Arboles," Mr. Anderson said politely. "Mistress Anderson will provide the empty chamber that belonged to our son to you, mistress."

"That will be suitable, Master Anderson. Thank ye," Seamus said.

"Indeed, Your Grace," Mr. Anderson replied.

"We shall see tae ourselves, Master Anderson," Finley said. "Thank ye again fur yer hospitality." Mr. Anderson courteously dipped his shadowy head to the men. Then, the men started walking toward the barn, silhouetted in the dark rain.

"*Bitte,* come with me, mistress. My wife will properly see to your comfort," Mr. Anderson said, politely intimating for me to follow him. Seamus followed us toward the house until Mr. Anderson opened the front door for me to enter.

The log cabin appeared surprisingly spacious inside than was anticipated from outside in the dark. It smelled of cooking, burning logs, earth, and tobacco smoke. There was ale and broken bread with a dish of butter on the rectangular pine table in the middle of the room when we entered. Mr. Anderson solemnly introduced his wife to me as she stood from her wooden chair near the hearth. Now that I could view the couple clearly in the firelight, I saw they were of average height and seemed middle-aged with few years between them. The strain of hard country living was evident on their faces, making them seem older than they probably were. Yet in spite of their dour appearances, they were extremely polite and welcoming.

As tired and confused as I was with everything that was happening around me, I unexpectedly felt a sense of comfort in their home. While Mr. Anderson was unspoken and modestly reserved in my presence, Mrs. Anderson was slightly more sociable as she attentively placed a tin bowl filled with venison pottage and a mug of ale before me at the pine table. I politely thanked her and dipped my spoon into the pottage. After a couple of bites of the venison, I decided that it tasted very unusual and was too gamy for my taste. But rather than insult and starve to death, I began to devour it, realizing I could over-look the taste and smell in order to satiate my hunger.

After I had completed my meal, I thanked Mrs. Anderson again for serving me the food. She politely nodded her head once in acknowledgment, then proceeded to show me to the bedroom I was supposed to use for the night. It was a modest room, long and narrow, but clean and well suited for a good night's stay. I was happy to see a wash basin in the corner and a cotton towel neatly placed by it over the stand by the small twin bed. She explained to me that the room had once belonged to her eigh-teen-year-old son, who had joined the colonial militia under Colonel Ephraim Williams to aid British troops in the fight. According to her story, the men were attacked by French forces at Lake George and her son was "knocked in the head with a musket ball and promptly perished."

As sad as her story was, I eerily noticed how real her emotions struck me and how it evoked my sympathy. I also struggled to figure out what military engagement she was referring to—not to mention how confusing and strange it was listening to her tell me this tale in a manner different from the way people normally spoke in modern times.

When she had finished telling me her son's story, she apologized and properly laid out a plain, clean, coarsely woven knee-length white linen garment for me to sleep in, then left me alone in the room. I gazed at the garment for a moment. It appeared to be an old-fashioned shift of sorts. I gathered the plain shift in my hands to take a closer look at it. It reminded me of something that probably would have been worn by a cast member in the TV show *Little House on the Prairie.*

A sigh escaped me as I contemplated removing my clothes. A large part of me didn't want to undress, because I wanted what was mine to remain on me. But, as I considered it, my clothes were ruined. Logic told me that I could not sleep in this clean bed with filthy wet attire. So, I began removing Seamus's coat from my shoulders and placed it on the chair near the bed. Next, I began undressing. I put my perfectly ruined, pretty cocktail dress and shoes in a pile on the floor next to the chair. I lamented the broken heels of my expensive, mud-stained shoes as I stared momentarily at them. Finally, I folded my dirty, bloodstained coat on top.

Now only dressed in my strapless bra and panties, I used the wash basin to clean the dirt off my arms and legs, in addition to the grime beneath my nails. When I had finished, I suddenly became distracted and reached inside my coat pocket to withdraw my phone. I quickly threw on the shift and plopped onto the bed with my phone in hand. I lifted the phone into view, and the screen instantly illuminated. Still, to my dismay, it indicated no cell reception. The time and date did not register either. And it displayed what was likely only a couple more days of battery life before it would die and need recharging.

If it were to die on me, then I would certainly be out of luck. I couldn't make a call and reach anybody in that case. If that were to happen, I'd have to look out for someone that I could trust and reach out for help. I dropped my head onto the pillows, holding on to my phone as I tucked myself into bed. I curled up tightly beneath the quilt, wondering about the bizarre circumstances surrounding me, and I thought about the next opportunity to escape.

Later that night, I awakened from slumber, and had a hard time going back to sleep. I kept tossing and turning on the mattress because I was consumed with thoughts of returning home. I had become very anxious; the men had already taken me so far from the site where I had gone missing, and I was nervous about being moved farther away. Furthermore, I worried about the exact location where I had disappeared, since the car had vanished and the road had looked unfamiliar. There weren't any memorable man-made landmarks around the area that I could instantly recall. I began to panic, and I shot up from the quilt.

What if I can't find the exact location where I went missing again?

I tossed on my coat and shoved my feet back into my heels, which now suddenly felt uncomfortable to wear. I was compelled to escape again.

The cabin was dark and silent in the dead of night. I quietly crept across the floor and carefully opened the door. As I moved to cross the threshold, my leg unexpectedly bumped into a heaping, indiscernible mound on the floor. It obstructed my path and sent me suddenly flying into the corridor that led into the small sitting room.

"Oof!" the mound grumbled as I clumsily hit the floor with a *whump.* I landed flat on my stomach. I was brusquely grabbed from behind and whipped around onto my back. Something glinted in the moonlight entering from the window, and I caught the shape of a long, fierce dagger. Moonlight ran down the blade like quicksilver suspended high above my chest.

"No! Please don't!" I gasped, sharply frightened as I thought my life would end right then and there. A heavy weight rested immovably over me, and the shadows half revealed the stunned whites of Seamus's eyes.

"Guid Lord, lass! Whit the devil are ye doin'? I nearly killed ye!" he said. He drew the dirk away, tucking it into his boot. He pushed himself off me and knelt in front of me as I stirred to sit up on the floor. "Whit is the meaning of this?" he questioned.

"I, uh, I—I thought I heard something by the window outside the room, and I got scared," I lied.

"Och," he grunted. His hand moved over his brow in the moonlight, and he rubbed it back and forth. His palm fell away, and his shadowy head tilted slightly as he perceived me in the moonbeam coming through the window. "Ye heard a soond outdoors that frightened ye, eh?" The suspicion in his voice was clear.

"Uh, yeah—yes, I mean. I did hear something," I stammered.

"Humph… Weel, let us have a look. Shall we?"

I swallowed dryly as he stood before me. He grasped my upper arm, quickly pulling me to my feet, then released me. I turned back into the bedroom with him following directly behind me. His silhouette appeared large and intimidating in the small space of the room. He stepped across the bedroom toward the window and peered out. "It appears thaur isnae anything of concern outdoors tae cause ye fricht. So, ye neednae worry yerself. All is quite weel." His tone was even and unfazed, although his accent was strong.

"Oh," I muttered, slightly unsettled. "Well, um, thank you for making sure."

"Indeed," he said suspiciously. His face was unclear in the dark, but the moonlight caught the crease on the corner of his upturned lip. "I reckon it may prove unpleasant tae retire fur the remainder of the nicht attired in a coat and shoes."

I didn't respond as I glanced down at myself half dressed in the obscuring dark. I realized that he had a point. I moved around the bed toward the chair in order to set my coat there again. Seamus lingered a moment as I put my coat back and removed my shoes. He then moved toward the threshold, leaned down to collect his blanket off the floor just beyond the entrance, and then closed the door with him still inside the bedroom. He whipped his blanket out across the floor, placing it directly before the door.

"What are you doing?" I asked guardedly as I watched him.

"I shall see tae it that ye may rest assured nae longer spooked by strange soonds in the nicht, mistress," he said straightforwardly while beginning to make himself comfortable on the floor.

"You don't have to. I'll be all right," I replied uncertainly as I moved toward the bed.

"I reckon that if I remain haur, I shall likely hear whit strange soonds in the window that micht be of concern tae ye and mind so that yoo're not scared," he said.

"Oh," I said, stupidly realizing that I should have made my first attempt escaping through the window instead of using the door.

"Now git tae bed, lass, and sleep weel." His voice resonated softly with reassurance in the dark. He settled more comfortably on the floor by the door, and I dubiously turned toward the bed. I crawled beneath the quilt, tucking it close around me despite the clammy air. I located him motionless on the floor by the door, bathed in the moonbeam entering the room from the window. The room went quiet, and I stared at him for a while, feeling really unsettled, before I closed my eyes and tried to sleep.

AT DAWN, Mrs. Anderson entered the room and awakened me from my slumber. As I rubbed my eyes from sleep, I realized that Seamus was no longer in the room on the floor by the door. I noticed Mrs. Anderson had a bundle of clothing in her arms. She charitably donated the clothes to me, but there was nothing among the pile of clothing that I recognized. I inquired politely if she would instead loan me a simple pair of jeans and a T-shirt, to which she gave me a blank look and inquired deferentially, "What is that you request, mistress?"

"Never mind. It's okay," I said politely.

"Forgive my humble articles, mistress, but this is all I have to give to you," she said regretfully.

"No, it's all right. Don't worry about it," I assured her nicely. I nodded in acceptance, and she proceeded to dress me in simple fashion according to the eighteenth century.

It was an odd experience having someone other than myself dress me, as she covered the shift she had given me last night with a garment resembling a corset without the hourglass shape called *stays*. But before it went around my torso, I was first given a pair of plain cotton stockings to cover my legs, with strings for garters to keep my stockings from falling. The next thing that went on my person were a pair of simple leather slippers in place of my sadly ruined shoes. I wasn't used to this order of dressing, while Mrs. Anderson continued tying a rather sizable pouch around my waist, which was a *pocket* that remained unattached from the main garment. Then a plain white linen petticoat was wrapped over the pocket around my waist, followed by a simple brown twill petticoat on top. A neckerchief was placed over my shoulders and tucked in front of the stays. A garment resembling a short pleated jacket, known as a short gown, came over my torso and hung just below my hips as it was fastened in place by pins. Finally, a coarse linen apron was tied around my waist. Now I was properly dressed for the time.

It was an uncomfortable feeling, being weighed down by so many fabrics, particularly in this warm, humid New England heat. There was no mirror around for me to glimpse how I looked. But by the way these clothes felt, I wasn't fond of the sensation of their restrictiveness on my body.

When I emerged from the bedroom, Seamus was already seated at the table eating bread and butter. I perceived his unspoken reservedness in his expression as his eyes examined my new appearance.

"Come haur, lass. Git some food in yer stomach before we depart," he instructed. I moved toward him at the table and sat on the bench across from him. There were no plates set out on the table. So I carefully reached for the bread and broke a piece off. Seamus took the knife resting on the butter plate near him and cut a healthy slice for me.

"Thank you," I said gratefully.

"Aye, yoo're welcome," he replied. Mrs. Anderson approached me and gave me a cup of cider. It was the hardest cider I ever remembered having, and I sipped it sparingly to wash the tough bread down. After eating, Seamus stood from the table and reached in his satchel. He pulled out some silver coins and gave them to Mr. Anderson when he entered the cabin from outside. Mr. Anderson humbly received the coins.

"Thank ye, Master and Mistress Anderson, fur yer hospitality, and fur yer charity tae Mistress Arboles," Seamus said kindly.

"*Danke* most kindly, Your Grace," Mr. Anderson said respectfully. "Indeed, we are most honored."

"Fur yer trooble," Seamus indicated.

"*Danke schoen*," Mr. Anderson repeated appreciatively. Seamus then locked his eyes on mine as I remained seated at the table.

"Come along, lass. 'Tis time we take our leave," Seamus said. I stood from my seat and walked toward him as he waited promptly for me at the front door. He took me by the arm and escorted me outside as the rest of the men were already mounting their horses, readying themselves to leave the property.

As we approached Seamus's horse, the men glanced at me,

sizing me up and down. One of the men said something in Scottish while looking at me, prompting snickering all around. Seamus said something back to them in their language, and they stopped laughing. I fitted my slipper into the stirrup, and Seamus boosted me up over his tall ebony stallion.

Finley scrutinized me with his blue eyes. His square jaw was set sternly as he towered upon his sienna horse. "Humph," he grunted. He kept a doubtful eye on me as I steadied myself on Seamus's horse, then he turned to his brother, saying something in Scottish.

"Aye," Seamus replied, seeming to agree, as he easily hoisted himself up. He swung his long leg over the saddle, positioning himself snugly behind me. He continued saying something indiscernible to Finley in a subtle manner so that the others couldn't easily hear. Finley responded casually in the same kind of tone and gave his brother a particular look that appeared cautious. Then, Finley clicked his cheek and tapped his spurs, starting his horse off first among the group. The others followed ahead while Seamus secured us before starting. He wrapped an arm around my waist, pulling me in close against his well-built frame, and held the reins with his other hand, then gently urged his horse forward.

WE TRAVELED over hard terrain again for extended periods of time with few stops in between. On a couple of occasions when we actually took a break from journeying, I took the opportunity to examine the wounds on Fearghus and Seamus. I redressed the wounds with clean rags, which Mrs. Anderson had kindly supplied me with, along with some interesting botanicals said to ward off fever. I wasn't an herbalist, but was familiar with the known medicinal aspects of witch hazel, onions, gingerroot, and a vile of vinegar—all of which she had kindly provided me, and I could use to the benefit of my two patients.

But, I wondered in the back of my mind, why hadn't she simply given me some regular over-the-counter pharmaceuticals instead? I also found it very strange that she and her husband carried thick German accents. Their German dialects seemed authentic to me. They behaved in a manner, quite like my captors, that was strict and proper, which appeared obviously natural to them—unlike the lax way I was used to observing people behave in modern times. There seemed to be a huge contradiction or disconnect with these individuals, I thought. I didn't exactly know how to infer what I was witnessing, except that the world didn't seem quite the same as I had known it to be only two days ago.

It was beginning to dawn on me, aside from the ancient landscape, that I was not only with people who lived according to old and outmoded traditions, but by some freak of an inconceivable chance, by all accounts, I was in a location where the way of life corresponded to that of the eighteenth century during Colonial America.

At first, I thought I had accidentally stumbled upon a massive filming production, only to understand that was not the case. I then suspected that these people might have belonged to some kind of historical reenactment society for severe enthusiasts. But there were colossal discrepancies that kept defying that logic also.

When we finally arrived in a small village at dusk, reason seemed to really clash with my new reality. For starters, there was the complete absence of any evidence of modern technological advances associated with the twenty-first century. I didn't recognize my surroundings in the least bit as our horses trotted over cobblestones between brownstones and clapboard buildings that lined the streets and corresponded to the Colonial era.

It appeared that we had entered a town with a small but

comfortable population that was half rural. It seemed every dwelling had a small farm with cows, goats, sheep, and horses, along with vegetable and herb gardens. Most of the town had been cleared of trees, with them appearing only scattered here or there around the town. I noticed the architecture of these particular homes now were plain and colonial-looking. They were tall with high pitched roofs, or had barn-like roofs containing anywhere from two to four different chimney stacks common in Dutch design.

The layout of the town by all appearances very much reminded me of Old Sturbridge, Massachusetts. I had often visited that town with friends for fun while in college. Colonial Williamsburg, Virginia, also came to mind. I remembered the times we had visited extended family living in that area when my brother and I were kids on vacation with our parents. But as the sound of our horses' hooves clucked over these cobblestones, it eerily struck me as even more odd. I observed no indication of automotive transportation anywhere at all—not even a single parking lot.

I glanced at a small wooden sign mounted on a post in the center of the road at an intersection that read, "Johnker Street." *Johnker Street?* Almost too apprehensive to ask, I nevertheless pursued the question, "Where are we?"

"Albany, of coorse," Seamus replied in a calm voice behind me. I gasped as my heart sharply stopped dead for a second, and a deep chill came over me in the balmy early evening air. "Are ye alrecht?" he inquired, sensing my reaction.

"Yes—just a little tired, I think," I said. My blood ran cold, and I shivered.

"We shan't be much longer now, lass, whaur ye will be allowed tae rest," my captor said.

"Is this Yonker Street?" I asked.

"Aye," he said indifferently. I stopped short of breath. All of a sudden, I felt like I had been recklessly thrown off a cliff. My eyes still scoped around the area, looking for modern municipal infrastructure, but there was no evidence of any such development anywhere. No electric lampposts, no suspended telecommunication or electrical lines, no train tracks, no automotive vehicles, no paved roads or highways, no radio towers, no high-rise buildings, no cafés, convenience stores, or big chain stores—not even an individual on a bicycle…

It then suddenly occurred to me that I hadn't heard the sound of one jet airplane or helicopter in the air for two days now. The skies were deathly silent from all aircraft, as it had been on that surreal and horrifying day on September 11… Not a single sound from machines could be heard. Instead, in my expanding fear, I noticed that it was docile and tranquil all around.

The people roaming throughout town appeared homogenous, I also discerned. The men were clothed in knee-length coats and breeches topped with tricorn hats, as they paced the streets with black or brown walking canes. Also, the women appeared in petticoat gowns with caps or straw hats over their heads. The demographics also struck me as strange, with minimal Blacks walking the streets. No Latinos or Asians were seen anywhere. But of the few Blacks seen, man or woman, they were escorted through the streets like the Native Americans, who were more prevalent among the minority population here. There were no signs anywhere of mere tourists dressed in shorts, or jeans and T-shirts, sandals or sneakers.

If this were a staged community, it was certainly keeping within the context of historical accuracy and would have achieved its goal of providing a rich educational service to our nation. But something was inherently telling me that this place was not contrived.

So, where on God's green earth am I?

PART II
THE IMPERIAL AGE

As we trotted on our horses along Johnker Street, the main street where all the churches and public buildings stood rising up on a hill over a cobblestone path, the site of a large stone-laid fort emerged. We entered past the guards standing beneath the granite archway inside the courtyard. There was a large redcoat presence throughout the town, and even more so here, as this appeared to be the military base in town.

A sound force of soldiers moved around the area, entering and exiting barracks as others left and arrived on grounds. My captors started dismounting their horses as a stableboy hurried over to meet us. Seamus swung down off his horse and instructed the boy to leave his stallion. He handed the reins to Finley as he remained seated on his horse beside me.

"Make it quick, will ye?" Finley said to Seamus.

"Aye," Seamus said. "Take the lass with ye tae the Rasmussens'. She's weary now."

"As am I," Finley said in a crotchety tone.

"Guid, then go," Seamus replied. "I'll meet ye thaur." An unfamiliar man, presumably a high-ranking officer mounted high on his horse, made a sudden appearance before us.

"Your Grace," he greeted with a refined tone. Seamus turned toward the man, and the man faintly dipped his head.

"Laird Loudoun," Seamus greeted in return.

"Laird Kneep," Lord Loudoun said to Finley.

"Laird Loudoun," Finley responded in the same refined manner.

"Have ye lairds only arrived?" Lord Loudoun inquired.

"We have, general," Finley said.

"Then ye have made guid time." It seemed Lord Loudoun was also a Scotsman with an accent as thick as theirs. "Others from yer regiment arrived merely an hour ago, and presumably more will soon follow as a result of the surprise attack set upon ye."

"Aye," Finley said.

"Ye may report tae my aide-de-camp," Lord Loudoun said.

"His Grace will do so, Your Lordship," Finley said.

"Very weel, Sir Abercrombie will receive ye in his office." At this time, Lord Loudoun noticed me, and his blue eyes zoomed in, focusing on me. He slightly arched an eyebrow, and a look of interest came over his face. "Who, my lairds, have we brought with us?"

"She is Mistress Arboles, from Pennsylvania en route tae Boston, whom we have rescued from the attack of Indians along the way," Seamus informed him stiffly.

"Indeed?" His eyebrows lifted higher over his slim brow, and his lips slanted with musing scrutiny. "*Mistress* ye say?"

"Aye," Seamus responded shortly, with a note of what sounded like defensiveness.

"Hmm..." Lord Loudoun briefly paused, scanning over me once. "I dare say, she is quite fetching fur one of such coloring. From which part of the colony do ye belong, madam?"

My mouth dried slightly as he surveyed me with particular interest. "Philadelphia—that's where I'm from," I lied.

"I see..." His lips curled, making him appear derisive. "A far distance yoo've traveled, madam. I have yet to see Philadelphia.

Mayhap madam will indulge me with her company by telling me of it over a cup of tea?" It was more like a command rather than a courteous invitation.

"Mistress Arboles is quite weary from her journey, general. We micht allow her tae retire till the morn," Seamus suggested. I sensed Seamus's reluctance when he responded to Lord Loudoun.

"I am certain madam would care fur a spot of refreshing tea after an uncomfortable journey." Lord Loudoun sharply turned his blue eyes to me, anticipating my agreement. But I simply stared at him, caught off guard by his insistence. I supposed no response was acceptable except compliance, since he continued to say, "Please escort Mistress Arboles tae the comfort of my office, whaur she may enjoy a spot of tea. Thank ye, major."

Without an additional word, Seamus scarcely nodded his head toward Lord Loudoun. Lord Loudoun then lightly jolted his spurs into the side of his horse and started moving past us. Seamus turned his eyes up to Finley, high on his horse, and gave him a specific displeased look.

"Shall I bide fur ye presently, then?" Finley inquired.

"Nae, ye go on ahead tae the Rasmussens'. Inform them that I shall be thaur later," Seamus said.

"Alrecht," Finley replied. He turned to the other men still standing around. "Ye lads find yer quarters, and enjoy a hearty meal."

"Aye," they grumbled in unison, and dispersed.

"Take my horse with ye," Seamus said to Finley as he proceeded to reach for me around the waist and assist me down off the saddle.

"Ye dinnae care tae keep him with ye?" Finley asked.

"Nae, let Lachlan hold him, and tell the lad tae bide fur me," Seamus said.

"Alrecht." Finley clicked his cheek, and his horse started moving away from us, with Seamus's horse in tow.

Seamus let out a subtle sigh and wrapped a light hand around my arm. He looked at me, and I detected hesitation in his expression. "I shall see Sir Abercrombie before I deliver ye tae Laird Loudoun."

"All right," I responded. He paused momentarily and tightened his lips.

"He means tae interview ye," he said straightforwardly.

"Interview me? Why?" I asked, looking perplexedly at him.

"Do ye not suppose why?" he inquired curiously.

"I don't know," I said sincerely.

"He is a shrewd man. It is likely that he is curious about yer appearance," he said.

"I don't understand," I said, looking at him with confusion.

"He has not only perceived the fine look of yer skin and hair, but the jewels ye possess versus the rags ye wear," he said. I mechanically raised my fingers to my necklace, and I realized that Seamus was warning me.

"Oh…" I whispered.

"Tread lightly with His Lordship. He is quick tae rise," he said.

"Why are you telling me this?" I asked naively.

"Ye have spared my cousin, Fearghus, from certain death and have graciously aided my own injury, fur which I am grateful," he said squarely. "And… I dinnae wish fur ye tae be misjudged by him." I studied Seamus for a fleeting moment. He seemed genuine about what he was saying.

"Thank you," I said thoughtfully.

"Aye," he replied softly. "Weel then, now—let us go."

Guiding me by the arm, he led me across the courtyard toward one of the barracks I supposed was meant for high-ranking officers. Just outside the granite wall of the barrack at the entrance stood a pair of redcoat guards with towering black bear fur bonnets on their heads. Each soldier on either side of the doorway stood immobile, like stiff mannequins, holding muskets in one hand with the butt pointed toward their feet.

Upon entering, Seamus directed me to stand inconspicuously in the corner of the office, which belonged to Sir Abercrombie. I noticed the white-wigged commanding officer seated behind his desk, scratching a quill over a seemingly large piece of parchment. He appeared to be an older man in his fifties. Distinguishing the staunch expression of his slightly square jaw, accompanied by the dour wrinkle between his eyebrows, as he scraped the quill over the paper, I sensed he was a man of very little humor and lacked sensitivity overall. I felt a sort of disdain from him as he continued to scribe without making a mere effort to glance up from the page to acknowledge that an individual was advancing toward his desk.

"Duke of Monteith haur, sir, tae report his arrival," Seamus announced once he'd removed his tricorn hat and tucked it beneath his arm as he stood at attention in front of the desk.

"Major," Sir Abercrombie acknowledged without peering up from his scribing hand. "'Tis guid tae see that ye have soondly arrived, fur I was informed of the waylay set upon ye."

"Aye, sir," Seamus responded. "The Earl of Kneep has also arrived unharmed."

"Hmm… Aye." Sir Abercrombie seemed to finish up the last word on the parchment as he lightly tapped the nib and inserted the quill into the inkwell on his desk. His amber eyes turned up to Seamus as he repositioned himself more comfortably in his nicely fashioned baroque leather chair. "Have any of yer men suffered injury?"

"Aye, Captain Fearghus MacLeod took a musket ball near the shoulder," Seamus informed him.

"That is most unfortunate. How does he fare?" Sir Abercrombie asked.

"He's a strong lad. I reckon he may survive," Seamus said, without elaborating further.

"Guid. See tae it that he is delivered tae hospital. We have a surgeon haur tae look efter him," Sir Abercrombie said.

"Aye, sir," Seamus replied. I found it odd that he didn't include himself among the injured and kept his responses to a minimum.

"Very weel, ye may take yer leave till further notice. Guid evening, major," Sir Abercrombie said.

"Guid evening, general," Seamus said. He then turned and paced in my direction. His hand carefully came around my arm, and he proceeded to lead me toward the threshold.

"One last word, major," Sir Abercrombie said just as we'd started out the door.

"Aye, sir?" Seamus responded, turning his eyes back to the general.

"Who is the lass thaur with ye, major?" he inquired.

"She is tae see Laird Loudoun at his request," Seamus said expressionlessly, failing to give the man my name.

"Och, very weel, then," Sir Abercrombie replied, seeming unimpressed, and waved an equally dismissive hand. "Ye may continue taking yer leave." Seamus resumed guiding me out the door with him and led me to the adjacent office.

As we entered the office between two guards posted at the threshold, Lord Loudoun could be seen in the process of delivering to a soldier a leather tube that held correspondences. I noticed a very dark Black male youth, possibly no more than eleven years old, dressed in fine courtly attire, beginning to prepare tea over a gilded rococo-style stand next to the desk.

"Och, Mistress Arboles, it appears ye have come in time tae join me fur a nice spot of tea," Lord Loudoun said courteously as the solider received the tube from him and departed the room. "Please." He gestured to one of the two blue-and-gold brocade silk-upholstered chairs in front of his desk. "Please take a seat and make yerself at ease. I am certain that ye must be raither weary from having traveled a fair distance and will care tae have a moment of comfort."

I quietly paced over to the chair and sat. I naturally crossed my ankles and folded my hands in my lap, aware that Seamus had stepped aside accordingly and stood attentively at a slight distance beside me. I glanced up at him, noticing his tricorn hat tucked beneath his arm with a hand folded around the brim and the other hanging at his side at attention.

"Thank ye, major. That will be all," Lord Loudoun said shortly to him.

"If it is of nae consequence tae ye, general, I request tae remain present," he replied coldly. Although his demeanor seemed respectful, there was a hint of contradiction that came through his tone. Lord Loudoun's face hardened, correctly inferring Seamus's disposition.

"Ye may take yer leave now, major," Lord Loudoun returned pointedly, giving him an incisive look. Seamus clenched his jaw, appearing stone-faced, and rigidly dipped his head like a tin man to the general. He turned, and our eyes locked for a split second as he started retreating from the room. Lord Loudoun instructed the boy servant to close the door after Seamus, leaving the three of us alone together in the room. "That is better," he said with satisfaction as the boy proceeded to return to the corner in the back of the room, where he remained standing innocuously. "Now, perhaps ye and I shall enjoy a nice quiet conversation alone together," he said politely as his light blue eyes stared at me. A thin smile slanted his lips, and I silently scrutinized him then.

He appeared to be a well-polished man of well above average height and weight, whose looks were inoffensive and slightly better than normal. He also didn't appear too aged a man for an individual of his advanced years, approximately in his early fifties. Although he seemed courteous, there was a certain indescribable detachment I detected in his eyes that made him appear to be acutely hard and insensitive. Granted, I didn't know the man, never having seen him before in my life, and had nothing really on which to base my quick presumption, but it was merely an instinct I had.

"Allow me tae introduce myself, Mistress Arboles," he began

as he moved toward the tea on the stand and drew the cups. He positioned them accordingly on the tray. Modestly watching him, I wondered what this was all about. "I am His Lordship, Johnathan Campbell, Earl of Loudoun, Commander in Chief of the Armed Forces of British America, at yer service," he said. I stared vacantly at him, pretty much in disbelief.

"I see. Well, it's nice to meet you," I said scrupulously, as it seemed he was duly convinced of who he was in the role I thought he was playing.

"It pleases me tae make yer acquaintance. I welcome ye tae Fort Frederick." He perfectly poured the tea and took up a silver spoon.

"Thank you," I said politely.

"Will ye care fur a bit of sugar?" he inquired, indicating the sugarloaf in the petite white porcelain bowl.

"Yes, please," I said. He took the sugar nips between his fingers and broke a small piece off the sugarloaf and placed it in the tea. He lightly stirred the tea, then set the spoon back on the mahogany tray. He'd proceeded to pass the cup to me when he happened to notice my wedding ring as I received the warm teacup and saucer from him. "Thank you," I said as I collected the tea from him.

"Indeed, madam," he said pleasantly. "Ye are a wed woman, I understand."

"Widowed, actually," I informed him automatically while carefully settling the teacup and saucer on my knee.

"I am sorry fur yer misfortune." I detected a slight lack of genuine sincerity in his tone.

"Thank you," I said, nevertheless. I noticed a distinctive air about him. He had an unabashed disposition of Byzantine haughtiness, often ascribed to European snobbery, that was associated with wealthy individuals of the upper crust.

"May I?" he inquired interestedly, indicating he wished to have a closer look at my ring.

"Yes, of course," I said politely. I held out my hand, and he proceeded to take my hand in his. His hand, I noticed, was very smooth and not calloused.

"Och, yer fingertips are quite dainty. Yer skin is exceptionally fine—soft as a lady's," he commented with some surprise. "A diamond," he said, observing closely, catching the brilliant, glittering luster of the flawless stone in what was left of the sunlight entering through the window. "A pink one at that... Why, it is most exquisite... Quite an uncommon stone... and it is of a notable size. I huvnae seen such a setting. Whit sort is it?"

"It's a Tiffany's setting," I said carefully, feeling some reservation.

"Tiffany?" He turned his scrutinizing blue eyes to mine.

"Yes," I said, examining him too as his eyes were keenly investigating me.

"Hmm, curious," he said, and returned his attention to the stone. "The metal appears unique as weel. Whit sort is it?"

"It's platinum," I disclosed.

"Och, aye—*platina*. That is the name the Spaniards have given it. Is it not? I have heard of such a metal originating from their colonies located in South America, but I have not seen it till now," he said, holding a steady eye on me. "I understood it tae be described as an ugly metal. But yer *platina* is quite the contrary. It is, instead, raither exceptionally pleasing tae the eye."

"Thank you," I said modestly. I was beginning to feel uncomfortable as he studied my ring, so I carefully removed my hand from his.

"Aye, weel," he said as he sat back in his leather chair. I carefully brought the teacup to my lips and took a little sip. It wasn't exactly the best tea I'd ever tasted. It was slightly bitter black tea sweetened with sugar. His eyes briefly seized upon the gemstone necklace half concealed around my neck, and the quality earrings dangling from my earlobes—and the sparkling gem bangle around my wrist. "It seems yer departed husband must have been a man of considerable means." A thin, derisive grin curled his nice-looking, slightly full lips. "And he was a man, apparently, who had considerable taste in uniquely bonnie women, I micht add."

"Thank you," I said demurely, and drew the cup to my lips, sipping from it again.

"Ye appear tae be an original woman. Tell me, madam, have ye ever visited a fort?" he inquired, getting up from his desk and returning to the tea stand.

"No, I have to say that this is my first time visiting any fort," I said.

"I see." He turned to face me again and presented a petite porcelain plate to me that held a slice of some kind of flat oat bread with strawberry preserves smeared over it. I politely accepted the plate from him. "I have quite seen my share of forts, I assure ye. It is not the most favorable place fur a man tae have tae reside whilst in military service. And it is certainly the least favorable place fur a prisoner who must spend mayhap weeks haur under lock and key," he continued to say.

"Oh," I acknowledged, trying to figure out the point of this conversation. However, I was beginning to get the unfettered feeling that I was actually being interrogated—for whatever reason unknown to me—despite his subtlety.

"However, I have personal accommodations that are fairly suitable tae me haur, in order that I may accurately perform my duties as commanding chief officer."

"Well, I suppose it's good to have that kind of advantage, if it helps to be effective in your demanding profession," I replied, feeling out of place.

"Indeed... indeed." Lord Loudoun returned to his chair behind his desk and sat down comfortably. He leaned back in his seat, facing me. I was aware of him observing the unrefined clothing I was wearing and the crystal clips holding my loose ringlets in place at the side of my head. "Tell me, madam, as I am only acquainted with New York town, Boston, and Albany at present, whit are the traditions held in Philadelphia?"

"Oh—well… the customs there, I suppose, are like anything else found around the country," I said.

"Is that reit?" His light-brown eyebrows rose, making him look surprised.

"Well, yes, of course—we all speak the same language, don't we?" I replied honestly. He unexpectedly laughed, appearing genuinely amused. His response caught me silently off guard and made me feel a little more concerned.

"Yoo're a clever one, I must admit," he said as his laughter waned. "I believe ye amuse me, madam." He composed himself and sipped a bit more from his cup. I watched him replace his teacup on the desk as I nibbled on the bread, despite the fact that I had no appetite at the moment. "I raither enjoy being diverted. I am little charmed of late, and yoo're fortunate tae have such an effect on me." I smiled cautiously in response. His face straightened again, but the grin lingered as he stared at me now with a look of derisive admiration. "Ye colonials are a much different breed, I have found," he remarked in a disapproving tone. "But ye, madam, have interested me."

"Is that so?" I replied.

"Indeed." He again leaned back in his chair, propping an elbow on the armrest, and pensively stroked his clean-shaven upper lip with his forefinger. "Returning tae the topic, however," he continued, dropping his hand from his face. "Amongst my travels since arriving in the colonies, I have found great differences amongst the regions. Fur instance, spoken English amongst the folk haur is vastly different from one region tae the next. Yet yer case, fur one, is quite peculiar, as I've not yet met one with quite yer accent."

"Oh?" I responded curiously.

"Indeed."

"I see."

He paused momentarily as we gazed at each other. "Fur one belonging tae the feminine sex, I find it unusual, as I see it, that yer speech appears confident, and it is used forwardly. Yer English is indeed weel spoken, but it is not quite that of an English lady."

"Well, I'm not English. I'm American, of course," I said kindly, despite not liking the haughtiness of his tone.

"Mmm, of coorse." He narrowed a pensive eye on me.

"And you're Scottish, apparently?"

"Indeed."

"But both of us speak English comparatively well, don't we?"

"Mmm, aye... But whilst yers is not spoken precisely like that of an English lady, nor is it spoken as a typical subject in general from these parts. Instead, it appears that yer English is spoken lightly through the nose, as the French would speak."

"Is that how it really seems?" I asked sincerely.

"Indeed," he said frankly.

"Oh," I replied.

"Interestingly, I wulnae say that I find it offensive tae the ears. Quite the contrary, I regard it as uniquely intriguing. Which is why I am presently wondering, as I have met a man in recent days claiming tae have been born in Philadelphia who didnae sound a bit like ye."

"Really?" I replied.

"His Hessian inflection perfectly corrupted his English," Lord Loudoun said observantly.

"I see. Well, I suppose we wouldn't have shared the same sort of accent if that is the case, since my first language is English—obviously. Wouldn't you agree?"

"Conceivably," he mused. "However, isnae the land of Pennsylvania fairly dominated by Hessians, as one perceives haur in Albany?"

At that point I decided to take a considerable bite out of the heavy bread and chewed. I needed to buy a little time just to compose my thoughts. Working the thick bannock between my teeth, I finally swallowed and took a long sip of tea too, aware of him watching me. Taking a little breath and giving him a nervous little smile, I thought this was as good a time as any to confront the obvious issue as best as possible without disclosing too much about myself.

"You know," I started, as I placed my teacup next to the remaining piece of oat bread on the saucer balancing perfectly on my knee, "I must tell you that I really haven't the slightest clue why I'm here."

"Is that so?" A doubtful smirk lazily tilted his lips.

"Yes, I have absolutely no idea."

"Curious. But I have offered you tea. Is that not why ye are haur?"

"Yes, but that's not what I mean, really."

"Pray, do tell."

"Well, sure. One moment, a couple of days ago, I was traveling in my own vehicle, minding my own business, and the next minute, I find it stolen from me, leaving me suddenly stranded on the road without any help in sight."

One of his eyebrows arched high over one eye. Lord Loudoun appeared piqued with interest. "Is that reit?"

"Yes."

"Thieved by whom?"

Stick to the story, I told myself.

"By bandits—three of them. They took everything."

"Did they?"

"Oh, absolutely. They even stole my maid—and killed my chauffeur." *God help me, here we go.* I began telling him my colorful lie. I disclosed to him in vivid detail everything that had happened to me, from the moment I was stranded, the ambush and skirmish that followed, to the hand-to-hand combat between the Duke of Monteith and the Indian brave. Lord Loudoun listened to my tale completely engrossed, without blinking an eye.

"I see," he said when I had finally finished divulging my story. He paused momentarily, and his musing stare deliberately skimmed over my clothes. He spotted my ankles and noticed my simple leather slippers. "But I remain slightly puzzled," he hinted.

"Yes?"

"How is it that a bonnie young woman of means such as yerself would choose tae travel in the absence of armed guards on a perilous frontier road in attire that contradicts her social rank?"

Uh-oh… I did not think of that. I stalled answering the question with another sip of tea.

"Well, you see, these clothes were donated to me by a farmer's wife along the way." I continued explaining how my original dress had been totally ruined as a result of the ambush, and the trek we had made through the forest.

"A pity," he commented observantly.

"It certainly is." I looked disappointedly at my feet, missing my own shoes.

"I see…" His hands clasped together over his desk as he leaned forward, supporting himself on his elbows. The calculating, sardonic tension that had been lingering on his face suddenly eased into an indulgent smile. "I shall like tae speak quite plainly tae ye, madam," he said without reserve.

"Please," I agreed. A slight sigh of relief escaped me, and I realized that I must have been holding my breath. His smile widened, exposing the yellow incisors behind his lips. The smile didn't seem completely benign, however. Instead, it looked rather lascivious and sinister. The look didn't sit well with me.

"I believe that ye and I micht have more in common than perhaps I first believed," he said.

"How's that?" I inquired curiously.

"Weel, I perceive that yoo're more refined than ye imply. And as I have found the subjects living haur tae be raither simple and dull as compared tae the superior experiences acquired in Europe, I find myself hindered in this place from customs usual tae me."

"I see."

"Micht ye also perceive yerself in a similar position at present?"

"Well, I suppose so—everything is a little strange," I admitted.

"Indeed," he agreed, smiling uninhibitedly. It seemed he was attempting to convey something with the pleased expression on his face that had unexpectedly transformed his disposition into an attractive older man. "I recognize that it is complicated fur lasses in yer position tae find the reit sort of friend. Lasses at yer level of trade, I understand, are discreet—as weel as they must be tae secure the reputations of their patrons. But I also believe that yer prudence is a further measure that ye have taken in order tae safeguard yerself from these pious simpletons by which we discover ourselves surrounded. Therefore, I must inform ye that ye have found an ally in me." He lifted his light-brown eyebrows above his wide blue eyes with an eager expectant look.

"Excuse me—I'm sorry, but what profession are you referring to that you think I'm associated with?" I asked with some uncertainty.

"Come now, *Mistress* Arboles, ye neednae be coy with me. I assure ye that yer secret remains safe," he said, still smiling.

"I am extremely confused," I said, giving him an obviously muddled look. He chuckled, appearing sincerely amused—and charmed. But I was far from seeing any hint of amusement myself.

"Perhaps yoo're the most appealing courtesan I've yet encountered. My mistress, Madamoiselle Laurent, will not be pleased in the least bit once she learns that I have decided tae take on anither beauty. But that won't be too trooblesome, fur she will have nae choice but tae be yer friend also," he expressed with a level of certainty that instantly alarmed me.

"Oh my goodness!" I gasped. The man was seriously convinced. "There has been a huge misunderstanding. I think you've gotten the wrong impression about me."

"Whit is yer meaning?" He looked at me with a persuaded grin.

"I'm not a prostitute." I giggled awkwardly, looking at him preposterously. "I'm not at all like that. My field is pediatrics. I'm a pediatrician," I told him, suddenly growing hysterical with laughter over the insanity of this whole ordeal. "In fact, do you want to know something that's absolutely even crazier than being mistaken for a prostitute?"

The irreverent grin on his face faded slightly, but did not vanish altogether. "Pray tell. I wish tae know the source of yer levity."

"Well, the men that I've come into town with have actually abducted me," I said, while composing myself.

"Abducted ye?" He stared at me with a mixture of partial amusement and heavy interest.

"Yes, they just took me against my will and refused to let me return on my way, because they thought I was a covert op."

"A covert op?"

"Yeah, a secret operative."

"A spy, indeed?"

"Yes! Isn't that incredibly absurd? I mean, it is totally insane. And the completely bizarre thing about it is that they really seemed sincere," I explained ridiculously. "Truly? Espionage? Why on earth would they seriously consider me to be that? What for? First of all, who would I be spying for? And why would I care to do that? What interest could I possibly have in playing silly war games all day? No offense meant to any of you who seem to enjoy those sorts of games, but it's enormously far-fetched. I mean, I suppose everyone needs some kind of outlet from the pressures of reality these days and a forum for entertainment. Whatever floats one's boat—as long as it doesn't hurt anybody, right? But, c'mon, do I even *look* like I could possibly be a mole or sleeper agent in any way? Actually, I couldn't even be a DHS agent. Really… I'm positive that I can find much more important things to do with my time than to be involved in whatever the heck is going on around here—like tending to my practice as a pediatrician, or even going grocery shopping, for example. I can seriously say that I find all of this to be an immensely strange situation, which should not involve me," I blurted out, laughing. Lord Loudoun simply stared absurdly at me, seeming to be at a loss for words.

"*En effet, il semble que vous se trouvent dans une circonstance inhabituel dans ce cas,*" he finally said in perfect French as he stared deliberately at me.

"*Oui, oui, exactement. C'est tout un malentendu,*" I said, with some relief that we had reached some sort of understanding. I went on to say civilly, "I'm prepared to completely overlook this mistake and consider it never even happened. That is if I may, however, ask for your extended kindness and consideration by giving me the opportunity to return to the place where I was abducted. In which case, I would be extremely grateful."

"Mmm, aye…" he muttered, sounding somewhat doubtful. "First, may I compliment ye on yer French? It is perfectly spoken like a French lady."

"Thank you," I said. "Yours is well spoken also."

"I am quite familiar with the French and their ways."

"That's nice," I said simply. "But, again, if you wouldn't mind being so kind—"

"Tell me, madam, yer Spanish, I presume, is as keenly spoken. Is it not?"

"Well, sure."

"Will ye not indulged me by allowing me tae hear ye speak it?" he insisted with a piercingly contemplative eye.

"All right… What do you wish for me to say?" I felt this was a little odd, but I thought, *What the heck, I'll go ahead and indulge him.*

He waved a flippant hand and said, "Say anything ye wish."

"Okay. *Muchos gracias por el té. Fue muy agradable de usted para ofrecer lo a mí.*"

"Indeed, my pleasure."

"Do you speak it as well?" I asked, surprised.

"Mayhap not as skillfully as ye, madam. But I recall the tongue weel enough," Lord Loudoun said.

"Oh."

"So, ye are knowledgeable in multiple languages, I see."

"Yes."

"Are ye literate in all of them?"

"Yes, of course," I said simply.

"Then, ye are quite educated."

"Well, sure—but most people are."

"It may be the case fur some men, but not fur a woman."

"Excuse me? But there are plenty of well-educated women," I said, disagreeing exceptionally.

"Mayhap they are educated concerning their husbands and domestic duties. But ye, madam, are apparently unique." The lingering sneer on his face vanished and was replaced with a hard, cheerless expression as he stared at me.

"I see," I said. I cleared my throat.

"Ye are awaur, of coorse, that France and Spain are allies, whilst they both remain enemies of England?"

I couldn't help looking at him with a sense of mounting uncertainty.

"I suppose—within this historical context—they might be," I acknowledged.

"They *micht* be?" His light-brown eyebrows lifted noticeably. "Curious choice of words. I reckon 'tis raither an uncommon affair fur a Spaniard tae dwell peaceably in British territory.

Furthermore, I find it quite intriguing that a simple colonial lass could possibly be quite so knowledgeable in three different languages as ye have proven tae be. Such knowledge is uncommon in general. Particularly fur a lass, though she micht come from suitable breeding—let alone tae encounter one with such breeding haur from these colonies is unique." He spoke in such a superior manor, implying that he held real disdain for the people living here.

"Oh," I realized.

"Indeed."

"Well… I assure you that I'm completely American—obviously."

"Hmm—*obviously...*" he echoed doubtfully. "Yet the women I have known tae be so weel educated are those that I have discovered belonging tae a particular circle common tae Europe."

"You don't say?"

"I raither do."

"Well, we actually have a pretty good educational system here too, believe it or not."

A sudden outburst of chuckling escaped him. His cheeks flushed, brightening his demeanor and alleviating some of the intensity in his expression as he appeared half entertained.

"Charming," he remarked as he collected himself. I looked at him strangely. *A bit weird,* I thought. He seemed very eccentric, I assessed. "Have ye been tae France or Italy?"

"No. I haven't. Have you?" I asked.

"Allow me tae suggest that 'tis not ye but I conducting this interview, madam," he said sternly.

"Oh—okay—it's just that I don't understand the purpose of all this," I said. He narrowed his light-blue eyes on me.

"In that case, I shall be more candid with ye, madam. Courtesans are quite valuable tae men as myself. In fact, I have enjoyed many of them and have kept them quartered safely under my protection. I have traveled with one from England who I keep with me now. She is originally from France. However, one must keep in mind that they are employed women and therefore are untrustworthy. They are duplicitous. Many of them are spies fur their employers, as ye micht weel already know."

"No—actually, I would not know any of that." My throat felt dry, and it scratched when I swallowed.

"Ye dinnae say?" Lord Loudoun responded doubtfully.

"Yes, that's right. I wouldn't know anything about what you're trying to suggest." A sinking feeling came over me, and I wanted to just leave, but I couldn't. I felt bound and constrained to the chair I was sitting in as he willfully locked his eyes on me. An incongruous grin crept over his face.

"I see," he said pensively. He tapped his long white index finger over the mahogany surface of his rococo-style desk. "Very weel. I am obliged tae tell ye, madam, that I do not much care fur play unless it is in the bedchamber. Thus, when I ask ye a question, I expect a truthful response. I shall like fur ye tae reveal whit was meant when ye mentioned DHS agent?"

Oh no... I took a deep breath.

"The Department of Homeland Security, of course," I risked stating as my confidence diminished.

"The Department of Homeland Security—of coorse," he echoed deliberately, without an ounce of his previous humor. He paused for a moment, staring meditatively at me. Then, a faint, sardonic grin came over his face, but was shortly replaced by a bitter look. "Weel, then, it certainly seems that we indeed have much in common efter all, madam," he said derisively. I kept my eyes steady on him, ignoring his intimidating tone.

"Oh? How do you figure?" I asked. The mocking grin slithered over his face again.

"Yer choice in words strangely amuses me. Apparently, I cannae consider ye fur anither dull colonial Puritan or Quaker lass. Yoo're far more than that, indeed." He flippantly waved his hand, sneering at my appearance. "Yer charade with me is finished, madam. As fact would have it, yoo're not a poor farmer's widow, as yer attire would have me believe. Nor are ye merely a lady's maid, as ye dinnae assume the proper temperament. Ye have contradicted yerself quite weel. Ye have earned my sincere applause, madam. Felicitations." He lifted his teacup in appreciation and took a sip. He then set it down again on the saucer and continued, "Instead, ye are unexpectedly quite learned. Ye presumably have wealth in yer background—plenty of it, I believe."

He eyeballed my ring and the gems dangling from my neck and ears again.

"I am of the persuasion that ye are indeed a courtesan of significant education. And, as I have stated prior, I dinnae mind courtesans in the merest—especially when they are in my employ. I am also certain that ye are indeed a spy. In which case, ye have placed me in a particular predicament." He clasped his hands in front of himself with ease on his desk. In addition to his alienating European arrogance, there was something really distasteful I felt about him also as he kept staring directly at me. The quiet lasciviousness was discernible in his eyes. "My request is fur ye tae abandon yer employer, and align yerself with me. Tae do so will be tae yer advantage by sparing yer imprisonment. I micht inform ye that the weaker sex appear tae have more difficulty surviving such harsh conditions than their male counterparts. I doubt that ye would desire tae experience such harshness. Is that not so?"

My throat was so dry that I found it difficult to swallow. "No. I don't think that would be a very good experience," I said faintly.

"Aye, it would not. Therefore, I thought ye micht agree fur a better resolution. My wish is fur ye and I tae get along—preferably weel—above all else..." Lord Loudoun paused, seeming to consider his words carefully. He appeared calculating and imperious. I certainly did not like what he was proposing, and I felt extraordinarily uncomfortable. I nervously toyed with the rings on my finger in silence as the sound of his voice kept fading in and out. "I am not necessarily a dreadful man, madam. In truth, I can be quite indulgent. Ye will come tae perceive that I am practically reasonable with anyone who chooses tae be mindful of me... Now that I have granted ye a choice in this matter, I advise ye tae cooperate, as ye are in grave peril with me, madam... However, I am an honorable man. Therefore, I shall assure ye that if ye choose tae remain sensible with me, then I shall see tae it that ye remain unharmed... and cared fur within my protection."

I thought at this point that reality was starting to sink in a bit. My heart began racing as I realized with alarm the imminent danger I was suddenly facing. He had no intention of letting me go free. Furthermore, he was sexually propositioning me, and there was no way in hell I was ever going to prostitute myself. And to top it all off, he thought, for whatever reason, that I was a secret agent posing a threat to him.

My head started spinning. There was no way out—it was becoming slightly hard to breathe. I mechanically shifted my empty teacup and saucer off of my lap, aware of his scrutiny. The porcelain rattled helplessly as I leaned over to place the cup and saucer on the edge of his desk.

Without warning, one of the doors to the room flung wide open, abruptly disrupting the uncomfortable silence. His aide-de-camp, Sir Abercrombie, flew into the room, appearing obviously flustered.

"I beg yer pardon, my laird," Sir Abercrombie said uneasily.

"Aye. Whit is it?" Lord Loudoun said, apparently annoyed as he finally took his eyes off me and glared at Abercrombie.

"Governor Shirley and General Winslow of the colonial militia are present in my office, my laird. They have urgent news that cannae be delayed," General Abercrombie informed him hastily.

"I see," Lord Loudoun replied shortly. He sighed and flippantly waved at his Black boy attendant, who had been silently standing in the corner of the room during the entire course of our meeting. The boy promptly responded, moving across the room, and opened the front door. "Lieutenant!" Lord Loudoun called to the guard now seen standing directly outside the threshold. The soldier turned and entered. Lord Loudoun stood tall from behind his desk, appearing distinctly imposing. His frosty blue eyes returned to mine as he gave me a practiced smile. "Please excuse this intrusion, madam. I assure ye that we shall continue our discussion at a more suitable time during my leisure." He elegantly motioned for me to rise from my seat and ordered the young officer, presumably in his early twenties, to come forth. "Escort Mistress Arboles tae my personal quarters, whaur she may recover peaceably from her journey. See tae it that she isnae disturbed and that she comfortably remains upon my return."

"My lord?" The lieutenant questioned as he glanced skeptically at my appearance.

"I shall not repeat myself, lieutenant."

"Aye, my lord," replied the soldier, who had an English accent.

"And do not permit Madamoiselle Laurent tae take entry tae my chambers. She is forbidden. Is that understood?" Lord Loudoun ordered stoutly.

"Aye, my lord," answered the soldier.

"Very weel. Inform Madamoiselle Laurent that she is tae return tae *la petite maison,* whaur I shall meet her at a later time in the case she micht appear. Is that also weel understood, lieutenant?"

"Aye, my lord."

"Ye are tae remain posted at my personal chambers until further instruction." He turned his sharp eyes to me again. "We shall not wish fur Mistress Arboles tae become fearful by the notion that she has been left unguarded. Would we?" A trained grin faintly curled his lips, contradicting the sincerity of his expression. "I am quite anticipating the continuation of our conference later at length, madam. Until then, pray make yerself content in my chambers." He shifted his eyes back to the young solder now standing near me. "Ye may now escort Mistress Arboles, lieutenant."

"Aye, my lord," said the lieutenant. "Madam?"

I suddenly looked up at the young hazel-eyed soldier from my chair, realizing he was urging me to proceed out of the room with him. In utter disbelief, I glanced back at Lord Loudoun and noticed the restrained, cynical look on Sir Abercrombie's face. In expert fashion, Lord Loudoun turned his eyes from me with immediate attention to Sir Abercrombie.

Following the lieutenant out of the room, I was led through a series of stone corridors until we arrived at a flight of steep wooden stairs. I followed the guard up the staircase to the top landing, where we immediately faced an oak door. He turned the copper handle fixed high up on the door and opened it. Crossing the threshold, I entered an entryway that was unexpectedly luxuriously furnished according to the rococo style of the eighteenth century. The decor took me by surprise.

I suddenly whirled around to face the door behind me upon the sound of it instantly shutting closed. I glanced around, realizing that I had been abruptly left alone. My gaze fell to the pinewood-planked floors, and I had no clue what to expect next. But I knew that I couldn't risk sticking around and waiting for Lord Loudoun to come through that door.

Seamus was right: Lord Loudoun was shrewd—dangerously shrewd.

I reached deep inside my pocket folded within my skirts and grabbed my phone. The screen illuminated. Thank God! But to my severe disappointment, it was still incapable of linking to a cell network. The screen continued to just read, "Service Unavailable." Furthermore, the date and time were still not displayed. I also noticed the battery life was at 20 percent. It was getting too low, and I needed to conserve its energy, so I turned the phone off.

"*Crap!*" I cursed under my breath, and unhappily shoved the phone safely back into my pocket. As thoughts quickly ran through my mind, I knew there was no way I could simply escape through the front door with that armed guard standing right there behind it. I spotted the window beyond the entryway at the end of the short corridor. I hurried to it and peered out, estimating the approximately fifty foot drop straight down below to the ground. Without any ledges or anything else to grapple onto along the wall, it would prove to be a devastating fall that would result in a broken back and cracked skull.

I turned from the window and paced through the lavishly decorated apartment, anxiously assessing all the rooms for an alternate passage of escape, ignoring the surrounding antiques that otherwise would have fascinated me. Unfortunately, as I discovered, despite the few rooms, it seemed the only way out of this place was through the front door. Then, it occurred to me that maybe by chance there was a landline telephone, or a computer, hidden somewhere in all of this eighteenth-century rococo decor. In that case, I could then contact the authorities, and they could locate me in no time at all.

I discovered Lord Loudoun's private office and couldn't help being struck by the extravagant gilded furniture embellishing the room. To my wonderment, the furniture appeared authentic in detail.

My eyes sharply landed on the baroque desk. I approached it, and there was no indication of a telephone or computer anywhere. In fact, as I scrutinized the area, there was not even a sign of a single electrical outlet set in the walls. An abrupt wave of fear unsettled me.

I scoured the entire apartment looking for outlets and wires. Then, I abruptly stopped dead in my tracks and stared patently at a beautifully handcrafted glass lampshade. The lamp was not made to receive electricity, but to burn a candle. And as it appeared, none of the lanterns, be them sconces on the wall or placed on a stand, were adapted for electrical use.

I took a deep breath and decided to slow down for a second, thinking that I was quickly getting ahead of myself. Logically, I thought that the players in this charade had intentionally established living conditions, which were in keeping with true historic form. Except when I returned to Lord Loudoun's office, taking stock of the quill in the inkwell on his desk, I gathered one of the four sealed correspondences between my fingers and read the address to Sir William Shirley in elegant calligraphy. The neatly folded parchment paper was thick and heavy. I flipped it over and observed the large carmine-red wax seal that had an embossed crest and a stylized *L* in the center of it. Turning the correspondence back over, I placed it back on the stack of correspondences as I had found it and began searching for indisputable evidence based on an irrational hunch that I had gotten since initially arriving here. There was no indication of either a newspaper or magazine, but fortunately, there was a row of books spread over the oak mantelpiece high above the fireplace.

I randomly grabbed one of the leather-bound publications without noticing the title and opened it. There was no copyright information inside, except for a single date printed beneath the title and author's name. I lightly thumbed through the first few pages. The date read 1749. I lightly thumbed through the first few pages. Odd for sure, it appeared to be a bonafide piece of work displayed by the very fine print and the ragged page edges. Although, the pages seemed in very good condition, and the print still smelled of ink. I closed the book. I placed the book back into its slot and retrieved a different one. The date: 1706. Putting that one back, I took another: 1750. Shutting the book and returning it, my hands landed on a thin paperbound book that appeared worn and soiled. It was flimsy, I noticed, and appeared like a pamphlet as I carefully pulled it forth. Opening it, I located the date: 1692. My hands began to quake as I closed it. I placed it back with the others. I had never held publications so old.

An icy chill shivered sharply down my spine, and I felt the little hairs on the back of my neck stand up as the realization of the circumstances surrounding me began to unfold and started taking shape.

No sign of electronics. No remote indication of the latest publications as recent as the 2000s. No support of any kind related to the modern world as I knew it while examining Lord Loudoun's impressively neat and orderly, luxurious apartment suite. In fact, as I'd noticed, it certainly seemed he was a man of considerable opulence given the obscene wealth displayed for the time period in the decor of his living space—which begged me to ask myself: *where on God's green planet am I?*

Just as I slipped the pamphlet back into the slot between the other books, I heard the front door unlatch, with heavy footsteps entering over the pine floors. The door closed, and my heart pounded with serious alarm as I heard boots clunking down the corridor, headed in my direction. I quickly returned to the sitting room area and stood near the window, trying to appear natural—not exactly knowing what to do. The only thing I could think of was to see if I could somehow manipulate my situation with Lord Loudoun to my advantage.

The spurs clinked and ceased at the threshold. My eyes landed on the very tall figure now standing in the same room, suddenly startling me.

"Pray, dinnae be alarmed," Seamus urged cautiously. I stared unexpectedly, shocked to see him. I was utterly speechless as he continued to enter the room. "Ye must come with me, lass."

"What?" I replied unwittingly.

"Pray, we dinnae have time tae waste," he urged anxiously.

"I don't understand," I said, completely confused.

"It is not prudent fur ye tae remain haur with His Lordship," he answered.

"I know. Look—I just want to go home," I said innocently.

"I dinnae believe that is possible reit at present. Yet if ye remain haur, he will harm ye," Seamus said. I knew he was right about that, but I didn't respond. "I ken he believes that yoo're a spy."

"How do you know that?" I asked, somewhat surprised.

"Loudoun takes all colonials fur spies."

"Oh."

"He has placed ye haur in his quarters. He means tae discover the truth about ye fur himself, and when he has—" Seamus abruptly broke off, appearing urgent. "Heed me. He is not a man with much patience or kindness."

"But I'm not a spy," I insisted.

"It disnae matter whit ye say. He's knoon tae bend men tae his will… and will accuse anyone of treachery if it serves him. He will show ye nae mercy, as he is convinced—despite the fact that ye are a lass. He will take ye as he pleases."

Suddenly, my mouth went really dry again. "But I'm not a spy, for the millionth time already."

"So ye have said."

"Because it's true."

"Therefore, ye must make haste and come with me," he said adamantly.

"But why should I go with you? I don't even know you," I replied uneasily.

"Aye—I reckon ye dinnae," he responded. "Yoo've merely knoon me fur three days and two nichts longer than he. But I shall not harm ye as I have not already."

I hesitated, torn whether to leave with him or not, and uncertain if I could really trust him.

"Ye may risk yer chance with His Lordship. Or ye may risk believing whit I tell ye and take yer chance with me."

I continued to hesitate a moment longer. It was hard to think, but I had to quickly decide.

"Okay," I said spontaneously with a faint nod. "I'll go with you."

"Come, then," he said. He slipped his sturdy palm around my upper arm and proceeded to guide me swiftly out of the room back through the corridor toward the front door. Quietly pulling the door open, we stepped out into the main passage.

"Oh!" I gasped unexpectedly, tripping over something unseen and dense lying on the floor before my feet.

"Take care," Seamus warned cautiously as he simultaneously grabbed me by the waist and prevented my fall onto the unconscious guard stretched out on the floor.

"Did you do that?" I asked, completely surprised.

"Aye," Seamus said indifferently as he continued to urge us through the passage.

"Is he—" I started.

"He'll be alrecht. Now come along," he replied impatiently.

Without any time to regard the details of our escape, we simply moved down the staircase and passed through a couple of short, musty corridors. We nonchalantly moved through random groups of conversing and joking soldiers, who were clueless about our breakout. Following his lead, I paced along beside him as discreetly as possible without detection, or cause for concern. When we reentered the courtyard, Seamus steered us clear of Lord Loudoun's front windows into his office. A collection of laundresses appeared on their way to exiting the fort entrance, and Seamus hastily maneuvered me toward them, merging me into the group with him walking closely beside me.

Once we had crossed over the bridge, I realized as I took a breath that I hadn't been breathing the whole while we were making our way out of the fort. We continued walking with the women for several moments longer, when I felt Seamus easily seize my arm and disband us from the group. We proceeded on our own for a couple more blocks through town in the opposite direction of the fort. Soon, we arrived at the nearest tavern, where I recognized Lachlan lingering with two horses hitched at the post. He glanced up from smoking his pipe, noticing our approach, and waved at us.

Lachlan began unhitching the horses and mounted his horse the minute we arrived ready to depart. Seamus easily tossed me up onto his horse, Blaze, then effortlessly swung himself up behind me on the saddle. Once again on horseback, we set off at nightfall over the cobblestones through town.

CHAPTER 8

Within minutes, we had arrived at a nice-looking two-story Dutch Colonial brick dwelling. We dismounted our horses, and a stablehand led them away. Upon entering the somewhat large, orderly house, we were greeted by the owners of the property, Mr. and Mrs. Olaf and Hannah Rasmussen. Apparently, they were familiar with Seamus and were deferential as they kindly welcomed him and his small company inside their home.

Finley entered the Egyptian blue foyer from the sitting room, joining us once he heard new voices. The brothers briefly spoke to each other in Scots. Seamus then turned his gaze to Mr. Rasmussen and said, "I fear Mistress Arboles is quite weary as she has journeyed from afar at grave peril and would care tae rest without concern."

"Indeed," Mr. Rasmussen said politely. He indicated to his straight-laced wife, and she acquired their maid, who was attentively standing close. Mrs. Rasmussen briefly instructed her maid, and in a moment, the maid retreated. Mrs. Rasmussen subsequently encouraged me to follow her up the oak staircase. She led me through a corridor to a room at the end of the passage. The bedroom was noticeably neat, tidy, and pleasantly decorated with snowflake-white wainscoting, burnt-umber walls, New England lace, and modest, beautifully hand-crafted Shaker furniture over checkered wide-planked oak floors.

"I shall hope that you rest well after your tiresome journey, Mistress Arboles," Mrs. Rasmussen said in a stilted, genteel manner with a thick German accent.

"Thank you for your kindness, Mrs. Rasmussen," I responded.

"*Bitte.* You are welcome, Mistress Arboles," she replied modestly, then turned to leave the room, closing the door behind her. After a few minutes, the door opened again, with two Black maids entering the room. One of them was the maid I recognized from downstairs to whom Mrs. Rasmussen had given instructions.

"My name is Mary, and this is Hope, mistress," one of the maids informed me simply.

"Hello," I replied politely.

"We been expectin' you, mistress. A bath been drawn for you," Mary said.

"Thank you," I replied kindly. I was internally grateful to learn that I would be able to wash the outdoor grime from my body. I followed the young maids toward a door inside the room, antici-pating there would be a regular bathroom. But as the door was opened, I discovered it was actually a simple closet that had a washbasin and copper tub with a chamber pot in the corner. It became apparent that the two women were going to wait on me as I entered the privy closet.

"Thank you for preparing the water," I said gratefully. I was slightly uncomfortable as I sensed they were there to wait on me. "But you needn't stay. I'm okay being alone—if you don't mind."

"You is excusin' us, mistress?" asked the younger maid of the two named Hope. They both appeared uncertain and surprised.

"Yes, you've done plenty already. Thank you," I said gratefully, knowing it wasn't easy lugging large pails of steaming hot water upstairs to fill the tub.

"Is you certain, mistress?" Mary asked.

"Yes," I assured. "I hope I'm not being rude. It's just that I prefer having a bit of privacy, if you don't mind."

"If it be pleasin' you, mistress," Mary said. The two slender maids bobbed a curtsy and retreated from the room, leaving me to myself.

It took longer than a typical moment to untie the various fabrics constituting my plain attire. Finally, after completely undressing, I stepped into the tub. The lukewarm bath water was very shallow, but I was extremely glad to simply have the opportunity to sit privately in quiet with the comfort of being left alone while I bathed.

I SLEPT well the whole night through and awakened rather late the next morning as golden sunlight entered brightly through the windows. I groggily wiped the sleep from my eyes, thinking I was still at home. Until I noticed the ticking clock over the oak mantelpiece and read the time: nine thirty. Then, reality set in, and everything came rushing back, forcing me to realize this was not simply a bad dream.

Extracting myself from beneath the blanket, my bare feet touched the hardwood floor, and I paced toward the uneven glass window to peer out. The day appeared crystal clear with warm morning yellow hues spread across the fresh blue sky. Not a cloud could be seen as I gazed out into the distance. The Hudson River sparkled in the sunlight past the rural areas. The trees divided properties over the landscape and made the scenery appear like a peaceful pastoral painting reminiscent of the ones created by Thomas Cole.

My stomach growled, and suddenly I realized that I was

starving. I stirred from the window, deciding I needed to dress appropriately in order to make my way down to the kitchen. But when I glanced around the bedroom for my clothes, they were oddly nowhere to be found. It occurred to me that perhaps one of the maids might have entered the room earlier this morning while I slept and had taken the soiled clothes for them to be laundered. The sudden thought of my phone having gone missing alarmed me. I darted toward the bed and removed the pillow on which I had slept. To my utmost relief, my phone was still there.

A gentle knocking came from behind the door, and I replaced the pillow over my phone. I strode to the door and pulled the brass handle. It was Hope standing before me, holding a tray of prepared food.

"Good morn, mistress," she said respectfully as she entered the room and set the tray down on the tea table by one of the windows.

"Good morning, Hope," I replied. "Thank you for bringing this."

"You don't concern yoself, mistress. I is to see you is fed," she said shyly.

"Well, thank you very much. It's awfully kind of you," I replied genuinely. She straightened from the tray and looked at me a little surprised.

"Yes'm, mistress." She bobbed a curtsy. "The household normally don't take their meal till noon, mistress. But His Grace says you is ready ta take a bit of food right now."

"He did?"

"Yes'm, mistress."

"Oh—I am a bit hungry, actually. Thank you."

"I'm goin' ta return soon when you is done with yo meal, mistress."

"All right," I said gently. She curtsied again, then left the room, closing the door behind her.

I strode over toward the window and sat down at the small

Shaker tea table in front of the tray of food. I broke off a piece of oat bread and proceeded to spread a scoop of soft butter over it. There was a little dish of marmalade, I gladly noticed. I took my knife and lopped up a portion of it to spread on my buttered bread. The bread was dense and started filling me. It had an unusual flavor, but as I ate it, I decided that it didn't taste half bad. After I had finished eating the bread, I cracked open my hard-boiled egg and ate it while I gazed out the window beside me, admiring the view of surrounding apple trees.

When I had completed my meal, I realized that I hadn't had anything to drink and had grown thirsty. I reached for the mug without realizing what the contents were and took a huge gulp. My mouth was instantly set ablaze as the ale went scorchingly down my throat. It caused me to have a coughing fit, and I hurried to the privy closet to drink some fresh water out from the water pitcher next to the washbasin on the stand.

When I came out from the closet, I peered out the window again and caught a glimpse of Seamus standing at a distance just beyond the vegetable garden between the apple trees, gazing at the duck pond while puffing away on his pipe. A girl appearing in her late adolescence carrying a parasol strolled outside and soon joined him. That was Grete, the eldest Rasmussen daughter at eighteen years old. She had seven sisters, to my surprise. They were Elsa, who was seventeen, Heidi was fifteen, Kristen was twelve, Claudia was eleven, Kaethe was nine, Olga was six, and Frieda was two years old—and not a single boy among them.

They were a clan of alabaster-skinned rosy-cheeked platinum-blonde blue-eyed Fragonard cherubs appearing like most of the people and their children here. I, on the other hand, pretty much stood out like a sore thumb—ethnically speaking. My complexion was naturally tan, and my black Shirley Temple ringlets loosely hanging just below my shoulders made me realize that I was not in a place that was as ethnically diverse as any large city would have been in modern-day America.

The Rasmussens were one of the most respected families in town, I learned, as a result of their successful textile business, which had seeded their wealth. Mr. Olaf Rasmussen was a middle-aged gentleman in his forties and appeared to have a fair sense of humor, though he seemed to run his household like a tight ship. Mrs. Hannah Rasmussen was a staunch woman appearing near my own age. It was obvious to me, and perhaps to her, that she and I had little in common, although she was very kind to me.

A knocking came from behind the door while I was observing Seamus beginning to accompany Grete on a morning stroll. She looked pretty in the morning light, dressed in her pastel-green silk gown and large-brimmed pale-yellow ochre straw hat that was embellished with matching green satin ribbons swirling in the light breeze. As the two of them disappeared among the trees, I turned from the window to answer the door.

"How do you do, mistress?" Hope asked as she entered the room carrying a collection of brown linen wrapped packages.

"Fine, thank you. And you?" I replied, watching her place the articles on the edge of the bed.

"I is well too, thank you, mistress," she answered kindly. She started untying the cord around the parcels.

"That's nice," I said genuinely as I strode toward her. She dutifully proceeded to remove the contents from the parcels and revealed a pile of brand-new clothing. I stood near her as she intently laid the garments on the bed, and noticed the beauty of her mocha skin. Her complexion was smooth and unblemished, giving it the appearance that it was probably silky to the touch. Her features were fine, but her lips were perfectly full and closely reminded me of the image of Queen Nefertiti's bust.

After Hope finished organizing the garments on the bed, I pulled my new clocked stockings over my legs and secured them with fresh pink satin ribbon garters around each thigh. I gathered one of the slippers in my hand before slipping it on my foot and admired the detail of the simple peach silk brocade two-inch heel. There was no brand name associated with it, but it was very pretty and well-made. After I had slipped my new slippers onto my feet, Hope proceeded to outfit me in eighteenth-century fashionable undress as she encircled the stays around my torso over the clean fine linen shift I had slept in. After lacing the garment up my back, I was surprised how much support it gave, as much as a bra, although it was constricting. Next, she secured my new linen pockets around my waist. Then came the lace neckerchief around my neck and tucked over my bosom.

Once my pockets had been secured, an under petticoat was tied around my waist. Afterward, Hope tied a nice peach-colored cotton top petticoat around me, then she secured a pretty light-pink rose chintz short gown around my torso. Next, a delicate white muslin apron came around my waist, nearly completing the look. She then placed a dainty lace cap over my ringlets. At last, she finished dressing me by attaching a nice, petite straw hat with corresponding peach-colored silk ribbons around it on my head.

After I was finally properly dressed, Hope collected the dishes and left me to myself once more. I glanced at myself in the mirror and couldn't believe my image. I thought that I looked like a ghost stuck in time. It startled me. I moved away from the looking glass and departed my room.

While walking through the hallway, I noticed a door open to one of the bedrooms that I was passing by. I hesitated for a moment. I perhaps should not have, but I was compelled to enter the room. I had discovered one of the girls' bedrooms and noticed that it was nicely arranged. It was bright with golden sunlight entering that enhanced the snowflake-white wainscoting, the rose distempered walls, and the cheerful floral bedding with lace curtains.

Apparently, this was Grete's room, I surmised, as my eyes landed on the beautiful penmanship scribed in a letter that she appeared to be in the middle of writing. I was a little surprised to see that it had been addressed to His Grace, Duke of Monteith. It was modestly written and benign, but it left me with the amused suspicion that the girl had a crush on him.

But my light amusement quickly dissipated when I noticed the date written on it. My heart utterly stopped, and my breath left me as I read the date on the page: 1756, August 15. The year **1756** shot off the page like a ballistic warhead and seared my brain with the heat of a branding iron. The bones in my legs went like gelatin, and I collapsed into the chair before the small Queen Anne writing desk. The blood coursed through my veins like ice water, and I couldn't stop the uncontrollable trembling in my hands and legs, and my quickening breath.

The sound of Mrs. Rasmussen's voice talking to her maid on the staircase caught my attention, and I jumped unstably from the seat. I unsteadily hastened out of the room.

In my confusion, I had forgotten which direction my room was and mindlessly headed toward the stairs. Mrs. Rasmussen noticed me as I rushed past her and Mary on my way down the staircase.

"*Bitte.* Is anything the matter, Mistress Arboles?" Mrs. Rasmussen inquired worriedly.

"Oh, no, no—everything's fine, thank you. Just want to get some fresh air, that's all," I stammered, aware of my tremulous nerves. I continued mindlessly down the stairs as she stared after me with a questioning look.

Without really knowing where I was going, I wandered through the first-floor corridors in raw shock and discombobulation. Somehow I discovered myself outside meandering through the garden past the apple trees and rows of large lilac bushes. I had no idea where I was going, but I just kept moving. Finally, I discerned a wrought iron bench hidden between a band of sap-green maple trees, and I collapsed onto it, facing the small pond before me.

The sparrows chirped all around in the trees. The air was still, and I could hear my own breath heavily escaping me. I didn't understand how any of this could be possible, and I was striving extraordinarily hard not to freak out any more than I already was. But all sorts of thoughts were spinning wildly through my head. How was it at all possible for a temporal displacement to exist? And for a time warp to exist that I could experience and survive? Even though quantum physics explains its theories, I never thought it could be real. The physical reality of it could not be proven—until now. How could I even be alive if I had not ever been born yet?

The thought of my mom and dad, my brother and sister-in-law rushed to mind. Certainly they were searching for me by now. I was sure that they were already so worried, because they had no idea where I was. I knew they were going to spend a lifetime grieving, since they were never going to be able to locate me.

Oh my God, what am I going to do?

Nothing made sense. The thought entered my mind that I very well could never see them again. It hit me with such unforgiving force that I essentially could not believe the icy new reality I was now facing.

I might not ever see my family again... My life that I had—it's gone... All of it—gone. How did this happen? Why did this happen to me? Why?

Everything that I had seen and experienced from the time of my arrival in this place was real. The blood that had been spilled in the ambush was too much to handle all of a sudden. My vision blurred as tears filled my eyes.

A twig on the ground snapped at close proximity, and I glanced to the left of my shoulder, unexpectedly recognizing Seamus's tall presence. I quickly brushed away the tears welling in my eyes and strove to stifle my emotions.

"Have I disturbed ye?" he inquired considerately.

"No," I responded quietly, shaking my head a little. He observed me as he paused.

"May I?" he politely inquired, gesturing to the empty space next to me on the small bench.

"Sure," I replied, and shifted a little over to create more room. He sat close to me, and it was quiet between us for a second.

"Yoo're dismayed," he said.

"No—well, I…" I was on the cusp of tears and had to stop myself. After a fleeting moment, I decided to ask in spite of my shaking voice, "Do you mind if I ask you a silly question?"

"Nae," he encouraged attentively.

"What year is it?"

"Whit year?" He looked at me a bit odd.

"Yeah."

"Why, it is the year of Our Lord 1756, of coorse."

"Right, yes, of course… of course," I stuttered breathlessly, feeling my eyes uncontrollably welling up.

"Whit is it?" he inquired with real sincerity.

"I just… Well, I… I just miss… Forget it—it's okay… You wouldn't understand," I replied.

"Would I not?" he inquired carefully.

"No," I replied faintly, shaking my head a little with tears in my eyes.

"Are ye certain?"

"Quite certain."

"Ahh, but I see now. 'Tis yer husband that ye miss, is it not?" Seamus's tone was compassionate. I couldn't bear it and lost my composure. "Shhh, now… I understand the grief. It never ceases, but it will ease in time… All in time… Take heart, lass." Listening to him only made it worse, and I was completely overcome with emotion. I covered my hand over my face, hiding my streaming tears. I felt his arm gently come around my shoulder in an effort to console me. I just collapsed, sobbing helplessly.

Seamus proved to be very kind just then, however, as he

pulled me against him, allowing me to bury my crying head in his chest. His breath came close over the top of my head as he began repeatedly muttering calming words to me in Scots. I completely gave in and sobbed terribly over my confusing situation and utter terror. He soothingly stroked and caressed the back of my neck and shoulder while letting me seek consolation in his broad, firm chest.

It took a good long moment before my weeping began to subside. He shifted slightly and retrieved a handkerchief from his waistcoat. He lifted my chin and started dabbing at my moist eyelashes and cheeks as he spoke incomprehensibly to me. After a moment, I strove to calm myself.

When I glanced up at him, with our gazes so close, it suddenly occurred to me that there might have been more intent in his expression. Not knowing if I was misinterpreting him, I stirred from him and stood. I continued wiping the tears from my eyes with my fingers. He flushed, and I became really uncomfortable.

"Thanks. Thank you, I mean—for being so nice. But you really don't have to—I mean, it's okay. I'm okay—I'll be okay. I mean, I —I don't want you to think that I—" I rambled, backing away from him. My face felt like it was on fire. He was as flushed as I felt, but he didn't seem at all disturbed. He reached out and seized my hand. He gently pulled me back toward him so that I faced him directly while he remained sitting.

"Ye neednae fear me, Sylvina," he said quietly.

"No—I'm not afraid of you," I admitted, strangely enough.

"Yoo're not?" He seemed surprised.

"No," I said.

"Guid. That is guid," he responded satisfactorily. He contemplated for a moment. "Did Laird Loudoun frighten ye?"

"I don't think he's a nice person," I replied.

"He's not a nice man. He frightens everyone—particularly the lasses," Seamus revealed, as he released my hand.

"Oh." I nodded understandably.

"Aye," he replied. It became quiet between us for a moment, and the feeling was awkward. He seemed contemplative or hesitant. I couldn't tell which one. His gaze slightly shifted to the glinting water behind me. "It will please me if ye waur tae personally address me," he continued as he returned his eyes from the sparkling pond to gaze steadily at me.

"Personally?" I asked unknowingly.

"Aye," he said.

"What do you mean?" I asked.

"It would please me greatly if ye waur tae regard me by my first given name," he said deliberately.

"You mean Seamus?"

"Nae." He shook his head slightly. "Leif," he disclosed.

"Leif?"

"Aye. Seamus is my middle name," he explained. "Leif is my first name. Nae one addresses me by that name. 'Tis always Seamus. But it would please me if ye waur tae address me by that name."

"Sure, if you prefer," I agreed simply.

"I do," he said politely.

"Okay," I replied, nodding a little bit.

"Guid," he said, seeming satisfied. A slight pause in the conversation ensued, and the discomfiture emerged again. "Please, won't ye sit?" he continued, tapping the empty space next to him on the bench. "I shall not bite ye," he joked. I smiled a little, realizing that I was starting to feel a little bit better. I stepped toward him and returned to my place on the bench close to him.

"So," I started thoughtfully, trying to calm my spirit some more, "you're Scottish."

"Aye," he said, nodding his head.

"And Seamus is your middle name," I said, attempting to start a simple conversation.

"Aye. I was named efter my father and grandfather on my mother's side."

"Oh, that's nice."

"And ye? Efter whom micht ye be named?"

"Actually, I'm named after my paternal grandfather's mother," I said.

"Is that reit?" he replied interestedly.

"Yes."

"I see." He paused momentarily, and a lull in the conversation happened again. "May I inquire about yer departed husband?" he continued tactfully, breaking the silence. I looked directly at him, a little hesitant to broach the subject. "I shall like tae ken a little about him—if yoo'll please."

"Well…" I started softly.

"If ye dinnae care tae, then it is alrecht," he said.

"No, it's okay. I can tell you," I said honestly.

"Alrecht."

"Well, what do you want to know?"

"I suppose, whit was his name?" he asked.

"Matt—Mathew, really. But everyone called him Matt," I said.

"Och. That's a guid name," he said. I nodded accordingly. "Whit else will ye tell me of him."

"Well—" I thought momentarily. I realized that I couldn't fully disclose much about my late husband without the possibility of raising too many questions that I couldn't answer, because it might jeopardize my troubling predicament.

"Weel?" Leif encouraged gently.

"Well, he had a good disposition."

"Mmm. That's guid."

"He also had a positive outlook on life," I revealed.

"That's fortunate," he said.

"Yes," I agreed. "He liked the outdoors a lot."

"Did he?"

"Yeah. And he liked to travel. We took a lot of vacations together."

"Is that reit?"

"He had a good sense of humor—and he always made me laugh."

"Then he was guid tae ye," Leif surmised.

"Yeah, he had a good heart. He was nice to people—and he was always kind to me. We had a good relationship," I revealed.

"That is important."

"Yeah."

"I assume that he was a man of leisure and didnae have tae make a living."

"No, he made a living. His job paid him well."

"Och, whit did he do fur a living?"

"He worked as a university professor."

Leif furrowed his brow a little. I realized momentarily that I had to stop telling him any more information about Matt, because it was leading to more questions that I ultimately could not answer.

"He was a tutor?" Leif asked curiously.

"Yes," I said.

"Hm, curious," he said pensively. "Whit did he lecture?"

"Anthropology," I ventured hesitantly.

"Anthropology?" He appeared puzzled.

"Yeah."

"Curious," he replied with an unintelligible expression. "I huvnae heard of anthropology. Whit micht that be?"

"It's the study of various cultures and their evolution," I revealed.

"Och," he responded thoughtfully. "Did yer departed husband agree with the classical arts?"

"I suppose you could say he did," I said. Leif paused momentarily, seeming meditative.

"And he was a Spaniard also?"

"No," I said. "He was American."

"American? Ye mean he was a colonial. A Spanish subject?" Leif asked. I slowly nodded my head, convinced that if I told him the truth, he would not believe me or understand. "I see," he responded pensively. "May I inquire how he perished?"

"He, um, he was hit by a vehicle while crossing the street. The driver was drunk." My eyes started welling up again. I quickly whisked away the tears filling my eyes.

"Och, mercy—stampeded," he said. "My greatest sympathies."

"Thank you."

It grew quiet between us again. I simply sat staring out at the water before us, watching the sunlight glinting over the rippling pond.

"How long whaur ye wed?" he started again.

"Not long at all," I answered.

"Indeed?"

"Only a year. But we knew each other for a good while before we got married. So, that was nice. At least I was fortunate to have known him for some time before he passed away."

"Och, aye. Indeed," he said thoughtfully. "How long ago did this tragedy occur?"

"Three and a half years ago," I replied honestly.

"Och," Leif responded contemplatively. "How old was he?"

"He was thirty-six."

"Whit a true pity," he said, shaking his head. "Again, my greatest sympathies."

"Thank you."

"Aye," he replied thoughtfully. "How did ye ken him prior tae yer marriage?"

"A friend of mine introduced us." I couldn't tell him that we met at a New Year Eve's party through a mutual friend in Boston when I was a medical student at Harvard and he had just acquired his position as a professor at UCLA.

"That is nice."

"Yes, it was."

He drifted into silence for a moment. "I shall like tae thank ye fur yer conversation," he said.

"You don't have to thank me."

"I do indeed," he insisted.

"All right, then, you're welcome," I said. His lips tilted slightly upward, and his expression mildly relaxed.

"Would ye mind if we waur friends now?" he inquired thoughtfully. I considered the offer.

"I don't mind—I think that might be okay," I agreed politely. A gentle grin eased over his face attractively. Leif held out his large masculine palm for me to take. I slipped my hand into his sturdy hand, and he gently squeezed my hand.

"Thaur now, we're friends," he stated kindly, and released my hand.

"I guess so," I concurred.

"Guid."

I felt my lips slightly turn up, and I suddenly felt a bit better. He smiled gently at me in return.

"Now tell me," he commenced again, "whit exactly does 'okay' mean?"

"It means 'all right,' 'affirmative,'" I said.

"Och. I've never heard of it used till ye said so."

"Oh," I said. He simply smiled at me again, and I smiled accordingly.

THAT NIGHT in my room when I was alone with my thoughts, I kept fixating on my situation. I just couldn't figure out how I had arrived in 1756. Quantum leaping was just science fiction. No one ever thought that it could be an *actual* occurrence. Yet, again, I was living proof of it happening. I simply didn't understand how I could physically survive such transportation and arrive here.

I felt an immense sense of isolation and loneliness so profound that I fundamentally did not know what was going to happen to me, despite my new friend that I had acquired. I was *alone* in the universe. This feeling that I had was distinctly different from the loss that I had experienced when I unexpectedly lost Matt; then I at least had had my family and friends with me. I'd still had my life to live. But now, my family, all that I had ever loved and known, was gone. All of the things I used to do in my life that helped make me who I was had vanished.

I retrieved my cell phone, the one bit of remaining proof outside of my own mind that told me I was not crazy. I turned it on, and noticed how little battery life it had. I tearfully accessed my photo album and began thumbing through the pictures. I came upon several videos taken of friends and family. It became too much for me to bear, so I turned off my phone and shoved it back beneath the pillow. That night, I cried heavily until I fell asleep.

CHAPTER 9

The next day, I joined the family with Finley and Leif for a noontime meal. The children were very polite and demure, and uncommonly well-mannered compared to children of my time. I was aware that I stood out like a square peg in a round hole with my medium-length coal-black ringlets loose over my shoulders and my tan complexion and saturated green eyes. I knew that my mannerisms also differentiated me, and I struggled to fit in. I was apparently an individual of interest to the children as we sat across from each other at the dining table. The little ones simply stared at me with open curiosity. The older girls exchanged quiet looks of uncertainty. Mrs. Rasmussen minded her children at the table, ensuring that they stayed in proper, strict accordance while they kept watching me.

Occasionally, I noticed the eldest child, Grete, gaze demurely at Leif. There was no mystery there; he was obviously good-looking, and I guessed that he was probably in his early thirties. Looks aside, he seemed genuinely kind, respectful, and noticeably intelligent. Grete was attracted to him, I deduced, as she blushed when he happened to glance her way during the conversation he was having with Finley and her father. Leif smiled politely at her, but then his eyes shifted and fastened onto me. His civil grin lingered momentarily. His incisive gaze held mine for a minute, and I knew then that he was certainly looking at me.

I abruptly averted my eyes from him and took a sip of my tea. I did not know why I had suddenly become nervous. But I was. I was very nervous. Mrs. Rasmussen chided the girls, Grete and Elsa, for whispering to each other at the table. No doubt, I easily conjectured that I was the topic of their subtle exchange as Elsa gave me a suspicious look. I finished the rest of my meal in silence, feeling very much insecure about myself in this foreign situation.

AFTER EATING, I decided to go outside. The clearing was wide and open, and the air was hot and humid. Not a cloud floated in the rich cobalt-blue sky, and the sun shined really bright. The air smelled fresh and different. The woods encircled the grass clearing, where there were three Native American women servants doing loads of laundry off to the side of the house. The sunlight reflected brightly off the clean white linens tousling in the light breeze. At a distance, I recognized the glimmering pond at the foot of the bordering trees, and I started walking in that direction.

My mind wouldn't shut off, and I kept mulling over the series of irrefutable cataclysmic events that had recently taken place in my life. To think that I had been transported from the twenty-first century to 1756, before the conception of the United States of America, to an era when these territories were occupied and claimed by England, France, and Spain, with all of them vying for imperial superiority, was very hard to believe. A large part of this territory was under British rule and was where lawful slavery existed among all the European imperial nations here. This was a thought that went beyond mind-boggling for me; it was completely foreign.

I was trapped living in an era more than a century before the Civil War, the Industrial Revolution, and before the Wright brothers took humankind on its first flight. It would be more than a century before Thomas Edison harnessed electricity to make the first light bulb, before Alexander Graham Bell did the same for the telephone, before Henry Ford was the first to bring the automobile to the road, and before Madame Curie discovered radioactivity.

Furthermore, it would be two centuries before women would have the right to vote, or before the discovery of penicillin and other modern-day antibiotics, and three centuries before antiviral medications would come to be. It would also be two centuries before we harnessed the energy found in an atom, before the Civil Rights movement, and before Neil Armstrong would ever step foot on the moon. Such advanced technologies as those found in medicine, physics, and other sciences, transportation, telecommunications, and computers were all discoveries far off into the distant future.

I was trapped in an era that was out of touch with my own personal social norms and values, and everything else that defined me.

Seeing as how I did not know the exact conditions that had transported me back to this time period, I had no way of knowing if I could possibly return home again. And considering that problem made me think that the actuality of ever returning home was closely unachievable, if not completely impossible.

I am stuck here... Lost in this era—maybe forever.

I had never felt so utterly despondent and depressed in all my life. I had to face the cold hard fact of my new reality. I was so homesick that it physically hurt me, and I was so overcome that I started to break down again. I was on the verge of uncontrollably sobbing as I stood by the shore of the pond. I had no inkling what I was going to do, or what was going to happen to me.

"Are ye alrecht, lass?" a voice unexpectedly came from behind me. I suddenly turned and unwittingly realized that Leif was standing there. "I beg yer pardon. I didnae intend tae frighten ye," he apologized. I quickly wiped my face with my fingers. He retrieved a handkerchief from his waistcoat pocket and kindly offered it to me.

"Thank you," I sniffled, patting the tears from my eyes.

"Aye," he said simply. He didn't say anything else but remained quietly standing near me, and it felt noticeably uncomfortable in the commencing silence.

I shifted away from him, stepping away to sit on the cast-iron bench by the shore beneath the great evergreen limbs shading me. I strove to collect myself and noticed him stepping toward the bench also. He sat beside me, and I was aware of him sitting close.

"Please take heart, lass," he said gently. I turned my gaze to him and simply stared at him in my unspoken, tormented disbelief. Leif shifted his gaze from the glistening water over to me, and our eyes met. "It will be alrecht," he assuaged.

"I don't think you can promise me that—but thank you for saying so," I replied, discouraged. His ultramarine blue eyes appeared vibrant in the sunlight, I noticed. Without speaking further, he studied me for a moment. I nervously glanced away and tucked behind my ear the wayward ringlets blowing into my face by the gentle breeze.

"Mayhap," he ventured carefully, "ye micht believe that all will be weel in order that it may be so." I returned my gaze to him and briefly considered his words.

"Yes, that could be true," I replied.

"Aye," he said. It fell quiet between us again as we continued sitting uncomfortably next to each other on the bench while we both gazed out at the rippling pond.

After a moment, I regained some sense of composure. I turned my gaze to him again as he remained sitting motionless at my side.

"You're mending well," I noted.

"Och, aye," he replied, shifting his blue eyes back to mine.

"But you shouldn't be on your leg so much," I reprimanded.

"Och, I feel weel, however," he expressed confidently.

"But you could accidentally reopen the sutures," I reminded him.

"Aye, but it appears that ye did weel sewing my leg. And I'm not fond of simply lying about," he said.

"Oh. Okay, well, just be careful, then."

"I assure ye that I shall," he replied convincingly.

"Okay. And we must make sure it stays disinfected," I said.

"Aye… Apparently, yoo're a fine healer," he complimented.

"Thank you," I replied appreciatively.

"Yoo're welcome." He gazed searchingly at me for a moment. I was suddenly feeling uncertain again, and I turned my gaze toward the glimmering water in front of us. "I need tae tell ye something, lass." I returned to looking at him. "Ye need tae keep clear of him," he warned finally.

"Of whom?" I asked, confused.

"Laird Loudoun," Leif said.

"Oh," I replied, nodding my head a little. "I agree."

"Aye. I've already told ye that he is a dangerous man. I'm telling ye again as ye must stay clear of him."

"Thank you for telling me. I have no intentions of meeting him again," I said truthfully.

"He believes ye tae be a spy."

"But I'm not a spy," I responded certainly. Leif stared at me, musing over me for a moment. "Why would I spy?"

"Money."

"Money?" I gave him a ridiculous look.

"Aye."

"Listen to me, because I'm being very serious. I am not a spy. Do you understand? I have no reason to be one at all," I said clearly. He simply looked at me without saying a word. "Do you believe me?"

"The others are not certain," he responded.

"They're not?"

"Nae." He paused. "I suppose we shall discover whether ye are or aren't, however, will we not?" This time I stared at him for a moment, at a loss for words. "In the meantime, yoo're safe with us."

"I am?"

"Aye. None of us shall harm ye. Ye may trust all the lads yoo've met, including me." His complexion turned light pink. "Recall? Ye and I are friends, is that not correct?"

"Yes, I remember."

"Guid. Then, ye have nothing tae fear."

"Okay—thank you."

He nodded subtly. "Indeed," he said politely. I smiled nervously at him. I unthinkingly pulled my hair back—a typical habit of mine when I suddenly became self-conscious—as I was under his observation. I twirled it around into a loose ponytail at the back of my head. I was uncomfortably aware, as he studied me, that he could now see my neck and the pink tourmaline and diamond earring dangling from my pierced ear. I abruptly released my hair, and it fell back into place over my shoulders. His ears turned hot pink, I discerned, when he returned his gaze to the glittering pond. We didn't discuss Lord Loudoun after that moment, and the conversation drifted into silence.

"Would ye care for some tea?" he asked, interrupting the silence.

"Yes, thank you," I replied politely. Leif stood from his seat on the bench and stretched out his large hand toward me. I slipped my palm over his, and he clasped it. He gently helped me to my feet, and then we proceeded to walk beside each other back toward the house.

Early the next morning, we left the Rasmussens' residence. The men were headed north to Fort George. We were rejoined by the brothers' cousins as we left Albany. They had mentioned Fort Carillon also in their conversation a few times, which had no meaning to me as I wondered what they were talking about.

It took us a day traveling on horseback through dense forest to reach Fort George. While I was glad that we had arrived at a building for shelter and would not be camping outside tonight, fort living appeared to be really uninviting. This fort was not like the one we had left in Albany that was made of masonry. Instead, it was primarily a wooden field fort that was stale and rank with crowded inhabitants.

As we entered the officers' quarters, conversation ceased momentarily while the men seated around a stretched pine dining table curiously looked me over. Several officers inaudibly whispered to each other as Leif pulled a wooden chair out from the table for me to sit. He then pulled a chair out for himself and sat next to me. We were surrounded by eleven officers, who had already begun their afternoon meal. After a minute, conversation recommenced around the table. I sensed two other officers at the opposite end of the table had locked eyes onto me. I had noticed, as I was helping myself to a flavorless bannock and some butter, that there were no other women seated at the table except for me. And as it seemed that I had drawn some attention with my presence, I couldn't help feeling slightly self-conscious and out of place.

Leif reached for a bottle and filled my small glass with claret before filling a glass tumbler for himself. I naturally thanked him, and he responded in kind in Scottish. He snatched up a couple of hard-boiled eggs and passed one over to me. He proceeded to crack the one he'd kept for himself and began peeling it from its shell. I noticed an older officer seated at the head of the table looking directly at me with an unreadable gaze as he took a sip of claret from his wineglass. The officer next to him, who seemed slightly younger, had leaned in close to him and said something inaudible. The officer at the head of the table didn't respond and gently placed his wineglass back on the tabletop. They both wore English-style white wigs, unlike the other men, who chose to wear their hair uncovered and tied with a black ribbon at the back of their heads. As I determined from the discussions around the table, the men were a mixture of Englishmen and Scotsmen.

"Will you not introduce us to your beautiful wife, major?" inquired the officer seated next to the officer still gazing at me from the head of the table. Finley, who was sitting across from Leif, raised a brow at him.

"We're not wed," Leif said stiffly, and finished the claret in his glass. He reached for the bottle containing the red wine and refilled his tumbler.

"You don't say? Then who might she be otherwise?" asked the officer at the head of the table in his perfectly well-spoken London accent, who appeared to be in his late thirties.

"A bonnie lass," some other officer replied. Some of the men chuckled around the table.

"Are you telling me, then, major, that this lovely woman does not come with a name?" asked the English officer.

"Her name is Mistress Arboles," Finley answered curtly. I was quickly beginning to sense that some animosity existed between these particular men.

"Ah, what an unusually charming name," the English officer remarked. "I greatly apologize, but allow me, Mistress Arboles, to properly make your acquaintance amongst certain civilized men. Colonel Darby, and it is my pleasure." He courteously gave a brief nod toward me.

"Thank you. It's nice to meet you," I said politely.

"Tell me, I pray that your journey here was not perilous?" Colonel Darby inquired as he casually circled the rim of his glass with his forefinger.

"Actually not," I answered.

"How fortunate." He gazed at me with consideration and paused for a moment. Some of the other men exchanged mocking knowing glances with each other as they listened to our conversation. "You have an unusual accent. Where do you originate amongst the colonies?"

"From Pennsylvania," I lied.

"You do not say?" he asked interestedly.

"I happen to be familiar with Pennsylvania," said the officer sitting next to the colonel.

"Oh, really?" I remarked calmly, silently worried.

"Indeed," he confirmed. "I had the opportunity to encounter a man from that colony. He was a member of the colonial militia."

"Allow me to introduce Major Hansen to you," Colonel Darby said.

"Mistress," Major Hansen replied doubtfully. I gave him a meek smile. "I notice that your accent is unusual," he commented in his English intonation. "From whereabouts in Pennsylvania do you originate?"

"S-Southern Pennsylvania—near Philadelphia," I stammered,

hoping he wasn't familiar with that location. I took a sip of claret from my glass.

"I see. I have not yet had the opportunity to travel there. Curious," he said. "You are certainly a considerable distance away from your home, are you not?" Major Hansen looked at me with intriguing suspicion.

"Yes, fairly," I said.

"Then, if I may be of any assistance to you, I shall gladly oblige aiding you in anything you may require," he suggested.

"She wulnae need any assistance from ye," Finley interrupted gruffly.

"I beg your pardon?" Major Hansen stated clearly.

"She's not haur fur any lad's pleasure," Finley responded specifically.

"I am merely implying that perhaps the young woman may appreciate a friend, as she is so far removed from home. These are troubling times, major. Or have you forgotten?" Major Hansen said in his perfect London accent.

"A *friend*? Is that whit ye call it?" Finley asked. "I ken your sort. Yoo'll not be taking anything else that disnae belong tae ye under my watch."

"Watch your rank, *major*. You will not address me in that manner," Major Hanson retorted with displeasure.

"I'll *address* ye as ye are—a lecher and a coward," Finley snapped heatedly.

"I will have you removed from this fort!" Major Hansen threatened scathingly.

"At *ease*, gentlemen! That will be *enough!*" Colonel Darby, the commanding officer, interrupted with serious displeasure from the end of the table.

"Aye. That is enough," Finley grumbled angrily. Finley disgustedly shoved himself away from the table. He stood and paced out of the room.

"Come along, lass. This meal is spoilt," Leif said audibly in the same distasteful tone. He reached for my arm and clasped it, urging me up from my seat. He steered me out of the room and down the corridor. "Ye will go tae my quarters, lass, and bide till Finley or I return. I'll have a maid bring ye the rest of yer meal," he said sternly. With those last words, he swiftly escorted me to his room.

After a few minutes, Kezia, one of the few maids here, returned with a wooden tray of food for me to eat. I sat alone in Leif's room on the bed, rather glad to eat from the tray without company. When I had finished, I waited awhile alone in the room. Time seemed to be moving slowly, and I was beginning to feel restless. So, I simply curled up on the thin hay mattress and retrieved my phone. I opened the photo app and started the slideshow of pictures, which contained images of my family and friends. An image of Matt and me together popped up on the screen, and I abruptly stopped scanning through the picture index.

It was a picture of me and Matt sitting together on the beach. It was taken the day we found out that we were pregnant with our child. We were so stunned and happy beyond our wits about the news. Matt decided to take me out for ice cream on our way back home from our OB-GYN visit, so we had stopped at a gelato place near the Third Street Promenade in Santa Monica. While enjoying our ice cream, we had decided to take a walk down toward the pier, where we ended up pacing along the bike path on the beach. When we had reached a suitable place, we went out onto the sand, where we sat looking out over the warm aquamarine waves of the ocean. The weather was nice that day— it was July and warm. I had decided to take a selfie of us together right then and there. And as I snapped the photo, Matt had leaned in and planted a warm kiss on my cheek.

I felt a tear escape my eyelashes and roll down my face. I turned the phone off. I slipped it back inside my pocket and wept.

God, why am I here?

AT DAWN THE NEXT MORNING, Finley and Leif were suited up and packed with their horses, ready to leave as they waited outside the barracks. They were joined by Angus, Cole, Roy, Lachlan, Bearnard, Liam, and Derek, while Fearghus remained at Fort Frederick in Albany recovering from his musket ball wound. Leif's injured leg seemed to be recovering well from the arrowhead wound on his upper thigh. He gave no hint of discomfort, though he slightly limped occasionally after being seated for extended periods. The cousins in uniform were standing around each other talking in the courtyard as I exited the front of the barracks.

"Over haur, lass," Finley said as he waved a hand, motioning for me to approach the group. He paced toward me and told me, "Ye will ride with Seamus," as he started guiding me through the courtyard toward where the men were waiting with their horses.

"Alrecht, lass. Haur we go—we've got anither long trek headed out fur us," Leif said plainly as I approached him. He placed his hands on my waist, assisting me onto his horse. Once I was seated just so in the saddle, Leif swiftly swung himself up and over behind me on Blaze. He budged a little, adjusting himself more comfortably in the saddle. He closely fitted himself behind me, with his muscular legs hugging mine and his chest against my back. His long, masculine arms encircled me, creating a cage around me and securing me on the horse as he held the reins.

"Tick, tick," Leif uttered, clicking the inside of his cheek. Blaze started moving. In an instant, the horses began trotting over the dirt path, and we were off now heading out of the fort. I had a sinking feeling about this trip; I was very worried about being

taken even farther away from the flash point of my disappearance back in the Berkshires.

We had entered a lonely dirt road in the wilderness. The trail was level for a while as we slowly wound through the mountains. The trees towered high above all around us, and the large maple leaves fluttered like crinkling paper in the light breeze. Thick white cumulous clouds floated in the cerulean sky like scattered cotton balls. Sometimes the basalt rock outcropped from the mountainsides along the path, and soon we were following the path along the Hudson River going north.

Today was another hot, humid day with no shortage of noticeable gnats, dragonflies, junebugs, and mosquitoes. The swaying of the horse lulled me as we moved along. Compounded with the heat and the two and a half hours we had already traveled, I was beginning to feel drowsy. I felt my body unintentionally beginning to relax against Leif's chest as my head bobbed gently on his shoulder.

"Bear up, lass. We'll rest in a wee while. We must clear the rocks first," Leif said gently against my ear, steadying me with his arm around my waist.

"Okay," I muttered, succumbing to rest my head against his shoulder. I decided to close my eyes for only a moment.

THE NEXT THING I remembered was being roused from a nap by the sound of Leif's voice.

"Sylvie… Sylvie," he muttered softly in my ear.

"Hmm?" I mumbled, suddenly awaking just as we had come to a halt at a small grassy clearing at the bank of the impressive rushing Hudson River.

"We have stopped fur a respite," he said.

"Oh. Where are we?" I inquired tiredly, gazing confusedly around our new location.

"We are near the falls," he informed me.

"Oh," I said. I looked around and saw nothing remotely resembling settlements.

"I apologize fur the hardship," he said, beginning to dismount first from his horse.

"I'm okay," I replied sincerely.

"Guid," he said. "Haur." He stretched his arms up, taking me by the waist, and considerately pulled me off Blaze, planting me firmly on my feet on the ground.

"Thanks," I said.

"Aye," he replied.

The other men drifted slightly away with their horses, where they proceeded to sit on the grass near boulders. Casual conversation in Scots started between them. Cole said something, and they started laughing with glances in our direction.

"Come along, lass," Leif suggested. He turned his head, saying something in Scots back to them. They all glanced back at Cole, laughing heartily. Cole didn't seem too pleased, by the scowl on his face. Leif tugged his leather satchel off the back of the saddle and proceeded to walk down a small incline toward the boulders on the riverbank. I followed him down the slope until he chose a place for us to rest on one of the small boulders just over the water beneath a gigantic pine tree. "Would ye care fur oat bread?" he asked, pulling the heavy bread out of his leather pouch.

"Sure," I replied.

"Very weel," he said. He proceeded to break off a piece of bread. He winked at me as he gave me the piece. "Come, let us sit." He indicated a spot on the small limestone boulder for me to sit. I went ahead and took my place on the rock, and he sat next to me. We quietly ate the dried salted ham and bread. "Haur," he said, holding out his canteen toward me. "Wash it down with this." I received the canteen from him and took a single drink. I coughed a little at the burning sensation of the rum going down my throat. "Guid, is it not?"

"Water will do for me, thanks," I replied hoarsely. He chuckled.

"Next time wee sips first," he suggested.

"Yeah," I agreed. His pink lips tilted agreeably, and his expression grew warm. "So," I started curiously.

"Aye?"

"What was it like growing up in Scotland?" I asked interestedly, trying to start a simple conversation.

"'Twas fine," he answered simply.

"So you had a nice upbringing there?"

"Och, aye. I have fond memories of it."

"Oh—that's nice," I replied, breaking off a bite-sized piece of bread and putting it in my mouth. "Do you miss it?"

"At times."

"Do you think you'll ever go back?"

"I reckon likely not," he answered, shaking his golden-haired head a bit.

"Why not?"

"Weel, I have a life fur myself haur."

"As a British officer," I said. He nodded in response.

"I have been reinstated in the army," he informed me.

"You were reinstated?"

"Aye. The Crown ordered it."

"Oh," I replied. "Well, how do you feel about being drafted?"

"Whit does it matter? I'm fulfilling a duty," Leif said resolutely.

"Oh," I replied simply.

His face grew flush, and he turned his gaze toward the rushing river in front of us. We sat momentarily in silence. As we were snacking, I ventured to ask curiously, "So, how long ago did you leave Scotland?"

"I left ten years ago," he informed me as he took a swig from his canteen, still looking out over the water.

"Oh, it's been a while," I noted.

"Aye."

"So you and Finley came to America together?" He returned his gaze to me, and our eyes met.

"Nae, Fin departed three years prior tae my arrival haur. He met and married an Anglican lass in Massachusetts Bay Colony, whaur he settled."

"Oh, what part of Massachusetts?" I inquired.

"A place called Northampton," he said.

"Northampton?" I echoed surprisedly.

"Ye have heard of it?" He looked at me with surprise.

"Yeah, actually I have," I replied.

"Och," Leif responded as he stared at me.

"I just heard someone talk about it once in a conversation. They had passed through there while traveling. Something like that—I think that's what I overheard," I lied.

"Och," he responded contemplatively as his steady ultramarine eyes held mine.

"So, is that where you settled too?"

"Aye. My brother and I own a portion of land thaur."

"That's nice," I said. "So, when do you think you'll return?"

"Before winter, I reckon."

"That'll be nice—there's no place like home," I acknowledged wistfully.

"Quite reit," he agreed.

"Do you have any nieces or nephews?"

"I have two nieces," he disclosed.

"Oh, that's nice."

"Aye, Mairie and Doireann are delightful," he said fondly.

"How sweet. How old are they?" I asked interestedly.

"Weel, Mairie is six years now, and Doireann is five."

"Those are such cute ages," I remarked kindly.

"Cute?" Leif asked inquisitively with a puzzled look.

"I mean, adorable."

"Och." He nodded.

"I bet you and Finley can't wait to see them again. I'm sure Finley's wife must really miss him."

"Och, aye, she must," Leif agreed. "And ye?" he began again after a drink from his canteen.

"Me?"

"Aye. I reckon that ye have nae bairns of yer own, I mean." I sensed his reticence about asking the question.

"Uh, no. No—I don't have any kids," I said awkwardly.

"Goats?"

"I mean, children. Kids are what we call children where I'm from," I replied, gently amused.

"Och, I see," he said, looking at me in a strange way. "Do ye like bairns?"

"Oh, of course, I love kids. I wouldn't be a pediatrician otherwise."

"I see," he replied musingly. "Weel, perhaps one day, yoo'll have bairns of yer own."

"Well, um, I'm not too sure about that," I responded uncertainly.

"Why not so?"

"Well, I think you'd have to be married for that," I said, considering the social norms here. Leif nodded in acknowledgment. He glanced out to the water again. I looked away too and listened to the trickling of the ravine as the water rushed by.

"Mayhap," he began again, returning his eyes to mine, "one day yoo'll wed again."

"I don't know," I replied skeptically.

"Mayhap ye micht not yet ken it," he said modestly. I detected his masculine cheeks turning pink, but he appeared nonchalant.

"Maybe. Who knows about anything, really? Life is so bizarre. But I feel my chances of remarrying are slim."

"Ye must truly have loov'd yer husband."

"More than anything," I said. Leif nodded his head lightly as I perceived his pensive gaze.

"Ye said that he was good tae ye," he mentioned thoughtfully.

"Very good."

"Indeed, that was a blessing."

"Yeah. It was a blessing."

"I reckon that yoo're a guid lass," he assessed.

"What makes you say that? You hardly know me," I responded.

"Yer loyalty tae yer husband."

"Oh. Well, it was easy—he was a good man."

"I reckon it does make it simple when couples git along with one anither."

"Yeah." I sighed wistfully. I ceased talking for a moment, and it became silent between us.

"Seamus," Finley unexpectedly interrupted. Finley glanced deliberately at me, then shifted his gaze back to his brother. "'Tis time we best be on our way."

"Aye," Leif acknowledged, and Finley turned away, walking back up the slope. Leif stood from his seat on the rock, swiftly collecting his satchel. He then took my hand, helping me up to my feet. "Come along, *àille dhubh*," he said easily, guiding me off the rock, and I followed him back up the hill.

The men had already started readying themselves on their horses as we crested the slope. Leif subsequently collected Blaze's reins. We mounted him, and the men resumed back on the trail.

CHAPTER 11

*L*eif and Finley lagged behind the rest of the men, walking and talking with each other in Scottish as they led their horses along the way while I continued riding on Blaze. I quietly observed the brothers as they spoke with each other. They both had the same kind of mannerisms, which only siblings could share, as they conversed. The brothers towered like Norsemen and were nearly the same height. Except I thought Leif might have been a hair shorter than Finley. I had never seen anyone with their kind of natural hair color. Finley's head gleamed like freshly polished copper. It was the deepest red that I had ever seen, yet it still was not dark enough to be labeled auburn.

Leif's head was even more brilliant as it gleamed like yellow gold beneath the sun. He had a head of thick, silky, straight strands that he wore just below his shoulders and kept tied back with a black silk ribbon. His shoulders were square and broad, I observed as I found myself admiring his formidable masculine stature. I forced my gaze away alongside the trail, trying to change the subject in my mind. Instead, I wondered where we were going.

In a while, the brothers had finished their conversation, and Finley swung himself over his horse. He trotted off ahead, joining the group, and Leif and I were once more left alone together. I watched him silently walk along leading Blaze for a little while. The air was thick with humidity again, but there was at least a light breeze that rustled through the trees, and it felt nice against my face. The sky was partly cloudy with large white cumulous clouds. I wondered if there was a chance of rain and hoped that the bad weather would wait until we had the opportunity to take shelter.

I asked Leif if he would let me down from his horse so that I could stretch my legs and walk too. He agreed and helped me down from the saddle. My legs at first felt a little wobbly and bowed as I proceeded to walk. But they soon straightened and felt normal as I continued to pace along. It felt good to stretch and exercise my legs while I paced quietly alongside him. I could see and hear the men several yards ahead laughing and joking with each other in Scots. I wondered what they were saying.

"Yoo're brooding," Leif observed.

"Hm? Oh—yeah," I replied, glancing up at him as I was unexpectedly interrupted from my thoughts.

"Micht ye care tae discuss it?" he asked.

"Well… I think it really doesn't matter at this point," I replied pessimistically.

"Whyever not?" he responded.

"I don't know," I replied gloomily, shrugging my shoulders. "It's okay—we don't have to talk about it, if you don't mind."

"As ye wish," he said respectfully. Silence fell between us, and I listened to the earth crunching beneath our feet as we walked. Jay birds were heard chirping high above in the sky as the breeze gently caressed my face.

"Tell me about Scotland," I started unexpectedly.

"Scotland?" Leif suddenly shifted his gaze to me, appearing somewhat surprised.

"Yeah, I want to know about it. What's it like?" I had always wanted to know what it was like there. Matt and I had made plans to visit the year he died.

"Weel," Leif began thoughtfully, "'tis quite bonnie. Ye can see fur distances… The land seems endless."

"Really?" I replied interestedly.

"Och, aye. Thaur is nae wilderness compared tae haur, but thaur is some forest. Thaur are glens that are vast and bonnie— and appear as if they can swallow ye whole without mercy."

"Wow, sounds amazing," I expressed attentively.

"Aye, quite similar tae the feeling these haur mountains give ye in this land. Also, the wind thaur can whip up somethin' fierce and blow ye about."

"Really?"

"Och, aye."

"That's amazing." He grinned at me, and the expression on his face was gentle.

"But if ye stand on a cliff," he continued, "and watch the river in the glen at sunset, it appears like heaven on earth."

"Sounds beautiful," I said, imagining it.

"'Tis."

"And you don't think you'll ever go back?"

"Nae. Thaur is nae reason."

"Oh… So, was it just you and your brother growing up? Are you the only two that your parents have?" I inquired interestedly.

"Aye. But I have a number of cousins," Leif replied.

"That's good," I said.

"Aye. They are as guid as brothers and sisters, I reckon."

"Yes, I suppose so too." He grinned at me again, and I naturally reciprocated. "So, when you first came here to live…" I started.

"Aye?"

"Did you experience any kind of culture shock?" I asked curiously.

"Are ye inquiring whether I found it quite different haur than from whaur I was born?"

"Yes."

"Weel, aye. I reckon I found it quite different."

"How so?"

"Weel, this is a vast land with many strange inhabitants," he acknowledged. I nodded a little. "But also, thaur is more ability fur a man tae create his own station in life."

"Right," I said, understanding.

"The nobility is less prevalent haur, so thaur's less rigidity regarding class," he said.

"I see," I said.

"And one is freer tae practice one's religion without being punished," he said. I nodded my head a bit in acknowledgment. "Save fur Papists, who remain persecuted," he said as he looked directly at me.

"Oh," I muttered uneasily. "So, do you go to church?"

"Aye, when I can."

"So, what religion are you?" Leif suddenly lifted his brow, and his eyes widened.

"Och, ye are certainly inquisitive, are ye not?"

"Oh, sorry, I didn't mean to pry," I said, realizing that I shouldn't have asked that particular question.

"Nae matter. 'Tis of nae consequence," he said unconcernedly. "I shall tell ye that I am familiar with the Anglican faith," he revealed evenly with a steady gaze on me.

"Oh," I replied simply.

"It disnae offend ye?" he asked strangely.

"What? That you're Anglican?" I looked at him strangely.

"Weel, in a manner."

"No. Why should I care what you are? You can be whatever religion you want," I said positively.

"Humph," he responded pensively.

"That's a weird question. Why did you ask me that?"

"I was merely curious whether ye had sentiments one way or the other," he said.

"Oh," I responded with uncertainty as I looked at him oddly for a fleeting moment. "Tell me about yourself before you were reinstated in the army. Like, what did you do with yourself?"

"Yoo're a raither bold conversationalist fur a lass!" he expressed unbelievably.

"Oh, please excuse me—again. I didn't mean—"

"Nae, it is quite alrecht," he said dismissively as he interrupted me. "I find it refreshing. I merely have never met a lass like ye, that is all." I perceived the genuine expression in his eyes as the sunlight illuminated the side of his face beneath the tricorn hat on his head.

"Oh," I replied simply.

"Never mind, lass. Yoo're fine."

"Okay." I hesitated.

"I shall reveal tae ye that I have always been a soldier since I was a young lad. So, being reinstated makes nae difference."

"Oh, I see."

"Do ye have any other questions fur me?" he asked.

"I guess I have one more question," I admitted.

"Aye, whit micht that be?"

"Well, I was wondering…"

"Aye?"

"I noticed that you don't wear a wedding ring."

"Och, aye. I'm not wed."

"Oh… So you've never been married?" I inquired.

"Nae. I have never had a wife," he admitted.

"Oh."

"Aye. Yoo're not like other lasses," he remarked subtly. "You hold a guid conversation. I enjoy speakin' tae ye—'tis plain." Leif winked at me, and I unexpectedly felt the temperature rise in my cheeks.

"Is it?" I asked shyly.

"Aye, 'tis."

"I suppose you're not so bad to talk to either." An obvious grin swept across his lips, making his face appear inviting and warm.

"Alrecht," he started. "Now, we best git on. Back up ye go on Blaze." Leif ceased walking and intimated for me to get back on his horse as he gave the animal a nice pat.

After I mounted his horse, he pulled himself up close behind me and steered the horse as we caught up with the rest of the men ahead of us.

everal hours later, after wandering through the mountains most of the day, we'd almost traveled twenty miles north of Fort George along the Hudson River. We approached a homestead in the distance. As we crossed over the pasture, smoke could be seen billowing from a humble log cabin house. It was quickly determined upon our advance across the field that the smoke we were seeing was not coming from the chimney. Rather, the house itself and the barn had been freshly burned to the ground. The air smelled of thick soot and ash. Cinder particles floated like dusty snowflakes in the hot, wafting breeze, and my stomach gave a sinking lurch.

The men ceased talking and began slowing their steps in a cautious manner as they exchanged alerted glances. The brothers glimpsed at each other as they stealthily paced over the clearing. Finley secretly signaled to the others, and the men began inaudibly spreading off in different directions as they watchfully walked through the grass, poised for something. Finley had vanished somewhere ahead when Leif reached up, stealing me off his horse, and planted me on the ground. We were left slightly behind the others, walking mindfully through the clearing, while

Leif remained silent, attentively scoping out the area as we kept our slow and steady pace.

"Do you know this place?" I asked him curiously.

"Aye, this is Jack McFarland's dwelling," Leif answered distractedly in a low voice.

"Where is he?"

"I dinnae see him."

As the men scrutinized the area while roaming the property, they ominously came to a halt near the cabin, and the answer to my question was immediately discovered. The shockingly unreal image of a bright red-haired bearded man lying scalped and bloodied with his throat slit from ear to ear stunned me. The sight knocked the wind straight out of me as I stood there gaping in horror. He was clutching his musket while he lay with it on the ground.

"'Tis Jack," Finley muttered to Leif as he knelt beside the dead man, checking him. He placed a compassionate hand on the dead man's shoulder.

"Nae one survived," Angus informed us from a slight distance away. He was bent over the lifeless body of a woman who had suffered the same horrendous fate. I strayed away from Leif and Finley toward Angus where the dead woman lay, seeing her with my own eyes. Strands of her sandy-blonde hair were dancing in the light breeze on one side of her head. The top of her skull was exposed and bloodied, along with a deep gash stretched across her neck. Her ashen lips were parted, and her eyes that had captured unspeakable terror remained wide open. She had seen the true face of evil upon her death. I simply stood staring in complete shock at this poor, poor woman; I just could not believe my eyes. After a moment, I glanced up and happened to see more corpses caught in the smoldering, charred rubble.

"*Oh!*" I gasped horrifically. "There're children!" I rushed over toward the hot cinders, incapable of doing anything to remove the three little blistered, limp bodies trapped among the smoldering debris. It was apparent that the three little boys were deceased, and I was paralyzed by the unimaginable sight of them. I tried to grasp what I was seeing and wondered, *Who in all the world, and why would anyone commit such a hateful act against innocents?*

"Indians," Derek said, turning to Finley.

"Aye," Finley responded unfortunately as he stood over the male corpse.

"Allied tae the French," Leif said stoically.

"Let's go," Finley directed.

"Wait a minute," I suddenly interjected.

"Aye?" Finley sharply turned his gaze to me.

"You're going to leave them here? Just like this?" I asked disapprovingly, filled with shock.

"That's reit," he said unquestionably.

"But you *knew* them. Shouldn't you at least bury them?" I inquired.

"Nae. We're taking our leave," Finley responded impatiently, and began walking away from the devastation. The men followed his lead and proceeded to cross the pasture. I abruptly snagged Leif by his billowy white linen sleeve, and he stopped in his tracks.

"How could you just *leave* them here like this and not take care of them? Isn't that a bit inhumane?" I criticized. Leif's eyes suddenly flashed with insult and anger. His face was hard and serious.

"Dinnae discuss humanity with me, lass. I have seen far too much in my life tae ken whit is *humane* and whit is not. Aye, we kent the McFarlands weel, and they wulnae be disturbed," Leif said evenly as his eyes ardently glared at me.

"Okay—it was just a suggestion," I meekly acquiesced after the unexpected sternness in his voice. I suddenly felt a bit intimidated by him. Leif shifted his steady eyes from mine and moved forward, walking in the direction toward the rest of the men.

NIGHT HAD FALLEN UPON US. We came to camp outside in the wilderness beneath humongous, towering trees. The crickets were out in full force, creaking all around, and the night air retained the day's heat and humidity. I could smell the moist earth and decaying leaves close to my nose while I lay on the ground on my side, quietly thinking. The horrendous images I had seen earlier in the day of the tragic McFarland family having been mercilessly killed had been disturbingly branded in the forefront of my brain. Every time I blinked or tried to close my eyes merely to rest, I could distinctly see the look of terror frozen perfectly on Mrs. McFarland's murdered face. And then there were the children... so innocent and helpless. Their sweet little lives cut short before they would have had the scarcest chance to know what it would have been like to have lived their own lives.

I rolled over onto my back and gazed at the starlit sky, seeing into the universe. I could see the Milky Way arc across the heavens like I had never quite seen before. It was crystal clear and saturated with celestial bodies. I recognized some of the constellations like Sagittarius, which lay in the southern portion of the sky, and Ursa Minor, where I found the Little Dipper. I had forgotten what the last star of the handle of the Little Dipper was called, but remembered that it pointed north. It was aligned perfectly with the brightest star at the top of the Northern Cross. I marveled at how everything in the sky above appeared perfectly the same as it had almost three centuries into the future.

Shooting stars, one after another, whizzed by, streaking across the dark, ageless sky before quickly fading into nothing. To look up into space and know that it enveloped the earth like a glass marble in an infinite ocean of celestial bodies, and that we existed in it—living and breathing, on a planet that had evolved by chance from primordial matter created by the big bang—made me feel comparatively insignificant. I knew as I gazed at the stars that I was looking back in time. *How could this all be real?* I wondered why God had cruelly thrust me three centuries back in time from my future existence. I was so tremendously confused and hurt by this mean twist of fate that I knew I might not be able to bear it.

"They are bonnie, are they not?" Leif muttered observantly all of a sudden as we lay next to each other.

"Hmm?" I glanced over at him.

"The stars—they are bonnie," he repeated, looking up above at the sky.

"Oh—yeah…" I muttered, shifting my eyes back to the stars.

"In the winter," he started softly, "in Scotland—at nicht the skies are alecht. It is said that when thaur comes peace upon land and sea, the nimble lads and merry maidens come forth tae dance in the northern sky. They are tranquil in form, but are all of grand stature… and still their dances are graceful. The lads first bow tae the maidens, and the maidens curtsy tae the lads. And when the dance comes tae hecht, some of the lads bound high and whirl about as they have become so merry. All the while, fairy pipers play enchanting music whilst the merry couples dance across the northern sky," Leif said in a low, soft voice. I lay quietly beside him listening to his tale while still looking up at the stars.

"You've seen the northern lights?" I asked amazedly.

"Is that whit ye call them?"

"Yeah."

"Aye. I have seen them."

"That's a nice story."

"I reckon it is also," he said mildly.

"I've never seen the northern lights in the sky," I said quietly. I had only seen them on TV, or pictures of them in magazines, or on the internet.

"Ye huvnae?"

"No," I muttered, shaking my head.

"Weel, they're bonnie," he said softly.

"I can only imagine," I replied. I turned my head toward him. He shifted his gaze from the stars, steadily meeting my eyes. I could see the details of his silhouetted face in the blue moonlight falling between the branches. "Are we safe here?" I whispered concernedly.

"They'll not come fur us," Leif assured me gently.

"How do you know?"

"We're on burial ground," he informed me, gesturing across the mound we had tucked ourselves against. I looked up over to my left and witnessed to my horror in the shadows several mounted pikes with impaled, decapitated human heads spaced apart in certain locations surrounding us on the large mound.

"Oh my God!" I jolted, completely shocked as I also noticed the previously unobserved numerous severed human limbs dangling by ropes in the trees to the side of us. "What's going on here?" I gasped in utter disbelief, appalled.

"The victims of their enemies tae honor their dead ancestors," Leif explained gravely in a low voice.

"*Oh my God!*" I wheezed at the incredible savagery. I was shocked beyond anything that I had ever seen before.

"Do ye think Europe has any better ways?" he asked in a demoralized tone. I looked intently at him, considering his question. He was right. The history of World War II put it into perspective for me. "War is war, nae matter which way it is perceived. It creates the same demons nae matter whaur it is conducted."

That was tragically true. I turned my eyes away from him, looking back up at the stars—thinking. I understood now what it truly meant to feel *helpless*.

"The McFarlands… You knew them well?" I asked curiously, feeling very despondent.

"Aye," Leif replied. His tone was melancholy.

"Tell me about them. How did you know them?" I returned,

looking at him, discovering that he was still staring at me as our eyes met again.

"I first met them nearly six years ago when I arrived in Northampton from Scotland. Jack arrived from Ireland as an indentured servant. He had sold himself intae servitude once his father passed away and could nae longer pay the farm debt his family owed. He served as a planter in Maryland, harvesting tobacco. That is whaur he met Mairie, his wife, who was indentured as a dairy maid," Leif explained.

"Oh…" I replied thoughtfully. "So, how were they able to come here?"

"Weel, once they had completed their servitude, they waur given their freedom… So, they waur free tae go as they pleased. They traveled north in search of land given tae them by the government that lay far north in the frontier," Leif explained.

"Oh," I said, understanding.

"Upon their journey, they came through Northampton, whaur Fin and I met them… Jack and Mairie waur weary from their travels—she was far along with a bairn on the way. So, as they had nae place tae billet, Fin offered fur them tae bide at his dwelling," Leif explained.

"That was very nice of him," I acknowledged.

"Weel, it was whit they needed… Mairie at length gave birth, but the bairn passed away. It was too wee… It was their first bairn," Leif disclosed solemnly.

"Oh, how terribly sad. That's tremendously hard to deal with," I said compassionately, knowing all too well how much I could relate to her pain.

"Aye," Leif agreed abstractedly. He continued holding my eyes steadfastly with his. I couldn't help the suddenly emerging tear in my eye and quickly wiped the droplet away as it was on the verge of rolling from my eyelash down my cheek.

"So what happened?" I asked.

"Weel, they stayed on some time at the invitation of Fin, since

Mairie especially needed tae return tae being fit fur travel. It proved tae be a guid circumstance fur them, as it gave Jack the opportunity tae be a sharecropper on Fin's land fur several years before Jack ventured on his own as a free landowner," Leif continued soberly.

"I see…" I muttered. I reflected some more about the McFarlands, and a faint sigh escaped me. "Oh, how terribly sad," I whispered.

"Aye," Leif whispered back. It fell quiet between us as I sensed his pondering also. "I reckon it is gettin' quite late. We ought tae git some sleep, lass," he suggested in a low voice.

"Okay," I uttered softly. He was right; it was late, and I was really tired. But as we started to drift into silence again, my thoughts kept reminding me of the horrific images I had seen today that remained branded in my mind. I rolled to my side away from him. A knot in my throat emerged, and my eyes began to fill with silent tears. "I am *so* sorry about your friends," I said in a faint, shaky voice. I fought back the tears as hard as I could.

"Aye," Leif muttered grimly. "It was a tragic fate fur them tae have met." I covered my eyes, whimpering quietly while tears streamed uncontrollably down my cheeks. "Shh, shh, *àille dhubh*, shhh," he muttered gently. I unexpectedly felt his hand carefully come over my shoulder as he attempted to console me. His thumb moved soothingly against the back of my shoulder, massaging me with compassion. I unthinkingly reached around with my hand and tearfully slid my fingers between his. I sensed his caution as he held my hand. Then, I felt his fingers lock tightly around mine. He shifted closer toward me, and I could feel his breath caress the back of my neck as I continued to snivel.

CHAPTER 13

We awakened to drizzle the next morning. It was an overcast and dismal day. The rain came down heavy at times, forcing us to stop and take shelter beneath the trees. The showers became so dense that it reminded me of being stuck in a tropical rain forest as the thick mud enveloped our every step. It was then that we were finally compelled to wait out the rest of the downpour beneath a large shale overhang. I felt miserable being trapped and drenched in my heavy, cumbersome clothing while exposed to the grime and dirt. I wasn't fond of being so vulnerable to the elements with no sign *anywhere* of clean shelter containing modern conveniences.

Oh, what I would give for a cleansing shower now. I could only dream about it.

The men were in no better spirits either. They were glum from yesterday's tragic and depressing discovery. Their usual high-spirited, animated conversations, which typically passed between them, were nonexistent today. Instead, they were quiet with little, if anything at all, to say to each other.

We were going to have to huddle in this dark, dank, musty-smelling cave for a while and wait for the torrential rain to subside. So, I propped myself on a medium-sized rock tucked near the back of the cave out of the breeze. A couple of other men found similar locations within the cave, while the rest had pulled out their collapsible army stools to sit. Several of them passed their time with a game of cards, while others simply decided to take a nap.

Finley stood at the entrance of the overhang just before the pouring rain, with Leif standing near him as he leaned against the cave wall. Leif took several swigs of rum from his canteen, and Finley placed a bit of snuff from his snuffbox on the back of his palm and quickly inhaled it. The two of them exchanged only a couple of words, it seemed, then simply remained silently standing still as they looked out into the pouring rain.

After a few minutes of just standing, Leif glanced around and spotted me sitting at the back of the cave. He paced toward me, and I made room for him to sit next to me on the rock.

"It's really coming down," I remarked.

"Aye, 'tis," he said, looking out through the opening as he positioned himself next to me.

"It's like the jungles in South America," I said thoughtlessly. Leif turned his gilded head and looked at me strangely.

"Have ye seen South America?" he inquired, astounded.

"No. I just read about it," I informed him.

"Och," he said, nodding slightly. Suddenly, a tremendous crackling sound of thunder erupted, crashing and rolling violently across the sky overhead, shaking the earth beneath our feet in its roaring wake. I jumped a bit at the fierce, unexpected sound. "'Tis merely thunder, lass—naught of which tae be afraid," Leif said reassuringly.

"Right," I agreed with a small grin. "It's just that it was *really* close."

"Reit overhead, I reckon."

"Yeah, the lightning strike must have been only feet away."

"How do ye reckon?" he inquired, looking curiously at me.

"Well, you can kind of tell, generally speaking, how close a lightning strike is depending on the time of the lightning strike and the sound of the thunder," I said.

"Is that reit?"

"Yeah, so if you saw lightning and you measured the seconds between that and the sound of the thunder, then you could estimate how many miles away you were from the original lightning strike," I informed him.

"Certainly?" Leif's eyes widened, appearing interested.

"Yeah, because light travels faster than—" I interrupted myself, realizing that I should perhaps not be telling him this.

"Faster than whit?" he continued curiously.

"Never mind. It doesn't matter." I waved my hand in a dismissive manner.

"Why do ye disregard such an interesting conversation?"

"I don't think it's that important," I said instead.

"But I do care tae ken whit ye waur saying. Pray, indulge me," he encouraged sincerely. I looked at him for a moment and considered continuing.

"Well—I was just going to say that light travels faster than sound." Some of the men were overhearing our conversation and glanced strangely at me.

"Ye mean tae tell me that the lecht I see is in motion? And so is soond—in motion, I mean?" Leif gazed at me in piqued surprise.

"Yes," I said certainly.

"And lecht moves more quick than soond?" he repeated wondrously, appearing confused.

"Yes," I said.

"Och, that is impossible," Cole disagreed surely, involving himself in the conversation.

"Aye," Angus agreed.

"Aye, how is it possible?" Leif inquired.

"Well, you've seen a rainbow, right?" I asked.

"Aye," Leif said.

"Okay, well, when light hits the water droplets in the sky, sometimes it causes the light to bend, and what happens is the white light splinters into the colors that you see, because it slows the white light down. It's called refraction," I explained simply. The men all stared at me with disbelief and confusion on their faces.

"Refraction," Leif echoed with intrigue.

"That's rubbish!" Roy scoffed.

"Aye, everyone knows that sunlecht is still," Cole said obviously.

"She speaks like a witch!" Derek interjected dubiously.

"Well, everyone once thought that the world was flat until Christopher Columbus came around," I mentioned. Leif's eyes widened as his lips tilted into a smirk.

"The lass has some reason thaur, lads," Finley admitted.

"Och, she soonds like a witch," Roy said disagreeably.

"I'm not a *witch*," I assured. But, observing their suspicious gazes, I saw that they appeared uncertain. Cole said something in Scots, and the men started laughing. As their chuckles echoed throughout the cave, I noticed Leif's complexion turn a deep red hue. He glanced back at Cole and replied in their language, sending more laughter between the men, and they started jeering Cole. Cole appeared embarrassed as he withstood their teasing.

"Alrecht, alrecht—that is enough, lads," Finley ordered soberly. All the joking started to simmer down between the men as they continued to exchange knowing looks. After a minute, they resumed minding their own business and playing cards again.

"Dinnae pay any mind tae them, lass. They only like making trooble," Leif said, with embarrassment visible on his face.

"Oh," I replied demurely.

"They're just lads. Dinnae pay them any mind," he repeated confidentially. I nodded a little. He winked at me. I smiled a bit, and a warm grin eased over his face. He leaned over for the saddlebag he had placed at his feet and drew it up over his knees. "Haur," he said, offering me a small pear. "Ye must be a little hungry."

"Yes, thank you. I am," I said politely as I gladly received the fruit from him. I watched him retrieve another one from his leather bag for himself. I bit into the pear, and it was nice and sweet.

"Guid, is it not?" he asked, noticing my reaction as I chewed the pear.

"Yeah," I replied lightly. He took a big bite out of his, and the pear he was holding already appeared nearly gone. I observed him chewing and swallowing his piece of fruit as we snacked.

"That was an interesting discussion we waur having a moment before now," he mentioned.

"Yeah," I agreed as I ate my pear.

"Whaur did ye acquire such information?" he asked inquisitively.

"I read about it in a science journal once." I didn't tell him that I had learned it when I was in elementary school.

"Curious… Ye appear tae be a clever lass."

"Thanks," I replied modestly as I watched him finish his pear. He glanced at me, and our eyes met.

"I admire that quality," he said plainly.

"You do?" I responded as I continued eating my pear. He lightly tossed his pear core to the side, and it landed in the musty dirt.

"Aye, indeed," Leif replied. He gazed meaningfully at me, and I felt my cheeks grow warm. A grin visibly swept over his attractive face, brightening his smiling eyes, and I nervously glanced away down to the half-eaten pear between my fingers.

∼

THE THUNDERSTORM PASSED in about a half hour, and the hammering rain turned into light, dismal drizzle. Once the rain had almost ceased, we resumed traveling through the dripping vegetation. The mud was waterlogged along the narrow path, sucking the horses' hooves in deep. It was going to take us forever to finally reach our destination at this hindered, arduous traveling rate. Every ounce of me felt like complaining, but I refrained. Instead, I cursed it all in my head.

I wasn't precisely sure what time of day it was. But I presumed it was probably somewhere close to three or four o'clock in the afternoon. I didn't know where our next destination would be, and I wondered how much longer we had left to travel before reaching our final resting place.

Because of the unfavorable conditions caused by the wet weather, the men were strongly disinclined to break from journeying except for the brief time when nature called for us to relieve ourselves. They were determined to push onward without further delay. So, needless to say, we were all pretty weary and hungry by the time we had at long last arrived at our next campsite.

Resting at Fort Edward was ideal at this point. *"The Great Carrying Place"* was how it was known to them, because it was the portal from Lake Champlain to the Hudson River. The fort was a Vauban-style stronghold constructed from granite surrounded by an eight-foot-deep, fourteen-foot-wide dry moat. There was a sutler right outside the fort's gates where, in the faint drizzle, a number of British soldiers could be seen purchasing plenty of booze and tobacco along with some other items of interest. We rode over the bridge past the guards posted at the gates into the fort inside the courtyard. There were several large barracks, four blockhouses, a couple of guardhouses, and a magazine.

Many of the provincial soldiers were camped at Rogers Island just across the way in the middle of the river. But the fort appeared well garrisoned with a larger portion of provincial troops than British soldiers, in addition to a mixture of Iroquois in military service. However, I had noticed once again that the number of women included inside the fort were few. The women were either soldiers' wives, indentured maids who assumed the roles of laundresses and cooks, or camp followers. The women, I witnessed, were also tirelessly and exhaustively charged with the taxing task of being the emotional and physical primary caregivers not only to their children, but also to the sick and injured soldiers as they assisted the surgeon.

Our horses were drawn to a halt in the middle of the court-yard, and we dismounted. As our horses were being led away by the stablehands, we walked toward one of the buildings and entered the barracks. I followed Finley and Leif into the commanding officer's briefing quarters, where Generals Lyman and Johnson, Colonel Smith, and Captain Gage were in the middle of a discussion.

"Ah, my lords, we meet again in good health, I see," General Lyman said suddenly, interrupting his conversation as he greeted Finley and Leif with a brief nod.

"Aye, how are ye, General Lyman?" Finley inquired.

"Well, thank you," General Lyman said. "And yourselves, my lords?"

"Well, thank ye, general," Finley replied. The general's eyes, like the other officers', had landed on me.

"This is Mistress Arboles," Leif said, introducing me to the officers.

"A pleasure to make your acquaintance, Mistress Arboles," General Johnson said plainly. I nodded gently in acknowledg-ment. In my nervousness, I fiddled with my ring and decided to keep it unseen beneath my traveling cape with my hands clasped together safely in front of me.

"So," General Lyman began sharply, shifting his gaze back to Finley, "where are my reinforcements?"

"Laird Loudoun has not dispatched any reinforcements," Finley informed him.

"Has he not?" General Lyman appeared surprised.

"I fear not," Finley answered.

"Did he not receive my correspondence?" General Lyman inquired.

"He has made nae reference tae it," Finley said.

"Does he not think we are in the middle of war? How could he *sit* in Albany and do *naught*?" General Lyman scoffed heatedly.

"He means tae first combine our forces," Leif said.

"I've heard it—and what will that do but disrupt the order of our men! Meanwhile, the French will have secured Crown Point. Thus, what am I to do but bide our time whilst we are attacked by the French and their savages!" General Lyman stood with his jaw clenched, clearly disturbed while trying to maintain his composure.

"Captain Gage here has only just returned from an expedition at Crown Point and informed us of the state of French affairs," General Johnson said. "I wonder if Lord Loudoun has wit enough to press matters more aggressively when I inform him myself of the grave situation."

"Yer concerns, general, micht be received lightly, fur I recently witnessed General Winslow attempt the same effort with His Lordship," Leif informed him.

"Is that right?" General Johnson asked.

"His Lordship dismissed his soond reason," Leif continued. Then, all of a sudden, speaking of the devil, a much-waterlogged General Winslow entered the room with two other companions —one being Major Israel Hendrix and the other being a Mohawk man named Otetiani.

"What a coincidence!" General Lyman expressed.

"My lords, sirs," General Winslow greeted when he had entered in dripping wet clothing.

"So you have arrived," General Lyman acknowledged satisfactorily.

"We have," General Winslow replied, removing his wet tricorn hat and cloak.

"Good," General Johnson said. "And you, Otetiani, how are you?"

"Well, thank you, general," the Mohawk man replied. He was attired in a regular white linen shirt and beige breeches with leather leggings. He had two long braids with eagle feathers tied at the ends, which dangled over the rest of his loose, long black hair down his back, and wampum beads across his chest, I noticed as I listened to the conversation. Everyone I had encountered so far spoke with strong accents, and sometimes I found it quite difficult to understand them.

"Glad to hear that you're well," General Johnson said to Otetiani.

"You as well, sir," Otetiani replied.

"Our company will lodge here for the night. Tomorrow we continue north and push on to Crown Point," General Winslow said.

"Good, good," General Lyman agreed favorably.

"In the meanwhile, I'm to return to Albany to see about the delivery of our reinforcements," General Johnson said.

"I wish you better luck on that request. Lord Loudoun is uninterested in our opinions and concerns," General Winslow said grimly.

"We shall see about that. If he has any scruples about this war, he'll do as I ask," General Johnson replied staunchly.

"So, what are your orders?" General Lyman inquired of Finley.

"We're headed tae Fort William Henry," Finley revealed.

"I see," General Lyman said.

"You may take your leave with my company as we must tour Crown Point," General Winslow said to Finley.

"Thank ye," Finley replied.

"Otetiani and his brother, Garakonthie, will continue forth scouting Lake George," General Winslow said, glancing once at his fellow Mohawk companion. Otetiani faintly nodded his head once in assurance.

"All right, then, 'tis settled. We get on with our aims at first light tomorrow," General Johnson said determinedly.

"Aye," General Lyman replied, along with everyone else's agreement. At that point, the meeting had come to a sudden conclusion.

That evening, I was placed in a small room within the officer's barracks. Living conditions at the fort were undesirable, to say the least. This whole camping adventure gave a new meaning to the idea of "roughing it"—and I wasn't fond of it at all.

The construction of the fort, though made of granite, was built with eighteenth-century technology, which invariably left a lot to be desired as far as the ease and comfort of twenty-first-century conveniences. The mortar holding the packed block stones in place was concocted from a mixture of mud, clay, thatch, and dung, and left a dingy, musty smell indoors. Instead of viewing a ceiling when I lay on my thin, straw-filled mattress, I saw large, thick rafters supporting a vaulted roof.

The one window in my room was made of thin, uneven glass, which was hardly capable of insulating from the outdoor elements and allowed moisture to collect around the window frame. A subtle breeze entered the room from cracks around the window. I imagined that living in this place during the winter months would likely be a brutal experience. Thank God, however, I considered, that the poor soldier who would inhabit this wretched room in the winter would at least be lucky enough to have a woodburning stove here to provide him warmth in those lonely, cold months.

CHAPTER 14

"Sylvie… Sylvie… awaken. Lass… awaken." I remotely heard Leif calling me from my slumber. He was gently nudging me on my shoulder as I groggily awakened.

"Yeah?" I mumbled drowsily, opening my sleepy eyes.

"Yoo're weeping in yer sleep, lass," he said softly. "Ye could be heard beyond the door."

"What?" I muttered. I rubbed my tired eyes and saw him hovering over me in the moonlight coming from the window.

"Ye waur having a bad dream," he whispered. "Ye waur weeping." The moonlight illuminating through the window trapped him in a luminescent blue glow above me, and he appeared like an apparition.

"Really?"

"Ye called out fur Avie."

"I did?"

"Aye."

"Oh," I said despondently. My dream had felt too real and was very fresh in my mind. I felt the residual tormenting effects of my nightmare as I remembered the accident I had experienced that had killed Matt and our unborn child, whom we were going to name Avie.

"Are ye alrecht?" Leif asked concernedly.

"Yeah," I muttered, rubbing my face a little for some clarity. "I'm sorry. I didn't mean to awaken you."

"Nae matter—ye were distressed in yer sleep. But are ye alrecht now?"

"Yeah."

"Guid. Better dreams, then." He gently placed his large hand on my shoulder and lightly caressed it.

"Okay—thanks."

"Aye," he replied in a kind tone. He shifted away from the glowing moonlight into the shadows. I closed my eyes again, but found it difficult to sleep. I restlessly struggled to quiet my mind and drift into peace. I turned over onto my left side, facing Leif while he continued resting on the floor against the door. He was stretched out over his scratchy wool blanket beneath the lustrous moonbeams pouring through the trees by the window. He looked like a silver ghost trapped in a shimmering state of suspension. His chest rose and fell with every even breath he took. I simply watched him there on the floor in the enveloping silence, aware that he was wide awake also.

WE LEFT Fort Edward early the next morning. It was a much better day for traveling. The sun was brightly shining, and there wasn't a cloud in the sky. But the earth remained damp and soaked in areas along the trail. The morning air was warm and comfortable and was a welcome difference from a miserable, rain-soaked day like yesterday.

We rendezvoused with General Winslow's company of about five hundred men. A moderate company, as I understood it, with the remaining half of the soldiers under his command staying at Fort Edward and detachments left at Saratoga.

We continued hiking higher in altitude through the Taconic Mountains. The scenery was stupendous, and I was flabbergasted as the trail exited from the forest out onto impressive flat slabs of ancient granite jutting forth from the mountainside to form sky-scraping cliffs that plunged endlessly toward the earth. The horses' hooves clucked along with the sound of soldiers' marching feet over the level rock. The sky was crystal clear with no hint of the smog pollution that was common from where I came. The bright sunlight was more intense than I had ever experienced. A pair of sunglasses would have done some good, I thought. Instead, I adjusted the large brim of my dainty straw hat to block the sun.

We could see for miles over the undulating forested moun-tains, past the immense blue lake water resting atop the moun-tain across the way. It was absolutely beautiful as it glinted like cobalt quicksilver beneath the sun.

I had done a lot of sightseeing and traveling across the United States, particularly with my parents as a young child and later as an adult, but I had never visited this part of the country. I was familiar with a lot of the beautiful landscapes, national parks, and historic places that this wonderful country had to offer. But I never in all my life had seen anything that compared to the complete and precise, perfectly unspoiled glory of this magnifi-cent scene that graced the earth like I was now seeing. A vision as beautiful and as striking as this could do nothing but inspire the sense of God.

I caught Leif staring at me as I was gazing across the land-scape. He gently smiled at me, and I smiled back as we walked beside each other while he led his horse. His gaze was intense and steadfast—and compelled my self-consciousness. I balked and nervously looked away again at the scenery. My eyes trailed downward toward the stone on which I was walking. I could still feel him staring, and I hesitated to look up at him again. When I finally forced myself to meet his piercing blue eyes again, his face further warmed with an engaging grin.

"What is it?" I asked insecurely.

"I'm merely enjoying the scenery," Leif replied casually.

"I see," I remarked diffidently.

"Aye."

"Oh."

"I merely wish tae imprint it on my mind before the view passes me by."

"Oh."

"Bonnie day, is it not?"

"Yeah, it is."

"Better than the rain."

"Absolutely," I agreed.

"Indeed," he said.

The conversation was oddly strained. I supposed it was due to a kind of blossoming, unspoken sense of mutual modest attraction for each other—which made me feel weird. I was very much aware of him gazing at me, and it drew forth my uncertainty.

"You're staring at me," I remarked clumsily, turning my gaze up to his as our eyes met again.

"I ken," he said confidently.

"Why?"

"I care tae gaze upon ye."

"Oh... Well—please don't do that," I stammered uncomfortably as I pushed some of my ringlets over my shoulder.

"Whyever not?"

"You're making me nervous," I admitted hesitantly.

"Am I?"

"Yes."

"I see."

"So—please look at something else."

"I dinnae care tae," Leif said. His boldness threw me for a bit of a loop. I glanced away from him and gazed at the scenery in front of me. I felt him still staring at me for a moment longer.

"You're making me uncomfortable," I said faintly. I looked at him again, and he grinned at me. "Well, just look at the trees ahead instead, please," I suggested self-consciously. The grin on his face widened, and the expression in his eyes clearly warmed.

"I'll watch ye fur however long I care tae, *àille dhubh*," he said plainly. I didn't know how to respond, so I glanced away from him again and looked at the undulating mountains. After a moment longer, I sensed him finally turn his gaze ahead.

WE HAD TRAVELED WELL over fifteen miles, and the day was growing old. Having grown weary of walking, I rode on Blaze with Leif pressed closely against me. I realized at that moment, with his hard chest touching my back and his firm arms around me, that maybe I was growing irresponsibly connected to him without objectively taking stock of the evolving situation. It had become apparent to me that our developing appeal for each other had become palpable between us in a short amount of time— even though I had been trying my hardest not to like him in a particular manner. There was no way that I could go against my better judgment and admit my emerging friendliness toward him; it was a pointless acknowledgment. Furthermore, it wouldn't have made an ounce of difference in my situation, or done either one of us a bit of good. So, I forced thoughts of him from my mind, and to the best of my ability, I concentrated on the way the sunlight spread beautifully over the landscape.

DURING OUR JOURNEY, we had crossed over twenty miles of undulating, winding, rocky terrain. The sun was beginning to set, and the weather had changed as we now climbed high into the Adirondacks. The atmosphere grew temperate. Clouds began rolling in across the sky and turned over the mountain peaks, draping them in mist. In minutes we had become surrounded by fog, and visibility across the landscape diminished. The men became shrouded, and began vanishing in the damp haze. I shivered a little from the sudden drop in temperature and drew my cape around my shoulders. Leif assisted in covering me better with my garment, wrapping it fully around me like a burrito. In the process of adjusting my cape, I accidentally shifted my weight improperly in the saddle, and he clasped his brawny arm around my waist to keep me from falling off his horse. He tugged me back, fitting me snugly against him again, and kept his arm resting casually around my waist. I automatically stiffened a little, and his arm slid from my side down to his thigh. We were aware of each other, and I was secretly uncomfortable about it.

WE FINALLY ARRIVED at Fort William Henry at dusk and lodged there for the night. It was a newly built log bastion standing atop a hill at the southern end of Lake George. The view from the upper deck was picturesque, with the setting sun highlighting the seemingly endless glowing water basin. The lake surrounded us, with mountain peaks jutting up from the shoreline in the horizon. It struck me suddenly that we were in the American frontier. Never had I seen such a saturation of various wildlife species roaming free and unfettered in their indigenous habitats. The land was virgin—raw, robust, untouched, and wild. The view made me compare it with where I had come from originally.

As we finished our meal with General Winslow and Major Eyre, who had been supervising the fort since its construction, a courier rushed up to the general with a correspondence in hand. The courier passed the correspondence to General Winslow, and he promptly proceeded to read it. The letter must have been brief, because the general had finished reading it in a matter of seconds. He abruptly slammed the parchment down on the cabin table, appearing significantly displeased with what he had just read.

"It seems Lord Loudoun is ill-informed of the urgency of this war, as he calls my return to Albany," General Winslow informed us disapprovingly.

"Yer return?" Finley questioned.

"My *prompt* return," General Winslow hissed irately.

"We must secure Crown Point and create an offensive," Leif interjected obviously.

"Of course! What does the man think? We've been attacked at the fort here at all hours every day!" Major Eyre blasted angrily.

"We must secure the frontier, or countless more will suffer Jack's fate, as so many others have already," Finley said certainly.

"The whole territory will soon be overrun by the French and their Indians if we leave it alone to that man," Major Eyre growled again.

"He'll not care until they'll have reached the gates of Albany," Leif reproached scornfully.

"Well, someone best light a bonnie fire under Loudoun's arse and get this war on the proper go!" Major Eyre retorted. "I beg your pardon, mistress," he suddenly said to me. I simply nodded my head.

"Well, I intend to speak a bit of sense into him and hope that he perceives my opinion upon my return," General Winslow said determinedly with noticeable aggravation in his voice. He abruptly stood from his seat at the table and left the barrack. Finley, Leif, and Major Eyre remained at the table discussing the state of affairs at the fort. When they had finished, Finley turned to me and suggested that I be excused to retire for the evening. Leif escorted me from the dining quarter through the threshold within the barrack until we had arrived outside. We climbed a flight of stairs and entered a sleeping chamber.

"Rest now, *àille dhubh*, our journey has not yet ended," Leif warned while opening the door for me to enter the room. It appeared he was not yet ready to turn in himself for the evening, since he remained standing at the doorway.

"What about you? Aren't you tired?" I asked curiously.

"Aye, I am. However, I have a bit of unfinished business tae discuss with Fin," he said.

"Oh. So you're going to leave me here all alone, then?"

"Fur the time being," he informed me. "Dinnae try anything foolish, fur a guard will be posted at the door whilst I attend other matters. Do ye understand?" I nodded a little. "Guid. I shan't be long." He turned, then disappeared behind the door.

I kicked off my shoes and sat silently on the thin, lumpy mattress. I could hear Leif strictly instructing the guard behind the door. I realized that I couldn't escape even if I did succeed at running away from the fort. Where on earth would I go after that?

So, I decided to recline on the bed and rest my tired head on the down pillow. It didn't take long before I closed my eyes and fell to sleep.

CHAPTER 15

At daybreak, the fort had awakened to an alerted barrage of musket fire. A shoot-out had occurred outside the fort, with a skirmish underway by French encroachment. Voices shouted out, and the British were in action as rushing footsteps scuffled around outside my door. I heard someone loudly warn that French Indians were attempting to scale the walls, when suddenly a thunderous cannon blast erupted. I leaped out of bed in alarm. My ears were ringing. The noise of the mortar fire was deafening and shook the barracks like a raging earthquake, causing dust from the ceiling to fall onto my blanket.

"They're attempting to scale the wall!" shouted a man outside at a distance.

"Make haste! Make haste! Pour it down on them, lads!" I heard an Irishman holler. Suddenly, there was a *swoosh* and ensuing tormented screams. Men were crying out in ultimate agony. "Again, lads, again! Git the tar ready! Git it on them grand!" Another *swoosh* and more tortured screams. I determined that the enemy was receiving a bout of medieval torture by being doused with boiling tar. It sounded like the fort was in a red-alert state of chaos, and I darted toward the window, wondering if I could see anything taking place. I could only see faint billows of smoke puffing up toward the sky at a distance behind the lookout tower. The door abruptly swung open, and Leif was promptly present.

"What's happening?" I asked anxiously, feeling quite startled as I stared at him.

"'Tis only a wee band of French and Ottawa," he answered.

"It sounds rather intense," I noted.

"Dinnae worry, the fort is secured," he said assuredly. I still looked at him with concern. "However, I reckon that ye ought tae place yer shoes upon yer feet."

"All right," I agreed. Realizing that I needed assistance slipping my shoes on my feet due to the restrictive stays around my torso preventing my ability to properly bend over, I asked him if he wouldn't mind helping me.

"Aye," he said, and bent down to assist me. I noticed the color seep over his ears, turning them red as he helped my shoes over my toes. Once I had my shoes on my feet, Leif offered for us to have something to eat. We then withdrew from the room, returning through the open corridor down the staircase toward the officers' dining quarter.

The skirmish seemed to last several minutes, until the armed exchange began diminishing as calm took over the fort once more. I gladly assumed that the enemy had fallen back—if not all of them having been completely killed to curb any more damage they might cause.

I joined the men for an early morning meal. There were a few other officers present at the table, with General Winslow absent. He had eluded the fighting, as he was on his return to Albany already. It was a brief breakfast, and once we had completed our meal, the brothers along with their seven cousins and Otetiani's brother, Garakonthie, and I exited the protection of the fortress walls. Lake George could be seen directly in front of us. The men pulled forth three large canoes from the shore and pushed them slightly into the water.

"In ye go, *àille dhubh*," Leif urged as he held out his hand to assist me inside the canoe. I slipped my gloved hand into his and sat inside on the bench near the middle of the canoe. Leif stepped in at the bow, and Garakonthie shoved us away into the water. He sloshed into the water as he stepped and climbed in at the stern. The canoe rocked noticeably from side to side when his weight shifted inside the vessel. Then, Leif took his oar and began paddling us farther from the shore. Finley and the rest of the men shortly followed in more canoes, quickly catching up alongside us. Garakonthie reached for his oar and placed it in the water, and the men began paddling north over the vast, frigid lake.

The morning was mild with a bit of humidity in the atmosphere. The sunlight had dawned with short yellow rays. A thin veil of golden mist lifted from the water, shrouding the lake in eerie, mystical foreboding. The shorelines from the east and west could hardly be seen through the low-lying clouds, and the mountains faintly emerged from the mist, hinting at land beyond the water. The lake was calm, and a deafening stillness enveloped us. The oars dipping and rising gently from the water scarcely disturbed the surrounding dense silence.

We glided effortlessly over the lake as the men took long, easy strokes with their oars. What would have been nearly an all-day trip to reach halfway around the lake on horseback took us half the time on water. By midday the mist had fully lifted, revealing bright blue sky embellished with stark white cumulous clouds. The lake was far and wide, stretching north as far as the eye could see. A breeze stirred, and the water grew slightly choppy, rocking our canoe over the breaks. After some time, we disembarked on a small, uninhabited island in the middle of the lake for a brief meal and to relieve ourselves.

After our break, we embarked again across the water with few other respites until dusk when we arrived at Rogers Rock, where the men had decided to make camp for the night. I had learned from what the men were saying that we were now deep in French territory. The men kept a low profile once we landed on shore. They had drawn the canoes onto land and covered them with nearby shrubbery, camouflaging them from the enemy. Instead of catching trout from the lake and smoking it over campfire, the men settled on bread and dried, salted venison that reminded me of beef jerky.

"Whaur does the fort lie?" Finley inquired of Garakonthie.

"Mm," Garakonthie acknowledged as he chewed on some venison. He pointed with his long index finger into the silt and began illustrating. "We are here," he said, pointing to the map he had drawn in the dirt. "Fort Carillon lies north from this point—about two leagues."

"Alrecht," Finley replied attentively.

"At the tip of the lake, there is a river. Travel the river upstream. Lake Champlain will not be too far. It is here, at the meeting of the river and Lake Champlain, where the fort lies," Garakonthie described.

"Guid. Alrecht, then. Seamus, ye go on ahead at first lecht. If all goes weel, we meet haur thereafter," Finley instructed.

"Aye," Leif replied pensively. He lifted his eyes from the dirt-illustrated map and glanced at me for a second. He appeared reticent or abstracted. He then shifted his glance back toward Finley.

"Ye agreed upon it," Finley reminded Leif.

"Aye, I ken," Leif said reservedly.

"Alrecht, then, at first lecht," Finley said unyieldingly.

"Aye." Leif dropped his eyes from Finley and stirred away from the group. He bent over and picked up a pebble. He tossed it up with his hand and caught it while pacing closer toward the shore. He leaned against a tree near the shoreline with his shoulder resting on the trunk and gazed out across the lake. I watched him muse over the pebble between his fingers, and after a moment, he tossed it far over the water. It skipped four times before it finally plunged out of sight into the crystal clear water. I decided to rise to my feet from where I was sitting on a log and walked toward him.

"Hey," I said softly when I came close to him.

"Aye?" His striking, deep blue eyes turned toward me.

"What's wrong?" I asked intuitively with a bit of delicacy. His expression changed, and he looked at me with some amazement.

"Why do ye believe aught is amiss?" he inquired oddly.

"I don't know... You just seem kind of—distant," I said cautiously.

"Distant?"

"Yeah—troubled, I mean."

"Do I?"

"Yeah."

"Och..." he replied vaguely. It seemed that he wasn't going to elaborate any further. I was feeling quite uncertain at the moment as I held my gaze on him.

"Are you all right?" I attempted to ask at least. He faintly grinned, but his eyes were remote.

"Ye dinnae need tae concern yerself about me, *àille dhubh*," Leif said evenly as he attentively gazed back at me.

"Okay," I acknowledged, nodding my head a tad.

"We best settle in. Nicht is falling," he urged.

"All right," I agreed automatically. I followed him back toward our camp. He spread out his blanket over the ground, and I found a place to rest on it.

AT DAYBREAK, Leif and I alone started out hiking through the forest along the lake. It was a treacherous and tiresome journey through the dense forest in the thick of French territory. At any moment, we could be unexpectedly detected through the trees and suffer an unknown fate if captured by Indians in league with the enemy. Leif and I hiked in silence nearly the whole way toward the northernmost end of Lake George. I wondered where we were going and why it was just us hiking, but I didn't feel that I could ask him, since it seemed he wasn't prone to speaking. So, I remained quiet too as we moved through the wilderness.

Leif alertedly scanned the area like a precision android as we trekked among the thick brush. He was prepared to defend us with his loaded bayoneted musket and pistols ready to fire at any sudden threat. The most apparent, troubling notion to me was that we weren't more camouflaged. The color of his scarlet military coat was a quick and easy target. I worried about this, and seriously hoped that we wouldn't be ambushed along the way.

Garakonthie was right; it was not too far a distance from where we had camped the night before to the tributary that streamed from Lake Champlain into Lake George. Just as we had approached the southern end of Lake Champlain, Fort Carillon appeared through the woods, perched on a clear-cut knoll overlooking the water. It was a formidable and impressive bastion constructed of gray granite and red clay shingles. Large cannons above jutted forth from the ports in the fortress walls. The structure itself appeared gigantic. It was far better designed and built than its British counterpart, Fort Edward, which now lay farther south of us, and obviously overshadowed wood-built Fort William Henry.

Suddenly, Leif stopped dead in his tracks, causing me to accidentally bump into him from behind. He instantly raised his armed pistol and aimed it straight at the concealing shrubbery. I heard a *click*, and within a second, a strange man dressed in a blue French military uniform promptly emerged from the foliage with his pistol pointed directly at Leif's face between the eyes.

"Capitaine! Capitaine! Ici! Dans le bosquet! Britannique!" the French soldier called out. In seconds, a rush of troopers swarmed around with their arms drawn at us. Leif held steadfastly and stone-faced, pointing his pistol at close range toward the French soldier's chest who had discovered us. My heart suddenly began

pounding and raced, pumping the sting of fresh adrenaline throughout my veins as I stared alarmingly at the Frenchmen instantly surrounding us.

"*Saisissez-les!*" fiercely commanded the French captain just as he arrived. Suddenly, a strange hand grabbed me around my upper arm, and I reacted, snatching my arm away from an unfamiliar French soldier.

"*Allez! Allez!*" urged the soldier abrasively with his pistol pointing directly at Leif.

"*Donne-moi à votre Général Vaudreuil. Dit-lui Majeur Monteith est ici pour le voir,*" Leif demanded cooly in flawless French.

"*Enlevez-les! Maintenant!*" shouted the captain. Leif slightly slackened his grip on his pistol, and a soldier standing next to us snatched the weapon away from him. Another soldier stole Leif's other pistol from his holster, hostilely yanking it from him. The French soldier also took the loaded musket slung over Leif's back. The soldier who had discovered us still stood before Leif with his pistol directed at Leif's face. He gestured with it for us to start walking toward the fort. "*Rechercher la région pour les Britanniques!*" ordered the captain as he intolerantly waved his arm for his men to search the remaining area. "*Faites vite! Deplacez-vouz!*" the captain ordered impatiently. He shoved Leif on the back with his hand to hasten his steps.

"*Je ferais attention de cette main a vous, capitaine—vous pourriez le regretter,*" Leif threatened in a cold and level tone. The captain didn't respond, except to warn the guards ahead to make way as we approached the active fort, with French and bare-chested Indians dressed in feathers, breechclouts, and leggings everywhere around.

As we arrived, surrounded by the captain and his four other soldiers, we marched through the guarded gray stone archway between two large cannon ports above into a fairly large courtyard. Just by superficial observation, the setting inside the fort appeared noticeably better organized and in better hygienic conditions than the British forts I had seen. Although, it looked like a number of the soldiers were slightly emaciated, and some were obviously sick with severe colds. Nevertheless, Fort Carillon appeared to be the crown jewel of forts as far as I had seen.

The well-garrisoned barracks were to the right, left, and behind us. We continued through the rectangular courtyard catty-corner toward a staircase at the back of one of the barracks.

"*Arrêt,*" ordered the captain when we came to the bottom of a staircase, and we were stopped abruptly in our tracks. The captain marched up the stairs and entered the barracks on the second story of the building. After a brief moment, he reappeared and gestured to his men. "*Apporte-les,*" he directed them, and we began walking up the steps.

When we came to the top landing, we were led by the captain through the door inside the general's quarters. The captain flamboyantly bowed in front of the general before spinning on his heel and closing the door behind himself. Leif and I were left standing together in front of a stout, pudgy man who appeared to be in his early fifties attired in his highest-ranking white-and-blue French army uniform. He, too, wore the fashionable white wig and had brown beady eyes, a long, straight nose, and a small, round mouth. He remained seated behind his desk and extravagantly twirled his wrist in a greeting gesture.

"*Je suis Général Pierre de Rigaud de Vaudreuil, Marqui de Vaudreuil, Gouverneur ou Nouvelle France, et Commandant-en-Chef des Armèes Francaises,*" Lord Vaudreuil gruffly introduced himself. "*Bienvenue à Fort Carillon. Entrez.*"

"*Merci, Général Vaudreuil,*" Leif replied civilly as he tucked his tricorn hat beneath his arm. "I am Major Seamus Stewart, Duke of Monteith, of the Royal Highland Regiment serving His Royal Majesty, King George the Second of Great Britain."

"*Un plaisir, Majeur Monteith, de faire votre connaissance,*" General Vaudreuil said. Leif respectably tilted his head without any sign of emotion. "To what do I owe the pleasure of your call, Majeur Monteith?"

"Mistress Arboles," Leif said mechanically.

"Mistress Arboles?" General Vaudreuil promptly turned his beady brown eyes onto me as he stood from his rococo desk and paced around it, directly facing us. "A wonderful pleasure, madame." General Vaudreuil smiled pleasurably and extended his pudgy hand. I placed my gloved hand into his accordingly, and he bent forward, placing his little round mouth on the back of my hand.

"*Merci, Général Vaudreuil,*" I replied uneasily. General Vaudreuil raised his eyes to me again and looked curiously at me.

"Yer emissary, Mistress Arboles, has been discovered amongst us and is safely returned tae ye unharmed," Leif stated professionally. General Vaudreuil furrowed his brow slightly and unemotionally glanced at me before returning his unreadable eyes to Leif.

Emissary? Suddenly, I was feeling insecure as a sinking sensation came over me. How could Leif think that I was a spy? And as it quickly dawned on me that his intention was to leave me here, a sense of panic rose inside me. I realized now why he had been acting strangely yesterday and today.

"France is grateful for her safe return, Majeur Monteith," General Vaudreuil said politely. "And as a demonstration of our gratitude, I shall assure your safety from my fort."

"*Merci,*" Leif replied impassively, appearing straight-faced and mechanical. I precipitously slid my hand into his and automatically squeezed it tight. Leif didn't respond, but I believed that he sensed my panic. He imperceptibly glanced down at me. I didn't want to let go of his hand. *Please don't leave me... Don't leave me here... I'm alone... Don't go... Please!* I silently implored him. Instead, he undetectably forced his hand loose from mine. He respectably slanted his head toward Lord Vaudreuil, spun an about-face on his heel, and was directly gone out the door.

Leif left the room in a blink of an eye. He didn't even glance at me. Just like that… he was heartlessly gone—and I was abandoned. I was left standing there all alone, very much feeling like I had suddenly been punched in the stomach, while looking at the face of this new, strange man.

"*S'il vous plaît, Madame Arboles, installez-vouz conforablement dans cette chaise*," General Vaudreuil said kindly, pointing to the blue-and-gold damask rococo chair before his desk.

"*Merci, Général Vaudreuil*," I said politely as I moved to sit in the plush chair he courteously offered me. My heart was pounding quickly in my chest. I didn't know what was going to happen to me next as I gazed around at my newest surroundings. The general's quarters were noticeably clean and very well kept for fort standards, I noticed. He appeared to live more than comfortably in his nice quarters—more like in the lap of luxury. His office had a lovely view overlooking the beautiful landscape. The seemingly boundless Lake Champlain surrounded the panorama.

I sat primly and quietly noticed one of the huge cannons protruding from the port just outside the window to the right of us. I swallowed hard as General Vaudreuil casually paced around the back of his beautiful mahogany desk, where he comfortably sat in his matching decorative chair. He leaned to the side for the silver tea tray and proceeded to pour a cup.

"*Merci beaucoup*," I said gratefully as he passed the lukewarm cup of tea to me.

"*Mon plaisir, madame*," General Vaudreuil replied roughly, but in a civil manner. It was apparent that Lord Vaudreuil was not a stereotypical Frenchman who had a refined and suave air. Instead, he seemed rough and uncharacteristically blunt with little cultural sophistication. He was course and reminded me of a colonial trailblazer. Also, somehow I got the further impression that he was another man with a short fuse and a hot temper. He spoke with a slightly different French accent that wasn't indigenous to France. Still, it appeared to me that everything about him embodied imperial France.

I felt extremely uneasy; I was so far removed from anything familiar to me. I foresaw this interview as a treacherous circumstance and only hoped that I would not lose my head over it— quite literally.

He reached for a small, delicate round rose-petal-painted porcelain dish filled with decorated chocolates. *"Voudriez-vous un chocolat?"* he offered pleasantly. I stared at the deliciously decadent truffles, thinking, *How could I not?* It was one of my biggest food weaknesses; I used to love See's Candies and always stopped to get a small box of their delicious assorted truffles every time I went to the mall.

"Oui, merci avec bonté," I replied appreciatively, and nervously gathered the little truffle embellished with tiny pink polka dots between my ungloved fingers. He waited for me to take a bite of the candy. He watched with anticipation as I sank my teeth into it. "Mmm," I remarked favorably.

"Aimez-*vous* ?" he asked approvingly.

"Oui, il est vraiment delicieux. Il goûte comme la chocolat Viennois à moi," I said positively, recognizing the silky smooth texture of the milk chocolate.

"Oui, il est, directement arrivé de Vienne à moi aujourd'hui," he responded generously. *"Vous connaissez ce chocolat?"* he inquired, looking at me with substantial curiosity.

"Oui—j'aime le chocolat," I said modestly. He grinned considerably at me.

"Oui, toutes les femmes aiment le chocolat. Ç'est bon que J'ai leur fasse plaisir." He laughed briskly, and his double chin jiggled like a walrus. I daintily took another bite of my truffle and smiled demurely at him in response. He maintained his studying eyes on me, scrutinizing me like an insect beneath a microscope. *"Avez-vous été en l'Autriche?"*

"Non," I lied. I had indeed visited Austria once, but I didn't feel safe to admit it.

"Ah, quelle honte—Vienne est une belle ville."

"Est-il?"

"Oui."

"Comme ç'est bien."

"Oui." General Vaudreuil continued to silently scrutinize me with his little round, dark eyes. *"Êtes-vous Créole, n'etes-vous pas?"*

The chocolate I had let melt deliciously in my mouth unexpectedly went down my windpipe as I swallowed it. I coughed a little. So, I sipped a bit of tea from my petite teacup.

"Êtes-vous d'accord, madame?" General Vaudreuil asked concernedly.

"Oui, merci, pardonnez-moi," I said appreciatively with a scratchy voice.

"Certainement. Vous êtes Créole?" he continued to inquire.

"Eh, um... Pas exactement," I replied as I cleared my throat. He pursed his lips and slightly narrowed his eyes in a thinking manner. He appeared suspicious of me.

"Humph. Où habitez-vous en Nouvelle France?" He was inquiring of my origin in New France, and I was not sure exactly how to answer the question. I couldn't very well say that I was from Quebec City or Montreal, for that matter, without raising any more suspicion. Nor was it safe for me to say that I was from New Orleans without raising concerns over the tremendous distance I would obviously have traveled. Furthermore, I had drawn a historical blank and could not come up with any plausible cities that would have been well colonized during this period in time that might have placed me in the best ethnic demographic. So, I sat there facing the general for a second, literally put on the spot to come up with a reasonable lie.

"Oui, bien, vous pourriez dire que je suis de la Nouvell-Orleans," I decided to say after all, telling a lie.

"Humph. *Mais ce que je pourrais dire n'a pas d'importance. Alors, ce que vous dites est ce qui comple*," he cautioned precisely.

"*Oui, naturellement,*" I replied.

"*Bien. À quelle distance êtes-vous de la Nouvelle-Orléans?*" he persisted keenly.

"*Oui,*" I answered, very much aware of his exact questioning.

"*Je vois,*" General Vaudreuil responded guardedly. "*Vous parlez Français tres bien.*"

"*Merci.*"

"*Vous parlez Français la manière qu'il est parlé en France,*" he noted.

"*Merci.*"

"*La façon dont une dame Française parlerait la langue.*"

"*Merci.*"

"*Êtes vous déjà allé en France?*"

"*Non.*"

"*Je vois. Jamais?*"

"*Non—Jamais.*"

"*Curieuse.*" He twiddled his pudgy thumbs and paused speaking for a moment. I placed the last bit of chocolate in my mouth and sipped some more of my tea. "*S'il vous plaît, ayez un autre chocolat.*" He extended the dish of chocolates, offering me another truffle.

"*Ah, merci,*" I replied graciously. He nodded his head once in polite acknowledgment.

"*Le nom de votre mari est Espagnol,*" General Vaudreuil began again.

"*Oui,*" I acknowledged, biting into my second truffle.

"*Parlez-vous Espagnol aussi?*"

"*Oui,*" I answered.

"*Je vois... Bien, si vous dis-moi de votre mari, Je lui livrerai volontiers sans préjudice,*" he generously offered.

"*Merci beaucoup... Je suis, malheureusement, une veuve.*" I felt no choice but to disclose to him the truth that I was a widow.

"*Est-ce vrai?*" His brow lifted slightly in surprise.

"*Oui, tristement ç'est vrai.*"

"*Mes condoleances.*"

"*Merci beaucoup.*"

"*Oui, naturellement,*" General Vaudreuil replied abstractedly, and paused for a second. "*Bien, vous êtes une distance de votre Novelle-Orleans a la maison,*" he observed.

"*Oui, je suis.*" I had forgotten to be cautious and thoughtlessly reached for my teacup in my lap with my left hand. His eyes gawked surprisedly at my diamond engagement ring and gem-covered wedding band.

"*Quelle belle alliance votre défunt vous a offert,*" he noted, admiring my ring.

"*Merci... Merci beaucoup,*" I said politely.

"Mm-hmm," he grunted with acknowledgment. "*Dites-moi, comment s'appelle ton mari?*"

Why did he want to know my husband's name? A rush of uncertainty coursed through my veins.

"Mathew Arboles," I answered truthfully.

"Mathew," he echoed thoughtfully.

"*Oui.*"

"*Comment a-t-il été tué?*"

"*Mon mari a été tue dans un accident. Il a été difficile. Ç'est une pensée terrible dont Je me souvens,*" I answered desolately.

"*Je suis terriblement désolé pour votre perte, madame,*" he said sympathetically.

"*Oui, merci beaucoup.*"

"*Ainsi, vous travaillez actuellement comme espion pour nous.*" He believed that I was a spy for the French, and I found myself wretchedly sinking deeper into this quicksand mess of misunderstanding. "You are young and extremely beautiful—a perfect decoy candidate. You appear as fine as *une dame Française*. It makes me wonder why a Spanish nobleman would allow his wife to arrive with him in New France in such dangerous times when he was alive? Quite irresponsible of him, *non?*"

"Yes, well, we couldn't be apart… We loved each other," I replied stoically.

"*Oui, naturellement, amour,*" he mocked obviously. "So… you speak *Anglais* with much skill."

"Yes."

"Your accent sounds quite natural."

"Thank you."

"I am unaware that we have such a lady in our service. Tell me, which one of my *officeurs* employed you?"

What was I going to say? He was the governor of New France and commander in chief of all of its French military forces in the territory; he was perfectly familiar with all of the men serving under him. Therefore, it was not as though I could just simply toss out a made-up name and hope for the best. I had to name someone, but how could I do that without being found out, which would ultimately jeopardize my fate—if not my very life? I had to think quickly in spite of my inability to recall the details of my early American history.

"You see, that is just the thing," I decided to say offhandedly, nervously laughing a little.

"What is the thing?" he inquired.

"Well, this is very extraordinary," I started a bit comically.

"*Oui?*"

"Well, for some *odd* reason, I have been unfortunately presumed a spy by the English simply because I speak French. Isn't that ridiculous?" I laughed peculiarly. General Vaudreuil's eyes narrowed on me. He did not appear to be the slightest bit humored.

"You have been delivered to me by the British upon the claim that you are indeed a spy. It would not be only because you speak *Francaise*. Take into account your dialect, madame," General

Vaudreuil said suspiciously. "How did you come into British hands?"

"I, um, I was found," I replied.

"Found? Where were you found?"

"In the woods—I was lost."

"You were lost? In *Anglais* territory?"

"Yes."

"Why were you in *Anglais* territory?"

"I can't really say," I said sincerely.

"You cannot say? Or you *will not* say?" It was seeming that the general might soon lose his patience with me as he glared with pinched lips and narrowed eyes, looking obviously dissatisfied. "Let me make clear to you, Madame Arboles—if this is your true name—you are treading quite treacherously. I assure you this is *non* game. I see you are flawlessly fluent in *Francaise* and *Anglais*. You also say that you are knowledgeable en *Espagnol*, and I reasonably assume that you speak it as effortlessly as the other languages. You are apparently an unusual femme—if only by the mere look of you. Only a lady or a courtesan could be so finely kept. Yet you explained to me that you are widowed. Why, then, do you not wear black?" Sure enough, a point that had never in the slightest occurred to me as I glanced down at my cheerful chintz short gown. "Unless you are in truth not a Papist but a wayward heathen Protestant. So, which are you?"

"Which am I?" I echoed perplexedly.

"*Oui*—lady, or courtesan?"

"I told you. I'm widowed," I said factually in an even voice, feeling significantly insulted.

"Ah, so you say. Courtesans may marry also," he replied sarcastically.

"You listen to me—I'm *not*, nor have I ever been, a whore," I responded firmly, despite the nervousness I felt rising within me.

"You are a heathen no less, ah?" he continued to challenge.

"No, I'm not." I was aghast by his persistent affronting interrogation. He was trying to pinpoint where he wanted me with his accusation.

"Do not tell me, then, that you are a Papist?"

"As a matter of fact, I am Catholic."

"Mm-hmm… What, then, is the name of our Holy Father?"

I cleared my throat. "I'll say Pope Benedict the Fourteenth," I guessed on a whim, truly having no clue.

"*Très bien.* However, it is *non* secret who is *le Pape*," General Vaudreuil said obviously. "What if you present to me your *chapelet* instead?" To my detriment, I didn't have a rosary on hand to prove to him my Catholicism.

"I, unfortunately, do not have mine to show you," I replied as I finished the last piece of my chocolate.

"You do not?" It was easy to detect that he was growing even more suspicious of me.

"No—I lost it in the forest," I lied.

"Mmm…" He paused momentarily with his chubby fingers entwined over his desktop. "Can you name for me the number of Holy Sacraments?"

"Yes, there are seven."

"*Très bien.* Please, won't you list them?"

"Sure." Remembering this part was easy for me. "The first Holy Sacrament is Baptism, then Penance, followed by the Eucharist, then Confirmation, next Holy Orders and Matrimony, and finally the Last Rights."

"*Bien,*" he commented. "Now, recite for me *les Beatitudes.*"

All of a sudden, I felt like a child in catechism all over again. I could not remember the last time I'd had to recall the Beatitudes. I actually was not a strict, devout, practicing Roman Catholic.

"*Oui, uh, les Beatitudes,*" I began thoughtfully. "'Blessed are the poor in spirit—for theirs is the Kingdom of Heaven… Blessed are the meek, for they shall possess the land. Blessed are they who mourn, for they shall be comforted. Blessed are they that hunger and thirst after justice, for they shall have their fill… Blessed are the merciful, for they shall obtain mercy. Blessed are the clean of heart, for they shall see God. Blessed are the peacemakers, for they shall be called the children of God. Blessed are they that suffer persecution for justice's sake, for theirs is the Kingdom of Heaven.'"

"*Très bien...* 'For theirs is the Kingdom of Heaven,'" General Vaudreuil responded, better swayed. "*Oui.* You are *Catholique...* and you are either *Francaise* or *Espagnol*. However, I suppose that does not so much matter either way. We are friends, *oui?*" I took a deep breath and exhaled with some relief. "Now, tell me what you know of *le Anglais* defense."

"I beg your pardon? I am sorry, please believe me, sir, when I tell you that I don't know anything about the English," I expressed genuinely.

"*Assez!*" he shouted unexpectedly, and I jumped as his fist slammed angrily on his desk. "I am *non* longer entertaining your silly impertinence! You do know *something*! And you *will* tell me all that you know, *Madame Arboles*. Do I make myself *clear* to you?"

"Very."

"*Bien. Le Anglais* have built a new fort at the south end of Lac du Saint-Sacrament. Now, tell me, what is *le Anglais* strategy?"

"Well... it seems that you know as much as I. I'm sorry, but I can't tell you any more than that," I replied moderately. Without warning, General Vaudreuil stood from his desk and paced around the front of it until he stood directly in front of me. He suddenly thrust his arm and latched a firm hand around my jaw. I gasped with surprise and fright. "You try to trick me!" His dark eyes instantly hardened like black onyx, and his face became flushed with perceivable outrage. "You want me to believe that you are a spy for us when you are truly *en league* with *le Anglais* instead!"

"No—that's—not true!" I said desperately between my aching

pinched cheeks as he tightly held me between his unforgiving fingers.

"As far as I see, it is *true!*" Without releasing my hurting face from his unyielding clutch, he forced me to stand immediately before him. "You seek French information to assist *le Anglais.*"

"No!" I gasped.

"Then what? What is your business? Your business here with me?" He stood closely, slightly above eye level in front of me, so that I could feel his heated breath scorch my face.

"You're hurting me," I uttered painfully.

"You will hurt much more than this if you do not speak."

"I've been trying to tell you that there has been a tremendous mistake in my identity."

"Then tell me who you are. Give me your full name."

"Sylvina… Sylvina Arboles."

"Who is your employer?"

"Nobody… I don't work for anybody!"

"Who sent you?"

"Nobody!" I gasped. He tightened his grip around my face, and I winced. "Let go of me!" This was quickly turning into a repeated scenario, and I panicked. I desperately tried to pry his fingers from my face.

"Then I shall force the information from you!" He abruptly turned my head, which forced the rest of my body around as he shoved me backward and instantly released his hand. I fell, landing hard with my back flat over his desk, injuring my tailbone.

"*Ow!*" I wailed.

"Now, you are going to tell me *everything* that you know," he said caustically. He grabbed me by the neck and pinned me down on his desk. I wildly began flailing my arms at him in sheer alarm, knowing exactly what was about to take place. "I admire your fire, madame!" he mocked coarsely. I could barely breathe, let alone get a mere word out. He was surprisingly strong and swift for a man of his plump physique.

"Get the hell—off—me! You syphilis French bastard!" I wheezed, striving mightily to remove myself from his grasp. A sudden hot sting burned my face as his hand forcefully struck the side of my cheek.

"*Putain!*" General Vaudreuil snarled furiously, and started aggressively tossing my skirts up high. In an instant they were at my waist, and I was completely exposed from my hips to my feet. "Whores are an easy provision in *Nouvell-Orleans!*" he erupted, sloppily spraying my face with saliva as he spoke. "*Aie!*" he abruptly shrieked as my thrashing nails unexpectedly clawed the side of his face. He suddenly released his hold on me as he clutched his round cheek. I sprang up like a grasshopper and darted across the room, coughing and holding my neck for air.

"You better damn well keep your filthy swine hands off me!" I exclaimed, coughing. He drew his hand from the side of his face and glanced at his bloodied fingertips. He appeared shocked, and angrier.

"*Chienne!* You do not tell me what to do!" he raged, coming toward me again.

"Do not touch me!" I warned excitedly as I quickly moved to another location in the chamber with my pulse running wild. "*Le Marquis de Saint-Veran* will not be pleased if he learns that I have been harmed in any way—especially by you!"

General Vaudreuil immediately paused in mid-step while coming toward me. An unpredictable expression of astonishment swept over his face.

"What do you know of *le marquis?*" he inquired brusquely.

"*Le Général Montcalm* will be extremely displeased if you hurt me," I bluffed, spontaneously out of breath as I suddenly remembered some vague aspect of early American history from high school.

"He has sent you to *spy* upon me?" General Vaudreuil growled outrageously. "How *dare* he! He has *non* right! I am supreme commander in all of New France, *not he*! I shall show him that he cannot threaten *me*!" All of a sudden, General Vaudreuil lunged forward without warning and violently grabbed my arm.

"You see this ring you admire so much?" I said anxiously, frantically thrusting my engagement ring before his eyes. "It is a *personal* gift from King Louis to me! The king favors *le Marquis de Saint-Veran* over *you*! Tell me, General Vaudreuil, do most generals like yourself serve in such luxury while their soldiers merely crave *food*? *Le Général Montcalm* is not a financial parasite like you! He honorably serves the Court! The king gives generous gifts to the Indians as a show of gratitude and plenty of currency for provisions to his soldiers. But you aim to profit even more off the king's goodwill by selling the king's intended gifts to the Indians and embezzling from the military budget. If you harm me in *any* way, *sir*, you will ultimately have to answer to the king. And, I assure you—he *will* be angry!" I ventured to guess wildly as I tried to remember the history of the region.

Suddenly, General Vaudreuil released my arm. I rubbed my reddened wrist. He paused for a moment, severely scrutinizing me, looking alarmed and tightly wound.

"I shall correspond with *le Marquis de Montcalm*. I shall inform him of your arrival at Fort Carillon. He will know that you have been safely placed in my protection," he said corrosively.

"No! I want to be *immediately* delivered to him," I risked demanding.

"Once we have communicated, then we may proceed," General Vaudreuil responded unyieldingly. "Until then, you will remain my guest. *Garde!*" Almost immediately, the door swung open, with a young lieutenant entering through the threshold. "*Enlevez-la!*" he staunchly ordered his guard. "Promptly escort Madame Arboles to our guest quarters."

I was seized around my upper arm by the lieutenant and immediately escorted from General Vaudreuil's quarters. I was led outside and down a flight of stairs across the courtyard. I could not say how tremendously relieved I was as I was being escorted away from imminent danger. I had surprised myself by the risk I had taken to accuse General Vaudreuil of thievery, and how lucky I was to have been correct.

However, my instant relief was very short-lived as I was steered toward the prison barracks and placed in a vacant holding cell. It was filthy and dark inside with no windows, the only light coming in through the gated doorway. Experiencing severe disappointment and worry, I wanted to sit, but the cell was empty of a single chair or cot. The floor was covered with old sod and hay. I supposed that was the material prisoners were expected to use to pile for bedding. A grotesquely reeking stench of stale booze, urine, and feces, combined with the lingering stink of unbathed men, masked the dungeon.

It was better to remain standing instead, I decided. I was compelled to simply lean against the cold stone wall. On second thought, I decided to resist the urge to touch the dirt-covered wall, and just stood for however long I possibly could. I paced slowly around the cell, knowing I was now quite conceivably in the worst heap of trouble since I had been initially transported here to this time period. I had no idea how I was going to elude the difficult mess I was in this time. What on earth was I going to do once General Vaudreuil discovered that General Montcalm had no notion of me, and that I had lied?

There was no doubt that he was going to discover my deceit if I didn't have the chance to meet with General Montcalm first. It was only a matter of time. I imagined General Vaudreuil was conspiring something and that time for me was of the essence. It would merely be a couple of days, I guessed, depending upon where General Montcalm's location was from the fort, until General Vaudreuil would be convinced of my treachery. I figured General Montcalm couldn't have been too far away in any case. General Vaudreuil was a nervous, easily provoked, suspicious, self-indulgent man—characteristics that when combined were volatile and dangerous—and I found myself in his crosshairs.

I now anxiously paced around my rank jail cell, realizing that I essentially had a day to somehow render my escape. *Perhaps I could gain some sympathy from a soldier to disappear from the fort?* I knew that wouldn't work without the use of my sexuality, since it was now my only recourse. I'd have to trick him into letting me go. And once I had gained my release, how was I going to safely find my way back to Albany? I had no horse of my own, so I was going to have to try and steal one or I was going to have to hike the entire way by myself. The thought of the likely potential of being abducted by vigilant, bloodthirsty Indians in league with the French while in the forest entered the back of my mind. Still, what else had I to lose? I thought it was better for me to at least have given my escape a try. Only, while I continued to consider it, I knew I ran the very real risk of becoming lost in this perilous mountainous forest region if I quite possibly lost the trails along the way. They were often very narrow and obscured by uncleared vegetation. I could literally die of dehydration, starvation, and exposure, if I had not been attacked by a wild pack of wolves, or instead eaten by cougars or bears first.

My eyes landed on the soiled chamber pot in the corner of the cell, and a rat scurried around it. I jumped out of fright and quickly moved as far away from the pot as possible. I had to soon decide what I was going to do, and the pressure was mounting, disturbing me. I must have been held in the cell for close to an hour when a guard suddenly appeared and approached the gate. He inserted a key into the lock and yanked the rusty iron gate open. My heart began racing, and I froze with alarm. He firmly took my arm and proceeded to tow me from the cell.

"Laisse allez de moi!" I demanded him not to touch me, and I whipped my arm about to no avail as he thrust me into the corridor. *"Où moi prenez-vouz?"* I asked sharply, but he didn't answer me. *"Dites-moi! J'exige de savoir où vouz moi prenez!"* I demanded to

know where he was taking me as I excitedly tried to free my arm from his solid grip.

"*Shh!* Yoo'll have us discovered, lass!"

"*Leif?*" I precipitously stopped short in my step in sudden shock. I stared up at his obscured face overshadowed by the tricorn hat on his head.

"Aye, 'tis I," he assured in a low voice.

"What the hell are you doing?" I asked, astounded.

"Thaur's nae time fur discussion. Let's go!" he urged hurriedly, and tugged my arm again.

"Wait!" I paused in my step once more in confusion. But Leif had a lot more force and compelled me to move with a strong pull forward. "What's going on? Why are you dressed in a French uniform?" I asked breathlessly as he continued tugging me.

"I borrowed it," he said tersely.

"You *borrowed* it? What do you mean you borrowed it?"

"*Quit gabbing!*" he hissed. We instantly stepped outside of the barracks. Countless French soldiers swarmed the grounds. They surrounded us as they casually walked around the area. I nervously glanced around as Leif led me through the quad toward the fort entrance. "*Dinnae fidget!*" he hissed at me again. "We'll shortly be out of haur. Remain calm, lass."

I took his advice for both our sakes and tried my best to act normal. Leif's hand was securely clasped around my upper arm while he closely guided me like his possession among enemy soldiers. We were approaching the center of the courtyard, and my heart was galloping in my throat anticipating our escape. The archway at the entrance of the fort was clearly in sight and only several yards away.

"*Arret! Arret! Où prenez-vous son?*" shouted a loud, echoing voice from across the quad. I glanced over my shoulder. It was General Vaudreuil, noticing us as he had just come outside onto the upper landing from his quarters. "*Arret! Que faites-vous? Apportez-la moi!*" he screamed at us, ordering my possessor to cease and bring me to him. But Leif robotically ignored him and kept his eyes staring straight ahead past the onlooking soldiers as he hastily persisted in pulling me alongside him. *"Je vous commande—arret! Au nom de la France, vous devez s'arreter!"* General Vaudreuil continued to shout out. Leif moved swiftly—stone-faced and steadfast—with the aim of getting us out alive. *"Aretez-les! Dissident! Arretez-les—maintenant! Elle s'echappera!"*

The guards took immediate notice, and the sentinels at the fort entrance charged toward us. We were staring down the barrels of drawn pistols and bayoneted muskets as the guards rushed right for us. Leif imperceptibly had his pistol ready and instantaneously whipped it up, pointing it at the oncoming soldiers. They shouted at Leif to stop and drop his pistol. It was imminent that we were going to be arrested. There was no chance for escape through the entrance.

Without warning, Leif abruptly tugged me off to the side, and we were immediately running frantically along the barracks within the quad. Hand in hand, Leif jarred me along with him in flight around the back of one of the barracks, where we hurriedly trotted up a wooden flight of stairs, which placed us up on the stone-laid cannon deck. He rapidly scanned the area, promptly sighting a couple of guards on lookout duty at opposite ends of the deck.

"Allez! Allez! La vers le haut des etapes!" The chasing guards could be heard scrambling up the steps not far behind us.

"This way!" Leif hastily decided. He tugged me to the left, and we ran like the wind over the platform. The lookout guards spotted us and quickly understood what was happening as the ensuing soldiers promptly arrived from the staircase, chasing us. We rushed past the second story barrack windows to the left. To the right was a continuous row of evenly spaced grand cannons peering from their ports overlooking the lake. When we came to the end of the deck, we took a sharp left and continued following it until we suddenly turned right onto a wooden bridge connecting to a demilune.

There were three guards casually conversing on top of the demilune when we arrived. They abruptly detected our frenzied appearance. They looked at us with question and confusion. Before any of them could inquire, Leif suddenly shoved his pistol into his holster, then sharply positioned me at the start of the bridge in front of the wooden rail.

"We're going tae have tae climb down. Follow efter me, and I'll catch ye at the bottom," Leif instructed quickly. I peered over the edge of the rail into the ditch below and saw the distance from above was far enough away to break every limb in our bodies if we happened to slip and fall from the support beams.

I hesitated.

"Follow *exactly* as I do, and yoo'll be alrecht. Come—dinnae worry—I have ye," Leif directed me assuredly. He started to heave himself over the rail. I didn't see how it could be practically done to safely land on the ground. But he was already over the edge far enough below, advancing downward along the rafter. One of the soldiers on the demilune hollered out, asking what we were doing. He started toward me. The quickly approaching guards hot on our tail from the courtyard were soon going to be too close for a reasonable getaway, so I swiftly hiked my skirts up and threw my leg over the rail.

As carefully as possible, I concentrated on the protruding beam and slithered over the ledge. The three soldiers were excitably shouting after us, and the oncoming slew of guards from behind were merely seconds away from apprehending us. Leif and I were more than eager to arrive intact at the bottom in the ditch.

I mindfully slinked after Leif, attentively following his every movement down along the rafters. When we finally came to the last support beam, it was clear that we were going to have to jump the rest of the way down. The distance seemed closer to the ground, but still high enough to break a leg.

Leif lowered himself just so on the slanted joist and dangled near the ditch. He released his hands and collapsed into the dirt gully. He rebounded to his feet to my relief and quickly waved his hand for me to promptly edge myself lower on the strut.

"Make haste, Sylvie! Climb over, and I'll catch ye!" he directed me confidently. I wasn't so sure that he *could* catch me, because the distance was still too far. He could easily miss me, or I could land on him too hard, and he would drop me instead. "Hurry, lass —yoo're wasting time!" he said loudly with discernible anxiety.

I decided to trust him, so I very carefully waddled my way farther down the ridge of the joist. I slowly bent down, remembering the hazards of my cumbersome skirts, and worked around the beam to finally dangle myself from it. I glanced down at Leif, poised to catch me. I let go and fell...

"*Oof!*" he grunted, catching me in his arms within a flash like a football. "Guid! Come along!"

He hastily propped me onto my feet and rushed me away through the dry trench the very second the rest of the guards had reached the bridge. They peered over the rail and easily located us on the run. Horns sounded out in the fort, and commotion set off all around us, including the terrifying hooting and hollering of Indian war cries. Leif and I ran like hell through the trench as we scrambled over the dirt to climb out onto level ground. I could hear my own blood rushing through my head as Leif rapidly tugged me. We disappeared into the tall brush with the sound of our quickly stomping footsteps crushing vegetation beneath our feet. The alarmed soldiers were invisible among the trees and bushes, but could be heard chasing us from everywhere around us. I followed him blindly into the thick vegetation until we soon entered out onto the lakeshore. He swiftly hoisted me into a stolen canoe and promptly shoved us off from the pebbled shore.

Gunfire erupted after us as we were closely followed. Leif stuck his oar into the water and forcibly paddled with long, heaving strokes, pushing us fast and far away from the enemy shoreline. Musket balls hit and sloshed into the waves too close for my comfort, so I pulled out the spare oar and began paddling too. We were now being additionally pursued by a stimulated band of eager Abenaki and Huron warriors as arrows whizzed by our heads. Leif swung his arm around and fired his pistol back at the pursuing foes. A soldier instantaneously cried out in the canoe not too far behind us as the pellet penetrated his chest, and he suddenly slumped over.

My blood curdled with fear at the sound of the chasing Indians' impassioned, fierce, unwavering, warring shrill. I pushed the oar far into the water and thrust forth with all my fundamental might. The mere thought of being captured, raped, and killed was enough of an impetus to fight for my very survival, and so I heaved—and heaved with every stroke.

We quickly came upon a wave of rapids where Lake Champlain narrowed at the south end and were carried off into a tributary stream. The canoe recklessly bounced and rocked us around like an uncontrollable roller coaster. At one point the craft had tilted so far to the side, I thought we were going to capsize and be lost to our deaths in the rapidly flowing current. But the canoe was suddenly knocked the other way by the water and corrected the balancing craft. My oar hit a rock and snapped in half like a twig. Leif, seated behind me, clumsily scooted himself slightly toward me and centered his weight inside the craft as best he could. He attempted to skillfully steer the canoe with caution, managing us amid the white water.

We had gained some distance from our pursuers as a result of the rapid water flow. Still, they could be seen behind us. The water grew more turbulent, and I was aware that a waterfall was looming ahead as the waters began to thunder. I became progressively worried as I anticipated our approach. Within a matter of minutes, a thunderous roar of raging water sounded throughout the air. There was no doubt that the advancing waterfall was an impressive drop.

Leif strove to maneuver the canoe out of the quickly flowing water. It required a lot of his effort to manipulate our way toward the edge of the stream as we nearly crashed to our detriment into a huge boulder jutting out from the water.

Just as we avoided hitting the rock, the stream began carrying us back out into the heart of the flow. Leif worked, striving to pull the canoe the other way, fully aware that we were advancing dangerously close to the plummeting edge into the abyss. A sudden wave pushed us to the side, and Leif dragged the oar, pulling us into calmer waters. We soon came near the shore, and he leaped out of the canoe, splashing in the water as he towed it to the silty riverbank. He swung me out of the craft and planted me on the ground, then shoved the canoe back into the rapids.

The enemy was audibly detectable a fair distance behind us. Leif grabbed my wrist and drew his sword before tugging me into the woods. We hiked across a perilous path bordering the rushing river for a good distance until we were prevented by an obstructing outcrop sheering straight up into the heavens. Leif shoved his sword back inside his scabbard, since we had no choice but to climb a steep, rocky slope composed of silt and slate off to our side next to the abrupt igneous intrusion. The slope was slippery and cumbersome—particularly for me as I followed him in my hindering dress. My slippers could have benefited from having rubber soles, I thought, as he assisted me along the gradient.

When we finally arrived on level ground, we continued hiking hurriedly through abundant giant vegetation and dense forest. Suddenly, a single rallying call cried out among the trees in the distance, and Leif's attention piqued like hunted prey. His head turned in the direction of the sound. Close among the trees, an Ottawa war party was on scout and had just detected us. Leif summarily whisked us away with another war party close in pursuit of us. Everything became a precipitous blur as we huffed and puffed our way through the woods.

As we rounded the giant rock face, Leif retracted a portion of shrubbery at the base of the rock and tossed me inside a hole in the earth. He quickly pushed his way in after me into the tight, slightly deep chasm. We waited, hiding from sight—hoping.

Within minutes, I saw from below the legs of quite a few well-armed Ottawa braves passing us by. One of them did so much as promptly see the rift in the rock and peered inside. He scanned the area. Leif simultaneously whipped his large hand over my mouth, immediately stifling my gasp, and tightly pulled me back against his chest into the dark shadows away from view. He constricted me with a python grip, preventing my breath, as the brave surveyed the cave.

The Ottawa warrior lingered a moment, taking his time to gaze into the gorge. I was paralyzed with fear, and my pulse raced wildly. Finally, the warrior seemed satisfied with discovering nothing and moved along with the others. Leif continued his fast hold around me for moments longer after the war party had trailed off. He ensured my silence for our safety's sake in case a stray enemy might have been scouting close by.

At last, when it became clear that the Ottawa party had gone, Leif's grip around me relaxed and his hand slid from my lips. Then, he proceeded to climb his way out of the cleft. Once he was outside again, he reached down to assist me in making my way out.

Judging by the light in the sky, dusk appeared to be coming soon, and we continued winding through the wilderness. After a while, we arrived at a large gorge, where a steadily flowing stream lay deep below. It was apparent to me that Leif intended for us to take this route and climb our way down the steep rift. I was intimidated by the mere thought of attempting such a venture, because the slope was so very steep. We had no modern rock-climbing gear, or anything else that could have better secured our safety down into the narrow valley.

The slate was layered in an unusual fashion and appeared like small little brick-sized steps in some locations. In other areas of the formation, the rock overlapped in larger planes, which provided better targets for placing our feet as we climbed our way down. I conscientiously followed Leif with every step I took, hoping not to slightly miss my footing and tumble into the crevasse to a crippling death on impact once I hit the stream below. Leif skillfully manipulated his movements as he maneuvered while descending over the gradient. I was impressed by his natural agility as he met the demand of this course, rigorous, and hostile terrain; it seemed he had been physically prepared, or rather innately conditioned, for this type of environment.

In a little while, we safely arrived at the bottom of the ravine. The rivulet was turbulent. White water rushed over the submerged boulders and around protruding rocks. A series of large, somewhat flat rocks sticking out of the stream appeared like stepping stones. Leif sprang up tall on the first one closest by the riverbank and pulled me up next to him onto the sizable boulder. From my new perspective, the rocks appeared to rest questionably farther apart than I had originally thought. Because my legs weren't nearly as long as his, and because of the way I was dressed, I wasn't so sure that I could successfully achieve landing safely on a couple of the rocks without first falling into the water.

Leif took his first leap onto the second rock and easily landed securely on it. With his hand stretched out toward me and his feet well planted, I leaned slightly forward, taking his hand, and pounced off the rock toward him. My feet thankfully settled next to his as he tugged me reassuringly close to him. He then positioned himself to leap onto the next boulder. He bounded off. Again, his feet firmly attached to the rock, then he reached for me. I took his hand and flew toward him a second time, landing securely next to him. Leif poised himself another time and hurdled to the next rock. I followed him and landed next to him again.

The next jump did not appear as easy; the distance seemed a fraction too far, and the side of the rock facing us was an awkward shape. Leif took a concentrated second to balance himself before taking off. He soared in one giant leap, arcing his way across the stream like a great antelope. My heart stumped with relief as he landed on the rock without consequence. He stretched his arm out toward me and waved his palm for me to give it a go. Deciding not to think about it too much, I put my mind in concentration and focused on him being the target. With one big thrust, I pushed off the rock and took a flying leap. Suddenly, my tiptoes firmly hit the upper side of the rock, causing me to slip and lose my balance. I was headed for the deep, rushing, cold stream, which would whisk me away. But Leif simultaneously threw out a fast hand, grabbing my upper arm hard, and violently yanked me up over the rock against his chest. He secured me with his other arm around my waist, and I looked up at him with sheer relief. He gave me a nervous little grin with a sigh of relief too.

We calculatingly maneuvered our way across the rivulet with every anticipated leap over the stones. Soon, Leif and I came close to a shallow area where the boulders tapered off. We were then forced to step into the frigid water and made long strides until we emerged from the riverbank.

My shoes and stockings were now soaking wet, but only the hems of my skirts had become damp, since I was able to modestly hike them up high enough away from the stream. Leif's breeches also had become drenched from his lower thighs down to his boots as we moved out of the water.

We came to a pebbly shore, and our wet feet rolled and crunched over the small rocks as we paced along. There was a huge charred log obstructing our path when we came up the riverbank. As I followed Leif over the log, my ankle suddenly gave way beneath me.

"*Ow!*" I wailed, abruptly crouching down on the pebbles, holding my ankle in anguish from the sharp, shooting pain. Leif immediately spun around, looking at me crouched on the ground.

"Whit's the matter?" he inquired alarmingly, facing me. He at once noticed me clutching my ankle. "Och! Yoo've hurt yerself," he said quickly, kneeling before me.

"Yeah…" I moaned.

"Let me see," he urged as his hand gently began touching my lower calf. I apprehensively removed my fingers and let his cautious hand slide down toward my foot. He lifted my skirts a little to expose a portion of my leg to get a better look. I observed him examining it. "Ye didnae cut yerself," he noted while looking it over.

"No, it's my ankle," I whined. I actually felt like crying because it hurt so badly. It felt like nothing I had ever experienced. I bit my tongue and held back the temptation to whimper like a baby.

"Haur," he said attentively, and proceeded to gently stretch my leg over the pebbles. He mindfully removed my shoe, and I untied my garter. He proceeded to carefully roll my stocking down my leg and delicately removed it. I noticed the redness seeping over his cheekbones and quickly spreading to his ears.

"Ouch!" I gasped, sensitive to his probing fingers on my ankle. He looked concernedly at me.

"Can ye wiggle yer toes?" he asked.

"I don't know. I think so. Let me see." I successfully manipulated my foot.

"That's guid," Leif replied with relief.

"Yeah."

"Does it hurt when ye wiggle yer toes?" he inquired with a discerning gaze.

"No—I can wiggle them okay," I replied.

"Yoo've badly injured it, however. I can see by the swelling," he discerned.

"Yeah… it snapped when I twisted it… I think I might have torn a ligament," I replied worriedly.

"Let's see—can ye put yer weight upon it?"

"I'm not sure."

"Haur." He stood from kneeling and offered his hand. I slipped my fingers into his sturdy palm. He carefully pulled me upward to stand. I cautiously applied my weight on my hurt leg and was luckily able to hold myself steady.

"Guid," he remarked. "Now, can ye walk?" I proceeded to take a step, but couldn't complete it without wincing at the sheer agonizing pain. "Yoo're nae guid like this," he assessed absolutely.

"No," I replied, flinching.

"Alrecht, then. Git on," he said determinedly. He turned and slightly hunched, tapping the small of his back.

"Get on?" I looked at him in confusion.

"That's reit. I'm going tae have tae carry ye."

"Carry me?"

"Aye."

"I don't know," I responded skeptically.

"Weel, whit else would ye recommend?" Leif gave me an obvious look. I was wary about piggybacking on him. Except, apparently, there was no other choice in spite of my skepticism.

"Fine," I said reluctantly. But I hesitated.

"Weel?" he said expectingly.

"Okay," I said doubtfully.

"Ye first micht want tae hitch and fix yer petticoats," he suggested.

I stood self-consciously before him with his eyes steadily on me while I lifted my skirts and securely adjusted them above my knees. With his help, I also removed my other soaking wet shoe and stocking. Now bare legged, I stood ready in front of him with my skirts rolled up high above my knees and my wet stockings and shoes dangling between my fingers. He gazed unaffectedly at me, but I noticed his face had gone completely flushed.

"Guid. Alrecht, let's go," he said satisfactorily, then turned his back to me and squatted, lifting me up high on his back. With me on board him now, Leif started out again over the uneven terrain gently rising from the riverbank.

I stiffly rode on him, very much aware of the awkwardness of our closely engaged bodies. His brawny arms tightly hugged my bare-skinned legs encircled around his firm waist. I couldn't help wondering what sort of thoughts wandered through his mind as he carried me.

I peeped over his shoulder at my injured ankle wrapped around his waist. It was swollen like a purple gourd. I hoped that I hadn't really broken it, or I would be in *real* trouble. But I could only know for sure with a X-ray. However, I believed that I had most likely torn a ligament. In any case, I was rendered unable to walk and would have to find some way to remain off my foot. Fortunately for me, Leif seemed to have the strength and stamina to hike for long distances with me on his back through the forest.

After a little while, we arrived on more level ground, and the journeying was made less rigorous for him. My back had grown tired, because I had remained consciously stiff while he carried me along. So, I gave into my tiredness and relaxed fully, leaning my torso into his back. His shoulders were solid and square and made a great resting support for me. Based on his appearance alone, he seemed noticeably strong and forceful. But when I felt him holding me, there was no question of the intense fortitude he had regarding his fit, concrete physique. I let my arms slide down over his shoulders and comfortably tucked my chin into the curve of his perspiring neck.

His skin was hot and moist against my cheek. I could smell the salt and earth on him, and the odor of male labor. I was listening to the sound of his heavy breathing and watching my hanging shoes in my hands swing to the beat of each forging step he took along the way. Light strands of his golden hair whipped in the gentle breeze like feathers across my brow. Sometimes his wispy strands caught in my eyelashes, tickling them. I carefully pushed them away from my eyes to clear my vision.

"Why did you take me to Fort Carillon and leave me there?" I ventured to ask.

"I had orders tae do so," he answered tersely. "Laird Loudoun ordered it efter he was done with ye. And the lads believed that ye would be safe back in French hands."

"Oh… But I'm not French," I responded.

"Aye, so it appears," he said.

"I'm not a spy either. Nor am I a prostitute," I said surely. He didn't respond as he kept pacing through the forest. "Do you think that I'm those things?"

"I reckon that ye are not a prostitute," he said, huffing as he concentrated on his hiking.

"But you think that I'm a spy," I surmised.

"I dinnae reckon that I ken," he said honestly.

"Why did you come back for me?" I asked him. He didn't answer the question. "Why did you come back?" I repeated.

"I didnae feel reit leaving ye thaur with Laird Vaudreuil," he said. I didn't respond, and it grew quiet. "Ye looked at me before I left ye… Ye held my hand. Ye appeared afraid," Leif disclosed as he carefully moved over the terrain.

"I was very afraid," I admitted.

"I ken," he said subtly. I didn't respond. He became quiet also, and the conversation drifted into silence. So, I decided to put my chin back upon his shoulder in the comfortable curve of his neck while he continued carrying me. My eyes landed again on my swinging shoes over his chest, and my thoughts wandered while silence remained between us as we made our way through the forest.

CHAPTER 16

As dusk began to settle, Leif scouted a location safe enough for us to rest through the night. It was high alongside a mountain ridge beneath a cliff overhang. He carefully placed me down on the ground in the deepest area within the cave and casually sat next to me. It was certain that we weren't going to have the pleasure of a meal tonight. However, I supposed it really didn't matter, since all I could concentrate on was the throbbing ache of my bloated ankle. I moaned as I attempted to gently rub the pain away.

"Haur—have some of this. It will help ye," Leif suggested with his arm stretched out holding his canteen. I took it from him and had a sip. I winced at the biting hot alcohol scorching down my throat. I coughed a little afterward. "Yoo'll need more than that. Go on—take it," he insisted with an urging gesture. I put the canteen distastefully to my lips again and took a large sip of the rum.

"*God!* Where's the ibuprofen instead?" I coughed.

"Whit is that?" he inquired strangely.

"A good painkiller," I said, still coughing.

"Och. Weel, ye huvnae any of that. So, this will do," he said. He was right; after a little while, the liquor had begun taking effect and the pain from my injury began to quell. "How do ye feel now?" he asked.

"Better, I think."

"Guid. Ye shouldnae move yer foot, however," he suggested.

"No," I agreed.

"Alrecht, then." He suddenly pulled himself to his feet and started scavenging around the cave. He promptly found a long, sturdy twig and snapped it in two. He returned to my side, setting the twigs down, and removed his coat. He then began tugging at the shoulder seam of his linen shirt until it had completely torn off. With one fierce pull, he ripped the long sleeve in half. He reached down, scooping up the two twigs and positioning one on each side of my leg, then he began securing them as he tightly wound the material around my ankle and calf.

"Where did you learn how to make a splint?" I inquired, impressed.

"Och, when I was a wee lad, I fell off the barn roof and cracked my leg," he said casually.

"Ooh, that's awful." I winced.

"Aye, 'twas terrible when it occurred—but I was fortunate the bone hudnae moved through my leg."

"Yeah, that's very lucky. Sounds like it could have been a hairline or an incomplete fracture," I said.

"Och, aye," Leif replied blankly, nodding his head a tad. "A young surgeon came tae look at me and set my leg in such a manner."

"Oh," I said.

"Aye, it healed quite weel. I huvnae had a problem with my leg since that time occurred."

"That's good."

"Aye, 'tis," he said simply as he continued bracing my leg. In a moment, he was finished. "Now..." he resumed after completing his work, "that will suitably prevent any further movement from yer foot."

"Thank you," I said genuinely.

"Yoo're welcome," he said. I smiled at him, and just then I realized, quite profoundly, that he had honestly become my friend in spite of everything. He had risked his life to recapture me when he did not have to do it. He could have left me there at Fort Carillon, never laid eyes on me again, and not think twice about it. I remembered the first time he saved me from the Huron warrior, abducting me during the ambush. A knot formed tightly in my throat, and suddenly I found myself fighting back tears as I now looked at Leif's bewhiskered face.

I abruptly averted my eyes from him down toward my tattered, muddied hem and bandaged leg. I couldn't look at him, or I would have dissolved. After *all* that I had been through—the death of my husband, the loss of my pregnancy, the near crippling depression that followed, my physical rehabilitation from the car accident, and *most unbelievably of all*, abruptly being inconceivably hurled through a temporal warp that had landed me here in pre-American-Revolution times.

Since arriving here, I had been trekking by foot and on horseback while being exposed to the beating elements for days. I had surrealistically witnessed men being killed, while being wrongly accused of being a spy, delivered into the hands of perilous men, nearly raped, chased down and hunted by Indians, and all the while required to gaze upon these foreigners without allowing myself to connect with this stranger who was helping me... I couldn't handle it anymore.

"Yoo're distressed," Leif said, noticing. "Whit's the matter?"

"I'm sorry," I replied quietly. I returned my eyes to his and smiled at him.

"Whit's the matter?" he asked concernedly again. I simply shrugged a bit, inconsequentially shaking my head.

"It's nothing," I said, dismissively waving my hand. I felt an uncontrollable tear perch on my eyelid, and I immediately wiped it away with my fingers.

"But yoo're weeping. 'Tis something, is it not? Whit is it?" he urged gently. I couldn't respond. He tilted his head a little to one side and gave me an encouraging look. "Whit's trooblin' ye?"

"I'm sorry—I can't help it… I'm just feeling a little emotional —that's all. I'll be all right," I said unevenly, feeling the quiet tears roll from my eyes down my cheeks despite myself. I promptly wiped them away. "It's okay. I'm okay. I'm all right."

"Ye certainly dinnae appear it," he said, obviously unconvinced. "Tell me—whit is it?" I took a little breath and shakily released it, trying to sort my thoughts.

"I'm just… I'm just feeling overwhelmed, that's all—very overwhelmed," I said, sniveling. "I'll be okay though," I muttered, more or less trying to convince myself of that.

"Come haur," Leif urged as he gently compelled me against his broad chest and enfolded me in his muscular arms. "'Tis alrecht, Sylvie… Yoo're safe with me," he said tenderly. He held me with kindness and security. My emotions overcame me, and I buried my face in his strong chest. I disintegrated, releasing all of my pent-up, painful feelings in an uncontrollable flood of tears. I gradually held on to him with my arms wrapped tightly around his neck. He continued holding me with compassion for an undetermined time and just let me cry for as long as I needed to. His hand gently moved over my back, caressing and soothing me. He was solid and concrete. As I held on to him, he was tangible and real to my senses, to the point that it could not be denied.

"Thank you… thank you for—being my friend," I sobbed.

"Shhh," he whispered softly. "Yoo're safe with me now." I continued crying as he gently hushed me, soothed me, and reassured me. His hand roamed upward beneath my loose ringlets to the back of my head, lightly caressing my tangled tresses. His manipulating fingers comforted me in a way Matt had never had to do. Leif's hand roved closer to the side of my tear-streaked face. His large thumb began carefully stroking the side of my cheek, and he slightly pulled back. He lifted my chin and looked into my eyes. "Please dinnae weep, Sylvie. I'm reit haur fur ye. Yoo're safe with me. Do ye ken? Yoo're safe," he insisted. His intense crystal blue eyes acutely locked on to mine as he deeply and seriously looked at me. His gaze arrested me, and I started to calm.

"Okay," I whispered compulsively, feeling his other hand sensitively trail up over my shoulder until it warmly rested on the side of my neck.

"Guid… Guid," he replied. His thumbs lightly stroked my cheeks, wiping the tears away. He lifted his hand slightly and delicately pushed my wayward ringlets from my tearful face. He was looking at me with such meaningful concentration, I found it haunting and evocative at the same time. I wondered what he was doing… but I saw the wanting in his eyes. I was suddenly beginning to feel extremely strange. My blood became warm, and my heart was palpitating. A tingling feeling electrified my nerves, and I sharply felt an unusual rush of something latent within me stirring. My attraction for him was surfacing, but I wished to repress it.

His gently stroking hands persuasively encircled my face. They felt mildly calloused, but smooth enough and warm against my skin. His thumb wandered down toward my chin beneath my bottom lip and began lightly tracing the outline of my mouth. It went around again and swept over the lower half of my mouth, parting my lips. He drew me closer, and I could feel his warm breath caress my emotional face. He was searching me as I gazed back into his keen, impassioned eyes. I sensed him, and he silently brushed his soft, heated lips against mine.

Leif began gently and tenderly kissing me. It was a strange feeling. I didn't know what to think, but I let my hands slide up over his shoulders and around his neck, allowing him to kiss me. He responded and pulled me firmly against him. His careful lips became more eager and compelling over mine. He was exposing me to his desire and calling me toward him to confirm it. I reached around the nape of his neck and slipped my own caressing fingers deep within his luscious hair, affirming my connection with him.

His heated lips moved fervently over mine, with his anxious hands massaging the back of my head and neck. His zealous kisses trailed over my cheek and meandered to my neck. I felt my temperature rising by the mere touch of his lips on my skin. He was definitely experienced at kissing, I sensed. But what I was feeling from him was more than that: it felt honest and potent.

I realized that I was no longer weeping. I felt that there was a new physical correlation between us. A force that was tangible. I found myself wanting more of him. He sensed me and pulled me tighter against him, feverishly kissing me. He abruptly withdrew his lips from the base of my neck and ardently returned them to my lips. His breath had become shaky and heated. I gasped as he unexpectedly thrust his scalding tongue deep into my mouth, and filled it.

I automatically withdrew at once from him. I startled myself. I stared back into his unexpected heated gaze and saw that his face was flushed with perceivable yearning.

"I—I'm sorry. I'm so sorry, I didn't mean to do that," I gasped. I was suddenly embarrassed—and didn't know how to recover.

"Nae, I apologize. I shouldnae have been so bold and kissed ye," he said carefully.

"It's okay," I replied nervously. I suddenly felt like I was cheating on my late husband, as irrational as that sounded.

"Are ye alrecht?" He appeared so sincere and honest in spite of his scarlet face that I really felt horrible.

"Yes, I'm all right," I said. Leif nodded lightly, looking at me with an open expression.

"Guid. I apologize," he repeated genuinely.

"No—you don't have to apologize," I said honestly, very much aware of myself.

"But I must apologize," he said sincerely.

"No—seriously—I don't mind that you kissed me," I disclosed in a soft voice. His brow lifted with a mixture of surprise and uncertainty.

"Ye dinnae?"

"No—it was nice," I admitted uncomfortably.

"Aye," he agreed softly. A bashful grin gently tilted his lips.

"It's just… Well, I just think that—uh… we shouldn't let ourselves get carried away or anything, you know?"

"Och—aye, of coorse," he agreed, nodding his head in accordance. "Yoo're correct, it wouldnae be wise."

"No… It wouldn't, I think."

"Nae," he echoed calmly. A moment of embarrassing silence ensued between us. I had some experience to know how quickly things could progress from a passionate kiss. I'd strongly sensed the direction in which we were headed, and although I'd really wanted to proceed, I knew it wouldn't have been the best thing to do; I wasn't prepared for any complications or repercussions that were bound to arise as a result of succumbing to our noticeable and palpable temptation. Not only did I strangely feel really guilty about kissing him because of my late husband, but also because my Catholic guilt had gnawed at my conscience, preventing me from freely experiencing pleasure with him without consequence.

"Well…" I clumsily resumed, interrupting the embarrassing silence between us.

"Aye?"

"I'm a little tired," I said honestly.

"Och, aye. I too," he said gently.

I remained sitting close to him, looking down at my hands enfolded over my lap. Leif reached for my right hand and gently drew it over his muscular thigh, enfolding it within his large palm. His thumb tenderly stroked my palm as he silently examined my fingers between his. I watched his exploring fingers over mine as he separated my fingers and spread his palm over mine, noticing the difference in sizes between them. I lifted my gaze, and our eyes met. I smiled at him, and he grinned reservedly. His eyes returned to looking at our entwined hands.

"Such a perfectly fine, delicate wee hand. Look at that—so very wee in mine," he observed.

"Yeah…" I said softly. Leif quietly turned my palm over and raised it toward his mouth. His lips pressed warmly and tenderly over my knuckles. He returned my palm to his lap and held it in his before our eyes met again.

"I'm glad that I have met ye, Sylvie," he said genuinely.

"So am I," I agreed softly. His stubbly cheeks creased as his lips curled. My stomach suddenly growled, embarrassing me a little. "*Oops*," I whispered with a meek giggle.

"Yoo're hungry," he replied regretfully.

"Not too much," I said.

"Haur," he said, collecting his canteen again. "Have enough of it. I ken that ye dinnae favor it, but it will quell yer appetite—along with the pain in yer foot."

"Okay," I reluctantly conceded, watching him pass the wooden canteen over to me. I took it and braced myself to take several hearty swigs of the potent alcohol.

"That's it… Take a bit more," he suggested while he approvingly observed me drink. I took another couple of large gulps and felt that I had had enough. "Guid," he said, satisfied, then retrieved it from me and corked the rim.

He then stirred to his feet and prepared an area for us to rest for the night. When he had finished, he carefully gathered me up in his arms and placed me on a bed of fallen maple leaves to rest. As I made myself comfortable, he resumed sitting closely next to me with his back leaning against the cool rock and his legs comfortably stretched out in front of himself. I lay there watching him shift slightly as he retrieved his pistol from his holster and the leather pouch from around his waist. He began inserting a new piece of flint and twisted it down into the hammer.

"What are you doing?" I inquired curiously as I relaxed on the leaves.

"I'm making preparations in case we're alarmed," he answered, presently uncapping his powder horn.

"You're going to keep watch all night?" I asked.

"Aye." He half cocked the hammer to his pistol.

"But you must be exhausted." I yawned.

"I'm alrecht," he assured me while pouring a measure of gunpowder down the barrel.

"Well, we could change places, at least. I could watch after a while, that way you could have a chance to get some sleep," I offered. I had never fired a gun before in my life. But there were plenty of women in my day who were familiar with firearms and shot guns all the time. I thought I could do it too if I had to. A distant grin tilted his lips while he focused on arming his weapon.

"Thank ye all the same, lass. However, I dinnae recommend ye firing a pistol," he said.

"But I could do it—I'm not afraid," I said, yawning again.

"Mayhap yoo're not. Even so, it isnae a guid notion," he said.

"Why?" I continued, watching him as he wrapped a lead ball in a small piece of cloth. With a tool, he rammed it down the long pistol barrel on top of the gunpowder already inside. Leif paused in what he was doing and looked down at me beside him with an admiring expression.

"Yoo're noble-hearted, lass. But I'll mind us," he stated.

"I just want to help you," I said sleepily.

"I ken," he said gently. I detected a subtle grin relaxing his face. "Yer generosity is much appreciated, *àille dhubh*. However, I like ye fine with yer bonnie face intact," he said frankly.

"Oh—okay," I acquiesced drowsily.

"Now, be a guid lass, close yer eyes, and sleep," he urged affectionately.

"Okay," I whispered, faintly nodding my head. He winked at me and returned to the task at hand. I continued watching his fingers place a small amount of gunpowder in the powder pan. He snapped the frizzen in place over the pan before fully cocking the hammer. Locked and loaded. I finally closed my eyes for the night.

CHAPTER 17

J awakened the next morning to Leif softly caressing the side of my face with his thumb as he lay next to me, closely watching me.

"Guid morrow tae ye, *àille dhubh*," he greeted softly.

"Good morning," I muttered sleepily, gazing back up at him. His lips widened into an affectionate smile. I stirred, sitting up next to him, peering around our location.

"It rained last nicht," he informed me.

"Yes, I guess it did," I remarked, noticing wet ground outside of our sheltering cave. The air was pungent with the smell of damp earth. The vegetation was still dripping from the rainfall, and the droplets could be heard randomly pitter-pattering to the ground from the surrounding trees.

"But we remain unharmed," he said.

"That's good."

"Aye." He carefully uncocked his pistol and set it aside. "I reckon we ought tae move on. I need tae git ye fed." He mustered himself to his feet. My ankle looked like a huge black-and-blue gourd and throbbed like hell. I snatched his canteen before he collected it. I opened it and chugged like a collage frat boy. Leif's fingers wrapped around the container, interrupting me as I swallowed, and he pulled it away.

"Pace yerself, lass. Not too much—'twill knock ye reit off yer feet," he warned while promptly corking the canteen then slinging it over his shoulder.

"Aye aye, *captain*," I mocked lightly with a sloppy salute. It was amazing how suddenly warm I felt after drinking the liquor.

"Ye mean *major*, lass," he corrected frankly.

"Whatever you say, chief," I replied. I winked at him, and his eyes widened. A light chuckle escaped him.

"Look at ye already besotted on spirits," he scolded lightly. "Alrecht, 'tis time fur us tae go," he said as he towered over me. He placed a sturdy hand around my upper arm and carefully helped me to stand on my good foot. With one big, swift heave, he hauled me upward upon his back.

Leif set out walking across the muddy, uneven terrain through the woods with me piggybacking on him again. Although it had rained the night before, the sun was out shining brightly, illuminating the earth through the trees. It was warm and already very muggy in the morning. The birds were present in full force, chirping and singing throughout the forest. We had a fairly long distance to hike before we would reach Fort William Henry. I supposed that we were going to have to spend a few more nights in the wilderness, since we were resigned to traveling by foot—and because the extra weight Leif was now carrying slowed us down considerably. My biggest fear at this point, other than suddenly being attacked by a ferocious wild animal, was being tracked by our very competent enemy pursuers and ambushed along the way.

Leif walked along, attentive to his surroundings. The trees and earth were literally blanketed with moss, which enveloped everything the eye could see. It made the land soft and cushioned Leif's footsteps, stifling the sound of every step he took. The entire forest was insulated and seemed like an acoustical sound hall, allowing for everything to be precisely heard.

I found the place on his neck again and comfortably set my chin on the curve there. The sides of our faces touched, and his skin felt scratchy against my cheek. I rested at ease against his back, with my arms encircling his broad shoulders and my hands lightly folded over his firm chest. My mind was wandering, and I thought about what had happened last night. The kiss had been seared into my mind, and it was all I kept thinking about. It was as if my mind had tripped a circuit loop I couldn't stop.

Notwithstanding everything, I thought about how much Leif had swayed my emotions and influenced my affections in this very short amount of time. I discovered that I had grown interested in learning more about him and who he was as a person. And I realized the emergence of my newly discovered physical attraction to him. Furthermore, although he was completely different from Matt, I found that I could not help already feeling natural and comfortable with this strange man.

In spite of my apparent reservations and every other logical apprehension that I had, I discovered myself feeling oddly enthusiastic. Leif had acknowledged his own curiosity and attraction to me in a very definite way, and it inspired me. Despite myself and the feelings I still held for my late husband, and although my world had been turned completely upside down, everything unexpectedly felt fresh again, and a new hope came over me. I was glad. I hadn't felt this way in a very long time.

Simultaneously, however, I was all over the place with my thoughts. My delighted thoughts were also plagued by the fact that I could not totally disregard my responsibility regarding Leif. I couldn't ultimately just think about myself; the thought of hurting him made me feel extraordinarily guilty and shameful. The truth was, as I was forced to recognize it, that I still wanted to go home very badly. It was my priority. When the right opportunity permitted, I was going to leave him to ultimately achieve that goal.

I couldn't stop thinking about the situation in which I now found myself. The truth also was that, at the moment, I was enjoying his companionship. I decided that I wasn't going to allow myself to spoil it right now. I tried changing my thoughts and focused on the scenery as we hiked along.

"Leif?" I started thoughtfully.

"Aye?" he replied.

"So what's going to happen now?" I asked.

"I dinnae ken," he said.

"Oh."

"I reckon we micht have tae encounter Laird Loudoun one way or anither," he said seriously.

"Right," I muttered.

"Dinnae fret, lass. All will be weel," he assured, as he huffed along the trail. "'Tis fortunate that he disnae ken that I have ye. He merely knows that ye went missing."

"Right," I said.

"Aye, and we must keep it that way," Leif said certainly. I silently agreed with him. "I promise ye that he wulnae harm ye."

"I hope that you're right," I replied honestly.

"Dinnae worry, Sylvie. Ye must trust me now."

I didn't say anything else after that. Nor did he. Instead, a comfortable silence ensued between us, and I easily rested my chin on his shoulder against his neck as we continued along.

We had come upon a water hole fed by a small stream, where we decided to rest. Leif carefully set me down on a nice-sized limestone rock slightly away from the silt shoreline. He paced around the area, scoping out something. After a moment, he finally found a good enough bush and hacked off a lower branch with the tomahawk stuck in his belt. He pulled up the sturdy branch and briefly looked it over with satisfaction before he came near to sit next to me. He took his dirk in hand and propped up one end of the branch, then began whittling it away.

Soon, the end of the branch was shaved into a clean, sharp point, and Leif had turned it into a sturdy spear. He proceeded to remove his boots and stockings, then went toward the water and waded in a shallow area between several medium-size rocks in the stream. He stood there quiet and still, gazing silently into the water like a stone sculpture. His spear was raised just enough above the water, and he patiently waited. I wasn't certain how many minutes had gone by, but my stomach gave away my hunger and growled angrily. I leaned over a little, trying to quell the grumbling, when within the blink of an eye, he sharply drove his spear down into the water between his knees. He lifted his fishing tool and pulled out the largest rainbow trout I had ever seen. I grinned with sudden surprise, utterly impressed, as he quickly turned around in the water and faced me proudly, showing off his prize.

"*Bravo!*" I exclaimed, applauding him. "*Qué magnifico! Excelente!*" I poured on the ovation with my affected Italian accent in Spanish. His pleased face brightened further with a blatantly proud smile as he made his way back out of the water.

"A fair size, nae doubt," he said.

"It looks like it was on steroids," I commented.

"Steroids?"

"Never mind."

"Weel, at least ye ken that I can also feed ye, *àille dhubh*," he boasted.

"Yes, I suppose so. Thank you," I said gratefully.

"Alrecht, now let's prepare it," he promptly suggested.

"Actually, sushi looks very good right about now."

"Whit is sushi?" He gave me a puzzled look.

"Raw fish to eat."

"*Raw* fish? Tae eat?" he echoed with a disgusted look.

"Yeah," I said.

"That disnae soond fairly appetizing," he said, shaking his head somewhat. I laughed a little. "Ye eat yer fish uncooked?" he inquired oddly. He was staring at me with a shocked expression as if I were an extraterrestrial.

"Not really," I lied, shaking my head a little with a slight, uneven smile.

"Whit do ye mean, then?" he inquired curiously.

"Well, people in Japan do," I said unthinkingly.

"I beg yer pardon?" He gazed at me, astounded.

"I mean that I read about it—that they eat it that way," I said unevenly. I realized that I had to lie again.

"Och," he said strangely. "Weel, we Scottish folk care tae cook ours before we eat it." He winked at me, causing me to smile at him.

Leif was skilled with a tinderbox and quick with building a suitable campfire for our fish. Once it had finished roasting over the hot coals, we ravenously dug into the fleshy meat. I felt like a famished individual who had been deprived of nourishment for an undetermined period of time. I couldn't ever remember enjoying trout as much I did then. The meat was hearty, moist, and smoky flavored, and slid right off the bone like butter. Within several minutes, Leif and I had completely cleaned the fish from its flesh, leaving only the head and bones as evidence of its former existence.

My stomach felt full and happy again, and a nap would have been a nice thing to take right about then. However, since we were on the run from our skilled adversaries, it didn't seem like Leif was going to let us waste much time once our food had finally settled in our stomachs. We sat together in front of the water talking. Well, Leif mostly did the talking, and I gladly listened. He talked about several things pertaining to his childhood when he lived in the Scottish Highlands, and the adventures he had undergone on the European continent as a young soldier. All of it was extremely interesting, and I discovered myself engrossed in every detail. He also told several jokes that actually had me rolling with laughter—after he had to explain the gist of them to me. It turned out he was quite the comedian.

I studied his animated face while he spoke, and I liked what I was seeing. His eyes lit with warmth and enthusiasm. He was buoyant and presently unreserved. I could easily see that he truly enjoyed his life, and that he did not seem afraid of obstacles that arose in his life. The corners of his eyes wrinkled when he laughed, illuminating his face. The more I watched and listened to him, the more I gravitated toward him, and I was consciously aware that I had fallen within his orbit.

After about an hour or so of relaxation and nice conversation, he suggested we leave our lazy spot at the water hole and move on before we might be discovered. He doused the campfire with water and covered it with damp earth, and the blaze fizzled out, with steam billowing up into the air. He hauled me up on his back again, and we proceeded up an undulating incline of mud and rock.

In a while, we finally reached level ground and miraculously found our way onto a traveled path, which made for much easier trekking. The forest was dense everywhere around us and laden with giant ferns. The trees were mighty along the path, and moss carpeted their trunks and limbs, in addition to the scattered rocks over the ground. Poison ivy and wildflowers grew freely on the earth, appearing like a patchwork of quilted colors.

We entered into an area of mist among the trees and ferns, which came from a nearby waterfall. The whole scene appeared like something from a mystical fantasy film. The air felt a little cooler. All of a sudden, Leif sharply ceased in his step and imme-diately stared past the trees to the right over his shoulder. He silently stood there in the middle of the path, arrested with alarm and attention drawn toward the enveloping woods.

"What's the matter?" I wondered, quickly sensing his alert reaction.

"Shhh..." He lightly hushed me.

"Did you hear something?" I whispered faintly. Slick and fast, Leif dashed us off the path to the left among the trees. He rapidly galloped through tall vegetation with me still on his back. Saplings and fern branches mercilessly whipped across my face and stung my skin as he tore wildly through the undergrowth. Without warning, he dove us into a large thicket of fern bushes, and we landed roughly on the damp ground, concealed. He promptly knelt beside me, withdrawing his pistol and fully cocking it, ready to shoot. He was panting heavily while gazing sharply at the woods surrounding us. "What's wrong?" I asked anxiously.

Leif abruptly capped a palm over my lips, instantly silencing me. He communicated with a look, warning me not to open my mouth, then gently slid his hand away from my lips. He brought an index finger to his lips before pulling it away and gestured with his palm for me to remain still. I nodded accordingly and froze.

Armed with a loaded pistol in one hand and a drawn sword in the other, he waited with anticipation, perfectly motionless like a petrified fossil. The forest, once infested with singing birds, I noticed had unexpectedly muted into silence. Not a single sound was uttered from the trees for a length of time that seemed hyperextended.

Suddenly, a branch snapped at a distance a few yards away. Leif swiftly pointed his pistol in that direction toward the sound through the plants, ready to fire, when a young buck was seen through the trees, nipping at the greenery. A faint sigh escaped him as he half cocked his pistol, appearing only partially relieved. The buck twitched an ear in our direction before abruptly prancing off and disappearing between the trees. Leif fully cocked his gun again. In a second, the unexpected squawking sound of a lone blue jay sounded out. It squawked several times at a distance before he decided to suddenly uncock his pistol. He quickly sheathed his sword and stood tall in the foliage.

"Let's go," he said quickly, and swiftly took me up into his arms, carrying me from the thicket. He jostled me around a little as he hurriedly walked through the woods. We hadn't gotten very far when a redcoat unexpectedly appeared from the trees behind us, pointing his pistol directly at Leif's back.

"Dinnae take anither step or I'll lay one in ye, *French*," said the redcoat. Leif instantly arrested his steps, and I peered over his shoulder to look at the man.

"Is that ye, lass?" Angus asked, as he recognized me with considerable shock.

"Yeah, yes, it's me—and Leif. He has me," I quickly informed Angus.

"Leif?" Angus called perplexedly with his pistol still raised at him. Leif slowly turned around, facing Angus, still cradling me in his arms before him. "It *is* ye, Seamus," Angus said, recognizing him instantly, looking obviously astounded.

"Aye," Leif replied.

"*Jesus Christ!* I nearly blew ye away," Angus said, suddenly relieved. He lowered his pistol and uncocked it.

"Guid notion ye didnae," Leif said, also completely relieved.

"Aye. We thought we had lost ye, lad," Angus said, walking toward us. "Whit in *damnation* are ye doin'?"

"That is whit I care tae ken," Finley said unexpectedly, suddenly emerging from between the trees. Leif lightly shrugged his shoulders and gave Finley an unspoken sort of guilty look. "Whit do ye mean that ye dinnae ken?"

"Dinnae ken," Leif replied with an unreadable face. Finley doubtfully narrowed his eyes on his brother. Suddenly, the rest of the men were visibly treading hastily toward us from among the woods.

"Whit transpired?" Finley asked straightforwardly of Leif.

"The lass was in trooble," Leif answered candidly.

"In trooble?" Finley echoed skeptically with a questionable eye skimming over Leif's enemy uniform.

"'Tis whit I said," Leif said.

"We already ken that the lass is in a predicament," Finley countered with opposition.

"But I dinnae believe she belongs with the French," Leif maintained.

"Ye dinnae?" Finley questioned.

"Nae," Leif replied.

"Then, whaur do ye reckon she belongs?" Finley inquired.

"Dinnae ken at present," Leif said.

"Dinnae ken, eh?"

"Nae."

"Then whit do ye propose?"

"I dinnae ken."

"Whit do ye mean that ye dinnae ken? Did ye not reckon the position this puts us in with Loudoun?"

"Aye, I thought on it a wee bit."

"A wee bit?"

"Aye."

"Weel, ye ought tae have contemplated it fur much longer than that!"

"Mayhap."

"Mayhap, ye say?"

"Aye."

"Jesus, Mary, and Joseph, Seamus! Do ye not reckon that we're in a bind now?"

"Aye! I reckon."

"Then, whit?" Finley asked irritatedly. Leif merely shrugged his shoulders. "Humph! Weel, whaur is yer proper uniform?" Finley inquired, disgruntled.

"Switched with a guid French soldier," Leif informed him. Finley went silent for a brief moment and heavily sighed through his nose with sealed lips that were pinched into a line. He gave Leif a discernibly frustrated look. Then he resumed saying something obviously admonishing in Scottish to Leif. The brothers went back and forth, clearly arguing, for an extended moment.

"*Alrecht*—I ken!" Leif responded irritably to Finley once he had finally finished disagreeing with him. Finley rubbed his brow, and tense silence ensued between the brothers.

"Now whit?" Cole inquired, also visibly irritated.

"We best git on, then," Finley determined as his eyes unwittingly landed on my injured ankle. "She's maimed?" Finley gave Leif an unbelievable look.

"Aye, she twisted it somethin' fierce as we escaped a Huron and Ottawa war party pursuing us along the way," Leif informed him. Finley rubbed his chin, appearing further annoyed as he gazed at my ankle.

"Alrecht, then, we best git on now," Finley ordered in a disgruntled tone.

"We had an Ottawa party give us chase from the fort as we waited fur ye. I thought fur certain that they had ye," Cole said.

"We eluded them as far south as Rogers Rock, but returned in search fur ye. I didnae reckon ye would have the lass with ye, however," Finley said gravely, still appearing very annoyed.

Leif didn't respond. "Whit occurred tae Garakonthie?" he inquired instead.

"He went on tae inform Winslow's men of the Ottawa war party headed fur them," Finley informed him.

"Och," Leif replied, nodding his head.

"Let's go," Finley directed shortly.

"Aye," Leif agreed.

The men began moving through the forest and resumed navigating their way back onto the faint path.

Leif adjusted me in his arms several times as we passed over level ground for a while. The trail began sloping down a moderate gradient for aways, and soon Lake George could be seen through the trees. The path led us along a bend around a giant granite outcrop along the edge of a steep cliff. I hung on to Leif, very conscious of his mindful steps as he walked slowly over the narrow, uneven earth, praying that he would not misstep and accidentally slip over the crevasse to our likely deaths upon the merciless rocks below.

Everyone carefully crept along the untrustworthy downward slope. It seemed like forever before we would reach the stable end of the path. But, in cautious time, as we wound around the mountain, the trail changed at last and became level again. Soon, we had entered from the passageway out onto a pebbled shore in front of the lake. A couple of large canoes were beached several yards away, and we began approaching them. When we arrived at the vessels, Leif attentively swung me into the middle of one canoe as several of his cousins filed inside the watercraft beside me in the water, at the bow and stern, along with him. Then, the men shoved offshore, and we floated south over Lake George.

CHAPTER 18

I never thought I would be so glad to return to grimy, rustic wood-built Fort William Henry in one piece, secure again in British territory. We entered one of the barracks, where Leif comfortably set me on a dining bench and sat beside me as the others filled the empty spaces around us. A young Sauk maid, captured as a slave, readily entered the quarters prepared to deliver a hot clay pot of venison pottage. She placed a stack of tin bowls in the center of the rectangle table, along with the piping hot pottage and a large jug of rum. Without any hesitation, before she had finished placing the spoons on the table, the men unceremoniously grabbed the bowls and eating utensils as they began serving themselves.

Observing every man for himself, in that case, as they ate, I had no time to lose either and strove a reaching arm past my burly, boorish companions for a bowl and spoon. But the bowls remained out of my reach, and it seemed like I was going to be left out in the cold for a meal. So, I sat there for a moment, wondering how I was going to circumvent them to get something to eat. Just when I was convinced that I was probably going to have to wait like a pup for scraps, Leif stealthily slid an unexpected bowl full of the pottage before me and winked warmly at me.

"Eat up, lass," he encouraged.

"Thanks," I replied gratefully.

"Aye, yoo're welcome," he said.

I took my spoon between my fingers and began hungrily digging into my warm food. As Leif began serving his own bowl of pottage, the men were animated with agreeable discussion and in good spirits as a result of having safely returned to the fort.

In the middle of our eating, Sean, a lieutenant, entered the dining chamber. He briefly scanned the room and immediately locked on to Finley. He walked directly toward Finley, discreetly leaned toward him, and confidentially disclosed something into his ear. Finley glanced at Sean with an unreadable expression. He inaudibly said something back to Sean, and Sean nodded. Leif, sitting directly across from his brother, was aware of the two men quietly discussing. Sean continued saying something else to Finley, and Finley and Leif exchanged subtle glances. Then, Finley disengaged himself from concluding his meal and left the table, following Sean as he exited the chamber and disappeared behind the door.

LATER THAT NIGHT, I lay in Leif's bunk half asleep, trying to get some rest. I was kept awake by him and Finley in discussion over some political issues concerning the war, which fortunately had nothing to do with me this time. The brothers shared this particular officer's room, which was already cramped inside, and with me included made the space feel like a sardine can. Leif had stretched out comfortably on Finley's cot. Finley didn't seem to mind, since he remained seated in a wooden chair with his heels stretched out, resting on the edge of his cot. Their conversation faded in and out as I at last began drifting toward slumber.

"So, whit do ye reckon the governors are going tae do then?" Leif inquired.

"Cannae say as of yet… Most conceivably they will call an assembly," Finley replied.

"Och, aye… Soon, I pray," Leif said.

"Aye, the sooner, the better," Finley agreed.

"I cannae believe how mismanaged His Majesty has allowed this war tae be conducted. Who reckons whit is occurring in his court?" Leif questioned skeptically.

"His mistress is occurring in his court," Finley answered dryly.

"*Humph.* Weel, that isnae helping us haur any," Leif replied.

"Aye," Finley agreed. The conversation paused momentarily, then Finley continued, "So, now we must be on the watch fur Loudoun. He disnae ken that we have the lass as of yet, but that is reckon tae change… And when that transpires, he is going tae seek her out."

"Aye," Leif acknowledged.

"I reckon yoo've been thinking on it."

"Aye."

"Weel, now ye must think long and hard on how we are going tae remedy the situation."

"Aye, I'm awaur."

"Weel, I have my thoughts on it. Whit ye did was foolish," Finley chastised.

"Aye, but whit was I tae do?" Leif replied.

"Follow orders, lad…"

"Aye, but it wisnae the reit choice fur the lass."

"Humph. Orders must be seen through, however."

"In this case, I must disagree."

"Of coorse ye do, as I reckon that I ken the reason why… Speaking of orders, I meant tae mention tae ye that Winslow has been recalled tae Albany fur certain, as ye recall the correspondence he received."

"Aye."

"Aye."

"Do the men ken why he was recalled?" Leif inquired.

"Nae—as far as I'm told."

"His recall is preposterous!"

"Aye, weel, it continues tae worsen."

"How?"

"Loudoun not only recalled Winslow, but dismissed him also, according tae Sean," Finley informed him.

"*Dismissed* him?"

"Aye," Finley said.

"How is that reasonable?"

"My sentiments precisely. The men say that Loudoun has also dismissed Winslow's troops."

"All two thousand men?" Leif replied, sounding appalled.

"Every last one of them," Finley responded.

"Whit about those camped at Edward?"

"Them as weel."

"That is a total of four thousand men," Leif said.

"Aye."

"Damnation…"

"Aye," Finley replied.

"Whit sort of aim does he mean tae undertake?" Leif inquired with discernible incredulity in his voice.

"According to General Lyman, as this bit of information was given tae me by Sean, Loudoun means fur the lads tae practice military arts and plant cabbages," Finley informed him.

"Cabbages! He cannae be earnest," Leif replied.

"He's quite earnest."

"*Cabbages,*" Leif scoffed. "Is he not under the impression that thaur is a war taking place haur?"

"'Tis fur provisions in the intended siege of Louisbourg."

"Och! Loudoun is full of *crap*. Carillon is more imminent," Leif retorted.

"Aye, and quickly achievable… Thaur is sedition amongst

the ranks… He'll have a hard time employing his methods with us. Already the militia troops have broken ranks from the British, and the British are not thus far behind the provincials… Thaur is dissent as weel amongst the officers, ye ken," Finley said.

"I ken… Mass subversion will do nae guid," Leif commented.

"Aye," Finley agreed.

"So, whit are ye going tae do then?"

"I need tae meet with Governor Shirley," Finley answered.

"Yoo're going tae Boston?"

"Aye, I must."

"If Loudoun discovers it?" Leif pointed out.

"Aye, if he learns of it, I'll encounter him then," Finley answered.

"Be wise about it, however, Fin."

"Aye, ye neednae worry about me, lad."

"As ye say."

"But now as fur ye, we must decide whit we are going tae do haur," Finley said.

"Aye, I ken," Leif responded pensively.

"So."

"I reckon we shall head back with ye tae Northampton before ye take leave fur Boston," Leif said.

"I see… I ken whaur yer interest lies—and it wears petticoats," Finley hinted.

"Weel, it is far better than gazing upon ugly faces in the ranks," Leif said sarcastically. Finley lightly chuckled.

"I reckon the lads will be returning with us," Finley said.

"Aye, they wulnae be heading back tae Albany tae plant cabbages whilst on leave once we return from haur," Leif said.

"Indeed… Thaur is a small company of Braddock's remaining haur. I'll need tae return them tae Albany first, however, before continuing on tae Northampton," Finley said.

"Alrecht."

"So, I shall meet with ye and the lads at Fort Massachusetts once I take my leave from Fort Frederick."

"Aye," Leif said.

"I shall need ye tae stay on at *Taigh-Bheinn* with Elizabeth and the lasses once I take my leave fur Boston," Finley said.

"Aye, of coorse," Leif said soberly.

"Arrest any redcoat on sight who wulnae leave my property upon first request," Finley insisted.

"Aye."

"I dinnae want any enlisted dregs billeting on my land."

"Aye," Leif agreed.

"I dinnae care that Loudoun orders it. I'll be damned tae hell if any such one of them threatens my property. Loudoun has nae right tae circumvent the proper Crown laws of this country in place of his own absolutism," Finley said disapprovingly.

"Yet the Crown commissioned him," Leif said.

"Aye, weel, I have grave doubts about the man indeed," Finley replied.

"I also. Loudoun will have matters tae take up with us in that case, then," Leif said.

"I'm willing tae take that risk. Ye simply remain invisible from Loudoun till I appropriately handle the matter. We dinnae need tae give him any more cause tae come efter ye, lest ye be recalled tae London and face yer kin at High Court on the count of trea-son," Finley said.

"Nae."

"So, remain from secht fur now."

"Aye, I shall," Leif agreed.

"Now, get yer arse off my bunk—I'm dead on my feet," Finley said wearily.

"Aye," Leif scoffed lightly. Finley said something to Leif in Scottish, and Leif chuckled. I heard some shifting around the room as the brothers finally settled themselves for the night. I was glad the room fell quiet, and I thought it was good that finally now maybe we could all get some sleep.

CHAPTER 19

The next morning, the brothers and the rest of their companions were preparing to leave from Fort William Henry, along with General Braddock's men and a small English company originally encamped just south of Lake George. There was a strong sense of apparent discontentment involving all the troops at the fort. A visible proportion of provincial servicemen were vocal in their disgust and outrage, as word had gotten out about General Winslow's recall and dismissal of him and his troops by Lord Loudoun. Adding fuel to the fire, they were fuming over the grievous reality of England's inability, or lack of interest, to protect them from French encroachment on their frontier as many innocent lives were being lost. It was easy to conclude that the encamped English soldiers here had become the target of colonists' anger. A backlash of palpable resentment had erupted, and physical confrontation broke out between the men while we were readying ourselves for our departure.

The most vile and base curse words and name-calling I had ever heard went to and fro among the soldiers, as fists wildly began flying between them. It was quite a surreal and disturbing sight to witness. In seconds the hostility became contagious, and brawls began everywhere. Chaos was soon going to take control of the fort if someone did not quickly squash the conflicts.

Suddenly, arms had been drawn, with bayonets and pistols pointing all over the place. General Lyman, Finley, and Leif, along with four other lower-ranking officers, rushed out from the barracks into the courtyard on the sidelines of the feuding soldiers. Leif had simultaneously rushed me away back inside the barracks, where I was patiently waiting for him while seated on a wooden bench until it was time for us to leave the fort.

Suddenly, a tremendous cannon blasted out into the sky and roared like thunder just overhead, causing my heart to skip a beat. Dust drizzled from the ceiling over us as the building shook from the thunderous cannon blast. Within minutes the fort fell quiet, and General Lyman could be heard from outside excitedly ordering all disorderly men to drop their arms. I could see from the window soldiers obediently lowering their firearms. General Lyman went on scathingly chiding his provincial troops and ordered disciplinary action on them. Finley continued the severe tongue-lashing directed at the British soldiers once Lyman was finished speaking. He ordered every man involved in the brawl to remain under Lyman's command to protect the fort, and for any British soldier resisting Lyman's orders to be hanged without question for mutiny. I thought that was a little unsettling. Finley was obviously not a man to contend with.

In a moment, the contention among the soldiers had quelled, and Leif carried me back out into the courtyard toward Finley and their cousins. He proceeded to assist me up onto Blaze, then he mounted himself behind me. Once everyone had mounted their horses, we started out from the fort, following Braddock's leftover marching company south along the Hudson River toward Fort Edward.

～

WE HAD BEEN TRAVELING for approximately half the day and surprisingly were making good time with the regiment on foot. It seemed that we would arrive at Fort Edward by midday tomorrow.

By the end of the day, we had reached Glens Falls, where the brothers decided for the men to set up camp. I was so glad to finally be able to dismount Blaze; I was weary, and the day had been long on horseback. My ankle was still throbbing from the swelling of the severe sprain I had suffered two days ago. If only I had been able to place an ice pack around it and had the opportunity to elevate it at the same time, I knew that would have spared me most of the painful agony of it by now. Instead, I simply sat on the ground beneath a large pine tree before the waterfall, examining my injury and the splint supporting it. At least, I surmised, a bit of the swelling appeared to have diminished—but not as much as I really wanted.

"How does it fare?" Leif suddenly inquired, noticing my attention to it as he returned from his horse to make a place for us in camp.

"Um, I suppose it'll be all right. I still think that I might have torn a ligament," I assessed, thoughtfully studying it. Leif placed what he had gathered from his horse onto the ground beside me and knelt. He carefully took my ankle in his hands and examined the splint.

"Aye, yoo'll be maimed fur about a fortnecht," he said, scrutinizing my ankle.

"I know… Just what I need." I sighed disappointedly.

"Dinnae fret, *àille dhubh*, I'll watch ye weel and guid. Yoo'll be up and about in nae time at all," he replied reassuringly. I kept my gaze on my bandaged ankle. "Whit is it?" he inquired perceptively.

"Hmm?"

"Yoo're brooding."

"How do you know that?" I asked with surprise.

"I reckon that I have a notion about ye," Leif said reticently.

"Oh." I suddenly felt self-conscious again, and I bit my lip.

"Do ye care tae discuss whit is troobling ye?" he asked intently. I hesitated answering him.

"It's okay—it's just my ankle bothering me. I'm okay otherwise," I lied. The truth was that I was really homesick. I wanted very badly to return home, but I didn't see how that was easily possible right now.

"Is that it, then?" he inquired as he closely gazed at me. I sensed his skepticism when I glanced up from my ankle and looked at him.

"Yes," I responded convincingly. He faintly nodded and stared at me for certainty.

"I ken that traveling can be hard on ye. Bear up, lass. We shall soon be done with it," he promised. I gave a little nod.

"Where are we finally going?" I inquired.

"We're headed tae Massachusetts Bay Colony, whaur Fin's property lies," he answered.

"Oh," I said. He kept his gaze unwavering on me as he continued kneeling close beside me. He scooped up my hand into his and gently held it, warmly caressing my knuckles.

"Trust me, Sylvie," he said confidentially. "I intend fur ye never again tae be delivered tae the likes of those men," Leif promised.

"Thank you," I said appreciatively, perceiving his earnestness.

"Nae need tae thank me," he said. I merely stared back into his steadfast, meaningful gaze. His rugged cheeks flushed a little as he locked his eyes with mine. It was difficult for me to look away from him; I was aware of him—and myself—again. "Alrecht," he continued after a moment, "allow me tae complete setting up camp."

"All right," I agreed, nodding my head in shy accordance,

clearly understanding how he was beginning to make me feel. I averted my eyes from his and glanced at his strong, large hand covering mine. His palm slid from mine, and he rose tall to his feet. He turned away and resumed preparing camp.

CHAPTER 20

That night I slept inside the tent. Leif and Finley remained just outside, keeping watch, along with several other men posted around camp. For a while, although I was considerably worn from the journey, I lay awake listening to Leif and Finley talk. They preferred talking in Scottish rather than English, and the conversation between them was obviously familiar and friendly. They joked and laughed intermittently together in low voices.

There was something soothing in their voices as I listened to their hushed tones. A nice sense of true sibling fondness existed between them, which came through very well in their conversation. I recognized that kind of kinship I had with my own brother, and I grew more homesick. My mind wandered as I remembered home. But, consequently, the thought of Leif entered my mind. I remembered how good his lips had felt against mine. The thought of him embracing me the way he had the night we slept in the cave crept into my blood again, tempting me with further interest in him.

Only in our short-lived clandestine moments shared together while traveling, away from public observation, had he stolen an easy hand around my waist, or a covert caressing palm over my shoulder. At certain times, he imperceptibly pulled me more tightly against him while riding together on his horse. I could faintly feel the placement of his lips against the back of my head as he breathed in the scent of my loose ringlets. Once, he had even stealthily slid his palm over my hand, securely entwining his fingers with mine and wrapping our connected arms around my waist while on his horse. At that moment, I felt the warmth of his lips scarcely brush the side of my neck. It sent a sharp rush of electrifying adrenaline throughout my veins, and the pit of my stomach quivered with butterflies. He had excited me, and I was very aware of it. I felt like an adolescent girl who had a secret crush. I knew that I wasn't supposed to feel the way I was feeling. Not only did it feel impractical, but I also still held guilt that I was betraying the feelings that I still held for my deceased husband.

I had a hard time going to sleep, since my mind kept wandering. Finally, the talking outside my tent had stopped, and the camp sounded dead quiet. Except the croaking frogs could be heard nearby. The owls also hooted in numbers, and suddenly a large pack of wolves howled from a distance over the mountain. I stirred slightly at that particular sound with some alarm; I was definitely a city girl who took little comfort in the untamed wilds of nature.

The front of my tent unexpectedly opened, and a shadowy figure crawled inside. I popped up from my blanket, immediately startled.

"'Tis only I, lass," Leif whispered, coming through the opening.

"Oh," I gasped uneasily.

"I apologize that I frightened ye," he said sincerely.

"It's okay."

"'Tis alrecht that I frightened ye?" he asked, sounding confused.

"No, I mean I'm all right," I clarified.

"Och—guid," he replied.

"Are you all right?" I asked genuinely.

"Certainly."

"Oh… good."

"I'm merely minding ye," he informed me.

"Oh," I whispered, partially relieved.

"I thought ye would be asleep by now. Are ye certain that yoo're alrecht?"

"Yeah."

"Guid, very weel… The wolves awakened ye, then?" he asked in a hushed tone.

"Yeah—they did," I whispered back, feeling a bit uncomfortable as I lied.

"Weel, thaur is nothing tae fear. They are far enough away."

"Oh, okay."

"Alrecht, then."

"So, you're on the lookout now?"

"Aye… Then Fin will take my place efter a few hours."

"Oh—you'll get some sleep then."

"Aye."

"That's good. You won't be sleepy tomorrow in that case."

"Nae."

"Good."

"So, yoo're alrecht, then?"

"Yeah," I replied, and a yawn came over me.

"Very guid," he returned, as I discerned his shadowy figure by the entrance. "Then I shall take my leave. I'll see ye in the morn, lass."

"See you in the morning," I whispered.

"Good necht," he said softly.

"Good night," I replied faintly. Leif shifted, and the flaps of the entrance opened. In an instant he disappeared behind the canvas drapes.

I finally closed my weary eyes, and soon found myself drifting to sleep.

～

THE NEXT DAY we continued past Fort Edward going south along the Hudson River. We had traveled close to twenty miles today, which made for good timing for the cavalrymen, but fatigued the marching infantry. It took us another day and a half to finally reach the outskirts of Fort George, where the men had set up camp for the evening.

It felt like I had been roving for such an endless amount of time that the days began to blur together. I no longer knew what day of the week it was, or the day's date. It was so unimaginable to think of the endurance required to achieve such hiking through the elements in this wilderness that I was beginning to lose stamina. I never before considered myself a weak person, and thought I could realistically achieve nearly anything physically challenging because of my athletic background. But this experience was proving to be an extreme undertaking of constant will and emotional and physical strength, the likes of which I had never conceived before.

From Fort George the next morning, the group separated, since Finley set out on horseback to return a marching portion of Braddock's English detachments to Albany. Leif and the others proceeded east over rugged terrain along a narrow trail toward Massachusetts.

After nearly a day and a quarter, we began traveling along a river, and I wondered about it. As we traveled the distance, I began recognizing that the trail was taking us through the Berkshires. I had assumed we were currently trekking along the historical Mohawk Trail, and a sudden flicker of excitement and hope entered my mind as the road began appearing vaguely familiar to me.

It spontaneously occurred to me that we were absolutely returning on the very same trail we had originally taken toward Albany when I had first joined my captors. This path was leading me back to the epicenter of my temporal dislocation.

I wondered if I would be able to recognize any landmarks, which might indicate to me for certain the exact area where I had disappeared. Unfortunately, there were no apparent man-made structures that I could easily identify as a unique marker. I desperately hoped that some distinctive feature in the land would look familiar to me to show me the place I needed to find.

"Is this the Hoosic River?" I curiously asked Leif, looking down at the shining water rushing below us along the trail.

"Aye," Leif confirmed easily. "Ye recall it?"

"Yeah," I replied simply.

"Och," he muttered near my ear. "We are close tae our destination once we pass Fort Hoosic."

"Oh… Why are we going to pass Fort Hoosic? I mean, wouldn't it be easier if we just camped there tonight?"

"'Tis merely a blockhouse."

"Oh."

"Hold fast, lass, if ye can. We have only one league left before we arrive at Fort Massachusetts."

"Okay," I replied. "So, where are we ultimately headed?"

"Northampton, as our military unit is on leave presently," he said simply.

"Oh," I said.

Northampton. I had no idea what to expect when I got there, or what was going to happen to me finally. A mixture of feelings came over me. A portion of me was curious to see what Northampton looked like in 1756—especially because I had attended Mount Holyoke College, which was in the next town over in South Hadley. So, I was quite familiar with the five-college area as I had remembered it. But even though I wondered what Colonial Northampton might look like, it meant that I was going to be taken far away again from West Hoosic—later known as Williamstown. And I had a strong feeling that quite possibly I would not be returning to this location in the Berkshires for some considerable time to come—with the real likelihood of never seeing it again.

I cannot let that happen, I thought. I could not allow myself to remain stranded here for an indefinite amount of time if I could help it. Forever trapped here seemed *unimaginable* to me. I felt adamant about not letting the chance for my return escape me. Although I was uncertain if I could merely return home again to the twenty-first century, I had to try and discover that for myself.

As I rode along on horseback with Leif thinking about all of this, it appeared that my desire to go back home absolutely outweighed my sudden infatuation with him, regardless of everything that had happened. I realized that even now, as early into our kindred friendship as it was, I couldn't spare him any hurt feelings. I knew that he might feel a bit disappointed—and I felt bad for that fact. I didn't want to hurt him, no matter how faint the feeling would be, because I liked him. Still, as I continued to ponder it... *What other choice do I actually have?* At least I would have disappeared early enough into our friendship that he would have not known any deep sadness or resentment.

After a while, the road began bending, and we were passing a portion along the road that I suddenly recognized! There was that weird basalt outcrop again, which looked like a huge over-sized eye. The local college kids called it "Crazy Eye," since there was some sort of eerie folklore ascribed to this location by the town's residents, claiming that if a person remained in a certain location facing what appeared to be the pupil, his or her fate would be revealed. But just beyond the outcrop on the other side laid a keyhole grove of bloodroot blossoms against the rock, where I remembered regaining consciousness after my last recollection of crashing my brother's new SUV that fateful night.

Everything in me silently screamed in utter alarm for me to

come to a grinding halt and leap off the horse toward Crazy Eye for the thicket. I was compelled beyond my instinct to throw myself off the horse and run madly back into oblivion. But just as fiercely, I was sharply constricted with paralysis as Leif's arms remained firmly around me while holding the reins. The abrupt realization that it was incumbent upon me to act prudently came over me. Aside from my injured ankle that disabled me from escaping, I also couldn't risk raising any more suspicion about myself than I already had. It was too dicey a chance for me to take without endangering my security. So, I just sat there in internal shambles, literally incapable of doing anything to rescue myself from being marooned in British America.

I silently watched the grove in bewilderment as we passed it by, and I wondered if by chance I would ever see this place again. I held on to the sight of Crazy Eye for as long as I could until it fell from view, at which point, I finally turned my eyes away to the road ahead. My heart fell like stone as it dropped to my stomach and filled me with dread. I feared the unknown, as reality had gripped me with the hard understanding that I was likely stranded here for an indefinite period of time.

I must have released an anxious sigh, because Leif subtly responded by slipping an assuring hand around my waist and holding me close.

"Are ye alrecht, lass?" he inquired quietly against my ear.

"Yeah," I replied modestly.

"It wulnae be long now. We are near the fort," he informed me mildly.

"Okay," I said softly.

Soon we passed Fort Hoosic, which was exactly as Leif had described. It was nothing but a small blockhouse and stockade outfitted with a small militia regiment. But, at last, after about fifteen minutes, we arrived at Fort Massachusetts. It was a very small log-built fort stationed four miles east of West Hoosic, between what would later become the town of North Adams.

This fort was garrisoned by the British, and appeared somewhat overcrowded with pitched tents inside and outside the stockade.

There was only one building made for troop barracks, and it seemed significantly compact with a single captain and six lieutenants. Captain Wallace relinquished his quarters to the next highest officer camped at the fort, which was currently Leif. Angus, Cole, Roy, and Derek displaced four lieutenants into different quarters while we camped there for the night. Sleeping again in close quarters with Leif had become a familiar undertaking and complicated the obvious magnetic tension between us.

Tonight, instead of talking, all I wanted to do was sleep the minute my head hit the pillow. I presumed Leif must have felt the same way, because he was already sound asleep as soon as he lay on the floor by the door, seemingly beat.

Two days later, at daybreak, Finley came galloping alone into the fort. The brothers gladly greeted each other. A couple of hours later, all of us were off again on horseback, traveling east from the Berkshires toward the Connecticut Mountains. Leif and Finley road alongside each other as they trailed behind the others at a distance. They talked casually in Scottish. I was watching the men ahead of us as they chatted and laughed with each other. They appeared pleased to be heading home, and a mild sense of relief pervaded them.

"Did he interview ye about the matter?" I heard Leif ask Finley as I tuned into their conversation again.

"Aye, a wee bit," Finley said.

"He didnae threaten tae hold ye over the matter?" Leif asked.

"Nae," Finley answered.

"Och… Are we suspect, then?" Leif inquired.

"He's uncertain," Finley said.

"Suspicious," Leif said.

"Aye."

"I see."

"I reminded him that he never arrested the lass as a prisoner and detained her as such—that he merely had her placed under watch by an incompetent guard," Finley said.

"I see," Leif said.

"Aye, weel, I also told him that he might have himself tae account fur it, as the lass could have simply fled without anyone's notion in spite of the inattentive guard posted at the door," Finley said.

"So he took that intae consideration?" Leif asked.

"Not tae his liking."

"Hmm," Leif mused.

"Aye… So, now 'tis best that ye remain undetectable fur a bit of time, lad."

"Aye."

"I reckon the matter will diminish in wee time, fur thaur are many more pressing concerns promptly at hand tae which he must attend. The trooble with the lass will be overshadowed by some measure," Finley said, gazing pointedly at me. Leif did not respond, but I noticed Finley shift his gaze back toward Leif, and I saw him give Leif a knowing glance. Then, Finley trotted his horse away from us ahead toward the others, leaving Leif and me behind alone together, traveling in silence.

Two days later, we reached the Connecticut River Valley and followed the river south. At dusk the next evening, at long last, we arrived in Northampton. It was completely rural with a handful of settlements positioned sparsely there about the land. It appeared nothing like the way I had remembered. It was absolutely an agricultural-based parish, far removed from the academic foundation that would later come to support the economy of this town in the future.

We entered the area on the north side of the community and followed a more heavily worn trail leading toward the center of town. Suddenly, the road forked, and the cousins separated with friendly farewells. Leif, Finley, and Angus veered right while the others continued straight. After approximately a half mile down the road, Angus waved a send-off, and the brothers reciprocated likewise as he began trotting down another path toward the left. Currently, with only the three of us continuing on the road, it suddenly became noticeably quiet; a sense of particular calm and ease ensued between the brothers that I had not witnessed until now.

Within five to ten minutes after separating from Angus, we began approaching an expansive pasture where several cows and calves were grazing. Just ahead across the clearing was a large whitewashed clapboard farmhouse with many lampblack shutters and a sweeping veranda. At a distance, the small figure of a woman could be detected close to the house collecting laundry from a clothesline. There were two young girls running around screaming and chasing each other near the woman. I noticed another girl, appearing somewhat older than the other two, helping the woman with the laundry.

Finley quickly dismounted as he spotted the animated figures across the clearing, and began leading his horse with some eagerness. As we gradually came closer, one of the younger girls noticed us approaching from a distance and suddenly stopped playing. She turned and darted directly toward the woman, calling her attention from her chore. The woman ceased working as the girl pointed in our direction. The woman shaded her eyes from the setting sun with a palm, and the girl dashed like a jackrabbit in a beeline heading straight toward us over the pasture.

"*Da! Da! Da!*" the girl excitedly shouted out in her little voice, and Finley gladly hastened his pace. The woman looked on, watching as the excited child ran toward Finley, and began walking forward toward us with the other two children by her side. In a minute, the anxious girl had happily reached her father, and Finley promptly scooped her little body high into the air with a full bear-hug embrace. She was the spitting image of her father in female form, with very fair, rosy skin, light-blue eyes, and a shiny copper head.

"Ahh, how is my very bonnie wee lass?" Finley said joyfully.

"Well, Da, very well!" she replied gleefully.

"Aye, indeed—I can plainly see so," Finley said warmly. "Let me have a guid look at ye." He pulled the fair little face away from his neck and into view. "Och! How yoo've grown! I dinnae believe my eyes!"

"I'm a big lass now," she informed him proudly.

"I reckon so," Finley uttered delightedly.

"Yoo're back, Da! Yoo're back!" she said happily.

"Aye. I've returned, lass," Finley affirmed. Suddenly, the little girl noticed Leif standing behind her father.

"Uncle Seamus!" she abruptly shouted with further excitement.

"Aye. Come give yer uncle a squeeze," Leif responded gladly, and the girl happily leaped into her uncle's arms with a tight hug around his neck.

I sat there on Blaze observing the three of them. I couldn't help smiling; it was so heartwarming to see them greet each other after enduring such a long and uncertain separation. I had never seen this unguarded side of Leif and Finley—particularly Finley. Not until now did they appear essentially glad to be home again. It shed new light on them—and I liked what I was seeing. They were sincerely warm and affectionate with the little girl. The girl turned a shy eye on me and gazed at me with some doubt while still propped up high in her uncle's arms.

"Who is she?" she shyly asked her uncle.

"Her name is Sylvina," Leif replied gently.

"Och," she said bashfully to Leif. She timidly glanced at me again before shifting her attention back to him. "She is very bonnie," the little girl whispered. Leif's lips tilted reservedly.

"Is she not?" Leif said quietly.

"Aye," the girl agreed, and glanced at me again.

"Hi," I gently greeted her with a delicate wave of my fingers.

"She speaks strangely," the girl noticed instantly.

"I reckon we micht soond a bit peculiar tae her as weel," Leif said.

"My name is Mairie," she introduced herself to me, appearing rosy-cheeked and bright-eyed.

"It's very nice to meet you, Mairie," I said pleasantly.

"I'm six years old," she informed me proudly.

"Oh, wow, you really *are* a big girl," I replied. Mairie suddenly turned to her uncle and secretly whispered something into his ear. Leif smiled and looked at me.

"She reckons that yoo're kind," Leif disclosed.

"Oh, thank you. That's very nice of you to say. You seem really sweet to me too," I replied, and she smiled bashfully.

"Is she a fancy lady?" Mairie inquired openly to her uncle as she noticed the necklace still draped around my neck.

"Alrecht now, lass—that'll be enough of yer cheek," Finley interrupted, transferring her from Leif's arms into his own. The men proceeded to walk again, with their horses and me in tow. "Now tell me, how are yer sisters?"

"They are well," Mairie informed him simply.

"Guid. Tell me about yer mother," Finley said lovingly.

"She made bread this morn," Mairie replied innocently.

"That is guid. Whit sort?"

"Sweet oat."

"Ah, I like it."

"You cannae have any till suppa."

"That is a long time I have tae wait."

"Aye."

"Alrecht, then." Finley chuckled lightly.

I admiringly observed the family as we approached the house, with the three of them walking together ahead of me while I sat on Blaze with my injured ankle as Leif led the horse. It was clear that the family was no doubt from a homogeneous genetic pool; they all possessed the fairest alabaster skin I'd ever seen, light-blue eyes, and rosy cheeks. Mairie resembled her father with shiny copper hair, while the other two girls had hair the color of white platinum, resembling the wispy strands of hair that had escaped his wife's capped head.

As Finley crossed over the pasture, his wife trotted delightedly toward him. They greeted each other with a tremendous embrace as the two remaining girls were not far behind. The family happily exchanged affections while Leif and I were approaching.

"Where's the bairn?" Finley inquired happily.

"She's napping unda the tree," his wife pleasantly informed him in her strong New England accent. She pointed to the oak tree nearest them supporting the clothesline.

"Ahh, let me take a peek at my new heart," Finley said, and stepped over toward the quiet Moses basket beneath the large oak tree. He carefully lifted the youngest family member named Alice, who was a month old, into his arms. He carried her, still sleeping, back over toward his wife. Finley was proudly admiring the newest addition to the family, whom he had not yet seen until now. When Leif had come close, Finley's wife greeted him with a single gentle kiss on the cheek. She then shifted a modest, wondering glance over to me.

"This is my wife, Elizabeth." Finley properly introduced his wife to me, along with the other two girls curiously looking on. His daughter Doireann was age five, and his niece Amity was nine years old. "This haur is Sylvina. She will be staying with us fur a wee while."

"How pleasant to meet you, Sylvina. Welcome to *Taigh-Bheinn*," Elizabeth greeted demurely with a reserved tilt of her head.

"Thank you. It's nice to meet you as well," I said politely.

"Well, you must be weary from your journey," she said.

"Aye," Leif said. Leif reached up around my waist, pulling me off his horse and carefully cradling me in his arms.

"Oh! You're maimed," she expressed regrettably, suddenly noticing the splint on my slightly less swollen ankle.

"Unfortunately," I responded.

"What a pity," Elizabeth responded sympathetically. "Well, please do come inside the house," she urged affably. Finley carefully transferred the sleeping baby into his wife's arms as his two daughters and niece surrounded him like a school of fish. He then turned and took a minute to hitch the horses to the nearby pasture fence before we followed him and Elizabeth inside the house.

PART III
NORTHAMPTON

Two weeks later, my ankle had nearly made a full recovery from the bad sprain incurred en route from our escape from Fort Carillon three weeks ago. *Three weeks ago...* I couldn't believe that three weeks had already passed. That meant that I had actually been missing from my normal life for at least a week prior to our expedition to the French fort and had been living here marooned for an entire *month*! What an amazing reality pill to have to swallow; I could barely rationalize this fact as I lay dumbfounded on my four-poster bed one morning listening to a robin whistling while perched on a birch tree limb just outside my bedroom window.

With a slight remaining limp to my walk, I lightly hobbled toward the window and peered out past the birch tree down below and saw the golden cornfield glowing in the morning light. Sounds from the household could be heard already, and it seemed that I had slept in a little. I glanced at the clock on the Queen Anne dresser, and it read eight fifteen. I reached for my dressing gown hanging on the bedpost and put it on over my shift before I went downstairs to the kitchen, hoping to grab a nibble to eat as I was sure that I had already missed breakfast with the family.

Like I had anticipated, no one was in the kitchen when I entered, but I spotted a basket of fresh cornbread, crumpets, and blackberry preserves in the middle of the kitchen table. So, I paced toward the rectangular oak table, sat on the bench, and proceeded to help myself to the goodies in the basket. I began spreading some soft butter and preserves on the second half of my crumpet and took a bite as Elizabeth entered the kitchen nicely attired in her best dress. But I perceived the surprised look on her face when she noticed me eating the crumpet and detected the open jar of preserves in front of me.

"Good morrow," she greeted in a modest manner.

"Good morning," I replied. "How are you?"

"Well, thank you. Did you sleep well?"

"Yes, thank you."

"I'm pleased, then."

"These are very nice crumpets you've made," I complimented pleasantly.

"Oh, deah," she said lightly with her hand placed over her mouth when Leif simultaneously entered the kitchen, also appearing very well-dressed in civilian clothes.

"Whit's the matter?" he inquired simply as his eyes shifted inquisitively between Elizabeth and me.

"The basket," Elizabeth stated with some regret.

"Aye?" Leif responded. I quickly felt like a guilty child caught with a hand in the cookie jar as I gazed innocently at them both standing in the kitchen in front of me.

"The basket was meant fah you," Elizabeth informed Leif.

"In that case, the lass is welcome tae it," Leif replied carelessly.

"Miss Constance Pringle brought it auva fah you a short while ago," Elizabeth notified him awkwardly.

"Och," he replied nonchalantly.

"They ah fresh made."

"Och… That was considerate of her." Leif put his hands in his breeches pockets, appearing slightly uneasy as he shifted his stance to one side.

"Aye, she learnt of your return some days prior," Elizabeth informed him.

"Did she?"

"Aye, of course she did."

"Och," Leif said simply.

"I am so sorry. I didn't know," I abruptly apologized, realizing my honest mistake.

"Nae matter, Sylvie, go on and enjoy as many as ye like. It makes nae difference tae me," Leif insisted. I thought I detected a little pink emerge on his clean-shaven face as he gazed at me while I was not properly dressed.

"It's okay, I can get something else to eat," I said guiltily.

"Nae. Ye may have it yerself," he said.

"Are you sure?"

"Certainly."

"Oh—okay… Thank you," I replied sincerely. Leif simply nodded his head once in accordance. Elizabeth didn't say anything else about the basket or Miss Constance Pringle, but instead gave Leif a certain glance—which got me thinking a little bit. "Well, you both look very nice this morning. Are you going somewhere?" I inquired unskillfully, trying to ameliorate the discomfiture in the air.

"'Tis Sunday," Elizabeth said.

"Is it?" I replied unknowingly.

"Aye, the day of worship," she reminded me.

"Oh, right, yes, of course—silly me," I said ridiculously. She slightly furrowed her brow and was looking at me with an uncertain expression.

"Please, won't you hasten lest we are tardy?" she requested modestly.

"Oh," I replied unexpectedly. "But I —"

"Dinnae concern yerself with a guid frock, lass. Elizabeth has one awaiting ye," Leif interrupted reassuringly.

"Oh. She does?" I asked, a little surprised.

"Aye," he replied easily.

"Oh." I shifted my gaze to Elizabeth.

"Aye, 'tis a simple frock of mine, and it will do," Elizabeth said.

"Oh, okay. That's very nice of you, thank you," I replied. I was a little caught off guard, not realizing that going to church was expected of me. But how could I say no? My ankle was nearly completely healed, and I could carefully walk around. So, I felt obligated and did not see any way out of it without creating offense. "Okay. If you wouldn't mind giving me a moment to properly prepare, I can be ready soon."

"Indeed," Elizabeth replied, satisfied. I glanced at Leif as I got up from the kitchen table, and he subtly looked at me with some encouragement.

AFTER I SPENT several minutes washing up using the washbasin, Elizabeth entered my room to help me dress in a simple but pretty Naples-yellow silk taffeta gown and straw hat adorned with matching ribbons.

Within fifteen minutes, I was properly dressed and ready to attend church with the family. Everyone was dressed in their Sunday best and appeared crisp and sober. The girls were rosy-cheeked, pink-lipped, and were all dressed in pretty little white calico gowns with pink silk ribbons adorning their bonnets. They looked like pure little images out of a Reynolds painting. Elizabeth appeared fine but modest in her simple viridian-green silk frock, matching green bonnet, and cardinal cape, with her Bible in hand as she held her baby. She was walking closely next to Finley, who was strictly attired in a tricorn hat, black coat, burgundy waistcoat, and black breeches as we proceeded to walk from the farm toward the center of town.

I was used to seeing Leif attired in his military uniform, which was quite impressive and enhanced his rugged good looks. But it wasn't until we had arrived here that he began to wear simple breeches and a linen shirt that made him look more regular and comfortable. Today he appeared particularly nice—freshly shaven with his thick, straight golden hair neatly tied back into a queue with a black silk ribbon, dressed like his brother in a black coat. Unlike Finley, the color of his waistcoat was a rich sienna silk that complimented his black breeches, black coat, and nicely shined black buckle shoes. He was noticeably very handsome as the brilliant sun illuminated his black tricorn hat and square shoulders as we walked along, taking a shortcut through the property toward the main road into the village.

I felt Leif glancing down at me as we strolled behind the others. I peered up at him around the brim of my hat, and he warmly grinned at me. I gently smiled back at him and then demurely returned my gaze to the attractive foliage surrounding us.

"Yoo're bonnie," he expressed confidentially to me. I glanced up at him again, unable to help my shy smile. His teeth gleamed beneath the shade of his hat. I shifted my eyes away from him and gazed at Doireann skipping toward us to hold her uncle's hand as we walked. Instead, Leif gladly swept her high up into his arms and carried her along the way. It seemed he really did enjoy his little nieces; he was playful, sweet, and genuine with them, and had no reservations about showing his admiration and affection for them. At that moment, with Doireann happily perched in her uncle's arms, the thought occurred to me that one day he would make a really good father.

Luckily for me as I walked slowly and steadily with the aid of my cane, the trek to church, which laid on the outskirts of town, was not that far of a walk and had only taken us about fifteen minutes to arrive. As the whitewashed clapboard church began emerging from the trees at the end of the road, many members of the congregation had begun flocking up the stone steps inside the building. Although the town had strong Puritan roots, a small but robust portion of the town's people appeared to belong to this parish called St. Paul's Anglican Church. I had not realized that Northampton also had Anglican roots until now, as I later learned that the surrounding towns of Deerfield and Hadley were principally Quaker, Presbyterian, and Methodist congregations. The Quakers, Anglicans, and Congregationalists were in the minority compared to their evangelical Presbyterian and Methodist counterparts. However, most of Northampton's seven-hundred-member population belonged to the First Congregationalist Church in the heart of town.

As I later discovered, this particular First Congregationalist Church had experienced its own event of religious awakening revivalism through the Reverend Jonathan Edwards, which apparently had resulted in creating a stir of controversy among the split parishioners. The controversy had certainly made a stir throughout town. It caused large concern over the influence it might have had across town regarding St. Paul's Anglican parish.

This bit of information made me uncertain as to what to expect exactly. I was unfamiliar with an Anglican service and was curious to know what it was going to be like. I had gathered that it might be something like the procedures in a Catholic Mass. But I had to say that I was somewhat surprised when I discovered that the men and women were separated on either side of the aisle in the church, with the women and children placed on one side of the church in the pews and the men seated on the other side.

As we filed into the church, Elizabeth and I along with the children were guided by the usher into one of the pews. Leif and Finley trailed in after us and seated themselves askew across the aisle several seats behind us. Although the church was somewhat spacious, it was evident that the church would quickly fill with worshippers, with them ultimately spilling up into the gallery.

I silently glanced around my surroundings, curious about this place and its members. Inside was simple with plain glass windows and no familiar paintings or ornate adorations of images of Christ, His Apostles, the Holy Family, the Stations of the Cross, or any of the Saints. Except there was a single solid gold cross that stood erect on the altar over a limestone platform.

After everyone had collected indoors, the doors closed and the congregation quieted as Reverend Lock stolidly entered the pulpit. He was gray-haired, clean-shaven, gaunt with paper thin lips and round, deep-set blue eyes, and appeared as white as a ghost, contrasting with his black vestments. He stood erect, straitlaced, meticulous, and seemed to be a man without a sense of humor. Within a second after taking his place in the pulpit, Reverend Lock's voice promptly bellowed forth as he greeted his parishioners. Before he started the formal service, he primly began with a sincere welcome back to those members of the community who had returned from battle, and individually acknowledged them as he called their names.

After Reverend Lock welcomed back the last man, he turned his formal attention on me and also welcomed me into the congregation, in conjunction with expressing condolences regarding the death of my husband and the perils that I must have endured as a result. I sat there a little too aware of myself as all the unfamiliar stares shifted to me for a minute.

I silently noted how quickly news of my widowhood had traveled, and was surprised.

Reverend Lock then proceeded into the religious service. He began reading a selected passage from the Old Testament—about overcoming the Devil and evil. When he was through with the reading, he began preaching about evil, temptation and its adversities, and everything that will occur to a damned soul. It was quite a fire-and-brimstone lecture, but without the expected animated emotion customary of other Protestant religions. Reverend Lock's sermon delivery was rather unanimated, and I found it considerably dull. Furthermore, this service did not conclude in just forty-five minutes like I had been used to at my own St. Monica Church back home led by Father Hanley. Instead, Reverend Lock led a three-hour sermon that was typical in this day and age.

I was finding it a bit of a challenge to stay attentive to Reverend Lock's sermon because he was not inspiring, and my mind began to wander. I noticed that a few of the men had begun dozing. An usher came around with a stick. He prodded the sleeping men hard against the knee, and the men suddenly awakened from their snooze.

I had the distinct feeling that someone was intently watching me, and I faintly peered over my shoulder. My eyes immediately locked with Leif's as he had been staring in my direction. His lips slanted upward clandestinely. Before I could respond similarly, I noticed several other young men had also turned their quiet eyes toward me, and without reciprocating, I returned my gaze toward Reverend Lock in front still in the pulpit.

After a long while, when church was finally over, I felt like a relieved kid just let out of school, ready to scream and freely romp outside.

In customary fashion, Reverend Lock greeted his exiting parishioners at the front of the church, where they gladly flocked and loitered around the church grounds greeting each other. A reminder had been announced by the reverend upon concluding his service that the Porters were hosting a congregation dinner in honor of the returned soldiers. So, it seemed this was going to be our next event for the day, and soon the worshipping crowd had begun dispersing from the church property.

CHAPTER 23

The Porter family's property did not lie too far away from church. They were apparently a well-established family and pillars of the community, having found their early fortune in the pelt trade and recently in milling paper. Mr. William Porter had built his paper mill along a tributary off the Connecticut River between Northampton and Deerfield, which had won him instant success. Porter House, as it had been recognized by the community, was a fairly sizable house constructed in New England style with burnt-sienna clapboard and small lampblack shutters on all the windows. It had a number of rooms and was quaintly decorated with the latest style from Boston. According to Elizabeth, as she kindly sat with me by the window in the back of the fairly spacious and quaintly decorated, rich Naples-yellow distempered drawing room, the Porters had originally descended from the Mayflower through Mrs. Remember Eaton—a member of Mr. Porter's mother's branch of the family.

Mr. and Mrs. Porter originally had nine children between them, but had lost four of them in birth and illness. As Elizabeth informed me, I thought the symptoms sounded like influenza and scarlet fever, an infection caused by the strep bacteria and a highly contagious pathogen that would have been easily treated with antibiotics in my time. Of the Porters' surviving children, there were three girls and two boys: George was twenty-nine, Ann was twenty-five, William was twenty-three, Tilly was seventeen, and Alice was thirteen.

I had noticed as I gazed around the room filled with conversing guests that the girls were the only young Porters in attendance, and had learned that the sons were killed a year ago in an ambush by the Huron upon their garrison serving under Captain Ephraim Williams. This unfortunate event had severely harmed gray-haired Mrs. Anne Porter's spirits; it had landed her in a sour state of repressed anger, and with a severe resentment toward the Indians and French. Ever since, she had dressed in black and also had never been seen without her Bible in hand, in addition to the tight, wrinkled, somber expression that had settled over her grim face.

Elizabeth politely continued informing me about other members of the community attending the gathering and had kindly introduced me to her older sister, Suzanna, whom I had not yet met until now. She pleasantly joined us in our conversation and seemed slightly earnest for being only twenty-six years old. But so had most of the women here, who were already married with a number of children and a household to look after, I noticed.

Suzanna, a mother of two young boys, had a very pleasant disposition with very good manners. She seemed congenial and appeared to have a nice relationship with her younger sister, Elizabeth. Elizabeth herself was only twenty-four with a small litter of children to mind already in her early life. Also, as I had briefly calculated, Elizabeth must have been married at a very young age and given birth to her first child, Mairie, at the age of eighteen.

I sat there between the sisters, feeling very much out of my element even though they were very polite to me. It wasn't necessarily because of them in particular, but rather because I was displaced from my home, where customs and social norms were not nearly as confined as they were here in the eighteenth century—particularly here in Colonial America.

"I'm awfully sorry to learn about the tragic loss of your husband," Suzanna mentioned regretfully in her typical Massachusetts accent.

"Thank you," I replied soberly.

"What a frightful thing to be widowed. I don't know what I would do in such a case," Elizabeth said. "I would be quite uncertain living here alone without my husband."

"'Tis very dangerous living in the frontia. Why, about forty yeeahs ago, the whole of Deerfield was terrorized by raiding Abenaki," Suzanna said.

"What do you mean the whole town?" I inquired.

"'Tis what I said—the entire town was slaughtered and kidnapped by an Abenaki raid. They all came down the riva and surprised the town in the dead of night, terrorizing all out of sleep—burnt the whole town to a *crisp*!" Suzanna explained frightfully.

"Are you serious?" I replied with surprise.

"Oh, entirely!" Elizabeth said with wide blue eyes. "Not even women and children were spared death and being scalped!"

"Oh my goodness!" I gasped, utterly astounded. The sisters exchanged glances.

"Indeed! Fah, not even Heaven spared the community," Suzanna whispered carefully after a quick, prudent glance around.

"My goodness, that's so horrible!" I said.

"Oh, indeed! To have such a dreadful fate is unimaginable," Elizabeth lamented with a hand over her heart as she rocked her infant daughter.

"But a few young women were spared their lives, and were taken by Abenaki as slaves," Suzanna said dreadfully.

"Others suffered a worse fate and were sacrificed," Elizabeth added.

"Never heard tell of again," Suzanna interjected sadly.

"Is that right?" I replied.

"Indeed." Suzanna demurely nodded her head.

"That's wild," I said.

"A precise way to express it," Elizabeth said. It was incomprehensible to think that an entire town could be obliterated and stolen, no matter what era in time. The thought sent shivers down my spine.

"Has anything ever happened here?" I inquired curiously.

"Not since Governor Shirley had the fort built," Suzanna informed me with some relief.

"I see," I said. Baby Alice was having a bit of a difficult time settling quietly in her mother's arms, until Elizabeth discovered the source of the baby's discomfort was due to a soiled diaper. Elizabeth courteously excused herself to tend to the baby and left her sister and me alone sitting next to each other. Suzanna proceeded to inform me of the attending guests around the room.

First, Suzanna introduced me to her husband, Master Edward Mead, who had located his wife among the guests across the room. He had kindly delivered to us both a nice petite cup of sweet lemon water. Master Mead appeared to be fairly congenial, although quite sober, which could be ascribed to many of the New England population during this time. He stood slightly above average at a height of roughly five feet eleven and was noticeably slim with prominent rosy cheekbones. His hair was dark brown with eyes to match that were set deep in his head, and a pronounced nose that protruded well off the front of his face. His cheeks were sunken, and his chin was prominently square with a visible cleft carved right in the middle.

Master Mead's family owned and operated the local timber mill on the outskirts of town that was managed by his eight slightly thicker built adult brothers and their father. Master Edward Mead's role in the business was bookkeeper, and he seemed appropriately suited for the accounting position with the little round spectacles that rested precisely on his face. He retreated after presenting the two petite porcelain cups of lemon water to us and rejoined a couple of his brothers, who were engaged in a discussion with several other farmers. Subsequently, Suzanna continued telling me about the guests.

I coincidentally glanced at the threshold and recognized Leif staring at me from across the room with his hands casually tucked in his pockets as he leaned against the doorframe. His eyes warmly brightened with an accompanying grin when our eyes met. I automatically responded as my own lips gently tilted. He started forth from the doorway, appearing to come toward us, when a pretty young girl unexpectedly intercepted him, catching his attention before he'd merely crossed the room halfway. She was beautifully platinum blonde with bone straight hair that was properly tucked into a nice bun at the nape of her alabaster neck. The rest of her pretty head remained covered by a fine white linen cap and petite straw hat, with two stylized ringlet curls that dangled on each side of her pure-looking face. Her blue eyes, rose-petal-pink tinted cheeks, and thin lips contrasted perfectly against her extremely fair skin. Her demeanor was prim and genteel as she spoke with Leif. She appeared to have asked him something during the course of their genial exchange, and I thought I detected a bit of rouge seeping into Leif's cordial expression.

"That there is Miss Constance Pringle," Suzanna informed me as she noticed the direction of my glance.

"Oh," I said simply.

"Her family owns the milliner and tailor shops," Suzanna stated casually.

"Oh." I couldn't help noticing how comfortable Miss Pringle and Leif appeared to be with each other as they continued their discussion. "They seem to know each other well," I remarked indifferently.

"Aye, they are respectably acquainted with one another," Suzanna said.

"She seems nice," I said.

"She's a Pringle," Suzanna noted.

"What does that mean?" I asked curiously, as I detected a faintly ironic tone in Suzanna's voice.

"Why, of course she's pleasant, and she knows it. She's the fairest one in all of Northampton, with her two younger sisters following suit. Sarah and Mary are their names. They are over there by the harpsichord," Suzanna explained to me as she slightly indicated where the girls were in the room.

"I see." I spotted the two girls seated together, giggling by the harpsichord in the corner of the room across the way. They each appeared to be no more than fourteen to sixteen years old, with Sarah seeming a tad older than Mary.

"How old is Constance?" I inquired, curiously turning my gaze back to Suzanna.

"She's eighteen yeeahs of age—old enough to wed," Suzanna said.

"Oh," I replied. While observing Constance and Leif, Suzanna gently leaned closer toward me as if to reveal a secret.

"Constance fancies His Grace quite well, and has set ha sights upon him," Suzanna disclosed quietly.

"Is that right?" I replied with surprise.

"Oh, indeed. She's been fond of him for some time—and now that she's some years past sixteen, she wishes fah him to look upon ha with favah," Suzanna revealed.

"Oh," I replied.

"Indeed."

"Would you happen to know what his opinion is of her?" I inquired tactfully. Suzanna faintly shrugged her shoulders, appearing to consider the question.

"I cannot precisely say. But I'm certain that he must find ha pretty at least, as all the other lads do. He has been kind to ha, I know."

"Oh, I see."

"He assisted ha in the event of ha chaise having fatefully broken an axel upon the muddied road one rainy afternoon."

"Oh, that was nice of him to help her."

"Indeed." Suzanna grinned speculatively at me. "However, many of the lasses here favah him."

"They do?" I glanced back at Suzanna.

"Certainly. Do you not have any eyes?" Suzanna giggled demurely at me and gently nudged her shoulder against mine, giving me a knowing look. I unexpectedly felt my face grow warm. "Ahh, then you are not blind after all," she joked modestly.

"No—well, I just—I don't know." I thoughtlessly broke off, shrugging my shoulders a bit, trying to appear indifferent. But Suzanna just sat there by my side, smiling doubtfully at me.

"Forgive me. I do not wish to be rude to you," she said.

"No, you aren't—it's okay," I replied.

"Well, His Grace is of no consequence to me, fah I'm already wed. But all the lasses here greatly fancy him, and 'tis no secret why. His status suits his princely looks. Do you not believe so?"

"Well, I don't know," I replied reluctantly, and she lifted her eyebrows with an obvious expression.

"Is that what you say?" She giggled suspiciously. "Yet presently, a matter has been presented, and some would not be so fond of it."

"What matter?" I asked, puzzled.

"Why, you, of course—silly goose," she replied obviously.

"I don't understand. What does anything have to do with me?"

"The lasses will not like you," Suzanna said openly.

"Why?" I asked innocently.

"Your new presence has created a bit of a stir here in town, and the lasses do not appreciate a new rival," Suzanna explained.

"I don't perceive myself being a rival to anybody," I said honestly.

"Begging your pardon, Sylvina, but I do beg to diffa," she replied candidly. "Only beware, my deah, lasses may become quite envious of you—which may place you in a predicament. I shall doubt that you will find any friends amongst them," Suzanna warned, appearing quite honest.

"But I haven't done anything to anyone to warrant their dislike of me," I replied innocently.

"On the contrary, and I shall tell you why. It is because you have already captured His Grace's attention from them," she said candidly.

"Oh—I see. But it's all very innocent. There's nothing I want from him," I replied sincerely.

"It makes no difference, innocent or not. It leads to the same end, and lasses of courting age are prompt to discover these particular concerns."

"Oh." I wasn't sure how to interpret this straightforward information as I turned my gaze back to Leif, still conversing politely with Constance. Another girl named Emily, who was distinctively red-haired and seemed no more than twenty years old, had joined Constance and Leif in their discussion. Then a third brown-haired girl named Luisa, who also appeared to be within the same age range, joined their discussion. There Leif stood talking, now presently surrounded by three very young, wholesomely pretty girls demurely giggling as they batted their bashful eyelashes at him while fanning themselves in the midst of their conversation.

"Do you understand my meaning?" Suzanna hinted as she faintly gestured in Leif's direction. I didn't reply except to simply gaze at Leif and his surrounding company.

It was true what Suzanna said—Leif appeared popular with the girls. I didn't look anything like those girls or any of the other women in this town, for that matter. Everyone I had seen so far did not reflect my personal or ethnic background, and so I knew I stuck out like a sore thumb with my appearance. Because of the difference, I was aware of the many continuous stares I received nearly everywhere I went, which created for me a sense of uncomfortable self-consciousness that I wasn't used to, and at times made me feel quite uncertain. Sometimes I felt more like a freak or misfit rather than an attractive woman, which Suzanna claimed me to be.

In any case, I decided to take things as they came with a grain of salt and not to seriously ponder what she had said as I glanced away from Leif and his encircling admirers. Suzanna continued to point out more of the guests to me, like Master Rhodes, who appeared to be in his early thirties. He was tall and skinny and was the unwed schoolmaster originally from Hartford, Connecticut, currently seeking a wife. Similarly, Master Welles, the town crier and notary who appeared near forty, was a widower with two young boys of his own, and was also seeking a new wife.

Master Tuddle, who was stout and round, was the town's grocer and ran the business with his widowed mother. There was also Master White and his brother, also seeking wives. Then there was old Mistress Butterworth, who prided herself in the personal stake she had taken in the moral upkeep of the village, but who somehow knew everyone's personal business and was, according to Suzanna, quite meddlesome.

"And over there," Suzanna continued. She directed my attention with a glance toward the opposite side of the room at a young man standing near the window speaking with two other gentlemen.

"Who's he?" I asked casually.

"That there is Master Thomas Vinton, who has been gazing in our direction from the moment he entered the chamber," she politely informed me.

"Oh."

"He has not yet taken his eyes off of you since," she noted distinctly.

"Oh." I unevenly glanced away from Mr. Vinton when my eyes met his steady gaze.

"Master Vinton has three older brothers, George, Johnathan, and Richard, who are there, there, and there," she discreetly pointed out as they stood in different locations around the room.

"I see," I said simply.

"They are all wed save him and his younger brother, Ethan. Ethan is very good and kind, but lacks wit," Suzanna revealed unfortunately.

"Oh," I replied. "Is Ethan here too?"

"Aye, he's sitting beside little cousin Lottie on the bench at the window."

"Oh." Ethan appeared to be in his mid-twenties, and as I saw him sitting there contentedly with his young adolescent cousin Lottie, I noticed how gentle and innocent he appeared.

"Oh deah!" Suzanna said suddenly.

"What is it?"

"Master Thomas Vinton appears to be approaching this way."

"Really?" I shifted my gaze from Suzanna, and sure enough, Mr. Vinton was walking right toward us. He seemed somewhat tall in stature as Suzanna and I remained seated. Observing his appearance, I thought he looked to be close to thirty years old. With his dark chestnut-brown hair neatly tied back, clear complexion, well-proportioned facial features, and hazel eyes, he was agreeably handsome. He respectfully greeted Suzanna before turning an inquisitive gaze on me. He genteelly introduced himself to me as he properly took my hand in his. Instead of shaking my hand, which was my custom, he merely tilted his head in respectable accordance and lightly squeezed my hand.

"A pleasure to make your acquaintance, Mistress Arboles," Mr. Vinton greeted politely.

"Yours as well, Mr. Vinton," I replied.

"May I take the pleasure of your company?" he inquired graciously.

"Oh, yes, of course," I replied politely, gesturing to the empty chair to my left.

"Thank you kindly," he replied, also grinning a tad. He sat easily in the Shaker chair beside me.

"Well, I ought to discover where Elizabeth has vanished to. I mustn't leave ha alone and desperate with all the children to mind," Suzanna abruptly stated.

"Pardon?" I suddenly turned an awkward gaze to Suzanna as she started getting up from her seat.

"Elizabeth has not yet returned. I shall seek ha," Suzanna said.

"Oh," I replied.

"I'm certain you and Master Vinton will become nicely acquainted," she said demurely as she slipped me a quiet, knowing glance before turning away and proceeding out of the room.

At first, sitting with Mr. Vinton was turning out to be quite an awkward experience, since neither one of us had anything common to say to each other. I could sense his slight uneasiness, which in turn was making me feel somewhat self-conscious. It was obvious that he wished to talk, except all he could muster was an attempted glance in my direction. I caught his inquisitive eyes along with the diffident grin on his lips. Finally, I decided after a constrained moment to assist the conversation.

"So, Mr. Vinton, how are you today?" I asked. Mr. Vinton quickly shifted his eyes onto me from the socializing crowd.

"Oh, quite well, thank you. Yourself, Mistress Arboles?" he replied.

"Very well also, thank you," I answered politely.

"Splendid." He smiled uneasily with clear hazel eyes.

"Nice weather, isn't it?" Obviously, if I could have asked him about sports, I would have. But this conversation was beginning to feel like pulling teeth.

"Aye, splendid weather. Nice Sunday for church," he said.

"Yes, it is," I replied easily.

"The reverend gave a rather inspiring sermon, do you not believe?"

"It was interesting," I said.

"Indeed. I pray that you may find all of the reverend's sermons as inspiring every Sunday."

"Oh—yes," I replied.

"Reverend Lock has been with us for quite some time now," Mr. Vinton informed me pleasantly.

"Is that right?"

"Indeed—currently, for nearly ten years. He has done us all a good service here in Northampton, and we shall miss him when he retires," Mr. Vinton mentioned casually.

"He's planning to retire?" I asked simply.

"In a yeeah," he answered.

"Oh, I see. I suppose in that case, he will be greatly missed by the community."

"Aye."

"Who will be taking his place, then?"

"It is to be a Reverend Grinder who is to take his place, and we have not yet met. He will arrive some time next summer from London to become acquainted with our parish."

"Oh, I see. So, where will Reverend Lock go?"

"He will return to Scotland, from where he was born."

"Oh, I see."

"Indeed."

"Well, that will be nice for him to see his family again," I said.

"It will," he agreed genially. Mr. Vinton seemed like a nice young fellow, and although charmed with good looks, he seemed to be on the predictable and uneventful side. He continued talking about church for some time and how much he had enjoyed the relevance of Reverend Lock's sermon. He explained the legitimacy and importance of religion in a responsible and charitable society, which seemed to be a fair and reasonable opinion that I agreed with, and continued to express the importance of redemption for eternal salvation only offered through Christ. I respectfully thought I was back in church all over again listening to another oration, except Mr. Vinton's passion, I was able to see, was quite colorful like an evangelical.

Subsequently, he spoke of his family and how they fell into the profitable business of mercantilism three generations ago, beginning with his great grandfather who had traded in goods from Europe in Boston. It was his grandfather, Henry Vinton, who migrated west to Springfield, leaving his parents, brothers, and sisters behind to survey land for the government. As a result, the government had agreed to allot him a portion of Springfield land for his service.

Mr. Vinton further explained that his own father, Nathaniel, in a sense had mimicked his father's adventurism and pursued his stake in the northern Connecticut River Valley, which had placed him here in Northampton. It was here where the Vinton family had established their second mercantile shop with further success as it was indeed the only shop of its kind in town.

As I was listening to Mr. Vinton gladly explain more about himself, I happened to notice Leif pacing out of the room with Constance's hand gently linked around his arm. My eyes discreetly followed them as they glided toward the door leading out into the garden. As my gaze followed them out of the room, I noticed Mr. Hardy standing with a piece of minced meat cobbler in hand by a window near the threshold chuckling with another man. Mr. Hardy suddenly erupted into coughing when he began choking on a piece of his food. Within a second, some commotion had stirred as his face became beet red. It was immediately evident that he was unable to breathe, and he gripped his throat in a fit of fright and panic. The man next to him frantically scanned the room as troubled gasps were heard around their location.

"Quickly!" shouted Mr. Lawndale, Mr. Hardy's previously chuckling friend. "Someone fetch Dr. Kendall promptly. At once! At once!"

"What is it?" one of the women remaining nearby inquired excitedly.

"Master Hardy is having a fit! He is caught without breath!" Mr. Lawndale informed her.

"Heavens!" another onlooking woman gasped in fright.

"Archie!" screamed Mrs. Hardy as she hastened toward her stifling husband. His eyes were bulging from their sockets.

"What is the matter?" a middle-aged man who was rushing through the gathering in the room inquired urgently, appearing quite purposeful as he moved straight for the commotion.

"Right here, Dr. Kendall," Mr. Lawndale eagerly said, directing the doctor toward Mr. Hardy.

"It's Archie! Oh, dear heavens! Please help him! Don't let him be taken from me!" Mrs. Hardy cried in a complete frenzy. The conversation between Mr. Vinton and me abruptly dropped as the alarming distraction had seized our attention. Dr. Kendall attempted to help Mr. Hardy's choking by proceeding to slap a firm hand against his back as if he were banging on a door in a panic. However, the doctor's attempt with Mr. Hardy seemed unsuccessful. I looked on with concern, which quickly turned into horror as Mr. Hardy was on the verge of collapse.

"Wait!" I gasped with no ounce of decorum, and immediately bobbed up from my chair, giving Mr. Vinton my empty lemonade cup. I hurriedly moved through the crowd toward Mr. Hardy. Suddenly, a number of unexpected stares shot my way as I bullishly pushed my way among the guests toward the urgent situation. Apparently, it quickly appeared that I had gotten everyone's attention in the room, as expressions of surprise and shock had landed primely upon me due to my unanticipated outlandish intrusion.

"If you don't mind," I said urgently as I summarily pushed Dr. Kendall out of the way.

"I dare say!" he protested.

"What is the meaning of this, Mistress Arboles?" Mr. Lawndale retorted as he watched me reach around Mr. Hardy's girth from behind.

"Aye, I dare say! Mistress Arboles, what *do* you mean?" Dr. Kendall asked.

"I'm saving his life," I replied as I clasped my hands to form a reinforced fist and searched for the place right beneath the diaphragm just under the ribs.

"Step away and let Dr. Kendall do what he must for this man's life!" Mr. Kent insisted anxiously.

"No, I'm afraid I can't. With all due respect, Dr. Kendall, slapping him on the back won't help," I said assertively. I heard several people gasp as peculiar stares remained on me. Ignoring surrounding objections, I jerked my fists hard and fast against Mr. Hardy's upper stomach.

"With all respect that is due to *you*, Mistress Arboles, I am *quite* skilled at my profession," Dr. Kendall said disagreeably. "Now, if you will allow me, before this poor soul retires into the full graces of our Lord as we speak, I intend to preserve my dear friend Master Hardy's life!"

I disregarded what the doctor was saying and jerked my fist again against Mr. Hardy's diaphragm. There was no sign of the obstruction coming forth, so I quickly did the motion again as appalling stares remained on me. Again, there was no positive result. I repeated the motion with all my might and discovered that I was working a lot harder than I had anticipated. Aside from the fact that I had never needed to perform the Heimlich maneuver until now, Mr. Hardy wasn't the slightest of men. He was quite dense and wide, which made it a challenge for me to have first located the proper position to perform the maneuver. It was also quite difficult for me to keep my hands together in each attempt I made to force his chubby body to push out the obstruction from his esophagus. Furthermore, to gather enough strength each time to thrust my fists into his stomach cavity, I quickly felt myself beginning to perspire with every vigorous push I made to save this man's life.

Then, all of a sudden, the obstruction abruptly dislodged and made a sudden appearance from Mr. Hardy's mouth. The food went airborne and unexpectedly hit Mr. Lawndale square in the eye before the bit of obstructing meat bounced off into his ale mug where it finally landed.

"Good heavens!" Mr. Lawndale exclaimed shockingly.

"Indeed!" Mr. Mead echoed with surprise, staring down at the unexpected specimen floating in Mr. Lawndale's mug.

"Mercy me!" Mrs. Hardy gasped, utterly stunned over the conclusion. Her eyes rolled back in her head, and her stout frame went limp on the nearby Queen Anne sofa.

"Oh, Mistress Hardy!" Mrs. Butterworth expressed excitedly with apparent worry when she saw Mrs. Hardy unconsciously stretched out on the nearby sofa. Dr. Kendall stared categorically stunned at me for a moment, then promptly turned his attention to Mrs. Hardy passed out on the sofa.

"Are you all right?" I asked Mr. Hardy with concern as he began straightening himself from his hunched position. He was entirely red-faced as he gazed shockingly at me for a moment, still coughing and wheezing while striving to collect his composure.

"Aye… I believe that I am…" he replied, breathing heavily.

"Good," I replied with relief.

"Thank you," Mr. Hardy panted, still rubbing his chubby neck.

"It's all right," I responded easily, patting him a couple of times on the shoulder. "You should probably remember not to talk and eat at the same time, and to chew your food well before swallowing. You don't want to scare anybody again, I'm sure."

"I should say not—quite right, Mistress Arboles," Mr. Hardy

agreed, appearing to grow calm as he continued to gaze at me with raw disbelief and relief.

"Please be careful," I replied professionally as I proceeded to neatly straighten my skirts. The spectators encircling us reflected blatant expressions of outlandish shock as I pushed my ringlets back from my face.

Dr. Kendall used smelling salts to rouse Mrs. Hardy from unconsciousness. I assumed that the doctor could handle Mrs. Hardy without injury in this case, and I excused myself from the gathering. I felt many curious eyes following me out of the room as I crossed the threshold and vanished from the drawing room.

I found my way out into the vegetable and floral gardens. I strolled around until I had rounded the side of the house and spotted the road out front that would lead me back to my new residence. I decided to start walking toward the road. I thought it was just as well for me to return to Finley's property at *Taigh-Bheinn*.

As I headed toward the path, taking in the beautiful view of the surrounding oak trees, I happened to spot Leif and Constance walking quietly alone among the trees at a distance. He had his hands comfortably enfolded behind his back as he paced leisurely beside her. He appeared to be enjoying her company, and she also seemed to be enjoying her walk with him. I curiously slowed my pace as I gazed at them for a moment. I began to feel a bit odd about seeing him with her—disappointed actually... and a tinge jealous.

I averted my eyes back to the path and hastened on my way, limping slightly with my cane. As I moved over the path, I was suddenly in the midst of debating with myself... How on earth, first of all, could I let myself be jealous? It was a ridiculous idea. Obviously, Leif had a life here in this village before he and I ever met. So, of course he might have had some history with Constance—or with anyone else, for that matter. How could I have not recognized that fact?

Furthermore, he and I had only been acquainted for such a short amount of time—about a month or so, I supposed. So, we were by no means an exclusive couple. We hardly knew each other. It was a little stupid of me to have slightly hoped. He was free to live his life, and I was out of place for allowing myself to begin holding any ounce of expectation regarding him. I truly had no right to come between him and Constance; I supposed she was only picking up from where both of them had left off before he went to battle.

Except *why the hell did I let him kiss me?* And why did I kiss him back? *Ugh!* I wrestled back and forth between logic and my irrational feelings. I had finally concluded that in the grander scheme of things, the kiss was no big dilemma. I actually was no stranger to sharing a nice, inconsequential kiss with someone I had gone out with on a date before I got married. Therefore, I supposed I had to be fair to Leif about it, and not hold him to any expectations. The timing of the kiss was simply opportune, nothing more, nothing less. People have been known to behave thoughtlessly while high on emotions under desperate conditions anyway.

So, I decided that I was just going to stay out of it, and not get involved. Yes—that's what I had made up my mind to do. I was done with it. I didn't want any trouble, and I actually was not open to succumbing to my attraction to him anyway. The last thing I needed was to allow myself to become grievously hurt all over again—no way.

Most of all, I felt guilty. I wanted nothing more than to honor the memory of my late husband. The thought of betraying Matt's memory was as good as betraying him if he were alive, and that was something I would have an extremely difficult time coping with.

"Bide fur me, *àille dhubh*! I'll escort ye!" Leif suddenly called out from behind me.

"Oh my goodness! Where the hell did you come from?" I gasped, completely taken aback and arrested in my tracks. His eyes widened, appearing shocked over my choice words as he caught up with me.

"I merely cut through the wood," he answered, now standing tall directly beside me. I glanced up at him as he was now slowly walking with me. "I beg yer pardon, lass. I didnae intend tae frighten ye," he apologized.

"It's okay," I said.

"Ye accept my apology, then?" he asked.

"Yeah, of course," I agreed easily.

"Thank ye," he said genuinely.

"No worries," I responded. A slight grin came over his face, brightening his expression as I sensed his thinking. "What is it?" I inquired curiously. He shook his head a little.

"Only, I huvnae heard of that expression till now," he observed.

"Oh," I replied simply as I smiled at him a little. He grinned back at me, and I glanced away from him back at the road.

"Why did ye depart from the gathering?" he asked inquisitively. I shrugged a bit.

"I'm sorry. I didn't mean to seem rude. I was just getting a little tired," I answered truthfully. I turned my gaze up at him and met his ultramarine eyes.

"I see," he responded thoughtfully. "Is it yer foot bothering ye again?"

"No, it's okay. So long as I don't overexert it."

"Och. Weel, if ye had grown weary, ye should have sought me. I would have gladly left with ye," he explained.

"Oh," I responded, slightly surprised. "But you seemed preoccupied, and I didn't want to disturb you. So I guessed that I could just leave on my own."

"With whom was I preoccupied?" Leif asked, seeming puzzled.

"With Constance," I reminded him.

"Och," he said. "Weel, even so—ye could have come fur me. I would have obliged ye." He appeared certain as he gazed down at me.

"Oh."

"So, in future, if ye need me—dinnae hesitate tae ask me," he said surely.

"Okay," I replied, seeing the sincerity in his expression. Leif then turned his gaze ahead on the road. I glanced away also and kept my eyes ahead.

"I understand that thaur was a bit of ruckus in the drawing chamber," he began again. "I heard that Master Hardy choked on food."

"Oh, yeah," I replied.

"And that he would have certainly perished if it waur not fur ye." I sensed Leif looking at me again. I glanced back up at him and met his crystal blue gaze.

"Well, I'm glad that I could do what I could to help."

"Aye, nae doubt Master Hardy is indebted tae ye," Leif said. "I heard that ye had performed some sort of movement upon him that caused the food tae be expelled."

"Yeah," I replied. Leif nodded thoughtfully, appearing impressed.

"How did ye ken whit tae do in such an occurrence?" he asked inquisitively.

"Well, I told you that I am a physician," I reminded him.

"A physician?" he responded with a slightly surprised expression. "A physic?"

"Yeah."

"I reckon that ye claimed tae be a pediatrician, if I correctly recall." He looked quizzically at me, and I wasn't sure what he found slightly amusing.

"I am a pediatrician. I just happen to be a physician who specializes in children's medicine," I specified.

"Och, aye," he responded with a thinking gaze. I noticed the faint quizzical smirk lingering on his face. "Ye must have had a fine tutor."

"Yeah," I responded simply, nodding my head a tad.

"Humph," he lightly grunted as he maintained a musing eye on me. I glanced away from him, returning my gaze to the path. I momentarily sensed his gaze shift to the road also, and we continued walking together as our conversation lapsed into silence. We passed along a little creek until we finally crossed over a small foot bridge connecting the path on which we were walking and leading us out of the woods, ultimately returning us onto the road that directed us back to the farm. The house could be seen off in the distance. I winced a little and suddenly ceased walking. The pain in my ankle began to emerge again.

"Whit is it?" Leif asked, noticing me. "Is it yer ankle?"

"Yeah, it's starting to ache a little," I informed him.

"Och, I reckon I must carry ye now," he suggested. Before I could respond, in a single motion, he swooped me up high in his robust arms and proceeded to carry me the rest of the way to the house.

"Thanks for helping me," I said politely.

"Aye, of coorse," he said.

In about five minutes, we had reached the steps to the veranda. Leif went through the front door and entered the sitting room. He leaned down and carefully placed me on the wool damask Queen Anne sofa.

"Thaur," he said satisfactorily.

"Thank you," I replied gratefully.

"Och, aye. I reckon ye best remain off yer foot fur the time being."

"Yes, I think so too."

"Aye." He nodded a little. He sort of lingered for a moment, seeming to hesitate. "Shall I keep ye company?" he offered finally.

"If you want to. I don't mind," I said.

"Ye dinnae?"

"Yeah. But it seemed like you were really enjoying yourself at the gathering."

"Aye."

"Don't you want to go back and finish enjoying yourself? I mean, I'm not going anywhere. I'll be here when you get back," I said honestly. He lightly rubbed his square chin and the side of his masculine cheek.

"Nae. I ken that yoo're not able tae go far," he replied.

"So, I'm all right. You can go if you want to," I said. Leif seemed to stall some more as he remained standing before me.

"I would raither keep ye company," he said finally.

"What about Constance? Won't she miss you?"

"Aye, weel, I reckon that I shall see her anither time."

"Oh, okay."

"So, I would raither be haur with ye, if ye dinnae mind."

"Sure," I agreed.

"Guid," he said. He lightly scratched his head as he awkwardly glanced around the room. "Shall I read tae ye?" he asked.

"Sure, that would be nice," I said.

"Alrecht," he said. "I have *As You Like It* with me. Do ye like Shakespeare?"

"Actually, I do."

"Guid, then permit me tae fetch it." He swiftly left the room. After about a minute, he promptly returned with a leather-bound book in hand. He then sat in the chair across from me and opened the book to the first page. "Do ye enjoy comedies?" he asked before starting.

"Yes, I love comedies," I said.

"That is guid. I'm partial tae comedies as weel," he said enthusiastically. Then, he started to read, and I was interested in hearing the story. His baritone voice was soothing and animated at the same time, and I enjoyed listening to him read.

After a while, I grew sleepy, and I closed my eyes as I listened to the sound of his relaxing reading voice.

The next thing I remembered was being carried in his muscular arms up the staircase toward my bedroom. He entered my room and gently placed me on the quilt. My head sank comfortably into the pillows.

"Thank you, Leif," I muttered sleepily.

"Aye. Yoo're welcome, lass," he replied softly. I closed my eyes, and I felt his large hand carefully cup the side of my face as his thumb gently traced the arch of my brow. His warm hand lightly slipped from my cheek. Then, I heard the pine floor planks creak beneath his feet as he moved across the room, and quietly closed the door. The room fell silent, and I drifted back into slumber.

It rained through the night well into the next day, pouring down amid lightning and thunder. I had awakened to the sound of howling wind as the tree branches raked against the windowpanes. The temperature outside had started to cool in recent days. Except the leaves had not yet turned into brilliant colors. I sensed that fall would soon be underway, and my ankle had finally healed as good as new.

My room had grown cool overnight, and for me to leave my warm covers this morning was a challenge. All I wanted to do was stay cozy in bed for the whole morning, but my stomach was gurgling with hunger. The rest of the household was awake and stirring downstairs, so I felt that I had to be up and about too. Plus, the delicious aroma of freshly baked bread had also encouraged me to dress and join the family.

When I arrived in the kitchen, everyone had just begun seating themselves at the long wooden elm table. Elizabeth placed a fresh pile of bread rolls in the middle of the table beside the porridge and molasses. A round of apple cider served at breakfast had been filled in everyone's mugs. Mealtimes were generally a nice time. Everyone was relaxed, and the conversations were typically lighthearted and fun once the blessing over the meal had been said.

Finley was telling the girls a story at the table about a Scottish chieftain, which had everyone's attention except Amity's, who merely sat quietly in silence at the table. I listened partially to the story as I looked at Amity sitting across from me. I was more interested in her condition. Amity was deaf. She fondly reminded me of one of my best friends, Stephanie, from high school, who was also deaf. She was born that way, and I had learned how to use American Sign Language as a teenager so that I could communicate with her. I wondered how Amity had become deaf, whether she had merely been born with an auditory defect, or had she been badly impacted with a fever or a fall? I was curious. She had a sweet face full of freckles, platinum-blonde hair, bright blue eyes, alabaster skin, and a shy, docile, obedient disposition about her. She gazed up from her oat porridge and noticed me looking at her. I smiled kindly at her, and she bashfully returned her gaze to her bowl before she took a little sip of apple cider from her cup.

I shifted my glance over to Finley, seated at the head of the table opposite from Elizabeth and me, and discovered Leif gazing at me from the end of the table near his brother. I smiled timidly, and his lips curled a bit with a pleasant look in his eyes. He then turned his grinning gaze toward his little nieces, who were capti-vated by their father's story. It was during this time that I had learned that Leif and Finley were half siblings who shared the same mother, but had different fathers. Finley's father had died from influenza before Leif's father married their mother.

"Aye, now," Finley was saying as I began listening again, "thaur came one day when the laird came upon a fairy wood whaur he discovered a most bonnie maiden."

"How did she appear, Da?" Mairie inquired, mesmerized.

"Quite like Lady Sylvina, I reckon," Doireann suspected. Finley stammered, and the room went momentarily silent as he and his wife exchanged uncertain glances across the table. Leif's expression turned pink as his brother's eyes bounced toward him.

"Was she bonnie like that?" Mairie asked curiously.

"I reckon so," Finley said diffidently. "Let's get on with the tale, shall we? Now then, the laird fell whole heartily in loove with the maiden and pleaded her tae be his wife... The fairy maiden at last agreed on a single condition—"

"That he release her from mortal life," Mairie interrupted enthusiastically.

"Ahh, at the end of twenty years, mind ye. Thus, they lived happily in the great castle fur splendid years... Thereafter, one day as the two stood together on the bridge near the castle, MacLeod's lady reminded him of his promise, fur the day had come that she would return tae her fairyland. Yet the laird dearly loov'd his lady and grieved over the notion of her abandonment... He then strove fiercely tae hold her back. However, her fairyland beckoned in her ears, and it was far more powerful than the loove she bore fur her laird... She escaped his embrace and ran intae the forest before he could follow... Thereafter, she was never seen again. MacLeod was left forlorn with a mere piece of her cape clutched in his hand," Finley finished wondrously.

"That would be the magic Fairy Flag," Mairie said, enthralled.

"Aye, the magic Fairy Flag of Dunvegan," Finley said.

"Is it real, Da, have you seen it?" Doireann asked inquisitively.

"Och, aye, I've seen it. On occasions when I was a laddie," Finley said convincingly.

"Well, how does it appear?" Mairie asked, and Finley proceeded to describe it.

"That's a nice story," I said pleasantly to Elizabeth.

"Aye," she replied agreeably as she took a sip of her cider. "'Tis true, apparently."

"Excuse me?" I asked curiously.

"Aye. Fin never deceives us," she said with certainty.

"I see," I replied, silently doubtful that fairies existed. Then again, if someone had told me that quantum leaping was a fact, I would have laughed in that person's face. I caught Amity's glance again and smiled. I turned toward Elizabeth and asked politely, "Has Amity ever been able to hear?"

"I'm afraid not since she was two yeeahs of age," Elizabeth said as she broke off a piece of bread lightly coated with strawberry preserves and put it between her lips.

"Oh, so she wasn't born with a defect," I said.

"Nay. She was quite well—up and about like the rest of the children," Elizabeth informed me.

"Did she fall and hit her head or something?" I asked.

"Nay, 'twas a feva. The feva took my brother, Henry, and his wife, Sarah, and their three children. Amity was the youngest of the bairns. It was God's grace that restored ha life to us. We took ha in, and she's one of ours now," Elizabeth explained.

"I'm so sorry to hear about your loss," I said sympathetically. "What kind of fever was it?"

"'Twas grippe," she said.

"Oh, the flu," I said, nodding my head.

"Is that what you call it?"

"Yes, influenza."

"I see."

"So, she must have come down with an intense ear infection compounded by the flu," I conjectured.

"I see," Elizabeth replied with an incomprehensible look on her face.

"You see, sometimes nasal congestion from a cold or the flu can back up deep inside the ear. If the congestion is unable to drain, and instead becomes trapped, then it causes bacteria to grow, which festers, causing pain and pressure in the ear," I proceeded to explain to her. "Once the congestion is gone, but has not been resolved inside the ear, then it's that remaining blockage that ultimately causes the hearing loss."

"I see," Elizabeth responded. The conversation at the other end of the table had ceased as Finley and Leif had evidently been listening to my discussion with Elizabeth.

"You know, I was wondering—that is, if you wouldn't mind. I could teach Amity how to communicate with you, so that you can know what she's thinking, and vice versa," I ventured to offer.

"How do you mean?" Elizabeth inquired curiously with a confused expression.

"Well, I understand that you are teaching your girls to write their names and to read the Bible. If you knew that there was a way to grant Amity that same opportunity, wouldn't you allow her to learn what the girls are learning?" I inquired politely. Finley gave his wife a skeptical look.

"Well, aye, of course," Elizabeth said uncertainly.

"Well, there is a way to teach her," I said.

"How?" Finley interjected, appearing blatantly doubtful.

"There's a language that can be used. I would use my hands to teach her," I said.

"I've heard of the Indians using such ways," Elizabeth said unsurely.

"Certainly not! She'll have naught tae do with the Indian ways! Is that understood?" Finley said resolutely.

"But you misunderstand me. It has nothing to do with the Indians. It's completely different," I rebutted carefully.

"Is that reit?" Finley replied dubiously.

"Yes," I replied. "I mean, at least if you allowed her to learn it, she would have the opportunity to communicate with you and you with her. She could learn how to read and write."

"Weel…" Leif endeavored to say, "the lass does have some reason thaur, brother." Finley silently swung his gaze back toward Leif.

"Aye, my lord. What is to become of our poor Amity? Mayhap she might have a husband one day if she could express herself well," Elizabeth said delicately. Finley glanced back at his wife without saying a word. Then, his stern eyes shifted toward me again. He didn't respond, but appeared to be thinking.

"Very weel, teach the lass how tae properly communicate," Finley said finally. Elizabeth gazed contentedly at her husband as he returned his gaze to hers.

"My lady." He acknowledged Elizabeth with a slight nod.

"My lord," she returned modestly. Finley excused himself from the table. He got up from his seat, then left the kitchen. Leif also excused himself from our company and followed his brother out of the kitchen.

Subsequently, Elizabeth properly excused her children from the table and gave them some chores to mind. She explained to me, before we parted for the morning, that she would send Amity to me once the table had been cleared and the child had completed her needlework.

I DECIDED to tuck myself inside the sitting room for a while out of everyone's way as I waited for Amity to complete her tasks. I gazed at the library of books inserted into a built-in bookcase in the wall and lightly skimmed the volumes.

There were a lot of Greek and Latin prose, from Plato to Marcus Aurelius. I found Shakespeare, of course, and King James I. Also, Francis Bacon, Jonathan Swift, and Alexander Pope were among the library collection. My eyes landed on a series of folded newspapers tucked at the end of one of the shelves titled *The New-England Courant*. But what caught my eye was the pamphlet next to it. The printed name "Benjamin Franklin" pressed in bold colonial style lettering was on the front of the booklet, and I suddenly pulled it from the shelf. It was dated

1747, and I knew I was looking at an original publication of this article written by one of our country's founding fathers. I was stunned and impressed!

I began thumbing through the pages and tried to focus on reading some of the paragraphs, but my excitement made it too hard for me to read a line. In this pamphlet, young Franklin had written something to do with bettering military preparedness in Pennsylvania. I flipped through several more pages until a political illustration caught my eye. Footsteps could be heard coming down the corridor then, so I closed the booklet and hastily shoved it back into its rightful place on the bookshelf. I spun around and saw Leif entering the room. He was holding his pipe and tobacco box.

"Oh, hi!" I said animatedly. I swiftly swept my loose ringlets away from my cheeks, tucking them around my ears when I observed him drawing the double doors closed, leaving us alone in the room together.

"Hullo," he replied cordially. "So haur ye are."

"Yes," I said. "Were you looking for me?"

"Aye, in truth," he said.

"Oh," I responded with an inquisitive look as I sat on the sofa.

"I merely seek yer company," he said.

"Oh."

"Do ye mind?"

"No, sure," I replied pleasantly. He gently grinned at me and sat down comfortably in the green damask upholstered chair across from me. I clasped my hands properly over my lap as he pulled out his pipe and set the tobacco box on the small tea stand close to him. It was momentarily quiet as I watched him begin filling his pipe with fresh tobacco.

"You know, that habit really isn't good for you," I said thoughtfully.

"Is it not?" Leif asked lightly.

"No. It's not," I said as I observed him tilt the reed between his fingers toward the flame in the lantern and light it.

"Och, but it gives me comfort," he replied indifferently. He brought the flaming reed over his pipe and dipped it inside as he began to suck until his pipe steadily burned.

"It's still not good for you," I reiterated. He puffed out billowing smoke and quickly waved the flaming reed, putting it out.

"Whit brought ye tae that opinion?" he asked.

"It's not an opinion," I replied simply.

"Is it not?"

"No. I read about it in a medical journal."

"Is that reit?" he responded curiously. "And whit did ye read in the journal?"

"That smoking causes cancer," I informed him.

"Cancer?" he echoed uncertainly.

"Um, carcinoma," I said, remembering the likely term used for the times.

"Och, is that reit?" Leif replied with surprise on his face.

"That's what I read. It can occur over a period of time," I said.

"So, yoo're telling me that if I smoke fur the time being that I may be afflicted with carcinoma?" He gazed at me with some astonishment.

"It can happen over a period of a lifetime—if you continue to smoke, I mean," I informed him.

"Och. Weel, in that case, whit am I tae do? I reckon a little at a time wulnea cause any harm," he reasoned as he easily puffed on his pipe. I didn't respond, because I disagreed. I dropped my gaze from him as my fingers played with my wedding ring. "Ye did guid busy work yesterday, *àille dhubh*," he commented, referring to my having assisted Elizabeth with preparing preserves for the winter.

"Thank you. I didn't mind, actually," I replied.

"Ye waur of assistance, and that is guid," he said plainly. The smoke he exhaled billowed faintly upward toward the ceiling like translucent swirling strings. "The family will harvest squash soon."

"Oh," I said attentively. "So, is the yield meant for commerce?"

"Fin will sell it tae the military fur provisions," Leif informed me.

"Oh, I see..."

"So, ye are tae tutor Amity."

"Yeah, it should be nice."

"'Tis charitable of ye tae try tae help the lass," he said.

"Well, I could see that it would benefit her if she learned how to communicate."

"Indeed." Leif's attention drifted momentarily as he puffed on his pipe. I sensed that he was contemplating as he maintained a steady gaze on me. I turned my eyes from him, very much aware of his intense stare, and glanced out the window at a squirrel skipping up a nearby elm tree. "So," he began again, calling my attention back to him, "how will ye tutor Amity with your hands?"

"I intend to teach her sign language," I said.

"Sign language," he repeated interestedly.

"Yeah," I replied, nodding a little.

"So, whit do ye mean?" he asked simply.

"Well, I'll start by teaching her the alphabet."

"Och, how will ye proceed?"

"Well, I'll sign what the letters are—like, this is the letter *A*," I said as I held up my palm and carefully signed the alphabet letter with my fingers. "And this is the letter *B*," I continued slowly.

"Och, allow me tae try it," he said interestedly, and held up a palm. He attentively followed me signing the alphabet until we got to the letter *M*, where he had slight difficulty placing his three fingers over his thumb.

"Not exactly," I said gently as I noticed the wrong position of his fingers. I started from my seat across from him and approached his raised hand. I knelt before him and carefully slipped my hands over his large palm to correct the sign. "It's more like this," I said as I adjusted his large fingers. "There, that's it," I muttered as the sign for the letter had been corrected. I raised my gaze to his, and our eyes met. I noticed his concentrated stare, and the red hue seeping over his face.

"I see," he said faintly as he realized the correction. He released his fingers from the sign and lightly seized my hand with his. He pulled the pipe from his lips and placed it on the nearby stand without releasing his gaze from mine. I felt his palm steal up my sleeve and rest gently on my cheek. I didn't respond, since I was slightly caught off guard, and simply gazed back at him. His thumb moved deliberately over my lips, slightly parting them, and began tracing the outline. He leaned in close, and I could feel the heated flow of his smoky breath caress my lips. My temperature began to rise, and my rational thoughts escaped me.

"What's going on?" I whispered unevenly as I began to feel distinctly uncertain.

"Is yer meaning that ye wish tae ken whit is occurring?" he asked meaningfully.

"Yes," I uttered under my breath.

"Weel, I reckon that I wish tae kiss ye," he said softly. I sensed him, just as I had sensed him before when we shared the cave alone together.

"Well, I—" I hesitated.

"Whit is it?" he asked gently.

"I'm not sure about this," I muttered.

"Yoo're not?" Leif whispered carefully.

"No."

"Weel, nae need tae be concerned, fur I'm certain of it."

"You are?"

"Aye. I've been longing tae hold ye—and tae kiss ye again."

"Really?"

"Aye."

"Oh. Well, I—" He slowly leaned forward, and I felt his warm lips gently come over mine. His lips were noticeably warm and tender as he began carefully kissing me. My feelings were rising again. I couldn't trust myself with him. I was frightened and excited by it at the same time. I felt his hands beginning to roam deliberately over my shoulders until the tips of his heated fingers were buried among my loose ringlets. My dangling pink tourmaline and diamond earrings lightly rolled between his carefully examining fingers. His tender lips trailed to the side of my cheek down toward my neck, and my breathing became more heavy and unsteady. The more I desired to control my reaction to his touch, the more my blood began to stir, and I was futilely aware that I was being defeated. I was falling for him for sure.

I wrapped my arms around his broad shoulders, embracing him. He pulled me gently firm against him, and we were entwined. I buried my face in his neck as we embraced. I sensed his kissing lips over my neck as his desirous palms roamed along my back. His skin was warm, and I could smell the mixture of pipe smoke, dust, and salt on his skin. The odor was strangely arousing instead of averting. I snuggled my face further into his neck and drank in his scent as I kissed him back. I wanted to hold on to him for as long as I could, so I anchored my arms around his neck. He pulled me tighter into his chest, and I swear that I could feel his heart pounding against my breast.

Suddenly, a knocking on the door was heard, and we were abruptly interrupted. I instantly broke off our embrace and sprang to my feet. I hastily straightened my skirts and lightly brushed my palms over my face, checking my appearance, while stepping away from him. Leif swiftly stood as I went back to my original place on the sofa across from him. He glanced at me as he anxiously sputtered out, "Come!"

One of the double doors opened, and Amity shyly stepped over the threshold with Elizabeth. She meekly glimpsed at me, then at her uncle.

"Och, Elizabeth! Hullo," Leif greeted unevenly.

"Hallo, Seamus," Elizabeth replied politely. "I have brought Amity to see Sylvina for her lesson."

"Och, aye, of coorse," Leif said enthusiastically. "Amity, come haur, lassie." He stepped across the room toward her and kindly fetched her little hand in his. She glanced up at her aunt, uncertain, and Elizabeth gave her an instructional nod that also conveyed reassurance. Leif then turned with Amity and brought the little girl toward me. "It seems yer pupil has arrived."

"Yes, it does," I said, slightly winded.

"Weel…" Leif glanced down at Amity, and she turned her bright blue gaze up toward him. He smiled and lightly tapped the end of her nose with a gentle forefinger. She smiled a little, then Leif returned his gaze to me. "I shall leave ye both alone, then."

"All right," I replied.

"As shall I. Let's hope fah some measure of success," Elizabeth said.

"I think we'll do just that," I replied hopefully.

"Very well, then," Elizabeth said.

Leif released Amity's hand and gave us both a kind smile before turning with Elizabeth toward the threshold out of the room.

"Och!" he said, turning to me as he suddenly remembered something. "I am headed tae the village shortly. Did ye make the list of the items ye wish tae have?"

"Oh, yes! I'm glad you reminded me," I said breathlessly as I remembered the folded parchment in my pocket. I reached into my skirts and retrieved the small parchment. I glided toward him and gave it to him. He received it with a gentle grin and slight wink at me.

"Alrecht, then. I'll be off," he said.

"Thanks," I replied gratefully.

"Aye," he replied. He then turned and left the room with Elizabeth.

Now that Amity and I were left alone together, I closed the door, wondering how I was going to meet the challenge of teaching her. Where to begin?

In high school, after meeting my best friend, Stephanie, I volunteered my extracurricular time by working for a school for the junior deaf where I had originally learned American Sign Language. However, that was many years ago, and I had not practiced my signing since then. So, I knew that I was going to be a bit rusty at teaching it, but I hoped that I hadn't forgotten too much.

Amity remained standing for a moment longer after Leif disappeared from the room. I gently took her hand and smiled, wondering where to begin the lesson. I glanced around the room, thinking the best thing to do was to keep things simple for now. I led her over to the writing desk and placed her just in front of it. I had her watch my palm as I placed it on top of the desk and made the sign for "table" with both my hands. She only gazed uncomprehendingly at me. I clearly repeated the same action again with no response from her. I attempted it a third time, and still she gave me the same expressionless response. We tried the same method using several other objects in the room to no avail. After almost an hour of my uncertain attempts to form some kind of connection with Amity, I was beginning to realize the true extent of our work in spite of her apparent ability to have some level of communication with her family.

Making sure that she was watching me, I moved over toward the chair behind the writing desk and pulled it out into plain view. I then made the sign for "chair" using both my hands for her to see, and I noticed her brow scarcely furrow. Again, I distinctly repeated my action, and her grimace became more apparent. During the third attempt, I proceeded to take her hand and placed it for her over the seat of the chair. I demonstrated the sign with her own two hands. Her alert blue eyes bounced from me to her hands in confusion. Next, I took the quill from the stand on the table and held it up to her eyes before returning it. I then proceeded to make the sign for "feather." Suddenly, a shift in her gaze took place. She stared intensely at me. I could see something beginning to register in her expression. I gathered her hands into mine and demonstrated the "feather" sign again with her own hands. When I released her hands, she suddenly took it upon herself to mimic my motion.

"Yes!" I said excitedly, as I visibly nodded my head, very pleased. She vigorously slapped the table a couple times, demanding that I show her the sign for it again. As I did so, she copied me. Suddenly, it was as if a light bulb had been switched on in a place that had always been dark. The awakening had begun. It was remarkable to observe the abrupt intensity of her awareness run wildly across her face when she began to realize that everything actually had a name. I was startled by it, and glad too. I realized at that moment that it was as I had suspected before—she was, in fact, a bright child locked in a prison of silence. I sensed that she would be a quick study. Our lessons henceforth would go accordingly, I believed, and I was happy to see how eager she was to proceed.

Her thirst for knowledge was insatiable, which was going to force me to be on top of my instruction. It was going to be relentless and exciting work, for which I was up to the task. So, during the next two hours, our first lesson consisted of naming and recalling everything that was in the room.

CHAPTER 25

It continued to rain early the next morning. As I peered out of my uneven glass window, it seemed the clouds had grown thin in the distance, letting in bits of golden sunlight that bathed the land in brightness over the rolling blue mountains against the surrounding partly cloudy sky. It seemed the rain might soon break. I unlatched the window and propped it open for a better view. A burst of cold air coolly encased me as it entered the room. The landscape appeared beautifully majestic, a scene that might have been captured on canvas by the artist Thomas Cole.

After a second of admiring the beautiful scenery, the cold air notwithstanding, I shut the window, preserving the remaining heat in my room. I proceeded to dress myself, always cursing the stays and the rest of the undergarments I had to wear beneath my gown, which completed my dress. Once I had finished, I went downstairs for breakfast, which continued to not include the bacon and scrambled eggs I was used to, and for which I couldn't help longing in my moments of homesickness.

As we were all enjoying our breakfast, Leif discreetly kept glancing down the table in my direction as he and Finley were engaged in light discussion. I tried to ignore his eyes on me when I offered to take the fussing infant from Elizabeth as she tried to eat her meal. She gladly handed me the baby, and I started trying to quiet the infant. Within a minute, the baby had settled, soothingly cradled in my arms. I gently rocked and delicately stroked her plump, tiny face while Elizabeth was finally able to enjoy her breakfast porridge.

I sensed Leif's lingering eyes on me again, and I hesitantly glanced his way. Our eyes met, and his lips pleasantly curled with warm satisfaction, brightening his twinkling glance. Then, he returned his gaze toward the bowl from which he was eating. *I long tae kiss ye*, he'd said to me yesterday in the sitting room. My mind continuously recalled his voice as he said those words to me. His words had possessed my mind. I went to sleep last night with his words circling in my head. And now that I had confirmed my weakness for him, things between us were certainly bound to escalate. I knew for sure that I wasn't going to be able to handle the growing affection between us, and what naturally would transpire as a result. I needed to talk to him. I had to tell him that it was no good and that we must stop acting on our affections while we still had the chance.

Amity disrupted my abstracted thoughts as she caught everyone's attention by pounding on the table with her palm. She was calling for my attention, and when she saw that she had it, she made the sign for "more" and "cup."

"Whit is it?" Finley said, unexpectedly concerned.

"Okay," I signed to Amity, answering her before turning to tell Finley, "She wishes to have more milk." Everyone at the table was staring at Amity in shock. I spotted the pitcher at the other end of the table close to Leif and Finley as everyone remained stunned. "Would you mind passing the pitcher, please?" I asked of either brother—whichever one was in closest reach.

"Aye," Finley replied, duly surprised. He gathered the pitcher and slightly lunged passing it over the table toward me.

"Thank you," I said politely as I took the pitcher.

"Aye," Finley replied.

I poured Amity a bit more milk from the container. When I set it back down on the table, Amity signed, "Thank you."

"You're welcome," I signed. She brought her cup up to her small lips and sipped a little as everyone watched in awestruck silence. When she had had enough to drink, she set her cup back on the table in front of herself and began buttering a piece of bread.

"Is she content?" Finley inquired after a suspended moment.

"Yes, she's fine," I reassured. Finley merely nodded once in acknowledgment, and everyone remained incredulously staring in silence for a second longer.

"It appears that you have made some progress with Amity," Elizabeth said.

"Yes. She's an intelligent little girl. She learns quickly," I said.

"Well… we are certainly impressed with your tutorial talents, Sylvina, and we are deeply indebted to you," Elizabeth said.

"Well, thank you. It's a pleasure for me to teach Amity," I replied sincerely.

"We are most grateful," Elizabeth repeated cordially. I smiled at her. As I took my cup of water, I noticed Leif gazing kindly at me again. I reciprocated a faint but natural grin as I brought the ridge of my cup to my lips and sipped.

"Uncle?" Doireann began.

"Aye?" Leif answered, turning his attention toward his little niece.

"Do you suppose that you will wed Sylvina?" Doireann inquired innocently. Leif suddenly coughed, choking on the swig of cider he had just taken.

"I reckon that he might," little Mairie presumed. Leif's face went red as he tried to settle his coughing. I quite felt like I had the same reaction as my heart arrested for a split second.

"Oh, Mairie!" Elizabeth exclaimed nervously.

"But I rather like Sylvina," Doireann said.

"And we should be pleased if Uncle Seamus weds her, as she is bonnie and nice," Mairie added confidently.

"Children!" Elizabeth further exclaimed, appearing utterly mortified.

"Alrecht, lasses, that will be enough," Finley ordered in a tone only a father could take.

"It is not a proper discussion, do you understand?" Elizabeth continued reproachfully. The girls nodded bashfully together, saying, "Aye, Mother."

"Very well," Elizabeth said, then turned to me and apologized.

"It's okay," I assured her. I briefly glanced at Leif. He grinned unevenly, appearing embarrassed, and shifted his eyes down to his finger idly tracing the ridge of his mug. Finley glanced at his brother, and the two looked at each other discreetly for a slight second during the uncomfortable moment.

Then, Finley instructed the girls to complete their meal. When they had finished, he excused them from the table. At that time Elizabeth proceeded on to her daily routine of attending to the children and their morning chores before they had their Bible study. Once the brothers had finished eating, they left us in the kitchen to take care of our own tasks. As I was left with the infant still in my arms, I proceeded to lull the baby to sleep while Elizabeth worked nearby in the kitchen.

Once the baby had successfully drifted to sleep, I carefully placed her in her little cradle in the corner of the room not far from Elizabeth and left her to finish tending to her duties. I decided to seek out Leif to see if we could talk because I wanted to break off our budding affection for each other. Earlier while I was tending to the baby, I had begun thinking and gathered up some resolve to have a talk with him. So, when I had finished assisting Elizabeth, I left the kitchen, hoping to obtain a private moment with him.

I had peeked into a couple of rooms without locating him. As

I came around through the hallway, I could hear voices coming from the sitting room. I peeped through the crack between the doors and discovered Leif and Finley talking with each other in Scottish. It sounded like they were in the midst of a serious discussion. So, I turned away from the doors, deciding to walk back through the corridor, hoping to catch him another time in private.

SUNLIGHT HAD BROKEN through the clouds and was shining brightly through the windows. The rain had stopped, and I stepped out onto the back veranda. The air was cool and crisp. I sensed the season was on the verge of changing for certain, and I thought about home again. I wondered about what my brother and sister-in-law were doing at this very moment in time in the future. I also thought about my parents. I hoped that they were all right, even though I was sure they were worried sick about me. I thought about how my brother's nephews might be doing in school, along with their Little League and hockey games. Their lives were vastly different than these colonial girls' lives. My brother's nephews were very fortunate to have been born in softer times far off in the distant postmodern future.

I had been missing for almost two months now, and I just wanted everyone in my family to be well... because I did not know when I would ever return to see them again.

My vision became blurry. I wiped the teardrops from my eyes and noticed Amity and Mairie hanging damp laundry high up on the laundry line to dry in the sun. I went down the veranda steps toward the girls and offered my assistance, much to their surprise. There were abundant loads to hang out to dry. So, I surely didn't mind helping.

While I was in the middle of tossing a white sheet over the line, Elizabeth had come from the house, approaching me.

"I hope you don't mind," I said uncertainly as she noticed me helping the girls.

"I shall thank you fah your kindness," she said.

"It's okay," I replied affably. She demurely nodded her head in acknowledgment.

"But the Hardys have come fah a visit," Elizabeth informed me hastily.

"Oh," I replied simply.

"They request to see you," she said.

"They do?" I asked, a little puzzled.

"Aye," she responded. Her eyes quickly scanned over me, I supposed scrutinizing my appearance. "You must promptly receive them."

"Sure," I said, as I released the sheet I had just hung over the line.

"Come along," she said quickly. She started away, and I followed her back toward the house. As we walked across the veranda and entered the back of the house into the kitchen, she abruptly turned, facing me.

"You must wear your cap," she insisted.

"Oh, sure," I said mindlessly. I don't know why, but I frequently forgot to put my cap over my hair. I had just kept it tucked away out of sight and out of mind inside my pocket. I retrieved it from my skirts and placed it over my head. Elizabeth briefly eyed my appearance, examining it.

"I suppose that will do," she said with an uncertain look, regarding my loosely tucked hair. She proceeded to lead me through the hallway. We entered the drawing room, where Mr. and Mrs. Hardy were properly and comfortably seated along with a young man in their company who I had not yet met. Elizabeth gently intimated with her hand and said, "Here is Mistress Arboles," as we came forth.

"Mistress Arboles, how nice it is to see you again," Mrs. Hardy said pleasantly. Elizabeth began seating herself in a chair across from her guests.

"Mistress Arboles, indeed quite nice to see you," Mr. Hardy said genteelly, as he and the young man with them properly stood up from their seats.

"Yes, it is nice to see you both as well, Mr. and Mrs. Hardy," I said pleasantly. I sat down on the sofa near Elizabeth across from Mrs. Hardy. "How are you feeling, Mr. Hardy?"

"Indeed, very well, thank you, Mistress Arboles," Mr. Hardy said contentedly as he and the young man returned to sitting in their seats.

"That's very good. I'm glad to hear it," I replied as I sat properly before them.

"This is our son, Samuel," Mr. Hardy proudly introduced. He was a ruddy fellow with burnt-sienna hair and blue eyes, who appeared to be in his early twenties.

"Mistress Arboles," the young man greeted politely. "It is a pleasure to make your acquaintance."

"Thank you. Yours as well," I replied.

"Thank you fah your effort in preserving my father's life. It was most admirable and brave of you. We are indeed most grateful to you," young Samuel said in the same strong New England accent.

"Aye, most certainly grateful to you, Mistress Arboles," Mrs. Hardy said.

"Really, you don't need to thank me. I'm just really glad I was there to help," I replied honestly.

"Well, we cannot express our immense gratitude enough, and we wanted to pay you with our thanks," Mrs. Hardy said graciously. She passed over to Elizabeth a large basket of something baked and hidden beneath a white cotton cloth.

"Thank you," I said pleasantly as Elizabeth kindly received the basket.

"'Tis my maple nut bread, which I have made fah you," Mrs. Hardy said.

"'Tis most exquisite," Mr. Hardy added.

"Oh, how very nice. You didn't have to go to the trouble," I said graciously.

"'Twas no trouble at all. 'Tis the least we could do, fah we are forever in your debt," Mrs. Hardy insisted.

"Well, thank you, it's very thoughtful," I replied appreciatively.

"Mayhap I shall serve tea, and we may all enjoy the maple bread," Elizabeth courteously offered.

"Why, that would be lovely, deah," Mrs. Hardy agreed cordially.

"Very well, please excuse me. I'll prepare the tea," Elizabeth said.

"Indeed," Mr. Hardy said. Elizabeth stood from her chair, taking the basket in hand, and retreated from the room. Presently left alone with the Hardys, an awkward moment of silence ensued, and we simply sat there facing each other without a word except for a few friendly grins that were exchanged.

"Mayhap you may wish to know that our Samuel is a law apprentice," Mrs. Hardy began amiably.

"Oh, is that right?" I replied.

"Indeed," Mrs. Hardy said. I shifted my gaze over to young Samuel.

"So, where do you apprentice, Mr. Hardy?" I asked politely. He lightly cleared his throat and appeared rather stiff and erect while seated in his chair. He wasn't particularly tall, but instead was thin and slightly long-legged.

"Please, you may call me Samuel as all of our close friends here do," he insisted politely.

"All right, if you'd like," I replied kindly.

"I do," he said, and nodded genteelly. He had a noticeably serious disposition about him that far exceeded his youth. He appeared solemn and honest. I wondered if he had a sense of humor… Perhaps not, I gathered—or at least not one that I would have easily recognized as being "funny." But then again, he might have a dry wit, I considered. Although people with dry wits generally seemed to be of above average intelligence, they also tended to be strange in nature. In any case, he seemed to be a very decent, straitlaced sort of fellow, and I found him respectful and admirable. "Tell me, Samuel, where do you apprentice?" I inquired cordially again, aiming to keep up the conversation.

"I have an apprenticeship with Master James Otis in Lexington," Samuel informed me politely.

"Lexington?" I echoed interestedly.

"Aye," he replied.

"You're a Harvard graduate, then?" I asked.

"I am," he said modestly.

"That's a good school," I commented.

"It is an esteemed institution," he agreed humbly.

"May I ask you—that is, if you don't find it too intrusive…" I started.

"Aye, please continue," he said affably.

"Well, I was wondering what kind of law do you practice?" I inquired.

"Our interest lies in law enforcement," Samuel replied.

"Oh, so you arraign?"

"Primarily—but we have defended as well."

"I see. Well, that's interesting work."

"Aye, my sector is stimulating. I find that if a man is not properly versed in law, then he is bound by ignorance and therefore not liberated," he said.

"Yes, I suppose that's true," I agreed.

"My view is that law ought to serve the people justly," Samuel continued.

"Yes, certainly," I replied, observing the elder Mr. Hardy give his son a sidelong glance of pride.

"Our son intends to be a good lawyer serving the people once he passes the bar," Mrs. Hardy interjected politely.

"Yes, well, that's very good," I replied admirably.

"Sam's a bit of a radical in his ideas. Do not allow him to frighten you," Mr. Hardy said.

"I think it's good to be an independent thinker," I responded appreciatively.

"Do you?" Samuel inquired, intrigued.

"Indeed she may," Finley interjected impassively as he suddenly appeared, entering the room with Leif following. The brothers had their smoking pipes in hand as they kindly greeted their guests and comfortably seated themselves among us. Leif sat close to me on the sofa. I could sense his awareness of me, and I intended to ignore my compulsion toward him. He quietly glanced at me and stuck his pipe between his lips before returning his gaze toward the guests in front of him.

"Mistress Arboles was presently expressing her thought on free thinking," Samuel informed the brothers as they were newly joining the conversation.

"Is that reit?" Leif responded inquisitively. He returned his ultramarine eyes to me, along with everyone else. I suddenly felt a bit put on the spot.

"Well, what's the point of having a mind if you can't express it?" I replied.

"Indeed," Samuel replied admirably.

"Indeed, I feah that I have been surprised. This young lass here has wit!" Old Mr. Hardy chuckled heartily. His rotund girth shook like Santa Clause's belly amid his amusement.

"Aye, it appears she does," Finley said ironically.

"I esteem a man who takes a witty wife, for he will evermore remain of wit," old Mr. Hardy said cheerfully.

"Aye, as his circumstance will dictate him tae be so," Finley replied as he stuck the end of his pipe in his mouth and puffed.

"Precisely," Mr. Hardy said. My eyes turned toward Finley as he had made his comment, and I noticed Leif's ears turning pink.

"I, however, much prefer a wife who minds her wit by understanding her place next tae her husband's," Finley said plainly. This time I felt my own skin grow flushed with irritation as a result of Finley's backhanded remark.

"Well, indeed, all within reason—no gentleman desires an *outspoken* wife," Mr. Hardy responded, more collected now.

Elizabeth entered the room with Amity at her side. They each held a silver tray with everything needed for tea. Elizabeth placed the piping hot tea on a stand near the window, and Amity followed with her tray full of sliced maple bread and a pitcher of ale with several mugs.

"Mistress Arboles," Samuel continued as Elizabeth and Amity prepared to serve the tea, "I should like to inquire whether you have ever seen Lexington?"

"Uh, no, I have not," I lied. Amity came around and first served Mrs. Hardy a cup of tea with a proper slice of maple bread.

"Well, it is quite a stimulating place," Samuel commented.

"Yes, I imagine so," I replied politely.

"I expect a young lady such as yourself might find it nicely suitable," Mrs. Hardy interjected pleasantly. Finley and Leif were looking directly at me, and I sensed their scrutinizing gazes.

"Oh?" I replied simply as Elizabeth served Mr. Hardy ale and maple bread. The smoke coming from Leif's pipe near me felt thick in my throat.

"Why, yes, of course, my deah. It is a fine town," Mrs. Hardy said.

"Are there any theaters?" I asked. Amity came to me with a cup of tea, and I thanked her as I took it. Upon returning my attention to the Hardys, I noticed their odd facial expressions. The conversation seemed to have stumbled flat. I wasn't sure why. Perhaps they found my signing communication with Amity to be unusual.

"Eh, no, deah, we don't admire theaters in these parts," Mrs. Hardy informed me.

"Oh," I replied awkwardly. I decided to take a sip of tea from my cup. Looks silently flew between them.

"Were you once familiar with the theater?" Mrs. Hardy asked. I swallowed my tea suddenly. Her tone teetered on the verge of disapproval. Finley's brow raised as he looked at me with anticipation, and Leif merely fastened his eyes on me without any expression while he continued puffing his pipe, awaiting my response.

"I have seen a production of Shakespeare's *Macbeth*," I admitted as I placed my teacup back on the saucer I was holding.

"Och?" Leif muttered, surprised. He removed his pipe from his lips and examined my expression.

"A guid Scottish tale," Finley remarked, relatively impressed.

"Aye, I have read it several times," Samuel said curiously. "I understand, Mother, that there are playhouses in Virginia."

"Oh, I see," Mrs. Hardy said uncertainly.

"Is that where you have seen it?" Samuel inquired curiously.

"Not exactly—I saw it somewhere else," I replied simply.

"I met a gentleman once from Virginia, and he explained to me that going to the playhouse was one of his favorite pastimes. He enjoyed viewing plays made popular by the king's liking," Samuel said.

"I see," I replied, sipping more from my teacup. Amity had finished serving her uncles some ale and obediently acknowledged her aunt's gesture to depart the room.

"Henry Jackson was his name, and he had a drawl to his speech," Samuel continued. "Yet your speech is not at all quite like his."

"Well, then, you have guessed correctly that I'm not from Virginia," I said kindly. But inside I was beginning to feel unsettled with the direction of this conversation. I got the impression that theaters were taboo for some reason, and I didn't want to discuss my origin.

"Most interesting... Might I inquire where you were reared?" Samuel asked curiously.

"Um—well," I stuttered.

"Forgive me. I have been bold. I did not mean to pry," Samuel said.

"No—it's all right. It's very far away—where I spent my childhood. I suppose it doesn't really matter now though. I have experienced some tragedy in my life, and I don't like to think about the past," I said honestly.

"Aye, of course. I regret my mistake, and I am sorry fah it. I should not like to make you sad," Samuel apologized sincerely.

"Thank you," I said gratefully.

"I have a sista living in Lexington," he said, changing the topic.

"Oh, that's nice," I said.

"Ha name is Sarah, and she is a governess to a little Miss Anne fah a gentle family known as the Bradley family," Samuel explained.

"Oh, I see," I replied politely.

"Sarah frequently visits me when she has time fah herself. It might please you to travel to Lexington—when it suits you—to meet her," he invited kindly.

"Oh, that would be nice, I suppose," I said.

"She is in need of a pleasant friend," he said.

"Is she?"

"I'm afraid so. She doesn't have much opportunity fah friendship."

"That's too bad," I said regrettably.

"Aye, I feel that she may enjoy your company very much. It would greatly please ha."

"Well, that sounds nice. I would be happy to meet your sister if I'm ever in Lexington," I replied sincerely.

"Thank ye fur the invitation, lad, but I dinnae believe that Mistress Arboles will be leaving fur Lexington any time soon," Finley interposed.

"Oh?" Samuel replied innocently.

"Aye," Finley responded plainly.

"Aye," Elizabeth began cordially explaining, "you see, she is presently assisting us with Amity in orda that she may finally learn to communicate through scribing."

"Oh, is that not charitable!" Mrs. Hardy exclaimed.

"Aye, it most certainly is," Samuel agreed.

"How, may I inquire, will you manage such a task?" Mr. Hardy asked skeptically, although he was respectful.

"Mistress Arboles explains that it may be done first by enabling her to understand a series of hand gestures to communicate words," Elizabeth pleasantly informed him.

"How quite ingenious," Samuel said.

"I dare say, young lady, it appears that you may have a talent fah aiding people," Mr. Hardy praised.

"Thank you. I only do what I can," I replied modestly.

"You might consider it a gift from God," Mr. Hardy said plainly. I didn't wish to encourage the trend of the conversation, which was bound to head toward how I had acquired my knowledge, so I simply smiled and accepted his compliment.

The conversation continued lightly for a little while longer during the course of tea and pipe smoking. Afterward, the Hardys began to take their leave. As I proceeded to follow Elizabeth, who was properly seeing them out the front door, Samuel paced beside me and leaned slightly toward my ear, calling my name.

"Yes?" I asked, gazing back at his blue eyes as we momentarily halted in our steps before we arrived at the front threshold.

"I really cannot thank you enough fah all that you have done to restore my fatha's life," Samuel said quietly.

"Oh, really, please, you don't have to thank me," I replied sympathetically.

"Nonetheless, you must know that you are well regarded, and it would greatly please me, and my sista, if you were to ever visit with us in Lexington," he said very kindly.

"That's extremely nice of you, thank you," I responded sincerely.

"You must also know that if you are ever in need, please promptly think of us, fah we are happy to aid you," he continued earnestly.

"Well, that's very thoughtful of you. I'll remember that, thank you," I said appreciatively.

"My sincerest pleasure," Samuel said kindly. He respectfully bowed his head toward me. "Good day," he said politely as he straightened.

"Good day," I echoed automatically, and he smiled at me before leaving. As I watched the Hardys depart through the front door out into the sunlight toward their carriage, I rather thought that they seemed like a nice family and that if I ever had the chance to meet his sister, Sarah, it would be a pleasure.

Once the Hardys' horses trotted off with them inside the carriage, I spun on my toes to return inside, but accidentally bumped into Finley. I hadn't seen him standing there.

"Oh! Excuse me," I gasped, taken by surprise.

"Pardon me," Finley responded, unmoved. Apparently, he had been standing discreetly out of the way near the wall, observing with a discerning eye. I dropped my glance from his and hurried past him, intending to gather Amity in order for us to start our lesson—assuming that she had finished her morning chores.

When I rounded the corner in the corridor, I was suddenly caught off guard by Leif as he lightly snagged my arm and pulled me aside out of the passageway.

"Hi!" I gasped suddenly, feeling his hand around my wrist.

"Have I frightened ye?" he asked.

"Just a little startled, that's all." I panted slightly.

"I apologize," he said in a low tone.

"It's okay," I replied. He took a little step toward me, and I moved backward. My back unexpectedly pressed against the wall. I was aware that he was still lightly holding my wrist when he slid his other palm over my cheek and tenderly caressed it.

"I had tae steal a glimpse of yer bonnie face before I toil over duties," he said softly while his carefully caressing thumb faintly rolled over my lips and parted them. That strange sensation began seeping into my senses again as I gazed back into his crystal blue eyes. I recognized the swelling desire that came over his warm expression. I thought he was going to kiss me again. "I must speak tae ye, lass," he said in a muted voice instead.

"You want to speak to me?" I echoed unthinkingly, *very* conscious of his touch and the close proximity of his lips to mine.

"Aye," he muttered.

"Okay," I replied curiously. "Funny, I wanted to speak with you too."

"Is that reit?"

"Yes."

"We seem forever interrupted. Therefore, I'll wait fur a most private moment till we speak."

"All right… I think it's a good idea that we speak," I agreed.

"Aye," he replied. He gently traced his thumb over my bottom lip as he gazed admiringly at me. "How I long tae hold yer bonnie lips tae mine," he said gently. I could feel his warm breath caress my brow as he hovered tall before me. His stroking palm carefully moved around my neck. He shifted slightly so his hovering lips now lingered less than an inch away from mine. Then, I felt them sweeping lightly across my mouth. "May I kiss ye again?" he whispered.

"Why are you asking?" I muttered.

"I reckon that I ought tae," he replied faintly.

"Well, it didn't stop you before."

"Aye, ye have a notion." He gently seized my chin between his thumb and forefinger as he raised my lips to his. The warmth from his mouth weakened me and tore apart my resolve. I leaned into his kiss, and his hands stole around my torso. He held me snug against his chest as I buried my palms in the loose hair at the nape of his neck. All I wanted to do was to devour his kisses and feed him mine as I felt the growing heat between us.

"There you are, Uncle!" Mairie interjected unknowingly when she suddenly came trotting through the hallway. Leif abruptly stepped away from me out into the corridor in plain sight.

"Aye, lassie, whit is it?" he asked.

"Da has been requesting to see you," she sweetly informed him.

"Och! Of coorse. Please tell him that I'm promptly arriving," he responded.

"Aye," she said as she spotted me standing near her uncle by the wall. "Hallo, Sylvina," Mairie added politely with an innocent but inquisitive look in her eye.

"Hello, Mairie. How are you?" I asked amiably.

"Well, thank you," she said sweetly.

"Good," I replied. I glanced at Leif with his hands on his waist as he observed his niece.

"Now run along, lassie. I'll shortly come tae yer da," Leif instructed.

"Aye, Uncle," Mairie replied, and dutifully ran off back through the corridor, disappearing around the corner and returning to her father. Leif turned toward me, and I smiled gently.

"Aye," he said lightly.

"C'est la vie," I said.

"Indeed," he said with a warm grin. "Hmm," he muttered thoughtfully.

"What?"

"I merely wish tae spend more of my time with ye. That is all."

"Oh. You're very sweet."

"Nae. I dinnae believe that I am. But yoo're the one who is sweet." He covered my hand with his and fervently squeezed his palm around my fingers. "I shall see ye later," he said.

"All right," I agreed softly. Leif grinned benignly again, then released my hand. He started away down the corridor, and I went in the opposite direction through the passageway. I glanced back over my shoulder at his striding figure just before he vanished around the corner. Then, I turned again and continued down the hallway, aiming to begin my lessons with Amity, thinking it unbelievable that I had found myself kissing him again.

CHAPTER 26

*O*nce evening came and the children were tucked in bed, the day typically concluded with light tasks. Elizabeth usually darned stockings if she didn't prefer her beautiful needle-work, while the brothers typically enjoyed their pipes with whiskey as they discussed matters of interest in the sitting room.

The air was noticeably cool tonight, and a fire had been started in the fireplace in the sitting room. There was no one around when I entered the room. The warmth from the fire was inviting, so I stepped closer toward the hearth to warm my chilled fingers and toes. The season was changing, I recognized, and the trees had started turning colors.

After a minute of standing on the warm hearth, I decided to pull a chair near the heat when I happened to glance at Eliza-beth's baroque guitar resting on the window bench on the other side of the room. I straightened and walked toward the window. Out of curiosity, I grabbed the guitar by the neck. It certainly appeared like it belonged in the eighteenth century, I thought.

I was compelled to stroke it. So, I sat on the window bench and positioned the unusual instrument over my lap. I lightly strummed the strings once downward and noticed the strange pitch; the sound was hollow, and it was tuned to an open C chord. I was actually very familiar with playing a modern-day six-string guitar, but this one was slightly different. I had some classical music training when I was a little girl, learning to play the piano, guitar, and violin. But when I grew older, I really developed an affinity for more popular music like rock, jazz, and bluegrass. So, I focused my attention on contemporary music genres instead.

I picked at the strings a little and started tuning it to a more familiar sound created by an open G chord. Once I had finished tuning the guitar, I gently plucked a few cords and then started trying to play a song I remembered.

I heard footsteps entering the room. I stopped plucking the guitar strings and glanced up. Leif strode casually into the room and noticed me by the window with the instrument across my lap. I abruptly stood and replaced the guitar on top of the window seat just as I had found it.

"Nae, 'tis quite alrecht—pray continue," he insisted amiably, gesturing lightly with his palm for me to remain as I was.

"All right," I said, and returned to sitting on the window seat.

"So ye ken how tae play?" he asked interestedly.

"Um, a little, I suppose," I said modestly.

"Och," he replied. He approached and sat in the chair across from me with his heels stretched out on the floor in front of himself. "Do ye have a favorite ballad?" he asked casually.

"Well, I suppose there are a number of songs that I like," I admitted reticently.

"Och?"

"Yeah."

"Will ye play a ballad fur me, then?"

"Well, I'm not sure what to play," I said hesitantly.

"Anything will be nice," he said encouragingly. At that moment, Elizabeth and Finley entered the room and joined us by the fire.

"Oh, I see that you have discovered my guitah. I apologize, how thoughtless of me to have forgotten it there. I shall take it out of your way," Elizabeth said, and started to collect it.

"Nae, Beth, the lass plays," Leif said abruptly. Elizabeth stopped short and glanced at her brother-in-law.

"Does she?" Elizabeth asked.

"Aye, she was playing it nicely upon my entrance," Leif said.

"Is that right?" Elizabeth turned her eyes toward me.

"She was preparing tae play a ballad fur me," Leif continued to explain.

"Oh?" Elizabeth looked at me interestedly.

"Ye can serenade, lass?" Finley interjected good-naturedly as he took his seat in the Queen Anne leather chair.

"Yes, but I—" I started awkwardly.

"Och, dinnae be bashful now, lass. Go on and play us a ballad," Finley insisted.

"Well, I suppose it doesn't really matter," I said uneasily.

"Very weel, then," Finley replied expectantly.

"Except I'm not sure that I know any ballads that you might like," I said honestly.

"Pay no mind, I shall like tae hear one ye prefer," Leif said.

"Um..." I stammered.

"Dinnae be bashful, lass. Yoo're amongst friends," Leif encouraged.

"Aye, of course," Elizabeth said kindly.

"All right," I said reluctantly. I took a little breath. "Okay—I suppose I could play this one."

"Splendid," Leif replied, and smiled widely. He made himself more comfortable in his chair and sat back, relaxed. Elizabeth sat in a chair between me and her husband, with needlework in hand. Leif, sitting attentively on the other side of me, looked on with ready expectation.

I remembered a song that I had really liked that was written by Bruce Robison and was made popular by the Dixie Chicks. I started prefacing the song that I was about to sing to them by saying, "This song is called *'Travelin' Soldier'*, and it's about a shy boy who has newly joined the military. He's alone and afraid, and he befriends a young girl before going off to war."

"Very weel," Finley said approvingly.

"Okay—it goes something like this," I said, particularly conscious of their attentive anticipation as they gazed at me. I started picking individual strings and chords in close fashion to a banjo. After a moment as I set the melody, I began to sing the song in my first soprano voice...

As I continued playing the conclusion of the melody while plucking individual strings and chords together, I glanced away from my playing hands to watch my closely listening audience until the last note sounded.

"That was *very* bonnie," Leif commented first, appearing significantly pleased and impressed.

"Indeed, I have never heard a guitar played in quite that manner," Finley remarked. I wasn't sure how to interpret the unclear expression on his face.

"You have a lovely voice, deah," Elizabeth complimented.

"Thank you," I said meekly.

"Is it in typical fashion fur a lass tae play music the way ye do from yer origin?" Finley inquired curiously.

"I suppose so, yes," I answered.

"Humph," Finley grunted thoughtfully without seeming offended.

"Weel done, lass. Serenade us anither," Leif urged. He winked at me, then fleetingly shifted his glance toward Finley. Finley met Leif's glance and arched a brow. Then, Leif returned to looking at me.

"Aye, let us hear anither ballad, if yoo'll please, lass," Finley encouraged.

"Sure—if you'd like," I replied. I wasn't sure what to play for them next, but then I thought about a song written by Burt

Bacharach and Hal David that suddenly popped into mind. Performed by the Carpenters, it happened to be a favorite of mine when I was a small child. So, I started strumming and picking the guitar again with this new melody. Then, I started to sing "*(They Long to Be) Close to You.*"

When I had finished singing the song, I noticed Leif's complexion had reddened significantly as he gazed intently at me. I wasn't sure if the song was enjoyed, since my audience had remained quiet without an immediate response. I thought perhaps they might not have liked the song as my onlookers' eyes bounced back and forth between each other without a single word.

"You didn't like it," I said apologetically.

"On the contrary, lass, 'tis quite a bonnie ballad," Finley said.

"Oh, thank you," I said with relief.

"Aye, 'tis a very bonnie ballad," Leif agreed pleasantly, though the hue on his face was completely red.

"How have ye come by that particular ballad?" Finley inquired curiously.

"Oh, it's a song my father used to sing to my mother when I was small," I explained.

"Och," Finley replied curiously. Leif nodded slightly as he continued looking at me, entranced.

"Well, 'tis a lovely ballad," Elizabeth said kindly.

"I'm glad you liked it," I replied.

"Ye have a very bonnie serenading voice," Leif complimented, appearing bashful.

"Thank you," I responded self-consciously. I felt insecure as I returned my gaze to his and sensed the heat rising in my own cheeks.

"Indeed, you serenade beautifully," Elizabeth echoed.

"Thank you," I said, turning my gaze toward her.

"Pray, will ye serenade us anither?" Leif requested gently.

"Really?" I asked. His lips tilted softly as he gave me a heartened look.

"Aye, let's hear anither," Finley said persuasively.

"Okay," I agreed. "But I'm not sure what to sing next."

"Och, I'm certain anything will suffice," Leif said.

"Okay," I said thoughtfully. So, I started plucking the strings of the guitar again into a nice melody. I started the introduction to a song written by Stevie Nicks and made popular by Fleetwood Mac, then began singing the melody to *"Landslide."*

When I had finished singing and playing the guitar, I glanced at my listening audience, and they seemed pleased, judging by the nice expressions on their faces.

"Quite anither unusual but bonnie ballad," Finley remarked as he puffed contentedly on his pipe.

"Aye," Leif agreed softly.

"Indeed, but pray, what does it mean, I wonder?" Elizabeth inquired curiously.

"Well, the song is about how life changes," I started thoughtfully, "and essentially about how life may have unforeseen circumstances occur, which may overwhelm and tumble your whole world," I replied.

"Och, I see," Finley said.

"As confronting one's feah perhaps?" Elizabeth asked.

"Yes, I suppose so," I agreed.

"One may only find trust in the Lord God to securely surmount loss of faith," she said. Finley simply acknowledged his wife's statement with a slight nod as they glanced at each other, then Elizabeth returned to pushing her needle through her needlepoint embroidery. Finley lightly cleared his throat and turned his eyes specifically to Leif.

"Will you not, Seamus, serenade us now?" Elizabeth requested politely.

"Aye, if ye so wish," Leif agreed.

"You sing?" I asked suddenly with a combination of curiosity and interest.

"Aye, from time tae time," Leif responded.

"My brother has a fine voice, in truth," Finley said.

"How nice—I didn't know that you liked to sing," I remarked curiously.

"Aye," Leif replied, shrugging his shoulders a little. He seemed suddenly a bit demure as I smiled at him.

"What will you sing?" I asked.

"Och, weel, allow me tae decide," he said thoughtfully.

"He enjoys loove ballads," Finley teased. Leif ignored his brother and reached for the guitar, gently taking it from my hands. He put the pipe he was holding in his right hand down on the nearby oak stand and asked Elizabeth to play for him. She gladly agreed and put her embroidery aside to take the musical instrument from him. She placed the guitar over her lap and strummed it once.

"Oh! How strange," she said lightly, observing the unusual tuning of her instrument and proceeding to tune it back to her preferred open C chord.

Leif turned his golden head toward Elizabeth, observing that she had finished tuning her guitar and was now ready to play. He returned his gaze to me and said, "I'll serenade about a lass and a lad—'*Blow the Candle Out.*'"

"All right," I said pleasantly. So, Leif started from his chair and properly stood in position to sing. His eyes seized mine, and he began singing a chipper tune. Elizabeth followed his cue, intermittently strumming melodic chords over her baroque guitar according to the rise and fall of his voice. While I was enjoying listening to him serenade, I began paying attention to the lyrics and wondered about the words as he would not release me from his stare. I started feeling my cheeks grow warm as he sang when I realized the lyrics pertained to a young apprentice who went to court his love and spent one night with her, which left her pregnant with his child and unmarried to him.

When Leif had finished singing the nice ballad and Elizabeth had finished playing the guitar, I daintily applauded them with pleasure.

"That was very good, both of you. Thank you," I said. Leif appropriately bowed his head at his audience, then turned to Elizabeth and acknowledged her talent for the guitar. She reciprocated with her own nod to him.

"Thank you. I'm pleased that you enjoyed our entertainment," she said politely.

"Yes, it was very nice," I replied.

"Mayhap Elizabeth micht delight us with a melody of her own," Leif suggested pleasantly.

"I shall be pleased," she said willingly.

"Very weel," Leif responded satisfactorily, and moved to return to his chair across from me. He gently smiled at me as he took his seat. I returned his smile, feeling abruptly introverted, and shifted my attention to Elizabeth, who was now strumming a melody associated with the distant past.

After a while of diversion with ballads, recited poetry, and light discussion, the weight of the evening had begun taking its toll, and I could hardly keep my eyes open. So, finally, I politely excused myself from everyone's presence and decided to withdraw for the evening. After I arrived at the top of the staircase and entered my room, I began to undress. When I had finally finished, I was happy to sink into the pillows and comfortably fell to sleep.

CHAPTER 27

One morning began early with hard work in the field as surrounding farmhands, along with the help of some good neighbors, harvested the family's squash. Today Amity and I did not have the opportunity to review our lessons, as the children, Elizabeth, and I partook in assisting the harvest by serving meals and drinks to the men out in the field. It was an all-day, labor-intensive, consuming effort for them to harvest the squash. It was an effort that made all too real for me the extreme trials farmers experienced to produce food—something of which most members of my society, me included, were generally ignorant.

I was impressed with the stamina of the children as they labored in the kitchen and helped serve food to the neighbors and farmhands. I had never worked so hard, like a waitress, but I found that by pacing myself, the work came more easily.

I was made aware a couple of days ago that Finley would be leaving for Boston. He was going to leave at dawn the next day, so it was imperative that the vegetables were harvested and sacked before he left. Leif was going to drive the whole load into town early tomorrow morning to meet a regiment from the colonial militia passing through, ultimately on their way to Fort William Henry to deliver the vegetables.

With few breaks in between our tasks, and with the help of those good neighbors, the family had at last managed to successfully sack all of the vegetables by the end of the day. Normally, there were only two meals in the day, and dinner was typically in late afternoon, therefore "lunch" as I knew it did not exist. But we had all worked up a hearty appetite and were famished. So, we had a final meal of ham and pea pottage, which had been stewing in the kettle for a couple of days, to satisfy our hunger that evening.

The children were quick to bed before dusk had set, and by the time the stars were out en masse, I could not stand another moment of wakefulness. I followed the children's lead and slept like the dead the entire night.

THE HOUSE the next morning seemed quiet as a result of Finley's absence. He had left on horseback early before sunrise, headed for Boston. The destination lay slightly less than a hundred miles away, and he would not be returning for at least a month. When I went for my morning walk, I noticed that Leif was nowhere to be found. I remembered that he must have already left for town to meet the traveling militia to deliver the crop. I considered for the very first time while in my captivity that I was actually not being scrutinized or looked after now. *I could so easily wander off without anyone noticing*, I thought. But I was much too far away to try to successfully run away to where the future Williamstown would be. Even if I stole one of their horses, because I was unfamiliar with the area as it was, and without a map and compass or GPS, it would be difficult for me to navigate my way back over the trails to find the place where I had disappeared. So, the idea of escaping swiftly left my mind and left me in a state of home-sickness.

While out on my stroll, I noticed that many of the dogwoods, maples, and birches had begun changing colors. Their leaves were deep hues of alizarin crimson, cadmium yellow, and orange, and it dawned on me that it must be early November. *Could that be right?* I asked myself. I was stunned. My time away from home was growing more distant, and a sheer jolt of panic shot down my spine. *I could realistically be trapped here forever!* Startled, I realized that I was beginning to forget the desperation of my displacement, and the feeling of complacency had started filling the void of my burdensome urgency to leave. I was going to have to do something about my situation here. I didn't know how I was going to be able to change it just yet, but I was going to have to figure out a way to get home—the sooner, the better.

"*Psst!*" I heard someone whisper loudly as I walked closely around the side of the stables. "*Psst!*" I heard it again and arrested my steps. I saw a nice-looking blue eye peering between the planks of the stable wall.

"Hey, what are you doing?" I responded benignly, staring back at the peeping eye.

"I'm shoveling hay," Leif replied lightly.

"Oh," I said.

"I reckon, on the other hand, whit are ye about, however?"

"I was just coming back from a walk."

"Och, weel…"

"What?"

"Do ye mind keeping me company whilst I finish my chore haur?"

"Yeah, sure, I don't mind."

"Come about, then."

"Okay," I agreed, and I paced around the stables toward the front. I went inside and found him pitching hay in one of the rear stalls at the back of the barn. When I arrived, he stopped working momentarily.

"Nice tae see ye, lass," he greeted me.

"You too," I said. Leif grinned warmly and reached for a stool across the aisle. He brought the stool close for me to sit. "Thanks," I said, and took my seat on it.

"Aye," he acknowledged, and returned to pitching clean hay into the stall.

"Did you already go to town?" I asked.

"Aye," he replied simply.

"Oh."

"I also went tae Vinton's mercantile tae acquire the items ye requested," he informed me.

"Oh, thank you so much," I said.

"Aye, yoo're welcome. Except thaur waur a few items on yer list that had tae be ordered," he explained as he tossed more fresh straw into the stall.

"Okay," I responded.

"Thomas Vinton said that thaur is a shipment he's soon expecting of a couple of the items ye wished tae have, but he said the eucalyptus oil ye desire will be hard tae come by," Leif said.

"Oh," I said.

"So, I just as soon reckon that ye may wait on that fur some time as he disnae ken whaur tae acquire it just yet," he said.

"Sure..." I answered. A little lull ensued between us. I watched him pitch hay for a moment, thinking that this would be a good time for us to talk and for me to express some of the things that I've been wanting to tell him. But I couldn't quite find the right words to start out with as I continued admiring his laboring physique. "You said you wanted to talk—in private," I blurted.

"Aye," Leif replied as he continued working. I unexpectedly lost the gumption and could not find the nerve to lay out my reservations for him regarding us.

"Well—um, this seems like a private enough place to talk,

doesn't it?" I said carefully. He straightened from shoveling more hay and turned his eyes to me.

"Aye," he responded. He briefly dropped his gaze, wiping the perspiration from his brow with his billowy linen sleeve. He lifted his pitchfork slightly off the ground and placed it in the corner of the stall.

"So, what's on your mind?" I attempted to start the conversation. He looked at me with an unreadable expression. He put his palms on his hips and paced forward a couple of steps, keeping some distance between us.

"Weel…" he started. He bent to scoop up a piece of straw. He straightened and abstractedly rotated the straw between his fingers. He tossed the straw to the side, then lunged for the other stool hidden behind the post. He drew the stool forth, placing it directly in front of me, and sat. "Weel, I reckon that I have been wondering," he started to say.

"About what?" I asked curiously.

"I reckon I've been contemplating ye," he revealed. I noticed his thoughtful expression as he picked up another piece of straw and started toying with it between his fingers. He then returned to looking at me with intent.

"Me?" I responded curiously.

"Aye…"

"Well? What?"

"I wonder whether ye are content," he inquired sincerely.

"If I'm content?"

"Aye."

"What do you mean?"

"Simply whether ye are at ease haur—with us, I mean?" he asked earnestly.

"Oh, well, sure I guess so," I answered thoughtfully.

"Guid," he replied with a contemplative nod.

"Elizabeth is very nice," I said.

"Aye."

"And the children are so sweet. They're adorable," I said. Leif nodded in acknowledgment, but he was still distracted. He briefly paused and seemed slightly hesitant.

"How do ye reckon my treatment of ye?" he inquired, appearing diffident.

"I'm sorry?" I responded, slightly befuddled.

"I wish tae ken yer opinion of the way I treat ye," he repeated, with his face reddening. I shrugged a little.

"I suppose fine. You've been nice… You've been very nice to me," I answered honestly, feeling shy. He nodded.

"Then ye approve?" he asked.

"Approve?" I echoed, precisely aware that I sounded like an airhead at the moment.

"Aye."

"Well, sure, I guess—you haven't hurt me or anything, so… yes, you've been nice," I said. Leif nodded his head a tad again and paused momentarily in thought. I noticed his cheeks were really flushed now as he sat in front of me thinking.

"Therefore," he started hesitantly, "ye truly didnae mind my kissing ye?"

"Oh—" I responded unexpectedly. "I—no, it was fine, I didn't mind."

"Ye didnae?"

"No—I thought it was okay. I mean, it was nice. I liked it," I said unevenly. His expression brightened bashfully as one eyebrow arched, and the corner of his mouth tilted upward.

"Did ye?" he asked.

"Yeah," I replied quietly.

"That's guid," he said.

"Yeah," I agreed. He paused, and a lull ensued between us. I dropped my gaze from him and looked down at my clasped fingers in my lap. My fingertips toyed with each other. I sensed him gazing at the fire sparkling in my diamond as the sunlight entered through the cracks in the barn wall and captured the flare in the stone.

"Do ye still feel that ye may not take anither husband?" Leif asked. I suddenly returned my attention to him.

"Well, I don't suppose that I have given it much thought recently—actually," I said.

"I see," he said. His gaze fell to the straw he was playing with between his large fingers. I observed him pull the piece of straw apart and meditatively roll it to and fro between his thumb and forefinger.

"Why?" I asked curiously.

"Hmm?" he responded, returning his gaze to me.

"Why do you ask?" I repeated.

"Samuel Hardy admires ye," Leif said.

"Oh," I replied thoughtfully. "Should I be concerned about that?"

"Nae, he's a decent lad."

"Oh—okay…"

"He wishes tae court ye."

"What do you mean?" This was some surprising news to me.

"He wishes tae court ye," Leif repeated clearly.

"No, I know what you said, I just—how do you know?" I asked confusedly.

"He offered fur ye tae visit his sister in Lexington," Leif reminded me.

"So?"

"'Twas in hope that he may court ye."

"That's silly," I replied, looking at him absurdly.

"Why is that silly?" he asked plainly.

"Because I just met him only recently," I said obviously.

"So?"

"So, I don't know him—and he doesn't know me. So, he can't be serious."

"Indeed, he is most earnest," Leif responded. I couldn't help the unbelievable expression on my face. "If ye waur tae accept his invitation tae visit him in Lexington, he will see fit tae wed ye," Leif said.

"Excuse me?" I uttered unexpectedly. Suddenly, I was amused, and I covered my mouth, attempting to stifle my charmed expression. Leif apparently did not understand my amusement. So, I quickly tried collecting myself. "I'm sorry, I didn't mean to be rude. I'm just surprised."

"Why are ye surprised?" he inquired.

"Well, I guess that I'm just caught off guard, that's all," I said.

"Ye ought not be astonished. He's a young bachelor, and yoo're a very bonnie lass," Leif stated frankly.

"Thank you. But there are plenty of other pretty girls around town who could interest him instead."

"Aye, except he simply prefers ye," Leif stated.

"I see, well… I don't know what to say," I said honestly. Leif momentarily studied me.

"Being a barrister, Samuel is a lad who can afford his likely wife a gentle life," he said.

"Oh," I replied.

"Does that not impress ye?"

"Well, that's nice if he can do that—but why are we having this conversation?" I asked with puzzlement.

"Weel, I thought that ye micht begin considering his invitation tae court ye in order that he micht wed ye," Leif said.

"Really?"

"Quite."

"Okay, first of all, Samuel is too young for me, and secondly, no offense to him, but I have no interest in him at all whatsoever."

"Truly?"

"Yes, truly."

"Och…" Leif paused fleetingly, glancing down at the slender golden strip of straw he kept turning between his fingers. After a second, he returned to looking at me. "Thomas Vinton also fancies ye. Are ye awaur?"

"Not at all," I said.

"Och. Weel, he'll also wed ye," Leif said with certainty.

"Oh, well, how do you know that?"

"He makes an effort tae speak tae ye when he can efter church," Leif noted.

"Oh—well, he's just being sociable like everyone else," I replied.

"He is smitten with ye," Leif assured me. I shook my head at the ridiculous idea. "When he took my order at the mercantile, he inquired about ye," Leif revealed.

"Did he?"

"Aye."

"Oh, I wasn't aware."

"He also requested that I deliver this tae ye. I've been intending tae give it tae ye." Leif bent his head as he reached his fingers inside the pocket of his waistcoat. He withdrew a petite round pink silk pouch and handed it over to me. There was something hard in it. I loosened the yoke at the top of the little pocket and retrieved a pear-shaped crystal perfume bottle. It had a gold mount enameled with painted roses, and the inside of the container was filled with the liquid aroma. I was somewhat surprised to have received a gift as nice as this. I automatically opened the mount and carefully waved the bottle beneath my nose. The aroma was unique and very pleasant. I had never quite smelled anything like it and rather liked the smell; it lacked the minimal alcohol odor and synthesized aroma common in the abundantly manufactured perfumes of my day. I thought I detected natural tones of lemon and bergamot, but I couldn't place the other harmonizing scents.

"Wow, this is quite lovely," I remarked impulsively while recorking the mount over the small crystal bottle. "But I'm afraid that I can't accept this," I said, and carefully slipped the bottle back into its round, soft pink silk pouch. I stretched my arm out, holding the delicate pouch between my fingers for Leif to take. "Please tell him thank you for me and that it is very thoughtful, but I can't accept any gifts," I said.

"As ye wish," Leif consented, and wrapped his palm around the petite parcel. The tips of his fingers grazed mine as he took the pouch from me, and I noticed his masculine cheeks redden. I watched him put it back in his waistcoat pocket.

"So," he said simply when he looked at me again.

"So," I echoed. "Is that what you wanted to talk to me about?" I asked sincerely.

"I reckon," he replied. But he seemed pensive and restrained. I sensed that there was something else on his mind.

"Are you sure?" I urged.

"Weel," he began contemplatively. He tentatively shrugged his shoulders a bit, and I noticed how red his cheeks were at that moment.

"Yeah?" I encouraged gently.

"I recall something that ye said some time ago," he said.

"Okay?"

"Ye said that thaur was nae one that could speak fur ye."

"Speak for me?"

"Aye—nae family."

"Oh. Mm-hmm."

"Do ye still say that is true?"

"Yes, it's true—I don't have any family anymore," I said honestly. Leif nodded his head thoughtfully in response.

"Alrecht," he said.

"Why do you ask?" I inquired innocently.

"It remains that I must keep ye protected."

"Oh." I paused momentarily. "I'm sorry for placing any kind of burden on you."

"The only burden ye have placed upon me, *àille dhubh*, is the fondness I hold fur ye," Leif said directly. He tossed the hay strand to the side and stood tall from his seat on the stool. He reached for my hand and helped me up from my seat. He gently caressed my hand and smiled reassuringly. I smiled diffidently at him as I now stood immediately in front of him. "Now, I'm certain wee Miss Amity is awaiting her lesson with ye, as Beth nae doubt will be wondering over yer whereaboots," he acknowledged responsibly.

"Yeah, I guess I should get going," I agreed. Leif curled my knuckles around his large fingers and carefully raised my hand to his lips. He pressed a tender kiss on the back of my hand.

"Run along, lass. I'll see ye later," he said.

"Okay," I said. He gently released my hand. I smiled unevenly, and he grinned warmly. I took a couple steps away, ready to leave. "Bye," I said faintly.

"*Mar sin leat,*" he replied kindly.

I started away from the stall and paced out of the barn into the open air. I was thinking about our conversation as I walked back toward the house. I thought about how he'd verbally admitted his affection for me. I should have been further disconcerted about it, but in spite of myself, I was feeling glad inside instead. Everything seemed—I guess—better.

CHAPTER 28

Today I assisted Elizabeth in the garden. She had an extensive vegetable garden full of cabbages, radishes, carrots, onions, leeks, garlic, and pumpkins, which grew in the outlying field facing the sun. There were also herbs growing among the other plants. I recognized plenty of basil, comfrey, chamomile, hyssop, and violets. There were some other herbs that I had no notion of, and I wondered about them, when my eyes stumbled on one that I remembered.

"Is that foxglove?" I asked Elizabeth with concern as she was picking basil.

"Why, indeed," she replied simply.

"You should be careful of that. It's toxic," I warned. She unintelligibly stared at me for a fleeting second.

"Indeed?" she responded with a slightly strange expression on her face.

"What is it used for?" I inquired curiously.

"It soothes boils and head ailments. 'Tis also good for wounds," she said.

"I see. Well, just be aware that in large doses, it can arrest the heart," I said.

"Oh, I have never heard of it doing so," she said.

"What's that over there?" I pointed to a pretty cluster of bluish-purple flowers at a slight distance.

"That's herb Robert," she informed me.

"Oh," I said curiously.

"It aids in keeping mosquitos from biting," she said.

"Oh—that's good to have," I remarked sensibly.

"It most certainly is," Elizabeth agreed.

"And that over there? What does it do?" I inquired, pointing to another variety of flowers that reminded me of thistles.

"Teasel," she said.

"Oh, right—that's supposedly good for digestion." I remembered from my holistic health and pharmacology classes as a med student. Speaking of which, granted, I was not an herbalist, but I was certain that I was looking at pennyroyal right now.

"Ah, you're familiar with that group?" Elizabeth inquired, aware of the plant that had caught my eye.

"Isn't that pennyroyal?" I asked uneasily.

"Aye, it aids well with the vapors and flatulence," she informed me earnestly.

"Is that right?" I replied, amused.

"Oh, certainly, and it may also settle the stomach," she added.

"I see..." I said doubtfully. "But you should also know that pennyroyal is known to cause prenatal complications."

"Prenatal complications?" Elizabeth gazed at me as if I were speaking a foreign language.

"Yes, it shouldn't be handled by anyone who may be expecting a child," I clarified. She stared at me with alarm, but then laughed.

"Deah me, Sylvina, you are quite odd. You perceive me ignorant of my own garden. We have had such typical plants in my family fah generations, and we are unharmed yet. You need not concern yourself, I assure you," she said.

Yes, it is truly a wonder that anyone has ever survived a lethal garden such as this! It was truly remarkable! Conceivably, these people had no idea that they might have accidentally poisoned and just flat-out killed themselves throughout the ages by freely using plants like these.

While Elizabeth was kindly introducing me to the details of her garden, Mairie was suddenly seen galloping hastily over the hill.

"Mama! Mama! Mama!" she cried excitedly. Elizabeth abruptly stood, with her attention immediately directed on her little girl running toward us. The child cried out anxiously for her mother the whole way up the slope. Elizabeth hastily began moving away from the garden toward the fence as Mairie came closer. I was also startled and followed Elizabeth until we met her daughter just beyond the garden gate.

"What is it, child?" Elizabeth inquired of her little girl. Mairie was visibly out of breath, and panted uncontrollably for a moment before she collected enough air in her little lungs again to utter a word. "What is it, child?" Elizabeth demanded worriedly again.

"Mama… A number—a number of British soldiers are marching toward the house!" Mairie exclaimed breathlessly, pointing down from the little hill on which we were standing toward the direction of the house.

"Good heavens!" Elizabeth said frightfully. We could clearly see at a distance approximately two hundred redcoats marching from the east, headed straight for the house. "Have you seen your uncle?" Elizabeth asked Mairie sharply.

"He's in the stable shoeing one of the horses," Mairie responded.

"Fetch him—go! Not a moment longer—*make haste!*" Elizabeth instructed, with unmistakable panic detected in her voice.

"Aye, Mother!" Mairie gasped obediently, and, like a wildly frightened jackrabbit, swiftly took off running in the direction of the stables.

"We must make haste and return!" Elizabeth said anxiously,

and immediately turned from the garden. We rushed hurriedly down the small slope for the house.

We arrived at the house and swept inside, locking the three entrance doors inside. Soon, the throng of redcoats could be seen right out front from the drawing room windows. Elizabeth and I had all the children gathered around us as we peered expectantly out the windows. The lead commander on horseback was seen ahead of his marching soldiers coming closer to the front of the house. He raised his hand, signaling to his men to halt a mere twenty yards away from our front doorstep. He proceeded to dismount his horse just as we saw Leif entering the scene as he approached the men from the south side of the property.

As the commander touched the ground off his horse, Leif caught the commander's attention as he came forth. When Leif reached the proper distance for a conversation, the commander commenced speaking—presumably introducing himself. Leif replied, and I noticed that he was armed with his pistols tucked in the holsters around his waist.

The commander politely bowed his head to Leif once he had finished briefly speaking. The commander continued saying something else to Leif, then Leif responded. He gestured to the commander by waving his arm, pointing across the property on the opposite side. It looked like Leif was giving him directions, and the commander nodded as Leif spoke. The officer mimicked a small portion of Leif's hand motions, seeming to clarify given directions.

After a moment, once it was understood between the two men, according to protocol, the officer bent his head toward Leif and turned toward his horse. The commander mounted his horse and signaled to his company, and he proceeded to move out with his men away from the house in the direction across the field. Leif remained standing there watching the soldiers march onward until every last one of them had cleared far enough away from the house. Elizabeth released a slight sigh of relief, but her distress was still visible on her face.

Leif turned toward the house and began walking toward it. Elizabeth scurried to unlatch the front door for him as he came up the veranda and entered inside.

"What has happened?" Elizabeth asked anxiously.

"That was Captain Foster," Leif informed her.

"What does he want?" Elizabeth inquired.

"He requests quartering fur his men," Leif said.

"Oh, heavens!" Elizabeth gasped, placing her palm above her breast.

"Ye neednae fear. They wulnae be staying haur. I've directed them tae the property yonder," Leif said.

"That's your land," Elizabeth said surprisedly.

"Aye, the house thaur isnae in use. They may use it instead," Leif said.

"But if the soldiers wander onto this property?" Elizabeth inquired.

"As the captain is awaur that I outrank him both militarily and socially, he will heed my orders tae arrest any man of his found on this property, upon which I shall have him flogged," Leif replied resolutely.

"I see," Elizabeth said, appearing slightly more at ease. "They will want what we have in the garden, however," she said. "If they are ravenous, a soldier won't mind crossing our property for some cabbage, or corn."

"Aye, we shall provide them with rations, so not tae worry," Leif assured her. Elizabeth sighed reticently, but nodded her head in concert.

"As you say," she said, more settled, and withdrew from Leif, taking the children along with her. Leif caught me gazing at him as I stood observantly in the hallway.

"Ye mustn't concern yerself either, lass," he said assuredly.

"I'm not concerned," I replied sincerely. He grinned at me and gave me a gentle pat on my shoulder. Then, he continued down the corridor, and I turned, headed for the kitchen, and joined Elizabeth as she tended to the children.

PART IV
POSSESSION

This morning I decided to help Elizabeth with milking the cow so that she could tend to the children properly completing their chores. It was going to be a daunting task, since I secretly had no idea whatsoever how to milk a cow. The only time I had ever seen a real cow being milked was quite some time ago at the Los Angeles County Fair when I was a teenage girl. So, I knew that this task was most likely going to be an "experience" for me.

I entered the barn lightly swaying the large milk pails back and forth. Nelly was easily spotted in the first stall near the front of the barn. I lifted the latch to the gate of her pen and passed through the sill. I pensively scrutinized the large animal, wondering how I was going to approach this chore facing me. I caught sight of her udders and noticed that she indeed was overdue for a good milking. I spotted the stool in the back corner and retrieved it. I placed it close to her hind legs and sat on the stool. I positioned one of the pails beneath her udders just like I'd seen on TV.

"Okay, how hard can this actually be?" I muttered to myself, dubiously examining the large animal. I wondered what to do next. I logically thought to seize one of the udders, and I gently took one between my fingers.

"Whit the devil are ye doing now, lass?" Leif inquired abruptly, appearing unexpectedly in the stall.

"I volunteered to help Elizabeth with the milking," I answered, startled to see him.

"That is kind of ye. Now, move away from her—slowly," Leif strictly instructed. He was obviously concerned.

"Why? What's wrong?" I asked unknowingly.

"Apparently, I value that bonnie face of yers more than ye do. She's a full cow, and she's cantankerous. She'll knock yer bonnie smile tae kingdom come," he said seriously.

"Oh," I said, suddenly apprehensive.

"Now, take care and slowly move away," he instructed again. Without speaking further, I did just what he said. I ever so slowly removed myself from the stool and started backing away from the cow until I bumped into Leif's chest from behind. "Guid," he said finally with relief. I glanced up at him now that I stood next to him in the aisle, and our eyes met. "Did Elizabeth allow this?" he inquired unbelievably.

"Yeah, she said it would be helpful," I answered.

"*Och*, she should ken better than tae give her consent. I must speak tae her," Leif said, noticeably displeased. He then gently but firmly took me by the shoulders and completely turned me to directly face him. "Listen tae me, lass. Ye have a considerate heart tae want tae aid in chores as often as ye do. However, yoo're not made fur labor, and I raither not have ye hurt or killed. Do ye understand me?" The censuring tone in his voice mirrored the grave earnestness on his face.

"Yeah, sure," I responded innocently.

"Guid," he replied acceptably. "Now, do ye wish tae see how tae properly milk a cow?"

"Okay," I said simply. I felt his sturdy palms slip from my shoulders.

"Very weel," he said. He swiftly fetched another stool nearby. "Sit haur," he instructed as he set the stool down safely away from the animal. I moved to sit on the stool he'd provided. "Now, since Nelly is cantankerous, it will serve us better if I give her a morsel on which tae nibble," Leif informed me.

"Oh," I replied curiously while I observed him grab the large bucket, then pace to the back of the barn. He began climbing the ladder to the hay loft. In a few steps, he had nimbly climbed up into the loft. He briefly returned down the steps of the ladder with a bundle of fresh grass hay in the bucket. He came back to the cow's stall and calmly placed the hay before her. With some of the grass collected in his grasp, he gently cooed the animal as he rubbed her softly on the head and neck with one hand and tenderly offered her some hay with the other. The effect of his kind caresses and soft talk seemed to have relaxed and eased the animal.

When Leif believed that Nelly was contented, he moved to secure her with a halter at the post. He then took his seat on the stool next to her belly and wrapped his fingers around the teats, one in each hand at the base. He gently pressed, slightly pulling down on them along the way toward the end. *Viola!* The teats sprayed into the pail, and there was milk! It was captivating to watch his motions to achieve milk; he made it seem effortless. I was impressed!

Several moments passed as I contentedly watched him milking Nelly. The silence was nice between us as he worked; it felt comfortable and natural—as if we had always been this way with each other.

"So, you have a house?" I began curiously, simply making conversation.

"Aye," Leif replied easily, remaining hunched over as he milked.

"I didn't know that," I said.

"The property was abandoned fur many years, and the government seized ownership of it," he explained.

"Oh… Why was it abandoned?" I asked curiously.

"The folks that had once owned the land years ago waur stolen by Indians," he said.

"Oh my gosh! Are you serious?" I replied, shocked.

"I'm quite earnest."

"Well, what happened?"

"Abenaki raided the village—killed the husband and took the wife and bairns fur slaves," Leif revealed. I gasped awfully with a hand over my mouth.

"That's *crazy!*" I said, alarmed.

"Och, aye, 'tis a horrid fact," he agreed.

"How long ago did this happen?" I asked.

"Quite some time ago—I reckon fifteen years have passed since then," he said.

"I see. Deerfield had experienced a similar tragedy, if I recall what Elizabeth and her sister had told me," I said, remembering.

"Aye, that's reit," he said.

"*Unimaginable,*" I uttered.

"But, as I said, that was many years ago. I doubt the area will suffer anither fricht as that in spite of England's war with France," he said confidently.

"I hope so," I replied. Leif turned his eyes to me.

"As long as I'm haur with ye, *àille dhubh,* nae one is going tae carry ye off," he said with conviction. I wasn't sure if he had become flushed over working, or if it was due to something else.

"That's valiant of you," I said. He looked at me with a crooked grin that made him look boyishly bashful. "Well…" I drifted off, feeling pretty much put on the spot with my own shyness creeping over me. He kept his eyes locked on mine, seeming to anticipate more of a response from me. "Well, I'm glad," I finally said. His lips widened with a bold smile, then he dropped his warm gaze away from me and back to his milking hands.

"So, you bought the property from the government?" I continued.

"Aye, as thaur waur nae surviving kin tae lay claim tae it, the government seized the land and auctioned it. Thus, I purchased it," he explained.

"Why did you and your brother decide to live this far out in the country?" I inquired.

"When Beth and Fin were wed, Beth's sister had already been wed tae her husband, who is from these parts. Beth wished tae remain near her sister, so Fin purchased land haur tae suit her."

"So, you bought property here to stay close to your brother," I said, understanding.

"Aye."

"But you're not living in the house."

"Nae—my intention was tae do so… tae start a life haur with a wife. But it simply didnae occur due tae soldiering…" His ears turned hot pink.

"Oh… But that doesn't mean that you still can't live in the house, I suppose."

"It needs work."

"Well, you can handle that—easily, I think."

"Not quite, I reckon… Yet as I'm not wed, 'tis apparent for the moment that Fin and Beth need me haur more than I need tae spend my days alone in a large empty hoose."

"That makes sense. But do you want to be married?" He turned his head, looking at me.

"I've considered it," he said.

"Then, what's stopping you? I mean, I'm sure a guy like yourself could be married tomorrow. Connie would be happy to have you, and she's not the only girl—all of her friends think you're cute too," I replied.

"*Cute?*"

"Yeah."

"Whit does that mean?"

"You know—darling."

"Och," he said as he lightly chuckled, nodding his head a little with a quizzical grin. "I dinnae understand men tae be darling, however. Merely bairns and lasses are such."

"Well, in your case, it would mean handsome," I admitted. His expression turned pinker.

"Weel, thank ye," he said diffidently. "I reckon I dinnea ken how I micht appear tae the lasses. Be that as it will—I have nae feelings fur Connie. Nor do I have feelings fur any of her friends, fur that matter."

"Really?" Somehow I doubted him.

"Aye, truly. So, it makes the matter not as simple as it may seem."

"Hmm," I muttered thoughtfully.

"Furthermore, since the Crown has me in service, it disnae leave me much opportunity tae seek out a life I see fit fur myself."

"Oh," I said, considering. "Well, what sort of life would you prefer for yourself if you weren't in the service?"

"I would seek a quiet life with a guid bonnie wife and many bairns," he said.

"Oh. I see."

"Nonetheless, I shall manage," he said. Leif abruptly stood, picking up the stool by one leg, and moved around to the other side of Nelly. He propped the stool and sat on it, then proceeded to milk her other side.

We continued chatting for a while longer as he easily worked the cow. Our conversation was effortless and unguarded. It was a nice feeling being around him in this sort of quiet setting. I found myself truly enjoying his company. I laughed at some of the things he was saying to me, and he occasionally chuckled heartily at what I said. I sometimes thought that he thought that I was some kind of novelty, by the way he would occasionally look at me and laugh. It seemed we really got along, and it was natural. At one point, I was very glad to be in this moment, as I had realized how much I had missed sharing his company alone. It felt like we had become real friends.

"Fetch Nelly some more hay, *àille dhubh*," Leif requested.

"Sure," I agreed, noticing that the cow had nearly completed the pile of hay before her. I got up from my stool, grabbed the empty bucket, and walked to the back of the barn. I carefully climbed the tall ladder with my long skirts to arrive at the loft. Hay was plentiful everywhere on the platform. I collected a sufficient bundle of grass hay and started my return, but my heel unexpectedly sunk into the floor, catching me by sudden surprise as I nearly tripped over. I dropped the bucket full of grass and pulled up the hems of my skirts.

"Oh, no!" I said, seeing that my heel had been wedged between a missing knot in the pine floor.

"Whit's the matter?" Leif abruptly inquired from below.

"My shoe's stuck," I informed him.

"Och," he said as I heard him stir from Nelly. He paced toward the ladder and climbed it with no effort, swiftly arriving erect over the loft platform. In several long strides, he was easily towering next to me. His gaze naturally fell toward the floor to my hems. He knelt beside me. "Let me have a look." I gathered my petticoats and raised them halfway up my calf. "Indeed yoo're trapped," he acknowledged, observing the extent of my heel inside the hole of the floor. "Will ye remove yer foot from yer shoe?"

"Yeah." I instinctively placed my palm on his hunched shoulder for support and wiggled my foot free from my slipper.

"Guid," he said. He looked at the wedged shoe for a second. "Weel, ye indeed have got it deep inside the hole."

"It looks like it," I observed.

"Let me see if I can retrieve it without damaging the shoe," he said.

"Okay," I responded. I decided to take a seat on a nearby small bale of straw hay and watched him begin to delicately work the shoe from the wedge. After a moment, the heel gave a little, and the slipper popped out of its restraint wholly intact.

"Thaur we are!" he said successfully as he seized it.

"Great!" I said gladly as he started toward me. I observed him kneel before me with my shoe in hand.

"May I?" he inquired politely, looking down at me with his deep blue gaze while I sat on the bale.

"Oh—yeah, sure," I stuttered. It would have been a slight challenge from the restrictive way I was dressed for me to simply raise my leg and put the shoe on myself as I used to do at home. So, I lifted my petticoats a little, exposing my white stocking-covered foot and a small portion of my calf. I noticed Leif's ears turning red. He carefully encircled his fingers around my ankle and deliberately slid his palm up my calf. He proceeded to secure my shoe back over my foot. His complexion went bright crimson as my toes easily slid into the slipper.

"That's better," he said, returning his flushed expression to me.

"Thanks," I said, aware of his lingering palm around my leg. Suddenly, the temperature in my own cheeks rose. I knew he could see it, and I uncontrollably blushed some more. He glanced down again at the position of his hand and began lightly caressing the lower part of my calf. His bent head caught the glow of sunlight entering the loft window and set his hair ablaze like molten gold. He was incredibly attractive, I thought, as I watched his examining fingers mindfully massaging my leg.

He slightly straightened while still kneeling in front of me with his fondling hand remaining on my calf when he gazed at me again. I smiled unevenly. I sensed his other hand carefully encircling my waist. He was hesitant to let me go.

"What?" I muttered, beginning to feel warm and uncertain. He lightly shrugged his shoulders and grinned a little.

"Bonnie, sweet, kindhearted, *àille dhubh*," he uttered softly.

"Is that what you think of me?" I asked quietly.

"Aye," he replied. I smiled again, feeling the beat of my heart pound hard like a rapid drum within my chest. I felt my pulse rise further as I tried to control my breathing, and his eyes focused on my throbbing neck for a second, which only made my heart beat faster.

"What?" I whispered as I held his intense, steady gaze. His eyes smiled gently, and the warmth of his grin enticed me.

"Why do you say 'What?'"

"I don't know."

"Of coorse ye do. Nae one I ken says it. Now, why do you say it?"

"I don't know." I shrugged a little. "It's just something I say, I guess, when I'm nervous."

"I see. So yoo're nervous reit now, then?"

"Yeah, I suppose so."

"Why micht that be?"

"Well, you're—I—I mean, well, what do you want? From me?" I inquired, feeling very attracted to him.

"Anither kiss," he said gently.

"Oh," I whispered, staring back into his concentrated gaze. "Well, I—well, hmm…"

"Aye, whit is it?" he inquired longingly.

"Well, um, don't you think things are getting out of hand?" I asked.

"How do ye mean?"

"Well, I mean that things… I don't know—but the affection between us could get out of control."

"Och," he responded meaningfully. "But dinnae concern yerself. Thaur's nae reason fur worry."

"Why shouldn't I worry when things between us are certainly moving in a particular direction?"

"Ye neednae be concerned, since I shan't let anything ill become of ye."

"Oh… Well, I don't know. I still think things could arise between us that could be out of our control."

"I swear tae ye that I'll not let anything ill befall ye."

I paused for a moment, and considered him as I gazed back at his crystal blue eyes.

"Do you mean it?" I asked in a soft voice.

"Certainly, I do."

The attraction between us was palpable. His lips curled gently, and his hand began moving heatedly farther along my calf, lifting my skirts. His warm palm now came over my knee. He shifted, pushing my legs apart, and wedged his hips between my knees while using the hand simply resting on my waist to fully encircle me.

"Come haur tae me, loove," he said huskily. I smiled nervously at him as I let my hands trail up his rolled up sleeves along his muscular forearms and biceps toward his broad shoulders.

"You're strong," I mentioned as I gently massaged his shoulders.

"Am I?" He chuckled lightly.

"Yeah."

"Och."

"I like that."

"Do ye?"

"Yeah."

"Why is that?"

"Because," I said softly.

"Because?"

"Yeah."

"That isnae a proper answer," he said, smiling warmly at me. I smiled back at him, not revealing more of a response. He pulled me to the edge of the bale so now I was sitting closely against him with my thighs spread around his waist. He then methodically placed a hand around my other leg and pushed the opposite side of my skirts up, high over my thigh. This was definitely a seriously compromising position to be in, I thought. My skirts were currently immodestly high around my waist, exposing the bare sides of my buttocks, with him firmly pressed between my legs.

"Wait," I whispered, stiffening in his embrace.

"Aye?" he said heatedly.

"I don't think this a good idea," I said unevenly.

"Please, dinnae protest—I implore ye," he said.

"But I—just don't know."

"'Tis alrecht, Sylvie. I promise ye."

"You promise me," I muttered.

"Aye, I do." Leif held me tightly against him, and I could feel his steamy breath on my brow as he tenderly cupped the side of my face.

"Okay," I agreed, deciding to trust him.

"Guid," he said gently. He tilted his head and leaned in close, then tenderly pressed his soft lips over mine, further locking me in his clasp. Suddenly, I felt something firm, solid, and large restrained within his breeches push unmistakably against me between my thighs.

"*Oh!*" I gasped unexpectedly, a little alarmed even though I had some experience before in my past.

"Aye," Leif muttered coarsely against my lips. He stifled my breath with another passionate kiss before I could say anything. Locked within his embrace, he coerced me onto my back on the hay, and I felt his formidable weight come over me.

The hidden pressure of his groin between my legs was distinct and obvious. I felt a seismic shift within me, and my blood ran hot. I felt so incredibly strange. I parted my lips and received his desirous kiss as I moaned for him. I fleetingly thought that this could easily turn into something more than just a little kiss as I felt his hand intentionally wander higher over my stockings. His feverish palm arrived on my bare skin at the top of my exposed thigh and the rump of my right buttock.

"*Och,* Sylvie..." he groaned in a low tone. I started feeling unsure about what was happening, despite my enjoying every single heated kiss he was giving me.

"Leif?" I panted worriedly between kisses.

"Aye?" he replied feverishly as his kissing lips moved from mine toward my chin and down my pulsing neck. He was half aware of me as we were both increasingly growing caught up in the heat of the moment.

"Leif?" I started faintly again.

"Aye?" he mumbled between his trailing kisses as his lips moved toward the mound of my breasts just above my bodice.

"We're just kissing, right?" I had to make sure that this was all it was going to be.

"Aye," he replied rapturously. He raised his gaze to me. He put a gentle hand around my face, and a soft smile came over his affectionate expression as he gazed at me for a moment. "Dinnae fear, *àille dhubh.* I shall not let anything unfortunate happen tae ye," he said gravely.

His expression was completely real and sincere. I felt something suddenly form in my throat, and an unforeseen flood of mixed emotions nearly overcame me as I fought back tears. I could only nod a little in response. Still, a tiny tear escaped and began rolling down the side of my cheek. Leif tenderly placed the pad of his thumb over it and lightly wiped it away. He leaned in slowly, softly pressing his lips to the place where my tear had been. I brought my arms around his broad shoulders in a full embrace, fixing my body to his.

I allowed him to continue kissing me, and I gently kissed him on the side of his cheek, wanting to feel his lips on my burning skin. He moved his lips over mine, tenderly kissing me back. The heat between us only further escalated. Lucid thoughts ran in and out of my head, warning me to slow this event to a stop before it became a runaway train out of my hands.

Something was going to happen, in spite of what he had just

said—I could feel it. A frenzy had been worked up in him, and I was not far behind him. Leif fleetingly released his hungry lips from mine as he caught his breath, then replaced them on my lips as he abruptly thrust his tongue, causing me to suddenly gasp. When he finally released me from his powerful kiss, he turned my head to the side and began trailing kisses over my cheek down toward my neck again.

I had grown so consumed with the fervor of his emotionally charged lips and exploring hands that I had begun feeling extremely dizzy. A strange ache deep within my abdomen occurred. *This is no dream...* I was very aware of what was happening, and I drew him closer, fully and freely kissing him in return.

"*Och,* how ye weaken my resolve..." Leif murmured huskily while I kissed his slightly scratchy chin. He lifted his gaze to me again and shifted slightly to the side, but let his hand slide toward my inner thigh. I sensed his other hand lightly stroke my brow, clearing it from my stray ringlet tendrils. "Yoo're bonnie, so very bonnie," he muttered marvelously. I responded with an insecure little smile.

"Thank you," I said, and he grinned affectionately at me. His large hand purposefully slid farther between my thighs and unexpectedly cupped my exposed pubic area. Alarmed, I immediately threw my hand down over his, not wanting him to do anything else to me.

"Will ye let me tooch ye, Sylvie?" he asked tenderly.

"No!" I said, shaking my head also, on the verge of removing his hand from me.

"I swear on my honor that I'll not harm ye," he promised. He meant it; I could see the truth stark on his face as I stared back at him. Still, I hesitated. He did not persist, in spite of his palm still covering my small private tuft of hair. I decidedly shook my head no again.

"I don't want you to," I whispered back to him.

"Ye have my most solemn oath—I swear it tae ye," he said seriously again. I didn't know how to consider it. So, I was still reluctant. I didn't respond. He sensed me thinking. After a slight moment, he finally said in a very loving voice, "Pray, will ye trust me, Sylvie?" A faint sigh eluded my lips; I truly didn't know what to do. I mean, I wanted to—I *really* wanted to. But I didn't want to regret it later with a problem that I could not correct. "I swear I'll not hurt ye," he repeated softly.

"You swear?" I asked.

"I do swear it," he whispered honestly. I briefly thought about it—and considered him.

"Okay—I'll trust you," I spontaneously heard myself say to him.

"Fine," he said in a caring voice, and lightly kissed me on my lips. He returned his gaze to me, and his deep ultramarine eyes seized mine. I sensed his fingers begin gently moving over my private tuft of hair until he slipped one into the cleft between my legs. A little breath eluded my lips. His titillating fingers caressed and fondled me until one discovered my clitoris hidden between my legs, and I gave a faint moan.

"Aye, loove… I want tae please ye…" he groaned gravelly as his lips scarcely grazed mine. The sensation was affecting me as he searched with his gentle fingers to find me.

I wanted to look away from him and close my eyes. But Leif's gaze bound me to him, and I was forced to recognize him as he was calling forth an awareness deep within me. My head began spinning, and the distant ache in my abdomen grew more distinct and fierce. It felt like I was melting. My blood coursed hotly through my veins, eroding my forbearance with every delicious stroke his fingers executed against me.

"*Huh!*" I gasped suddenly as I felt the unexpected thrust of his large finger entering me.

"Yoo're like hot honey," he wheezed gruffly with wonder. His lips parted, and it seemed like he was going to seal his mouth over mine, but he merely held steady, looming over me ever so close. I felt the scorching, irregular panting of his heated breath breeze past my flushed face. Tiny beads of sweat began forming on his brow as he reached for me. My body began responding to his beckoning, and the moisture between my legs ran like a river. The dam holding me together had been sheered.

"*Mmm,*" I moaned uncontrollably when his finger continued thrusting rhythmically within me.

"Aye, that's it, *àille dhubh,*" Leif murmured hoarsely, while still fixing me with his passionate stare. He was determined to make me understand what he was doing to me, to make me buckle with every thrust and withdrawal of his fondling fingers on my sensitive clitoris. I was aware of how intensely attracted I was to him, and I didn't think that I was going to be able to withstand him much longer.

"Don't stop," I panted anxiously, instinctively tightening my own palm still covering the top of his hand down below between my thighs.

"I shan't," he uttered coarsely, and my body began taking control, leaving my thoughts behind as I now hovered on the precipice overlooking the edge of a great abyss. I gazed back into his eyes and perceived his awareness of me. He could see me for the first time, unadulterated and wanting. I willingly yielded to him and clutched his pumping hand, wanting to push him to the deepest, farthest place within me. I submitted and allowed him to dissolve the last of my fortitude, and I toppled from the height of the summit.

"*Ahh!*" I cried out, and he finally released my gaze, stifling my cry with his heated lips. I distantly heard his gravelly groan while falling mercilessly from my zenith. My thighs quaked uncontrollably. I was abruptly consumed by a tidal wave of deep-seated internal convulsions shooting like an electric pulse throughout my groin—and I didn't want it to cease. I closed my thighs around his palm, wanting to keep his touch on me as I continued to drift, rolling on waves of thrilling ecstasy.

Soon my body quieted from the rapturous tremors, and I floated back down to reality. I opened my eyes and gazed into Leif's ardent eyes as he lightly traced the outline of my lips with the pad of his thumb.

"Did I please ye?" he inquired hoarsely with a gentle grin.

"Mm-hmm," I muttered, half alert.

"Aye… I felt ye… I want ye, *àille dhubh*," he said softly in a hoarse voice. My mind was foggy, and I merely gazed dreamily at him. "I intend tae have ye… Yoo'll see," he uttered tenderly.

"You think so?" I whispered.

"Aye, yoo'll see…" He lightly pressed his lips over mine and gently brushed his slightly stubbly cheek over mine, bestowing more tender kisses across my warm face. I felt his fingers withdraw from the warmth between my legs as he started muttering affectionately in Scottish between his gentle kisses. I faintly heard him say in English, "I want ye, Sylvie… I'll make ye mine… Ye will be mine… Ye will belong tae me… Yoo'll see… Yoo'll see…"

He continued placing loving kisses on my face as I let my hands roam along his broad shoulders and around his back, embracing him. I buried my nose in the open collar of his linen shirt and took a deep breath, drinking in the scent of earth, spicy pipe smoke, sweet hay, and perspiration. It was an unusual odor, one that otherwise would have been repelling, but somehow further compelled my attraction to him. I sniffed him again, and it pleased my senses. Leif leaned back, gazing into my eyes again, and his flushed expression was generous and benign.

"You smell good," I told him.

"Do I?" He chuckled lightly with an amused look on his face.

"Yeah," I said, nodding my head a little.

"Sylvina?" Elizabeth unexpectedly called from below inside the barn. Without warning, I lurched up.

"*Och!*" Leif groaned abruptly in pain as my forehead accidentally collided with his nose and sent him rolling off me. "*Oof!*" he wheezed, tumbling off the hay bale, landing flat on his back on the hard floor. I swiftly lunged with concern over the side of the bale where he had landed.

"Oh, goodness! Are you all right?" I asked anxiously, noticing him clutching his hand over his nose.

"Och…" He moaned again, still in some pain. "Aye, I'm alrecht," he assured me.

"I'm so sorry," I whispered apologetically.

"Never ye mind. I'm alrecht," he replied. He withdrew the hand covering his nose and glanced at his palm. There was no noticeable blood, to my relief. "Ye have a bit of a hard crown, lass," he joked lightly.

"Sylvina? Are you here?" Elizabeth called out again. Leif promptly stirred to stand, but clumsily knocked the top of his head really hard this time on the plank of a wooden support beam just above, which firmly returned him to his backside on the floor.

"*Damnation!*" he hissed, not at all happy at what he had just done.

"Oh my gosh!" I gasped worriedly as I noticed him rubbing the top of his head.

"Hallo…? Is there someone up there?" Elizabeth called suspiciously up toward the loft in our direction. I simultaneously started to shift toward him, but unexpectedly pitched forward when his hand imperceptibly clasped around my arm and pulled me forward.

"*Humph,*" he uttered lightly as I landed squarely on top of him face-to-face on the floor. He pursed his lips and placed an index finger over my mouth, silently shushing me. I quietly nodded my head.

"Is someone up there, I say?" Elizabeth inquired suspiciously again. Leif removed me from him and placed me beside himself as he abruptly came to his feet, taking care not to knock his head again.

"Aye, Beth, 'tis merely I," he called back to Elizabeth below as he gestured for me to remain still.

"Oh, very well," Elizabeth responded with some detectable relief in her voice. Leif dusted himself off as he paced toward the edge of the loft and peered down.

"Is all weel?" he inquired.

"Aye, I merely came in search of Sylvina. I expected to find her milking Nelly," she explained.

"Och," Leif said with his hands positioned squarely on his waist, making his stance appear quite brawny.

"Yet I do not find her here," she said curiously.

"Aye, the lass has been haur," Leif disclosed.

"Where is she, then?" Elizabeth asked.

"She has nae business with Nelly," he said seriously.

"Why is that so?"

"The lass cannae milk a cow."

"Oh! Is that right?" Elizabeth sounded considerably surprised.

"Aye, she's much better suited fur tutoring Amity and naught else."

"I see."

"I reckon Sylvina will momentarily tutor Amity."

"Aye..." Elizabeth paused. "What are you about up there?"

Leif cleared his throat a little. "I, er, I'm fetching hay fur Nelly. I've already milked her halfway fur ye," he said.

"Oh, thank you kindly," Elizabeth replied gratefully.

"Aye, yoo're welcome."

"Well, I ought to fetch Amity at present. Sylvina will shortly wonder where she is, then."

"Aye."

"Very well. By your leave."

"Aye." Leif slightly backed away from the ledge as he kept his careful attention on the entrance to the barn. After a moment, he returned to me and assisted me to my feet from behind the bale of hay. I followed him toward the ladder and watched him step down first.

When he reached the bottom, it was my turn to come down. He waited, patiently looking after me as I carefully managed my way toward the first level. He took my hand as I approached him and helped me down the last few steps. As I came close, he then took me by the waist and completely removed me from the ladder, planting me on the ground.

With his hand still wrapped around mine, we paced through the barn together toward the front just before the entrance, where he stopped us. He turned, facing me, and tenderly placed his palms on my shoulders. I sensed his hands affectionately slide down the length of my sleeves until he took both my hands into his. He brought them to his lips, bestowing a tender kiss over my knuckles. When he lifted his lips and returned his gaze to me, his hands slipped comfortably around my waist.

"I want tae see ye later, Sylvie," he said fondly.

"All right," I responded receptively, nodding my head a little.

"Fine," he replied, pleased. He leaned down toward me and pressed his supple lips on mine. After his kiss, he gazed at me again. "Run along now, loove," he said. He released his hands from around my waist, and I turned away from him, walking out of the barn into the brilliant sunshine on a cool, crisp fall day.

I walked back toward the house feeling light-headed and floaty with delight as butterflies fluttered in my stomach. I was glad, and dare I say, even happy. I just wanted to hold on to these feelings for as long as I could.

CHAPTER 30

After our romantic encounter in the barn, I began looking forward to the next opportunity when Leif and I would meet again. Needless to say, that first occurrence spawned a whole host of stolen chances Leif and I clandestinely took to see each other. A lot of concealed kissing and hanky-panky started taking place between us. I wondered how far this sort of business was going to take us. It was only a matter of time before Leif would want to take things to the next level—and I was very reluctant to take such a large step as that. However, Leif never actually pressed the issue whenever we fooled around. So, I wondered what his feelings exactly were about what we were doing with each other. I thought if we could simply keep our "fun" with each other at a low grade, then maybe we would never escalate it to an end result. In which case, no one would really get hurt.

One afternoon after Amity and I had concluded our lessons, I went outside to hang clean laundry on the lines between the trees. A task I thought I could manage much better than milking a cow, or working to death in the kitchen to feed a bunch of hungry men working in the field. After draping a few rows of laundry, I was soon surrounded by glowing whiteness all around as the sheets tousled and snapped in the delicate sunshine breeze. The air was cool and sharp with the fragrance of earth and damp leaves. It was noticeably cooler in the shade beneath the oak trees, but the sun remained warm and it was nice.

I was humming a light tune I remembered while draping the next row of sheets over the laundry line. When I bent for the next large one and started hanging it, an unseen hand sharply caught my waist, unexpectedly pulling me around. Leif presently had me snug against him in his clasp with an arm fully encircling my torso. I suddenly stopped humming to myself as he took me somewhat by surprise with his stealthy appearance.

"What are you doing?" I inquired, a little winded. I was glad to see his fine face.

"I am searching fur ye," he muttered.

"Really?"

"Aye."

"Well, here I am," I lightly joked.

"Thus, I see," he said gladly. He clutched me tightly by the waist and stole a heated kiss from me.

"When may we meet again?" he muttered warmly over my lips as he broke from the kiss. I shrugged thoughtfully.

"Maybe in a little while when I'm through doing this," I murmured against his lips.

"Very weel," he said. "I shall be in the barn awaiting ye."

"Okay," I replied.

"*Okay*," he teased, and I laughed. He kissed me again, this time lightly on my brow, then released me from his snug hold. He retreated between the flowing, brilliant white sheets and vanished.

～

WHEN I HAD FINISHED HANGING the laundry out to dry, I strolled out over the green pasture toward the barn. It seemed the barn had become the standard place for Leif and me to be alone with each other without much worry about intrusion.

Arriving inside the barn, I paced toward the back to the ladder, anticipating him. When I reached the top step of the ladder, he was there standing tall over the landing, waiting for me and stretched out a helping hand. I slipped my fingers into his large palm, and he hauled me over the landing with ease.

"Hullo," he greeted kindly as I stood close in front of him.

"Hi," I replied, and out of nervous habit tucked a few wayward ringlets behind my ear. I tentatively began straightening my skirts. Leif was secretly relaxed, as he preferred holding my hand for extended periods. He proceeded to lead me across the loft toward a quiet corner where a full rounded bed of hay existed. When we arrived at the cushy pile, he allowed me to take my seat first on the hay, according to his usual good manners. He then lowered himself comfortably to sit next to me.

We started out talking this time before letting our excitement for each other take over. I liked it when we talked; it was a comfortable feeling—a natural feeling that was familiar and relaxing to me. Leif was charming, witty, intelligent, and could easily make me laugh. He reminded me of Matt in that respect—until now, it had only been Matt who could make me gleefully laugh and fill me with a good sense of mirth. But Leif was also gritty and tough with a kind of rawness imbedded in his character. Matt had very minimal facets of these characteristics. So, it was strange but captivating to see Leif with these aspects blatantly present in his persona. He sort of reminded me of a plainspoken cowboy with good manners.

"Tell me," Leif started.

"Hmm?"

"Whit was that bonnie wee melody ye waur humming earlier?" he inquired curiously.

"When?" I replied, a little puzzled.

"Earlier, when ye waur putting out the laundry," he reminded me.

"Oh!" I said, remembering. "It's a children's song I recalled."

"Och?"

"Yeah."

"It was quite bonnie."

"You liked it?"

"Aye."

"Oh."

"Does it have a name?"

"Yeah—it's called '*Rolling Acorn*,'" I said. I couldn't exactly tell him that the title was really called "*Donguri Korokoro*"—a Japanese song. So, I basically told him the English version of the title.

"'Rolling Acorn'?" Leif asked with a curious expression.

"Yes," I said, smiling at him.

"'Tis about an acorn, then?"

"Yeah."

"How curious," he said.

"You think so?" I asked as a large smile swept over my lips.

"Aye. I shall like ye tae serenade it tae me," he requested attentively.

"You do?"

"Aye," he insisted.

"Okay," I said. So, I began singing to him the song about a little mountain acorn that rolled from a hill and fell into a pond, where fish swam up to it and wanted to play with it. As the fish and acorn played together, the little acorn longed for his mountain home, and the fish were sad that he would finally go home.

Leif looked pleased once I had finished singing the English version of the song. He smiled widely with a thoughtful expression.

"There you have it," I said.

"Whit a curious wee ballad," he said, captivated. "I've never heard one like it."

"Probably not."

"But 'tis charming."

"It is," I agreed.

"'Tis quite capricious," he commented enchantedly.

"I suppose so," I said, smiling at him.

He gazed at me with appeal and amazement, as if I had come from another planet. I couldn't help it, I smiled freely at him; his innocent expression struck me with delight and attracted me. I noticed a bit of color exuding from his cheeks, and I looked away from him down toward my folded petticoats. My hands impulsively smoothed my skirts over my bent knees as I sat on the heap of hay. I was aware of Leif's fingers toying with my ringlets. I sensed them move gently around my ear as his fingers slipped a few loose tendrils just so behind it.

"How is it that yer locks are so very soft and silky?" he inquired, fascinated.

"Are they?" I asked, returning my gaze to his.

"Aye, softer than fox pelt—softer than anything I have ever knoon," he stated remarkably as his fingers buried deep into my hair and wrapped around the back of my head, lightly messaging my scalp.

"Do you think it's that soft?" I replied, oddly looking at him.

"Most certainly... 'Tis as murk as ebony and shines like black water beneath the moon at nicht," he complimented.

"Thank you," I replied.

"'Tis remarkable," he muttered. Then, he gently pulled me toward him from the back of my neck where his hand was currently massaging me and carefully compelled me to meet his tender lips. They were warm and inviting as he started kissing me. I responded and returned his kisses in the same soft manner. His hand started lightly trailing from my neck down my back and slowly wrapped around my waist and torso. He had me firmly clasped in his embrace. I instinctively reached my arms around his broad, square shoulders and buried my fingers at the nape of his neck into his silky, thick untied shoulder-length golden strands.

The pleasure in his kisses ignited a spark deep within me. I sensed him aware of me again, and his lips grew more heated. They trailed off toward my cheek, over my jaw, around my neck just beneath the lobe of my ear. My breathing became stifled, and I started to feel light-headed. Leif had me fervently fixed in his yearning embrace, and I recognized the strange feeling consuming my senses, changing me to suit the desire burning within him.

He easily shifted his weight and coerced me backward until I was flat on my back on the hay. I was conscious of his feverish hand roaming over my skirts as he quickly found the hems, and his large, slightly calloused palm wandered along my stocking-covered leg, pushing my petticoats higher over my knees. My lower half was completely revealed to him, and he began stroking his enticing fingers over the cleft between my legs, drawing forth the wetness from within me. I moaned slightly, growing anxious with his pleasing touch. He leaned over me and bestowed a heated kiss upon my lips.

"Aye, *àille dhubh*..." he groaned when he lifted his lips from mine. "Ye will be mine, Sylvie... I swear it..."

I was half listening to the things he was saying to me; I think he meant it. He sounded sincere—and convinced. The intensity in his voice was odd. I was being consumed by the wild spell of climbing ecstasy he was urging me to reach. I discerned the audible moan muttered from his lips as I simultaneously gasped upon the insertion of his thick finger.

"Och, Sylvie... Sylvie... Och, how I crave ye... I shall possess ye..." he heaved coarsely against my ear, allowing me to feel his scorching breath against my feverish skin. His fingers began their hypnotic motion, drawing me near to him as he had learned how to compel me forth. I started losing myself among his rapturous kisses and the emerging sensation of his adoring touch.

He shifted his weight a bit, and hovered closely above me. He unexpectedly withdrew his massaging fingers from me, and I partially apprehended the image of him adjusting his breeches. Suddenly, his strong hand carefully snagged my wrist in a snug clasp and tugged my unsuspecting hand toward his groin, wrapping my fingers around his newly uncovered, uncircumcised shaft. My hand abruptly splayed open, automatically reacting to release him as I instantly realized the sensation of his powerfully swollen shaft against my hand.

Leif promptly squelched my reticent gasp as he passionately sealed his mouth over mine like a gasket. I recoiled my hand from him, but his grip around my wrist was firm. He lightly yanked my wrist toward him again. He fixedly pressed my palm against him, intently wrapping my fingers around his erect shaft, and secured his palm over mine. Alarmed, I wanted to instantly let go, but he wouldn't let me. So, I wiggled my wrist a little within his unyielding grip, hoping he would be convinced to change his course a bit. Except the more he was kissing me, the more my senses became persuaded by him and confused me.

"Nae," he groaned unyieldingly in a scratchy tone. "Merely hold me, loove. 'Tis all that I ask… merely hold me… I assure ye that I shall not hurt ye," he promised.

I heard his plea, and for a fleeting, lucid moment, I thought that I should perhaps accommodate him; for a number of times after our first romantic encounter, he had been solely pleasuring me without ever asking for anything in return. So, I benignly squeezed him a little to let him know that I agreed to do as he wished. He responded and keenly reacted by slightly loosening his grasp around my fingers. His hand slowly released my palm and fell away as I started lightly stroking his engorged penis. My timid fingers worked around him as he situated himself more comfortably over me with the support of an arm propped next to my shoulder.

"Aye, loove—that is it," he uttered huskily against my ear. I felt his searing breath flutter against the side of my cheek. I recognized his heated hand touching the cleft between my legs again, drawing moisture from me with a command that I almost feared. He unexpectedly sheathed a thick finger within me, and I suddenly sucked in a deep breath. My stroking hand along his shaft automatically tightened in response. *"Ehh,"* he heaved hotly against my ear, and the blood in my body coursed through my veins like molten lava.

With every caressing motion my own palm mimicked around him, the less timidness I had, and his growing urgency emerged. As he continued drawing me forth, pulling me toward him, I intrinsically had the same wanting for him with each rhythmic stroke over his swollen shaft. Our hands in motion were in sync as desirous kisses passed between us, calling us to race together along an elevating journey.

I moaned, and his shaky breath heatedly caressed my lips. The intensity between us grew with a silent understanding. We were affectionately compelling each other, and the act started to morph into something else that was more powerful, complete, and real. Our fondness for each other began taking shape and manifested equally. He wanted to love me. I wanted him to love me... and I wanted to love him in return.

I was succumbing to the rapturous feeling he was giving me, and we were arriving together at the summit. Then the peak came, and I let go... falling into the raptures of oblivion.

I distantly heard Leif's scraping, low-pitched groan near my head as I felt him throbbing powerfully in my cupping palm. My insides convulsed euphorically around his fingers at the same time as I felt his essence escape him over the inside of my thigh.

My legs quivered helplessly as I rode the quaking waves of intimate bliss.

~

AFTER THE FLEETING orgasm between my legs dissipated, Leif collapsed with his full weight over me. His breathing was heavy and warm on my neck. He mindfully rolled to my side and pulled me snug, fitting me nicely against his solid body. His hand moved over my petticoats and carefully adjusted them to a modest position. Then, his arm trailed along my side, encircling my torso, where his palm naturally rested over my breast at last. I could still hear his deep breathing. It was heated against the side of my ear and neck as I was aware that my petticoats had partially wiped my dampened thigh clean.

Leif remained silently clutching me, and I wondered what he was thinking. But I didn't stir and disrupt the soft moment we were sharing, because it felt nice. So, I simply lay there spooning with him, wrapped in his arms in the hay. I lightly played with the linen fibers that were slightly frayed at the cuff of his billowed sleeve, pondering how easily we got along. And I was realizing that despite my personal reservations and the effort I had made to repress any feelings for him, I was now, on the other hand, feeling an emotional connection with him that was unavoidable. For whatever reason, regardless of my past, I had acknowledged my attraction to this new man.

I had started spiraling down a slippery slope on a journey that was falling further away from my grip, and would ultimately wane from my control the deeper Leif and I intended to explore our affection for each other.

I felt Leif's soft lips lightly bestowing gentle kisses behind my ear. I stirred and turned to face him, propping my head comfortably upon his shoulder. I smiled at him, and he pursed his lips over mine with a tender kiss. As he released my lips, he quietly stared at me with gently stroking fingers caressing my ringlets along the side of my face. His expression seemed both doting and pensive.

"What are you thinking?" I asked. The hue in his fair cheeks reddened, and he appeared slightly abashed.

"I'm pondering how I wish tea thank ye," he revealed uncertainly.

"Thank me?" I looked at him, obviously puzzled.

"Aye," he said.

"For what?" I asked curiously.

"Fur, eh… weel, fur doing whit ye did fur me," he replied hesitantly. The color in his cheeks abruptly deepened and seeped into the rest of his face.

"Oh," I responded unexpectedly, feeling sharply uncomfortable. "Well, you don't have to thank me for that," I said awkwardly.

"Yet I feel I must," he said thoughtfully, although noticeably self-conscious about it.

"No, really, it's okay—you don't have to," I insisted, embarrassed.

"Thank ye, loove, nonetheless," he replied, and pressed a nice kiss to my lips.

"Okay," I accepted sheepishly once he withdrew his lips. He intently gazed back into my eyes, and his expression was penetrating. I sensed him thinking as his thumb lightly traced over my lips, scarcely parting them.

"I enjoy feeling ye quiver amid my tooch," he disclosed affectionately.

"You do?" I whispered.

"Aye," he muttered.

"Oh," I replied, feeling awkward. He paused, thinking, and his face was entirely ruddy. He suddenly looked shy. "What is it?" I carefully prodded.

"Do ye enjoy it when I tooch ye?" he inquired thoughtfully.

"Y-yeah, yes, I like it very much," I stammered.

"Then, I can satisfy ye," he said.

"Yes, you do," I admitted. His lips tilted upward, and the grin on his face was pleasant.

"I'm pleased," he said genuinely.

"Me too," I replied.

"This time…" He pensively trailed off.

"Yeah?" I encouraged.

"Did ye notice?" I nodded a little. "Aye, it felt different… as if we coupled with loove betwixt us."

"I noticed that."

"That's guid."

"Yes, it is," I agreed softly. He grinned affectionately at me, and pulled me snugger against him as he carefully pushed his knee between my legs to hold me close.

"We culminated together as weel," he said in soft undertones.

"I know," I admitted.

"We can satisfy each other."

"It seems like it."

"'Tis guid whit we share—ye and I."

"Yes, it is." I paused slightly now, thinking of a question I wanted to ask him. "So…" I started uneasily.

"Aye?" His brow lifted.

"I, well, I… Are you sure you're okay with us not going any further than what we're already doing?" I had to ask; the question was troubling me.

"Och—aye," Leif responded unexpectedly. He seemed a little caught off guard and put on the spot. But then his expression changed somewhat as the redness visibly creeped back up into his face again. "I reckon it is fine at present," he said thoughtfully.

"At present?" I echoed uncertainly.

"Weel, I'm not gonnae lie tae ye, *àille dhubh*—I am merely a man, ye ken…" he began. "And ye are truly bonnie. I've told ye that I'm fond of ye—so, aye, I hope I may fully express my feelings fur ye one day."

"Oh," I heard myself reply remotely, aware of the uneasiness that slightly came over me.

"Yet I ken that yoo're not ready," he said keenly. "I ken that ye still think of yer departed husband... So, I shall bide till ye invite me."

That was very generous of him to say, because if he wanted to take it to the next level, I was sure that I could not withstand him and would ultimately sacrifice my better judgment.

"Thank you—that's really thoughtful of you," I said. Leif kindly lifted his hand to the side of my face and clasped my chin between his large thumb and forefinger, assuring that my gaze remained steadfastly fixed to his.

"I wish fur it tae be correct betwixt us," he said.

"I know," I replied softly.

"Are ye certain that ye ken?"

"Well, I—I guess."

"I ken that yoo're uncertain," he said perceptively. "I have given ye my oath that I shall not do anything tae harm ye. Ye must believe it," he said earnestly. I noticed that his deep blue eyes were penetrating. His gaze was intent and grave.

"I believe you," I told him. I *did* believe him. He was telling me the truth, and I knew it.

"Very weel—guid," Leif responded with satisfaction.

His fingers delicately fell from my chin, and he turned me to my side, pulling me against his powerful body. He kept me snugly fitted against his broad chest as my head comfortably laid on his shoulder. My hand instinctively slipped over his as I mindlessly played with the linen fabric of his loosened shirt beneath me. His muscular arm was nicely secured around my waist and held me with certainty against his formidable physique.

Nothing else was said between us, and silence ensued, surrounding us in a calm blanket of contentment. It felt normal and natural for us to be with each other like this as we cuddled together in the hay. It was as if we had always done so. I could feel his breath caressing my neck, and I began slipping into tranquility. Soon, the surrounding quiet began to sway like a lullaby as multiple birds chirped and sang outside the barn window. My eyes grew increasingly heavy, and finally, I decided to close them simply to rest. Then, I drifted miles away into a dream with him holding me.

CHAPTER 31

Today I went out for one of my usual morning strolls around the property. I crossed the pasture through a band of pine trees until I came upon a narrow dirt road. The air was noticeably chilly and crisp after the night rain. It was mid-morning, and dew droplets still covered the foliage like tiny glinting glass orbs. The sun shined brightly through the maple and birch trees lining the road and illuminated the dirt with intermittent dancing golden light. Alizarin crimson, deep cadmium yellows, and oranges burst forth in a rainbow of colors, enveloping me all around as I walked along the path. The maple, dogwood, and birch leaves had fully changed colors, indicating that the season was now deep into autumn. Soon, the leaves would fall, reducing those trees to a barren state for the winter.

I didn't really consider how much time had lapsed since I'd been here, as I paced along the path. Instead, all I could think about was Leif and the time we had been spending together. We had grown very close, and I discovered that I apparently felt glad inside that I had found more than a friend in him. In fact, as I was sorting through my thoughts and confronting my feelings, I had finally accepted the idea that I had real affection for him too.

Every day I looked forward to seeing him, and I felt secretly excited, and cheerful. It was as if I could escape with him to a place that was clandestine—away from the crazy, fast-paced, intensive, and hectic world I knew—to where I had no troubles, or had not known any pain. I felt the harsh reality of my past begin to vanish whenever I saw Leif. My fear of him subsided, and I had become myself again. A nice feeling had come over me as I continued to think about it like a silly girl.

I had come upon rolling beds of sneezeweed carpeting the forest floor beneath the maple trees. The fall flowers were in full bloom, showing off their brightly colored orange and yellow hues. I decided to stop along the path and began picking some of the bright flowers. I'd learned that they had advantageous medicinal properties and thought it would be a good idea to add them to my growing medical resources.

Leif's voice kept circling in my head like a corrupted recording stuck in a loop as I plucked flowers from the moist earth: *I crave ye... Ye will be mine... Ye will see... I shall possess ye...* When he said those words, they had seared into my brain, and I had trouble forgetting them. Leif's breath was burning as he had said those words to me. It spooked me a bit. People just didn't talk that way where I came from.

When I had finished collecting enough sneezeweed blossoms, I resumed walking along the path with a full and colorful bouquet in hand. I noticed at a distance a couple of British soldiers leisurely talking. They were perched on tree stumps drinking and smoking close to the bank of the pond, where I would soon be approaching on my way back to the house.

My stomach sank a bit with a sense of caution as I observed them with uncertainty laughing and talking in a loose manner. They didn't seem to be particularly upstanding soldiers as I would have expected servicemen to be. I could pick up bits and pieces of their boorish conversation as I advanced. Still, I had walked plenty of times through dark streets in the middle of Manhattan, and passed sketchy individuals without incident. So, I supposed passing by these soldiers would be similar. Besides, they really didn't appear to be nearly as threatening as the street thugs I had run across in the city.

The one on the tree stump whittling a twig with a small knife glanced up and noticed me approaching from a distance. He nudged his buddy in the chest with his elbow as he sat perched on the stump next to his friend, taking a swig of liquor from his canteen.

"*Ooo*, look at this dark beau'y comin' upon us now," said the one with the whittling knife to his pal.

"Oh, I've never seen the likes of 'er before now," his companion remarked roughly.

"Me naither," replied the first one in the same insensitive manner. The two were definitely from England, I could determine. They sounded and apparently seemed unrefined. When I had gotten close enough to them, neither they nor I could ignore each other's presence. I took note of their disheveled appearances and gazed at them long enough to remember their soiled, stubbly faces.

"Good morn, miss," greeted the one soldier who'd first noticed me as I was presently passing close by along the side of the road.

"Good morning," I said sedately.

"Good morn, miss," said the other one also.

"Good morning," I replied to him in the same manner. I noticed something about them that didn't settle with me quite right as I was passing them by.

"She's well pre'y. D'ya reckon she might stay and talk to us if we merely ask 'er?" one of them inquired while I tried ignoring them.

"I reckon mayhap. D'ya know that I seen one of 'em African

slave lasses before, and that one there ain't nearly like one of 'em. She's too fair, and did you see them green eyes upon 'er?" the former soldier replied.

"I did," the latter responded.

"Silky locks also."

"She doesn't appear like any of 'em half-breed Indian lasses naither."

"Nah… I don't mind though. I'll have a lass like 'er any time."

"She's pre'ier than any of the lasses I know back home."

"Aye."

This conversation I indiscriminately overheard was undeniably rude; they talked about me like I didn't exist, and rather that I was like a plain piece of meat to them. I instinctively hastened my pace, ensuring my full clearance of them. But after a minute of thinking I had gained enough distance from them, I heard the sound of walking steps over pebbles in the dirt at a minimal distance behind me. I glanced over my shoulder with some misgiving and saw them trailing nonchalantly not far behind me. I turned my view toward the path in front of me and hastened my stride.

Within a second, I detected their steps quickening. They abruptly appeared walking next to me, with one of them on each side surrounding me. I sensed something suspicious was going on with them and that they were up to no good.

"Lovely morn, would ya not say, lass?" asked the soldier on my right, pacing with me. He was slim and slightly below average height at about five feet, eight inches. He was fair-haired with a long, narrow, freckly face and razor-thin lips. I noticed his teeth were in really bad condition; they were stained yellow and brown. I felt fingers admiringly slip into my loose locks on my left side.

"Hey!" I retorted automatically, swiping away the other soldier's hand from me. His gaunt face lifted with levity and surprise. He stood approximately the same height as his buddy and slightly matched my own height at two inches taller as I glared nearly at eye level at him.

"*Hey!*" He laughed mockingly.

"Don't touch me," I said sharply. "I'm not bothering you, so you leave me alone."

"*Ooh*, she's feisty," said the one on my right.

"So I see," replied the one on my left.

"Careful, Nigel, she might clip your fingers," warned his companion. So, that was his name, then… Nigel glanced at his friend on the other side of me.

"Forgive me, miss. Please allow for a proper introduction. I'm Private Nigel Hawkins, and this eya is Private Edward Taylor—simply Eddie ter the rest of us. He's a nice lad, ya see," Private Hawkins said with theatrical civility. I doubtfully looked at him and his companion. "What is your name, may I ask?"

"No. You may not ask," I responded defensively. They looked at me with sudden surprise.

"We am merely tryin' ter make your proper acquaintance, and mean ya no harm, miss," Hawkins insisted as he dramatically drew a palm to his chest.

"Well," I began, "if that's the case, then you would simply let me pass in peace."

"Yet me and Eddie were wishin' ter pay ya a most kind compliment," Hawkins persisted. I didn't respond, except for the hasty steps I kept taking.

"Indeed," Taylor chimed in.

"Aye, see? Why, we merely wished ter say ter ya that ya have brightened our morn wi' your lovely presence," Hawkins said with showy kindness. I scrutinized his face as I subtly nodded my head in acknowledgment.

"Thank you," I forced myself to say civilly. "But I better be on my way. So, if you will kindly excuse me, I must go now."

"Is there someone awai'in' ya?"

"Yes, actually, there is—so I really must go, thank you," I said. Hawkins overtly slid his grubby palm over my shoulder and fixed his arm around me. I tried shrugging him off, but his arm was glued to me like an octopus's.

"Yet ya will merely be a moment by talkin' ter us," Hawkins said.

"*Don't*," I insisted contemptuously, as I wiggled from his touchy-feely clutch. But he unexpectedly snatched my hair between his fingers and held me tightly by the scalp, arresting me in my steps. "*Ouch!*" I gasped alarmingly. He sharply pulled my head back to face him directly, and the bouquet I was holding fell to the ground when I threw my hands over my head to wrench his clutch free from my scalp.

"Such a cheeky lass, ya are. But I like me lasses that way," he said brutally as he started tugging me off to the side of the road.

"Stop! *Let go of me!*" I exclaimed anxiously, feeling the pain on my scalp as he forcefully pulled me around by my hair.

"Christ! The lass is wed! Look!" Taylor said excitedly, noticing my ring as I struggled with Hawkins. He pointed out my ring to Hawkins, and Hawkins suddenly paused. The two of them briefly exchanged glances.

"Never ya mind! All the more reason ter sample another man's wealth with pleasure," Hawkins said harshly.

"She must be worth some ter husband, however," Taylor cautioned uneasily.

"Don't get daft now, lad! Ya know that we haven't had us a lass in welly six months. I'm dry about now, and I mean ter help myself ter this here bit o' fruit," Hawkins said determinedly. I wrenched around Hawkins's wrist and chomped down like a pit bull. He suddenly hollered as I broke the skin. He hurled me loose, violently flinging me across the path. I landed mercilessly in a patch of twiggy shrubs and knocked the back of my head against a small rock on the ground behind me.

I thought I unfortunately escalated the situation, as Hawkins returned to tower over me with inhumane, sadistic ire in his eyes. He was going to *hurt* me. I scurried backward as he advanced.

"If that is the way ya like it, lass—I will gladly oblige!" Hawkins growled cruelly. He lunged for my skirts, and I kicked vigorously at him to keep him at bay. It seemed that I couldn't get myself up from the ground fast enough to get away as his soiled fingers were trying to catch hold of my hems. Suddenly, his palm clasped my ankle. "No, ya don't! Get over eya!" he barked angrily, and harshly yanked me forward toward him. My skirts rode up over my legs as he violently tugged me closer to him.

He knelt down before me, and I kicked him in the critical spot in his groin. He suddenly groaned and bowled over in pain. I caught a glimpse of Taylor as he stood on the lookout on the road. I frantically stirred to get myself off the ground and anxiously crawled away from Hawkins while he held himself, moaning. But he unexpectedly reached a long arm out and fastened a viselike grip over my petticoats.

"Come back eya, you goddamn cunt!" he growled furiously. Hawkins all of a sudden tugged me back toward him with such unsuspecting force that I toppled onto my stomach as I was being dragged toward him. In a second, Hawkins had me at a disadvantage as he remained kneeling and ferociously hovered over me. He whipped me over onto my back, and I could clearly see his vehement, malevolent expression. An icy cold realization came over me, and I wildly flailed my arms around to protect myself. My nails caught the side of his face, and he shockingly lifted his hand to the side of his head.

"*Cunt!*" he shouted angrily again. He wiped his cheek and saw blood on his fingertips. With more ire, he promptly slammed his hands down on my wrists, pressing them into the foliage on the ground. It felt like my circulation was being cut off, and I frightfully screamed.

"Eddie!" Hawkins shouted back to the road.

"Eh?" Taylor responded alertly.

"Hold 'er down!" Hawkins scowled furiously. Taylor instantly swung around and swiftly replaced Hawkins's hold on my wrists with his own unyielding grip.

"Please… You don't have to do this! Please, don't do this!" I pleaded alarmingly.

"Oh, you're goin' ter beg? Well, I reckon I like that!" Hawkins said wildly.

"You don't have to do this!" I panted, terrified.

"That's it, Eddie, hold 'er fast—don't let 'er slip," Hawkins instructed, completely ignoring my pleas. "Once I'm satisfied, you may have a chance wi' 'er," he told his friend.

"Grand!" Taylor replied eagerly. I heard the latch of Hawkins's pistol belt come loose and snap from his waist.

"Please—don't! Don't do this!" I begged, panic-stricken. There was no way for me to escape; I was absolutely trapped between them at their mercy. *I was terrified beyond words!* They were going to do what they *wanted* to do to me, and there wasn't anything I could do to prevent them. I was alone in the desolate woods without a single passerby to intervene in the crime being committed. I screamed again with all my might with a carnal cry for help, sending echoes throughout the forest. Suddenly, I felt a burning, stinging pain across the side of my face. I momentarily saw stars… and I tasted blood from my lower lip.

"*Bitch!* Shut that mouth of yourn! You'll regret it if ya do that again!" Hawkins hissed furiously. "Now, let's get on wi' it!" He impatiently adjusted his breeches, and the front flap dropped open, exposing his stimulated shaft. I continued to frantically squirm, attempting to kick him away, but he brutally wedged himself between my legs and pushed my skirts high above my waist, obscuring my vision. He swiftly moved and lowered himself onto me. I felt him erect and ready as he grazed the tip of his shaft along the cleft between my legs in search of the right location.

I released a bloodcurdling cry from the deepest part of my being the moment I felt him at the point of entry.

Suddenly, I heard a *crack*, like the sound of a baseball splitting a wooden bat against the force of a hard swing. Hawkins went limp, abruptly falling over me with his full weight smothering me. I felt Taylor's restraint loosening from around my wrists as Hawkins's dead weight rolled off to my side.

"The lass haur isnae yer property fur the taking," said a firm, solid, unseen voice from above. A hand strongly fastened around my arm and pulled me upright to my feet. My skirts modestly fell back down, covering my ankles when I shakily glanced up, discovering Leif to my aid. He had his firearm stretched out with the hammer to his pistol fully cocked, directly pointed between Taylor's eyes. Leif pulled me aside, never taking his eyes off Taylor, who right now appeared extremely fearful for his life as he stared ashen down the barrel of a readied pistol. "Have they injured ye?" Leif inquired of me, while keeping his cold gaze fixed on Taylor. I shook my head a bit, unable to control my tremulous nerves.

"Almost," I replied. My mouth went completely dry when I gulped.

"Pass yer pistol tae me," Leif demanded. Taylor reached around his side and pulled out his pistol. Leif ordered Taylor to toss it low to the ground toward him. Taylor complied, and the pistol flew low, skidding close to my feet. "Pick it up, lass," Leif instructed me, and I bent to reach for it while he still aimed closely at Taylor's brow. I collected the heavy firearm between my shaking fingers and straightened. Leif retrieved the pistol from me and tucked it in his belt around his waist at the back. He then instructed me to collect Hawkins's pistol from his holster, and I did. Leif also took that firearm from me and tucked the second one next to the first. He continued ordering Taylor, "Take yer dirk out and drop it at yer feet." Taylor did as he was told, and Leif requested that I retrieve Hawkins's knife. Once I had it, I passed it to him, and Leif tucked it securely in his belt as he still aimed his weapon at Taylor's face. "Nae doubt yoo're Captain Foster's men," Leif concluded.

"Aye, we am," Taylor stammered uneasily, looking down the barrel of Leif's steady pistol. Leif's jaw was set square and taut. His eyes were shallow, hard, and unreadable as he soundly stood armed, ready to kill with heartless conviction. The only thing revealing a hint of emotion that I could detect was the crimson hue on his face.

"Give yer name," Leif demanded frigidly.

"Who am ya?" Taylor nervously inquired of Leif.

"Yer superior officer, and someone ye have crossed," Leif responded steadily.

"I see," Taylor said.

"I'll order ye once more tae give yer name," Leif stated again.

"'Tis, er, Ed-Edward Taylor," he said, appearing visibly uneasy at the loaded weapon pointing at his nose.

"Yer rank?" Leif demanded also.

"Private," Taylor answered.

"*Git* up!" Leif ordered.

"Aye," Taylor tentatively responded as he started to his feet.

"It is *major* tae ye bastards!" Leif said. Taylor's eyes closed with regret for a moment.

"I swear ter ya, major, that the lass is unharmed," Taylor assured urgently.

"Git him up!" Leif directed Taylor, referring to Hawkins, with his pistol steadfastly aimed at Taylor's head. Taylor complied without a word and struggled to gain balance as he lifted his unconscious companion from the vegetation. He heaved the dead weight and wrapped one of Hawkins's arms around his neck, stabilizing the limp man. I noticed blood dripping from behind Hawkins's ear.

"Back tae camp," Leif instructed expressionlessly, never wavering the aim of his pistol.

~

WITH LEIF MAINTAINING a steadfast grip on the trigger of his pistol pointing directly at the back of Taylor's head, I paced beside him as we followed the men along the road toward the encampment. Taylor struggled lugging Hawkins's listless weight over the path. Leif had no intentions of stopping to allow for Taylor to better adjust his companion, and so we pressed onward along the road.

After about fifteen minutes, the road forked, and we veered off onto a narrower path. Soon, a number of white canvas pitched tents surrounding a large, rustic two-story raw umber clapboard farmhouse came into view between the trees.

Attention among the encamped soldiers began stirring as we advanced through the property. Curious soldiers proceeded to approach us for a better look as we arrived closer to the porch of the house. Leif locked eyes with a young soldier who appeared no more than sixteen, and demanded for him to immediately collect the captain. The boy hastened to run up the doorsteps of the house and vanished indoors.

In an instant, the captain came stomping irately out of the house and down the steps. It seemed he was right in the middle of a shave, since soap lather covered half his face. He obviously was not in a favorable mood as he steamrolled his way through his curiously onlooking men.

"What the *devil* is this all about?" the captain exclaimed, recognizing Taylor and Hawkins while approaching us.

"Captain Foster," Leif addressed him stoically.

"Ahh, Major Monteith," Captain Foster acknowledged. The captain's questioning eyes rolled over his men, Taylor and Hawkins. His eyes briefly seized on to Hawkins, who was still rendered unconscious. "What is the meaning of this?" Captain Foster inquired suspiciously as he scanned the two men with some degree of uncertainty. Leif finally withdrew his pistol and uncocked it before placing it inside his holster. "Has there been an accident?" Captain Foster asked, scrutinizing Hawkins.

"Thaur has been an incident," Leif informed him unflappably.

"What sort of incident?" Captain Foster asked critically.

"Your men will inform ye," Leif said. Captain Foster furrowed his brow.

"Fetch water!" He scowled at the boy soldier, and the boy immediately disappeared among the other men curiously standing around.

"'Tis a private matter," Leif said.

"I see," Captain Foster responded tersely. The captain's gaze finally noticed me standing somewhat hidden behind Leif. I uneasily cast my eyes down from the captain. "I see," Captain Foster repeated perceptively.

The boy soldier promptly returned with a bucket full of water, and Captain Foster motioned for Taylor to release Hawkins. Hawkins fell to the ground like a wet noodle. The captain then motioned for the boy to dump his liquid load smack over Hawkins's head. The water drenched the entire upper half of him. Hawkins punctually began sputtering and coughing up water. He was restored vaguely to consciousness.

"Back to your duties, men! Back to your duties!" Captain Foster ordered abruptly to his inquisitive troops. The men started dispersing, and the captain irately glanced at Hawkins and Taylor. "Get him to his feet, private. You men come with me," Captain Foster commanded. Taylor began assisting Hawkins to his feet. Hawkins, drenched from the top of his head to his shirt, appeared slightly muddled. Captain Foster turned his gaze to Leif. "Major Monteith, if you will, please," he said accommodatingly, suggesting for us to follow him.

We entered the house. Leif was right about what he had said

regarding his property—the house on the outside was weathered, but indoors it seemed tidied and suitable for military accommodations. There were men working outside fixing some of the torn siding around the house. I heard hammering and shuffling high above on the roof as we stepped deeper into the corridor from the foyer. We rounded a corner, and Captain Foster ordered Hawkins and Taylor to remain at attention along the wall next to a couple of guards already posted. We followed the captain past the threshold, entering the sitting room, which had apparently been made into his office. The captain closed the door behind him, ensuring some privacy, and attentively stepped farther into the room.

"Please, major, make yourself comfortable. You have indeed afforded me and my men some comfort by your generosity, so please do not hesitate to be free," Captain Foster insisted solicitously in his proper London accent.

"Indeed, captain," Leif replied gravely. He ceased his steps just before the captain's letter desk. He stood erect and stiff as his eyes mechanically skimmed the room without turning his head. "I see the lodging is suitable fur ye," he noted.

"Yes, indeed—many thanks," Captain Foster replied. Leif gave a single acknowledging nod in response. Captain Foster's glance bounced nervously from Leif to me as I stood reservedly near him. "May I inquire who this lovely young woman might be who accompanies you, major?"

"Aye, this is Mistress Arboles," Leif introduced me in a businesslike manner. The captain cocked an eyebrow.

"A pleasure to make your acquaintance, mistress," Captain Foster said solicitously as he kindly took my hand and gently squeezed it. After releasing my hand, the captain shifted his gaze back to Leif.

"Ye may conclude yer personal business before we git on with the matter at hand," Leif said pointedly.

"Yes, of course," Captain Foster said, remembering the soapsuds still around his jaw. He excused himself and left the room, closing the door. Leif and I were presently left alone together in the office along with a soldier standing innocuously at the back of the room. Leif glanced at me with sternness on his face. He lifted his fingers and gently touched the side of my cheek.

"Are ye alrecht, lass?" he inquired intently.

"Yeah, I'm all right," I told him.

"Yet ye remain tremulous," he observed. "Are ye certain that they didnae hurt ye? Ye may tell me the truth."

"I'm not hurt... They didn't get the chance to," I replied honestly. Leif nodded once as he maintained an earnest gaze on me.

"Ye remain tremulous, however," he said. "Haur, ye ought tae sit fur a moment," he advised, and wrapped a hand around my upper arm. He thoughtfully led me to a chair by the letter desk near the window. I sat down in the wooden chair, not realizing until then how much I needed to sit in order to calm my shaking nerves. My knees trembled, and I felt cold. I pulled my cape tightly around my shoulders and glanced out the distorted glass window. I could discern some of the men practicing some of their military self-defense tactics.

Leif released a deep nasal sigh as he remained standing in the middle of the room with his arms folded over his imposing chest, waiting to speak to the captain. His jaw was clenched and set square. I could see that he was deeply meditative and didn't appear the least bit pleased. Although he seemed controlled on the surface, I sensed his resentment. I wondered how much further the anger actually ran within him.

Regardless of the hidden temper ignited inside him, Leif caught my gaze and stared at me intently. It struck me because I did not realize that he cared about me as much as he seemed to. He noticed the undisturbed tea tray placed on the captain's desk and moved toward it. He grabbed the teapot and poured piping hot tea into a small porcelain cup. When Leif had finished pouring the tea, he collected the cup then strode toward me.

"Take a bit of tea, lass. 'Twill warm ye some and settle yer nerves," he encouraged softly, leaning forward slightly for me to take the cup and saucer.

"Thank you," I said appreciatively, taking the saucer from his stable hand.

"I must ask ye tae be truthful with me," he continued, speaking quietly.

"Yeah?" I replied openly, looking at him with concern as I could read the gravity in his expression. He seemed as though he wanted to ask me something, except he was hesitant. I looked at him with cautious anticipation. Leif gazed at me very seriously.

"Are ye certain that ye waur not harmed?" he asked distinctly, appearing slightly uncomfortable for having asked the question.

"Yes, I'm sure," I answered honestly.

"Yoo're certain?" he insisted.

"I was almost, but I—I wasn't raped, if that's what you mean," I told him genuinely.

"Aye," he responded with a nod.

The door suddenly opened. Leif's posture straightened tall and square as a freshly shaven Captain Foster promptly entered the room, closing the door after himself.

"Thank you, major, for your generous patience," Captain Foster said as he paced farther into the room, headed for the chair behind his desk. Leif merely tilted his head in response to the captain. "May I offer you a chair, major?" the captain inquired civilly before taking his own seat behind his desk.

"I shall prefer tae remain as I am, thank ye, captain," Leif responded unemotionally.

"Indeed," Captain Foster replied uncertainly. "Ah, very good, Mistress Arboles is enjoying a spot of tea. Please accept my most sincere apologies for not offering it to you sooner... Very well," the captain continued. "Now, let us get to the matter at hand."

"Aye," Leif agreed resolutely.

"Pray, what appears to be the matter?" Captain Foster inquired professionally.

"I shall speak plainly, captain," Leif said.

"Yes, of course, major," Captain Foster replied with an anticipatory gaze.

"It is regarding two of yer men," Leif said gravely.

"Private Hawkins and Private Taylor, I presume," the captain responded.

"Aye," Leif said tersely.

"Yes, well, what of them?" the captain inquired attentively.

"I interceded as they waur attempting tae harm Mistress Arboles along the road just now," Leif informed him. The captain's gaze shifted toward me, and he turned a scrutinizing glance to me as I sat motionless with my tea resting between my hands in my lap.

"You interceded?" Captain Foster inquired, turning his attention back to Leif.

"Aye," Leif said indisputably.

"What *sort* of harm were they committing against Mistress Arboles?" Captain Foster asked.

"Bodily harm—apparently," Leif said. The captain's unreadable eyes shot over to me again as he put an elbow on his desk and lightly drummed his fingers once on the surface. "I caught them just as they waur about tae take their pleasure with her," Leif said grimly. The captain returned a serious eye to Leif.

"How unfortunate," Captain Foster said coolly. I observed his fingers lightly skimming the surface of the desk in front of him.

"Aye, *most* unfortunate," Leif echoed seriously. Captain Foster cleared his throat, appearing disturbed.

"Might I inquire of Mistress Arboles whereabout is her husband, as this case regarding his wife is pertinent to him?" Captain Foster asked plainly.

"She is widowed," Leif informed him.

"I see," Captain Foster said contemplatively. He turned his eyes to me once more. "My condolences to you, madam."

"Thank you," I responded demurely.

"Will you have some more tea?" the captain offered civilly.

"Yes, thank you," I accepted weakly.

"Allow me," Captain Foster replied politely. He stood from his desk, grasping the handle of the teapot. In a few short strides, he came around his desk toward me and poured some more hot tea into my cup. Leif silently watched the tea being poured. Once the captain had finished refilling my cup, Leif observed the captain return to his seat at the desk.

"Do you claim any injury, Mistress Arboles?" the captain suddenly asked me, as he poured himself a cup of tea.

"She claims that she has been unharmed." Leif had unexpectedly assumed speaking for me, and I was silently somewhat surprised.

"Indeed, that is fortunate," Captain Foster muttered with a measure of relief, when he concluded pouring his tea. "Then, I assure you, major, I shall properly look after the matter."

"The road whaur she was closely attacked occurred on Laird Kneep's property, and he will be most displeased when he learns of it," Leif informed the captain as he took a sip of tea. Captain Foster swallowed his tea a bit suddenly.

"Well, I assure you, major, that I shall indeed promptly attend to the matter," Captain Foster repeated, appearing slightly ill at ease as he replaced his teacup on the saucer on his desk.

"I shall bide tae see that it is done," Leif said determinedly. The captain appeared to have been overridden, and did not seem particularly keen about that fact.

"But I might have a proper word with my men," the captain respectfully suggested.

"Indeed," Leif said. Captain Foster signaled to the guard who had been standing like a wooden soldier at the back of the room. The guard promptly responded and paced to the front of the room. He opened the door. Hawkins and Taylor entered shortly, followed by two other guards. The men ceased their steps and stood at attention before Leif and the captain. Captain Foster clearly appeared disgusted, but held on to a degree of control.

"There has been a matter brought to my attention that involves the pair of you, concerning Mistress Arboles. Have you any notion of it?" Captain Foster inquired, staring strictly at the two men standing before him. Private Taylor fleetingly slipped a worrisome sidelong glance over to me as neither of the men were prompt to respond. "*Well?*" Captain Foster insisted, on edge, glaring tensely at his men from behind his desk.

"We meant no harm, cap'ain," Hawkins said uneasily.

"You meant no harm?" Captain Foster questioned.

"We meant nothin' by it," Taylor said nervously.

"To what are you *exactly* referring?" Captain Foster demanded.

"We merely wished ter become acquainted wi' the lass," Hawkins said.

"I see," Captain Foster replied, unimpressed.

"Precisely, cap'ain. We was merely meanin' a nice conversation wi' 'er as we met 'er on the road," Hawkins continued explaining.

"I see. Is that all?" Captain Foster said. The two men seemed rather hesitant to respond to the captain. Although, they both appeared clearly aware of Leif's presence and the steadfast, no-nonsense, disgusted glare he was giving them.

"Er, well, she paid us no mind—like she is be'er than us, and that we couldn't speak ter 'er or anythin' of a sort. She's a colonial, cap'ain—and we'm British soldiers, English, in fact. *How about a measure of respect?* I thought. But none come from the dark lass. We believe she was most out o' place, cap'ain," Private Hawkins explained.

"Is that right?" Captain Foster said dryly, with noticeable

displeasure in his voice. "Had it not occurred to either of you that you might have been discovered?"

Leif's fair complexion suddenly went a deeper shade of crimson, and his eyes narrowed on the captain.

"Is it yer policy, Captain Foster, tae permit yer men tae assault decent New England men by ravishing their women merely because they see fit tae do so, understanding that they will likely not be caught or held accountable fur their offense?" Leif asked irately.

"Why, no, of course not, Your Grace," Captain Foster said uneasily.

"Then, pray explain yer meaning," Leif said.

"Merely, ahem, that my men ought to exercise more scruples," Captain Foster said unevenly.

"Whit about the use of one's morality and honor? Has that not got any merit fur better judgment?" Leif asked reproachfully.

"*Indeed*, of course," Captain Foster replied, seeming somewhat insulted as the hue in his face rose.

"Then if such characteristics in yer men are merely lacking in yer charge, I urge ye tae promptly set a standard," Leif ordered tightly.

"Yes, Your Grace, I shall see that the order takes place," Captain Foster replied, though he was clearly incensed.

"These men will be swiftly sentenced fur their deplorable actions," Leif said coolly.

"Yes, they will be flogged for it," Captain Foster said with certainty.

"Fifty lashes each. I shall bide till the discipline is properly seen through," Leif said resolutely. Captain Foster's brow fleetingly lifted, then faintly furrowed.

"I assure you, Your Grace, the measure will soon take place," Captain Foster said.

"Not any sooner than at present," Leif stated unyieldingly. The captain seemed to be conflicted, but held his tongue.

"Very well," Captain Foster obliged finally, with some reservation depicted in his demeanor. The color had visibly drained from the perpetrators' faces as they realized their fate the moment the captain motioned for the guards to remove them from the room. Once the men crossed the threshold and vanished from the room, Captain Foster and Leif locked glances. Leif glared rigidly in silence at the captain. Captain Foster appeared to understand the code as he respectfully tilted his head toward Leif. Leif responded with a quick nod of his own, then Captain Foster proceeded out of the room.

The door closed after the captain, leaving Leif and me alone again in the office with the one guard remaining stolidly standing at the back of the room. Leif stepped toward the window where I was sitting and glanced outside, appearing to scan the grounds looking for something. After a moment, his eyes steadied. I leaned over in my chair a little, curious to see what Leif's gaze had seized on to. I followed his line of vision and witnessed Hawkins and Taylor surrounded by four guards, two in front and two behind. They were being led out over the grass toward a large oak tree, with Captain Foster following them not far behind in the distance.

My stomach clenched with some uncertainty as I suddenly anticipated what was about to occur. I felt apprehensive; I didn't know if this was the right thing to be done.

"Come away from the window, lass. Ye will likely not wish tae watch," Leif said. I suddenly glanced up at him, realizing that he had been gazing at me. He held out his hand for me to take. I placed my hand in his, and he helped me to my feet from my seat. I followed him across the room, where he led me to a more sheltered location off to the side opposite the window facing the field, and I sat on a bench in a niche.

Leif returned to the window, standing squarely before it with his feet spread at ease and hands clasped behind his back. I waited with dread as I tightly folded my hands in my lap. Shortly, a sudden audible cry came from outside. The noise was muffled inside the room and immediately compelled my attention toward the window. From where I sat in the niche, I peered motionlessly around Leif's silhouette facing the window. I could see Hawkins's bare back as he was bound to the oak tree about to receive a second lashing from Captain Foster's whip.

The captain whirled his whip. It snapped fiercely, and I gasped horribly as the tentacle snapped against Hawkins's unshielded back, slicing through his skin like a knife. Blood was easily drawn. I cast my stunned gaze down toward my knees as Hawkins hollered out in sheer agony. Leif remained still like a statue looking out the window, obstructing my view outside. But my ears were not spared the sound of Hawkins's continual painful cries. I couldn't help shutting my eyes at every sound of his audible screams as the whip struck his back.

I sat there quietly listening to the men being flogged, and my breathing grew harder; I felt like I was underwater. I just wanted the punishment to be over. I wanted the captain to stop. I could no longer stand hearing their cries. I suppose my expectations were reasonably low for crime repercussions of this sort; I would have expected merely a verbal reprimand, a possible demotion, and some jail time. The punishment was brutal and inhumane. Even though I unexpectedly had slight sympathy for my perpetrators, there was a real part of me that was glad to know that they, too, were receiving similar pain of the likes they would never forget, and therefore would be unlikely to commit the same deplorable action against another woman.

I was short of breath and nauseated to my stomach when the wailing sounds of the men receiving their penalty finally abated. Leif turned from his stance at the window and collected me from the niche. He took my teacup away to place it on the captain's desk, and then guided me out of the office. He stopped short at a guard posted at the front of the house just before the entrance.

"Tell the captain that I am presently taking my leave," Leif told him. The guard instantly rushed off the deck down the steps in search of the captain, then I proceeded down the steps following Leif. As we paced a little ways from the house, Leif glanced over his shoulder in the captain's direction. Captain Foster noticed Leif at a distance, and the men exchanged a silent code of acknowledgment in a mere glance.

Subsequently, Leif turned and protectively led me by the arm across the army camp and off the property.

There was not much conversation between me and Leif as we walked along the road back to the property belonging to his brother, the Earl of Kneep. In fact, we didn't even speak. I remained suspended and stuck in my own private troubling thoughts over everything that had just happened. I didn't know what I would have done if Leif hadn't come when he did. I couldn't begin to fathom the psychological consequences if I hadn't been rescued. I was so very lucky and grateful that he was there to help me. He saved me from being emotionally and bodily devastated. And the images and repeated sounds of my two perpetrators being whipped troubled my mind further and unsettled my spirit.

The colonists were correct, I contemplated, as Leif and I were now taking a shortcut through the woods; they were correct to fear British troops here. So many members of their military were extremely crude, crass, vulgar, and unsympathetic or ignorant of the humble culture here. There was this under-lying sense of arrogance, like they were owed something for their troubles for having to be here, and that they were innately better merely because they were English—or British from

Europe. It then all of a sudden dawned on me exactly at that moment the reason why the third amendment in the US Constitution Bill of Rights will have been written. *Will have been written...* I suddenly staggered in my thoughts. I was reminded again that this country was not my country, and that it would be another twenty years before the United States of America would even be given birth to.

Leif had slackened his pace as we walked along, now approaching one of the duck ponds on Finley's land. The house, obscured by surrounding pine trees, only lay five minutes away. Leif paused walking as he came to a large log on the shore beneath a row of cedar trees.

"Do ye mind if we sit haur fur a moment?" he asked unexpectedly, turning his attention to me.

"No," I agreed, subdued. He stepped around the log toward the front facing the glinting water bouncing sunlight like buoyant golden glitter, and sat. Leif gave the log a single pat, indicating for me to sit next to him. I moved around it and sat down. We sat quietly together for a bit as I watched him break off a dead twig from the log and toss it into the pond. I sensed that he was meditative, with his mind heavy in thought.

"Why did ye wander off, Sylvie?" he started pensively, as he shifted discernible, serious eyes to me.

"I just went for a walk," I answered.

"Ye shouldnae have wandered off alone," he said with disapproval in his voice.

"Maybe not—I had only intended to take a walk though," I said.

"But ye wandered too far," he said.

"I always go that way though," I replied reasonably.

"Ye micht have asked me tae escort ye. Why did ye not?" he asked earnestly.

"Well, you were busy with your letters—correspondence, I mean. I thought you didn't want to be disturbed," I said. He released a faint sigh and tightened his lips, slightly nodding his head as he kept his firm gaze fixed on me.

"Ye should have come fur me nonetheless. I would have gladly interrupted my business tae walk with ye," he said.

"I didn't know… I'm sorry," I responded contritely.

"'Tis nae longer safe fur ye tae be wandering so long soldiers are about," he said. I quietly nodded my head. "Do ye ken?"

"Yes, I understand," I said.

"Ye have been placed in my charge, Sylvie. It is my duty tae see that ye remain protected till further notice… Or till ye decide tae wed again… I must escort ye the next time ye wish tae go somewhaur," he explained explicitly.

"Okay," I agreed.

"Do ye understand?" he pressed.

"Yes," I said.

"Alrecht," he responded. The conversation broke off into silence for a moment as he contemplatively shifted his eyes over the sparkling water. It was cool and crisp outside with a faint breeze rustling through the fall leaves. But the sunshine still felt mild on my face, and the air smelled rich with damp earth.

"Thank you, Leif," I began shakily, feeling immense gratitude toward him along with a swell of other compounding emotions. Leif covered my hand with his and securely squeezed it while maintaining his gaze out over the pond. "How did you know where to find me so quickly?" I managed to utter on the verge of tears. I noticed his ear changing color and the redness emerging deeper over the side of his face.

"I saw ye out the window crossing the field whilst I was corresponding and decided tae delay business, since I wanted tae see ye instead. Once I arrived at the field and saw ye nowhaur about, I realized that ye had gone too far. So, I made haste and searched fur ye. I heard ye scream, so I hastened farther through the wood fur ye in the direction whaur I heard ye scream," he said.

"Oh," I replied.

"So, fortunately I arrived when I did," he said. He finally returned his thoughtful gaze to me.

"Oh," I said.

"I was reminded then how quickly ye can pace yerself, *àille dhubh*," he said.

"Oh."

"Indeed. Yoo're quick on yer feet," he remarked. He paused momentarily, staring into my eyes. He possessively drew my hand deeper into his lap. "I dinnae wish fur anything wrong tae happen tae ye, Sylvie," Leif said seriously.

"I realize that… Thank you for caring about me," I responded demurely, feeling guilty inside.

"Henceforth, come fur me, nae matter whit it is that I'm minding at the moment. Permit me tae take ye whaur ye wish tae go. I shall gladly take ye anywhaur," he insisted earnestly.

"Okay," I agreed.

"Do ye promise?"

"I promise."

"Very weel."

Leif changed hands over my fingers resting in his lap and slipped his formidable arm around my waist, pulling me close against him. I tilted my head against his shoulder and naturally rested against him as quiet ensued between us. Things had slightly settled between us as I sensed the tension in his shoulder relax a little. The perturbed frustration began to wane from him as I vacantly watched the burnt-sienna cattails on the edge of the pond faintly bending in the light breeze.

ANOTHER SUNDAY CAME, and we all went to church as usual. Once the service had concluded, the congregation typically collected for a short while around the church grounds. Greetings and polite mingling between the parishioners took place at this time. This Sunday, the Vintons were going to host Sunday dinner at their house for the small congregation to enjoy, and soon we would gather there for a good portion of the day.

Mr. Thomas Vinton had located us as Elizabeth and I mingled with her sister, Suzanna, and her family beneath the oak tree in the churchyard. He politely greeted us and inquired if we intended to join the gathering at his family's house. The consensus according to Elizabeth's family was that we would gladly attend, and Thomas seemed very pleased. He specifically glanced at me, slightly flushed in the face. He seemed anticipatory, as if he wished to speak with me. Instead, he merely said that he would be glad to receive us when we arrive at his residence, then departed from us in the churchyard.

After several moments of listening to the family converse among each other, I decided to search for the children, who had stolen away somewhere around the yard with Leif for a bit of lightheartedness. I strolled into the quaint floral garden and spotted the children in the distance, giggling by the little water-lily pond, peering at the frogs in and near the water. I noticed Leif was not with them as I approached. The girls and their two cousins, Henry and George, were happy to bring my attention to the animated frogs once I arrived. We were entertained as we watched the leaping frogs together for a moment.

After a little while, I finally urged the children to come along with me to meet their parents, who by this time, I was sure, were probably wondering where their children had gone. The children and I circled around the back side of the church through the yard, where no one was around except us. As we continued winding our way along the little pebbled path exiting the enclosure, I suddenly recognized Leif standing between the oak trees near a cast-iron garden bench, appearing deep in conversation with Constance Pringle. I immediately halted in my steps, and my heart dropped a little as I let the children continue walking the rest of the way without me.

Leif's expression was ruddy and intent. I witnessed their hands enfolded in each other's. He looked sensitive and engrossed as he was speaking to Connie. Her pretty cheeks were pink like rose petals. She daintily lifted her fingertips to her sweet face, and Leif followed with his own gentle touch on her cheek. He carefully stroked the side of her face then gathered both of her hands in his. He seemed extremely genuine as he spoke with her. He then carefully raised the back of her hand to his lips and bestowed what very much looked like a meaningful kiss. When he withdrew her small hand from his lips, he resumed tenderly caressing the side of her cheek.

I cannot believe my eyes!

Leif's glance shifted away from Connie, and he unexpectedly noticed me looking at them both from the path. He quickly released her hands. He was obviously caught off guard, and Connie quickly raised a palm over her little mouth, ill at ease as her eyes landed on me also. She abruptly withdrew from Leif.

All of a sudden, I stormed out of the churchyard altogether, leaving the premises without a word to anyone. I was filled with anger or jealousy—I couldn't distinguish between either emotion. I supposed they were one and the same at this point.

I raced out of the village entirely irritated and fed up with everything!

Not too far from Northampton village along the roadside lay Claude Lefebvre's land. I decided to take an even shorter route back to the house and cut through his farm, assuming he wouldn't have minded. He was an anchorite: a hermit who seemed harmless and nonthreatening to anyone. No one ever ventured to involve him in the community, since it was rumored that he was a contented recluse. Since coming to live here, I had noticed him once or twice tending to his garden. There was something remotely interesting about him—he had a reverent sense about him that made me view him in a monastic light due to the way he cared for his plants and animals. That was my initial impression of him the first time I saw him near his house from the road as we passed by his property headed into the center of town.

Soon, I had arrived at a fence surrounding Mr. Lefebvre's cow pasture. The fence ran for a long distance, and I realized there was no way for me to simply get around it. I heard Leif calling after me not that far behind me. I didn't want to speak with him! I didn't want to see him! I was so mad at him, I couldn't believe it! So, I ignored him. But I knew he would soon arrive close enough to me that I would have to acknowledge him.

I hiked up my skirts and tried placing one foot onto the lowest rail of the fence. I pulled myself up and awkwardly climbed to the second rail.

"Sylvie!" Leif called. I turned my gaze over my shoulder and saw him anxiously picking up his pace, jogging after me. He was swift and would shortly catch up to me. I quickly threw my leg over the top rail and clumsily worked to balance myself over the fence. Except when I stepped down onto the next lower beam, my foot caught the underside of my cape and I slipped. I completely lost my footing and flew backward, airborne, off the fence, plunging flat on my back into the soft earth. My body sank into the ground, and I realized my entire back was caked in mud. "Whit are ye doin', lass?" Leif called out to me outlandishly from his gaining distance.

"What does it look like I'm doing, *buddy*?" I called irately back to him, struggling to pick myself up again.

"Are ye mad?" he exclaimed unbelievably. I managed to stand upright and regain some footing.

"You betcha I'm mad! Go away! Leave me alone!" I yelled at him, even more annoyed now that I was now covered in mud.

"The earth isnae fit fur walkin' whaur ye are presently!" he warned.

"Tell me something I don't already know, *Sherlock*! Just go away!" I finally steadied myself on my feet. I started pacing forward, but didn't get too far when the earth sucked my foot in deep like a vacuum and I toppled over. This time I landed front first flat into the sloppy muck. The whole front of my gown was ruined with mud, and I felt some of the cool, wet earth on my bare skin over my upper torso. "*Shit!*" I cursed angrily. The ground felt like mushy dough as I strove to pick myself up again.

"Sylvie! Whit the *devil* ur ye doin'?" Leif said wildly. His Scottish brogue was even more pronounced as he spoke incredulously. I continued to disregard him and once again managed my way back to my feet. My heels sank deeply with every step I took as I tried keeping my distance from him. "The field spans wide— yoo'll not make it through!" Leif exclaimed as he huffed, now closely approaching me. I ignored him and kept going, determined to keep my distance from him. Suddenly, my arm was snagged in his noticeably firm clasp, and he whirled me around to face him. "Whaur ur ye goin', lass?" he asked, bewildered. He stared at me in sheer confusion and disbelief.

"Where do you think I'm going, *pal*? Obviously, I'm going back to the house!" I replied, visibly aggravated.

"Why?" he questioned, out of breath, looking utterly baffled.

"I don't want to talk to you right now," I said curtly.

"Whit in heaven's name is the matter?" he inquired, grimacing oddly at me.

"I can't believe you're asking me that!" I scoffed. He frowned and released a ridiculous sigh, appearing annoyed.

"I dinnae understand," he said.

"Oh, *please!*" I said sarcastically. He took a deep breath and sighed again as he rubbed his brow.

"Come along, lassie—we'll discuss whit is trooblin' ye at a mair suitable location," Leif decided conclusively. He then reached for my arm and seized it.

"No, we're not! *Let* go of me!" I demanded as I unsuccessfully tried wrenching my arm loose from his grip.

"Come now, Sylvie! Yoo're being childish," he said.

"*Childish!*" I exclaimed unbelievably. "Well, you look here, *mister*, you better let go of me or there's going to be a problem!" I tried freeing my arm from him again, but to no avail.

"If ye dinnae quit yer squirmin', I'll turn ye about and haul ye like a sack of grain off this plot haur," he said as he struggled with me.

"How dare you talk to me like that! You are *not* my boss!" I said vexedly. I purposefully tugged at him as I wiggled myself around to release his hand from my arm. All of a sudden, my foot gave way in the mud, and I slipped between his knees. Leif automatically lunged forward and swiftly took hold of my other arm to steady me. I quickly grabbed onto the lapels of his coat to keep from falling, and he lost his balance. I thought for sure he was going to smother me into the earth as he toppled. But he unpredictably planted facedown into the muck beside me.

He turned over and sat up in sheer disbelief, covered in mud now also. I angrily pushed myself up into a sitting position and attempted to get to my feet. But my efforts were made more difficult because the billowing skirts surrounding me were now weighted with mud and kept me from finding my feet.

"What a *splendid* day for an exotic mud bath!" I griped irksomely. I could feel the thick muck covering me from top to bottom along my entire back, weighing me down, making matters so much worse.

"Ye huvnae yet seen how I could treat ye," Leif warned.

"Is that a fact?"

"Aye."

"Well, I have nothing to say to you," I said as I watched him come to his feet again.

"We'll see about that. Now let's go," he urged. He decisively took a solid hold of my arm and pulled me straight up from the sloppy ground. In one swooping motion, he effortlessly scooped me up into his arms and resolutely carried me back toward the fence. When we returned to the fence, he swung me over the rails to the other side onto stable ground, then easily swung himself over the beams.

I scarcely regarded him as we now stood facing each other, smothered all over in smelly mud. Instead of acknowledging him, I chose to take off again, walking angrily away from him back toward the road. Now, I was forced to take the longer route in order to return to the house.

I sensed Leif fast on my heels as I stepped out onto the path again. He abruptly clutched my elbow, halting my steps, and spun me around to face him again.

"Whit is the matter? Why ur ye terribly cross?" Leif inquired exasperatedly, appearing quite perplexed. I studied him for a moment, considering my thoughts. "Pray, whit is it?"

"Okay, do you want to know what the deal is? Well, I'll tell you what the problem is, since obviously I have to spell it out for you," I replied shortly.

"Please do," he requested.

"*Fine.* First of all, okay—I get it—you obviously feel sorry for me," I began. He stared unresponsively at me. I took that to mean yes, so I continued to say assertively, "You feel sorry for me, and that's *why* you like me."

"That isnae why I like ye, lass," he replied.

"*Yes*, it is. I get it—I *really* do! So stop it. You don't have to *pity* me. I'm not some sort of charity case who can't figure it out!" I said crossly.

"Figure whit out?" he inquired confusedly. I sighed, very much annoyed by him.

"I can get along *without* you just fine," I said clearly. An offended expression abruptly passed over his face.

"I see," he said somberly, appearing somewhat hurt, I realized.

"You know, I have no problem if you want to play the field," I said frankly.

"Play whit field?" he asked innocently.

"People do it all of the time. I understand that," I said angrily.

"Whit do ye mean?" he asked.

"If you want to two-time and be a *player*, that's your choice, but you should have told me that's what you're all about, because I don't play that *game*!" I chastised.

"Whit game do ye speak of?" He furrowed his brow with apparent puzzlement.

"I don't go around sweet-talking people—whispering sweet nothings in one person's ear and then turning around and whispering the same load of *crap* to someone else!" I said angrily. His brow lifted with a mixture of additional offense and surprise.

"I huvnae sweet-talked anyone but ye—and I meant whit I said tae ye," he said, seeming insulted.

"Oh, spare me the Casanova junk!" I said disgustedly. Leif released a sigh, and his shoulders slumped slightly as he seemed to have come to a realization.

"Thaur has been a *grave* misunderstanding," he said.

"Oh, you bet your bottom dollar there's been a misunderstanding! I've obviously misunderstood *you*!" I responded sarcastically.

"Sylvie, I have been nothing but honest with ye," he said with a wholehearted look on his face.

"Well, where I come from, there's a popular adage that says, '*A picture says a thousand words*'—and I saw what I saw, and what I saw was you and Constance, and that told me *enough*!"

"Yet yoo're gravely mistaken. Thaur is nothing betwixt me and Connie, I assure ye."

"Well, she's obviously *infatuated* with you." Leif's bewildered expression flushed hot pink. "But I suppose it doesn't really matter anyway—it's not like we're exclusive or anything. I don't have any claim on you. You're a free agent. You are free to see whoever you want. You can be with anybody. I don't care—it's your prerogative. I'm not going to stop you. It'll be better for both of us if we just cooled things down between us anyway, and call it like it is—*quits*."

"Quits?"

"Yeah, that's right! So just forget about it."

"Forget about it?"

"Yeah, take a break from each other—you and I. Forget about it. I'm not doing it anymore."

Leif went speechless and stared at me for a minute. He genuinely looked confounded.

"If that is whit ye wish," he replied finally in disbelief.

"Yeah—that's what I want," I said flatly. The expression on his face dampened as though his feelings had been considerably bruised. I suddenly felt really awful. But there it was; I had to say what I had to say.

He hesitated to say anything else. So, I turned away from him and left him behind as I continued walking hastily along the road back toward the house.

I heard Leif's shoes crunching over the rocks in the dirt on the road as he trailed at a distance behind me. I griped and bitched silently to myself the whole way as I walked, until the welcome sight of finally seeing the farmhouse emerge through the trees. Both of us were miserably covered in sticky, smelly muck that reminded me so much of wet manure. I was glad to see the familiar whitewashed colonial farmhouse come into view at last as I crested the last small hill.

Arriving before Leif at the veranda, I angrily stomped up the steps. I managed to writhe my foot from my ruined, mud-caked slipper and kicked it off using the edge of the top step. I spitefully tossed the shoe off the veranda to the ground and strove to free my second foot from my other shoe. In a second, the slipper popped from my toes. Gathering the shoe from the top step, I chucked it far across the steps with contempt.

Leif gazed appallingly at my slipper as it bounced close to his advancing feet on the bottom step of the veranda and landed by his mud-caked buckle shoes. He turned his shocked expression up to me on the steps as I started scornfully removing my soiled cape and unfastening my muddied gown. He stared, blatantly flabbergasted, as I pulled my gown down until it dropped to my ankles. The smelly, wet soil had seeped beneath my gown and stained the next two layers of petticoats. So, I untied the first petticoat and then the second from around my waist, letting them fall to my feet. Leif's face immediately turned fuchsia as he remained standing near the bottom step, gawking astoundingly at me and utterly speechless.

"What are you looking at?" I said strongly in my standard American accent. He was gaping at me as I sidestepped around my ruined clothes before him now that I was covered merely in my undergarments. He slightly shrugged his shoulders, shaking his bright red face in transparent astonishment.

"I—I beg yer pardon, lass—but whit is the meaning of all of this? Yoo're out in the open unclothed!" Leif said outlandishly, looking steeply embarrassed.

"Well, I can't exactly go traipsing around the house covered in mud now, can I?" I said, burning with utter annoyance.

"I reckon not," he replied with wide eyes.

"*No—I can't!* Now, *excuse* me—I need to get cleaned up!" I abruptly turned my back to him as I crossed over the veranda and headed directly inside.

Once I came through the corridor, I marched up the staircase headed toward my room, griping ridiculously under my breath with several *choice* words to satisfy precisely how I was feeling.

When I entered my bedroom, shutting the door behind me, I caught a glimpse of my messy appearance in the free-standing looking glass. I placed a hand at the back of my head and felt the grimy soil clumped in my hair. I wondered with gross aggravation how I was going to successfully shampoo my hair. *I cannot believe this!* I regretted attempting to cross Claude Lefebvre's field. But I wouldn't have had to rashly decide to do so if Leif hadn't been ridiculously chasing me. *Now, look at me...* How utterly asinine!

I released a big sigh as I observed my dirt-covered self in the looking glass, thinking how foolish I had been to have allowed myself to grow attached to Leif. This was actually *all* my fault; I should have never let myself like him. At that moment, while pondering, I realized that I had become fonder of him than I had wanted to admit. I could not believe the actual depth my jealousy over Connie had run until now. It was ridiculous!

Now, I was really in trouble. I couldn't stand it! I was angry about the whole thing. Leif was a nice guy. He was always kind and fair with me—even though I was still technically his hostage. He never showed me any harm or ill will. He never hurt me in any way or forced his will upon me. Instead, he treated me well; he allowed me a good measure of freedom to do as I wished. He clothed and fed me well and bought me nice accessories to match several nice gowns he had designed and purchased for me. And how could I forget the several times he had rescued me from imminent peril? One of those dangerous times being only a few days ago. So, I hadn't the right to be too angry at him—not like I actually wanted to be.

I decided, finally, to move away from the looking glass and threw on my dressing gown, which was similar to a house robe. I paced back downstairs toward the kitchen and pulled the hot water pot from the flame in the fireplace. The pot was extremely heavy, but I managed without scalding myself to bring it into the privy closet and drew myself a much needed warm but very shallow bath.

~

CONSEQUENTLY, it was no surprise after that particular incident between me and Leif that we consciously kept our distance from each other. There were plenty of awkward instances between us. However, except for the occasional civil greeting and acknowledgment, Leif and I managed to respectfully avoid each other. Still, there were fleeting moments when we were by chance alone together that I sensed his desire to speak with me, and overall I pretended not to notice.

One day after Amity and I had completed our lessons together, I had gone out to the garden to collect some vegetables for Elizabeth's stew, which included several petite pumpkins, cabbages, carrots, snap peas, and radishes. When I had finished gathering all of the ingredients, I decided to take a little stroll around the front of the house and noticed Leif sitting on the veranda in a chair, spit shining his military boots. But as I further rounded the house toward the front of the steps, to my surprise, I discovered Mr. Vinton was seated across from Leif on the other side of the steps.

"Mistress Arboles," Mr. Vinton greeted politely, standing from his chair as he noticed me advancing up the steps. I automatically glanced curiously at Leif.

"Thomas calls tae see ye," Leif informed me with reservation on his face.

"Oh," I said.

"How do you do, Mistress Arboles?" Thomas inquired cordially.

"Well, thanks, Thomas. How are you?" I replied, returning my gaze to him.

"Very well, I thank you," he said gladly as he held a box of goods in his arms.

"Good, I'm glad to hear it," I said sincerely.

"I thought I might bring your orda to you, as it has newly arrived," Thomas informed me, lifting the box a bit in his arms for me to see.

"Oh, great—that's very considerate of you. You didn't have to come all this way to deliver it. I'm sure it was an inconvenience for you," I said.

"It is no trouble at all," Thomas replied.

"Well, thank you. You're very kind," I said. I was aware of Leif discreetly watching Thomas and me speaking with each other. He sat disconnected from us, seemingly preoccupied with his boot. "Would you like to come inside for some sweet lemon water? Elizabeth just made some this morning," I invited politely.

"Did she?" Thomas asked interestedly.

"Yes," I said.

"Why, that would be quite nice, thank you," Thomas replied appreciatively.

"Okay," I said courteously. I sensed Leif's silent gaze subtly watching us as he sat near the corner of the veranda shining his boot. I shifted a sidelong glance in his direction as Thomas proceeded to hold the front door open for me to pass through. Leif caught my glance, and I could discern the dissatisfaction in his ultramarine gaze. I dropped my gaze from him as Thomas and I entered the house.

Thomas followed me into the kitchen, where Elizabeth and the girls were preparing the next batch of pottage. Elizabeth gladly received the basket of fresh vegetables I had picked for her and put the collection in the middle of the table with the rest of the ingredients she was using to prepare the meal. She properly greeted Thomas as he placed my box of ordered supplies on a small, unobtrusive table in the back corner of the kitchen. He politely acknowledged Elizabeth, and they exchanged nice pleas-antries. Subsequently, I collected Elizabeth's nice silver serving tray with a crystal pitcher of fresh sweet lemon water and proceeded to lead Thomas from the kitchen.

"Pray, may I take that from you?" Thomas offered kindly to hold the tray when we entered the hallway from the kitchen.

"Oh, thank you," I said pleasantly. He retrieved the tray from me and gave me a nervous smile once he took it from me. I responded with my own polite grin.

Once we arrived in the drawing room, I showed him where to place the tray, and he carefully set it on the tea table. He found a chair to sit in near the table facing me while I began pouring a couple of glasses of the beverage. I passed a filled glass to him, and he graciously accepted it.

I sat in the upholstered chair across from him. An awkward moment of constrained silence ensued as both of us sat speechless facing each other, and Thomas smiled ineptly as I simply gazed at him. He put the glass to his lips and drank some of the beverage. I thought that was a good idea and took a sip from my own glass also.

"This is mighty fine lemon water," Thomas commented finally after he drew the glass away from his lips.

"It is good lemonade, isn't it?" I agreed.

"Is that what you know it as?" Thomas inquired amusedly.

"Yes. Except maybe lemonade has a bit more sugar in it," I answered.

"I see," he remarked. He took another sip from his glass. "Forgive me," he started again. "However, I am most parched."

"Not at all—would you like some more?" I asked, noticing that he had nearly finished his glass in a couple of gulps.

"That is kind of you, thank you," he said. I placed my nearly full glass back on the tray and moved to refill his glass. I noticed that he seemed a little fidgety.

"Is everything all right?" I inquired sincerely.

"Yes, of course," Thomas replied as I passed his refilled glass to him. He carefully took it from me. I sat in my chair again with my glass of lemon water in my hand on my lap.

"So, how is your family?" I inquired.

"Quite well—everyone is well," he said.

"That's good."

"Indeed."

"Will you be traveling anywhere?"

"No—I haven't any plans to do so," he said, with a slightly curious look on his face. "Why do you ask?"

"Oh, well, I just thought you might," I said simply.

"I see," he replied.

"Don't you like to travel, however?"

"I do not believe so."

"Oh."

"Quite honestly, if you don't mind my disclosing to you, I get ill when I travel. Therefore, I choose to fix myself to one place," Thomas explained.

"Oh, I see," I replied thoughtfully.

"I imagine that you might agree," he said.

"No, I actually enjoy traveling when I get the chance," I said instead.

"Do you?" His brow lifted with surprise.

"Oh, yes, I love seeing new places and meeting new people. It's exciting—it brings about a whole new perspective to a person's personal point of view, and makes a person more willing to accept other people's differences, I think," I said openly.

"How very intriguing," he responded, interested. "You're well traveled, then?"

"Just a little," I replied insecurely.

"What places have you seen?" he inquired attentively.

"It doesn't matter, really," I said modestly.

"I'm certain our little village hardly compares to the grand sights you might have experienced in your travels mayhap," he said.

"On the contrary, I think Northampton is among my favorite places," I admitted.

"Is that right?" Thomas replied, appearing surprised and pleased.

"Yes, actually," I said.

"I'm glad." He paused clumsily for a moment. "May I say to

you," he started nervously, "that I was quite anticipating your company last Sunday, and that I was instead disappointed to discover that you did not come?"

Suddenly, I felt a secret sense of dread washing over me. Leif was right. How could I have not noticed Thomas? He was really nice, but he was interested in me. It was unfortunate that I didn't feel the same way about him.

"I'm so sorry, Thomas," I began regrettably, looking at his handsome, slightly narrow, ruddy face.

"Pray, might I address you by your given name?" he inquired politely with an eager expression.

"Yes, of course," I replied. "You see, I had meant to arrive with the earl's family, but I had a bit of an accident, which forced my absence," I tried explaining.

"Oh, most unfortunate—where you injured any?" he asked concernedly.

"No, no, I'm all right," I assured him.

"Very well."

"Thank you for asking."

"Indeed."

"It's just that the mishap prevented me from attending the gathering at your house. I hope you understand," I said.

"Aye," he replied, thoughtfully nodding his head a little. "I merely hoped to show you our lovely gardens my mother keeps."

"Oh—that might have been nice," I said.

"Aye," he agreed. "We also have a pleasant duck pond that freezes in the winter months, upon which my brothers and I skate."

"Really?" I responded with noticeable surprise.

"Aye," Thomas said surely.

"Wow, that's really nice!" I replied enthusiastically.

"Mayhap you might wish to observe us one day once it freezes," he suggested.

"Maybe so," I said. Thomas smiled pleasantly, and seemed

hopeful as I noticed the ruddiness in his slender cheeks. "Do your sisters do it also?" He looked at me unexpectedly and chuckled lightly.

"I can't imagine my sistas ever being so bold," he commented.

"Oh," I replied, feeling slightly diminished. A fleeting moment of silence ensued. Thomas took a conscious sip of lemon water and cleared his throat, appearing to be fidgety again.

"I have been wishing to ask you a question," he continued uneasily. I noticed his face turning a deeper shade of pink.

"Yes?" I encouraged politely.

"I sent you a gift—some time ago. Did you notice it?" Thomas inquired curiously.

"Yes, I remember," I replied cautiously. He nodded his head.

"I was not certain that you were aware that I had given it to you," he said diffidently.

"Yes… His Grace told me that it was from you," I said.

"Very well," Thomas said with some discernible disappointment in his voice.

"I'm sorry," I said.

"Quite all right," he said.

"I hope you understand," I said.

"I suppose I do… I merely wished to please you," he said disappointedly.

"The perfume did please me. It was lovely, and very thoughtful of you to think of me. I truly appreciated it, and I thank you."

"Then you are not offended?"

"Of course not. How could I be offended when you were just being nice?"

"Then I am relieved."

"Yes, you shouldn't worry," I reassured him.

"However," Thomas said tentatively, "you did not accept my gift."

"Well—I—you are aware that I'm a widow?" I stammered uncomfortably.

"Yes," he recalled. "But you are young and lovely, dare I say."

"Thank you. But please understand that I have not forgotten my late husband."

"Not yet, at least."

"No," I said, shaking my head a tad.

"I understand."

"Good, I'm glad that you do."

"But you are still very young—and most lovely," he complimented again. "Mayhap one day you might see things differently."

"Who knows?" I asked rhetorically. "But for now, I'm content the way I am. I hope you understand."

"For now you say so," he agreed thoughtfully.

"Then, you do understand?"

"Aye, I realize your position. However, I will gladly endeavor to change your mind," Thomas said.

"Oh, well—we shall see, I suppose," I responded politely.

"It will bring me pleasure to please you," he said freely.

"You really shouldn't," I urged anxiously.

"Yet I shall," Thomas insisted with a smile. I was rather thrown off-balance by his determination and was unusually not witty enough to immediately reply. His hazel eyes shifted above my head toward the doorway, and I turned my gaze in that direction. Leif was entering the room. As our eyes met, I was certain he had heard a portion of our conversation. I nervously returned my gaze to Thomas. Thomas grinned at me, and began straightening from his chair. "Well, I believe 'tis timely for me to take my leave," Thomas said as he got to his feet.

"Oh, sure," I responded uneasily, and without delay, stood from my own chair, silently eager for him to leave.

"Thank you for the flavorsome lemon water. I most enjoyed my visit, Sylvina," he said pleasantly. I sensed that Leif was aware that Thomas had just addressed me by my first name, and I nervously glanced at him, realizing that my instinct was correct; I could see discouragement and frustration in his silent eyes.

"Your Grace." Thomas acknowledged Leif with a polite nod as he was taking his leave.

"Master Vinton," Leif reciprocated formally, politely nodding his head once as he settled into the room with his pipe. Thomas removed his tricorn hat from beneath his arm, ready to place it over his burnt-sienna-colored head once he stepped outside. I consciously moved past Leif, fully aware that his deliberate gaze was on me as I made my way to properly see Thomas out of the house.

Once Thomas retreated down the veranda steps, I closed the front door and peeped around the drawing room entrance, where Leif had made himself comfortable fixing his pipe to smoke. I dreaded that I would have to pass the open doorway on my way to the kitchen and that he would notice me. So, with imaginary blinders on, I swiftly entered the drawing room to collect the silver tray from the stand and moved over the threshold, completely ignoring him, and hastened toward the kitchen.

Elizabeth and the children were still tending to the cooking when I entered. After I had returned the tray on the kitchen counter, I immediately went to the corner table to collect my new belongings when something I did not remember requesting caught my eye, which rested on a small gathering of little glass bottles for my medical kit. I delayed promptly taking my things away and curiously retrieved the pretty, petite yellow brocade silk pouch. My heart suddenly sank, because I knew what it was. I loosened the yoke of the tiny purse and pulled out the fine crystal perfume bottle capped with an exquisite hand-painted yellow porcelain open rose.

"Deah! That's quite lovely," Elizabeth said, noticing curiously as she came around the table to collect the bowl with the raised dough in it.

"Yes, it is," I admitted disconcertedly. "Another gift from Thomas," I said, replacing the bottle into its pretty pouch.

"Do you mean he's giving you gifts?" Elizabeth asked surprisedly while holding the bowl in her hands.

"I wish he wouldn't." I sighed.

"He's fond of you," she suggested.

"Mmm, I guess so," I replied abstractedly.

"Do you wish not to have it?" she asked curiously.

"I just don't know what to do," I said honestly.

"Well, merely return it to him, if you do not fancy his gesture in the least bit," she said.

"Easier said than done," I muttered regrettably under my breath.

"Is it?" Elizabeth inquired curiously.

"I'm afraid so. He's rather persistent," I told her.

"Oh—well, I suppose that might make it a bit troublesome, in that case," she replied understandingly.

"Yeah, well, I'm going to have to give this back to him. I just don't want to hurt his feelings though," I said.

"Don't fret, Sylvina. Though he is smitten with you, he will mend if you do return it to him," Elizabeth said sympathetically.

"I suppose so," I replied uncertainly. She lightly patted my shoulder, and I left the kitchen with the wooden box in hand.

When I entered the corridor, I chose to go to my bedroom and organize my new belongings. While contemplating it, I ultimately decided to keep Thomas's gift to spare his feelings.

CHAPTER 33

Sleeting rain came down heavily late one evening soon after Finley's return from Boston. Elizabeth and Finley had just finished tucking the children into bed when a loud rapping came unexpectedly on the front door. The sound was obtrusive and sharply startled the household. Leif was the first to swiftly arrive at the front door. I stood motionless and startled behind the threshold of the corridor near the foyer as he answered the door.

"Master Kent!" Leif said, absolutely surprised.

"I'm indeed most regretful to intrude upon you this hour of night, Your Grace," Mr. Kent apologized profusely with obvious consternation in his voice.

"Whit is it, man?" Leif responded alarmingly.

"'Tis our boy, Nathaniel. He has the croup," Mr. Kent informed him desperately. Finley had just galloped quickly down the staircase and stood with Leif at the open front door.

"Their lad is ill," Leif informed Finley.

"We terribly regret learning this news," Finley said compassionately.

"Yes, he's taken a turn for the worse, and Dr. Kendall is currently in Lexington," Mr. Kent said, extremely distressed.

"I see. Who's with the lad at present?" Finley inquired concernedly.

"Merely my wife tends to our son. She has done all that she can for him, and we feah for him," Mr. Kent said anxiously.

"Whaur's the lass?" Finley abruptly asked Leif. Leif shifted from the door, starting to search. I emerged from the corner of the hallway, and Leif quickly noticed me.

"She's haur," Leif told Finley as I strode forth.

"Guid, bring her haur," Finley instructed. Leif faintly gestured for me to follow him to the door. "Come haur, lass." Finley beckoned me as I approached with Leif and stood by him near the front door. "'Tis Master Kent. Their lad is gravely ill," Finley told me.

"Yes, I heard. I'm so sorry," I said empathetically.

"The Kents need ye," Finley said urgently.

"Yes, of course," I said. "Let me just get my things." I then hastily trotted up the staircase to my room to fetch my traveling cape and medical bag.

"Whaur's yer horse?" I heard Finley ask Mr. Kent upon my returning downstairs.

"Our stallion recently went lame and was put down, and our mare is pregnant," Mr. Kent explained.

"Och, unfortunate," Finley said, sympathizing.

"Aye, indeed," Mr. Kent replied.

"'Tis a bit of a journey on foot," Finley said.

"I'll drive," Leif offered.

"Aye," Finley agreed as I stepped toward them through the foyer once I cleared the staircase. "Guid, she's ready," Finley said as I stood beside him.

"I'll ready the chaise," Leif said, and abruptly retreated from us. Finley offered for Mr. Kent to come deeper into the house for warmth and to wait by the fire in the drawing room. He poured Mr. Kent a glass of rum as I sat on the sofa waiting with them.

After about ten minutes, Leif burst through the house, promptly locating us to tell us it was time to go. His black great-coat and hat were soaked, dripping wet from the sleeting rain. He looked miserably drenched from head to foot.

We rushed outside into the bad weather toward the chaise. Leif helped me over the footstep, and I stepped inside the carriage meant for two very slender people. He shut and secured the door. Mr. Kent pulled himself up on top of the covered bench in front as Leif hurried around the horses toward the opposite side and hauled himself over the top next to Mr. Kent. I heard a *tick-tick* through the tapping sleet in the cabin, and in a second, the chaise jerked into motion amid the stormy, icy night.

IN APPROXIMATELY TWENTY MINUTES, we had arrived at the Kents' house. Once our wet garments had been removed and hung on the pegs by the door, Mr. Kent led us through their nice, modest home up the staircase over the second landing into their child's bedroom. Mrs. Kent immediately glanced up from her ailing Nathaniel lying in bed as we entered. Fear and angst were clearly expressed on her face. She also appeared noticeably weary from administering devoted round the clock care.

"Mistress Arboles," Mrs. Kent began with apparent relief, "thank you most kindly fah arriving. We did not know who else to call."

"Yes, it's not at all a problem. Thank you for thinking of me," I said concernedly. "May I?" I asked, seeking permission to examine their son closely.

"Aye, please," Mrs. Kent replied. I stepped away from Leif and Mr. Kent and crossed over to the other side of the room where their little boy was lying beneath the covers. He was a sweet-looking toddler with bright blonde hair and slightly pudgy cheeks.

I recognized the barking cough coming from him. It was definitely croup. I leaned slightly over him and gently touched my wrist to his forehead. His skin was damp, and the fever was high, I noted.

"How old is he?" I asked Mrs. Kent as I carefully started removing some of the blankets from him.

"Five years of age," she informed me.

"Would you happen to know how much he weighs?" I inquired.

"Three and a third stone," she said.

"Okay, so roughly forty-six pounds," I calculated aloud to myself. "Can you tell me about when you first recognized the symptoms?"

"Aye, he caught a chill about a fortnight ago. His nose became moist—he sneezed and coughed, but a fever came upon him two days after with the cough he has at present," Mrs. Kent explained worriedly.

"I see," I said. I gently lifted the toddler boy's back and adjusted the pillows behind him. I scooted and raised him back against the pillows so he now rested in a propped position. "That's better," I remarked. Without the invention of the stethoscope yet, I leaned over and proceeded to listen to his chest with my ear. There was surely congestion in the lungs, and his breathing was timed at short intervals. This case had the potential of quickly turning into pneumonia. Poor little Nathaniel kept coughing and crying in a hyperventilated manner as he gasped for breath. I turned to Mr. Kent and asked him if he smoked.

"On frequent occasion, aye," he replied.

"You might want to reconsider the habit, Mr. Kent, since young children in particular are highly susceptible to acquiring respiratory problems like asthma due to smoke inhalation," I advised.

"I see," he responded. Mr. Kent slid Leif a questionable glance.

"Has your son ever had a history of breathing difficulties?" I inquired.

"Nay, thank the Lord Almighty, our son has not," Mrs. Kent replied with visible concern.

"Okay, well, he does have a high fever—I'm guessing of about one hundred one to one hundred two degrees, and I recommend that he not be covered with any blankets except for possibly a very light sheet like this," I said, pointing to the delicate cotton blanket beneath one of the abundant quilts originally placed over him.

"Very well," she said willingly.

"Also, if you could continue to provide him with damp, cool compresses to keep over his forehead, that will be helpful," I instructed.

"Aye, of course," she replied observantly.

"Well, it seems that his condition was likely brought on by an acute viral infection as a result of his original cold—which can quickly transmute into pneumonia for small children if not immediately treated," I informed them. Everyone was staring at me with blank expressions.

"Has he pneumonia?" Mr. Kent asked alarmingly.

"At this point, I would not say so. You needn't worry, but you were really wise to contact me," I said.

"Thank Heaven," Mr. Kent said with deep gratitude.

"First, we just need to bring his breathing under control. Mrs. Kent, would you mind boiling some water for me, please?" I asked.

"Certainly," Mrs. Kent responded readily. She quickly got up from her son's bedside and exited the room where Mr. Kent and Leif remained standing observantly.

"I shall assist Mistress Kent," Mr. Kent said soon after his wife had left the room.

"That will be helpful," I agreed. Mr. Kent promptly vanished from his son's bedroom. Leif remained standing near the heating duct in the floor in the opposite corner of the room.

"Ye have yer work made fur ye, lass," Leif commented with apparent concern for the boy.

"Will you stay and help me?" I asked.

"Aye, of coorse," he replied.

"Thank you," I responded gratefully.

"Nae matter," he said sincerely. "Whit will ye have me do?"

"Will you simply hold him for me while I try to loosen and extract some of his nasal congestion?"

"Aye," Leif replied. He approached the bed as Nathaniel was coughing and wheezing among stifled cries. "Thaur, thaur, sweet laddie, haur we are... 'Twill all be better soon," Leif said tenderly as he joined the toddler on the bed and carefully collected him in his arms.

I had made a vile of saline solution to keep in my medical bag and retrieved it now. I poured a few droplets into a tiny glass funnel that I had fashioned, since syringes had not yet been invented, and carefully dripped a few drops into both of Nathaniel's nostrils as Leif securely held the sickly child. I had Nathaniel blow his nose to expel as much of the loosened phlegm from his nasal passages as possible. It seemed to have a slightly positive effect. More of the mucus had thickened into the back of the nasal membranes, I recognized. So, I had to create a kind of humidifier, which would help release mucus and quiet his cough.

After a little while, Mr. and Mrs. Kent returned with steaming water and placed the sizable wooden pales beside the bed as I had instructed. Leif helped me adjust the boy carefully near the steam so as not to burn him. Then, Mr. and Mrs. Kent retreated from the room and closed the door. Soon, the small room began to fill with a warm mist, in addition to the small cloth tent I had created for Nathaniel to breathe under in order for him to easily inhale the vapors. It seemed to help loosen his congestion and made him feel a little better.

Leif continued to keep a cool moist towelette over Nathaniel's feverish brow as I had advised while I made a mint mustard wrap to place over the toddler's chest. I also administered very small doses of ipecac at certain intervals to loosen the phlegm in his chest.

In a couple of hours, Nathaniel's continual barking cough began to subside and quieted. He had now grown calm enough to finally ingest a bit of lightly sweetened lemon water at fifteen-minute intervals. It was important to keep him well hydrated, I had explained to Leif, who was proving to be very astute in his assistance to me—something I was extremely grateful for. I wasn't sure that I would have been as swift with my effectiveness if it hadn't been for him.

It proved to be two whole days of round the clock care with sleepless nights. Leif occasionally offered for me to rest with a nap while he took my place monitoring Nathaniel and precisely watched him like a hawk.

On the third day since my arrival at the Kents', which was the fifth day of Nathaniel's battle with croup, the sickness seemed to wane. He had pulled through the worst part of the infection, well on the mend. His prognosis was good. A visible wave of gratitude and relief washed over Mr. and Mrs. Kent when I told them the good news of their son's recovery. An insurmountable weight was lifted from their spirits, and they were so overjoyed with gladness that both of them embraced as Mrs. Kent wept in her husband's arms.

"How shall we ever thank you, Mistress Arboles?" Mrs. Kent asked.

"Indeed, we are indebted to you for all that you have done for our boy," Mr. Kent said thankfully.

"It's not necessary—however, you're very welcome. I'm happy the outcome is good. I only request that Nathaniel continue to rest with no exertion of any kind. Also, make sure that he continues to take abundant simple lemon water that is not too sweetened to drink, and that he gets enough nourishment. A simple chicken broth is often good to have. And do not hesitate to call me if he worsens," I said.

"Yes, of course," Mrs. Kent agreed attentively.

"Many thanks to you as well, Your Grace," Mr. Kent said to Leif.

"Nae matter, 'tis quite alrecht," Leif responded genuinely.

Soon after, Leif and I left the Kents' residence, with me traveling in the chaise as Leif drove us back toward his brother's property, *Taigh-Bheinn*.

I WAITED for Leif as he unhitched the horse after parking the chaise in the coach house. When the horse was unharnessed, Leif placed it in the enclosure with the other horses, where it began trotting freely around the field in the overcast late afternoon. Once he had latched the fence closed, we started walking together toward the house in the distance.

"Ye do guid work, lass," Leif said unexpectedly, turning his gaze to me as we strolled together.

"Thank you," I replied appreciatively. He grinned subtly. "I think one day you'll make a really good dad," I observed. Leif looked at me with surprise.

"Do ye suppose so?" he wondered inquisitively.

"Yeah," I said genuinely.

"Whit makes ye believe this?" he inquired.

"Well, I've noticed how wonderful and sweet you are with your nieces—and you were so good with Nathaniel. It just made me think how nice you would be as a dad," I answered frankly.

"I see… Weel, I thank ye fur saying so. 'Tis very kind of ye," he replied, appearing somewhat flattered.

"Sure," I said simply.

"Weel, this is quite ironic," he said thoughtfully.

"What is?" I asked curiously.

"Merely that I was pondering something similar about ye as I was driving us home," he admitted. I noticed the side of his cheek appearing very ruddy beneath his tricorn hat as we were taking our time walking in the cold.

"Oh?" I responded curiously.

"Aye… I was contemplating how very weel ye cared fur the Kents' wee lad, and all the kindness ye have shown my nieces—particularly Amity and all that yoo've done fur her. 'Tis impressive… Yoo're sure tae make a fine mother one day," Leif said sincerely.

"Oh… Well, that's also nice of you to say… Thank you," I said appreciatively. Leif gave me a slight grin that seemed modest. I reciprocated with a little smile of my own. He glanced away again with his eyes cast down toward the grass-covered field as we paced together. He seemed reticent and pensive. I would have encouraged him to disclose whatever was on his mind, but I held back too.

"I dinnae wish fur thaur tae be any ill feelings betwixt us, Sylvie," Leif began to say. I turned my eyes up toward him, noticing him looking directly at me.

"Neither do I," I said honestly.

"It greatly troobles me that we dinnae speak as we once did," he said.

"It bothers me too," I admitted.

"I fear losing—" He suddenly broke off, seeming to reconsider his thoughts. "I dinnae wish fur us tae separate under animosity or misinterpretations."

"I don't wish for that either," I replied.

"Ye must ken that I highly esteem ye, and I would never betray ye," Leif said sincerely.

"I guess so," I said.

"I'm earnest," he insisted.

"But what about Constance?" I asked.

"She is of nae consequence tae me."

"But I know how much she really likes you," I said. The color in his face took on an even brighter hue.

"My fondness fur ye far exceeds hers," he said genuinely.

"Oh…"

"It pains me that we are nae longer friends."

I could perceive the sincerity in his eyes. His spirit was clearly bruised. I couldn't help feeling something for him. Plus, the truth was I was bothered by it too.

"So, then, what do you think we should do?" I asked.

"I wish fur us tae remain friends. 'Tis a burden when yoo're cross with me," he said with some difficulty.

I knew he was unhappy about my being upset with him. But I didn't expect it to have affected him this much. It struck me that I probably felt as bad as he did. I could perceive it written plain as day on his face right now that snubbing him had in fact afflicted him.

"I'm not mad at you anymore," I admitted finally.

"Yoo're nae longer vexed at me?" Leif inquired cautiously.

"No—I'm not," I assured him.

He gently grinned, with his breath lightly escaping him in relief. He seemed contented and satisfied.

"Thank ye. Ye have very much gratified me," he said genuinely.

"It's okay," I assured him. I paused for a moment, turning my gaze ahead toward the house we were closely approaching. "So, there isn't anything between you and Constance?" I asked him one last time as I shifted my eyes back to him.

"Thaur is naught that exists betwixt me and Miss Pringle," Leif said with straight certainty. "When ye saw us together speaking, I had explained tae her that since I am a soldier, I wouldnae make a pleasant husband fur her—and she was quite dismayed."

"Oh," I said.

"Aye," Leif replied.

"So, you're not interested in her at all?" I asked.

"Nae," he said, shaking his head.

"Oh… Okay," I said, accepting his word. "I'm sorry for the misunderstanding."

"I also. Yet 'tis of nae consequence so long as ye and I remain friends." I gave Leif a modest, reassuring smile, and he seemed comforted.

"We are friends, Leif," I quietly told him.

"Guid… It pleases me that we are," he said delicately. "I shall be lost if we waur not."

"Well, I don't want you to be lost."

"Yer words warm my heart."

"Yours do the same to me." He smiled at me, and I smiled back at him. He shifted his gaze ahead as we continued pacing beside each other.

"Sylvie?"

"Yeah?" I turned my gaze up to him and met his eyes again.

"I—" He broke off, appearing hesitant, as if he was considering his thoughts again.

"What?" I prodded carefully.

"I care," he said.

"I know you do."

"Do ye?"

"Well, I think so."

"Do ye understand that I care fur yer happiness?"

"Oh. You want me to be happy?"

"Truly."

"So, I don't seem happy to you?" I asked curiously. Leif grinned softly at me.

"I care that ye are happy, and I wish for ye to always remain so," he said.

"Oh… That's very nice of you to say."

"I speak more than words."

"I don't understand."

"It is how I feel."

"Oh—well… I wish for your happiness too."

Leif smiled warmly at me again, and I reciprocated with a nice smile of my own. He returned to looking ahead, and the conversation settled into silence between us as we continued walking together over the rich yellow-ocher field toward the house. I realized then that our friendship had grown deep and that I was overlooking a precipice: standing on the edge of forever.

PART V
PRIMITIVE

CHAPTER 34

Finley and Leif packed the family's travel belongings onto their road coach and loaded us all inside for the journey to Concord. We were to visit Elizabeth's parents and extended family there for the winter months, since it was their annual tradition. Elizabeth's sister, Suzanna, and her husband, Edward, along with their two small boys, were also to visit. They had arranged to rendezvous with us at the east end of Northampton just beyond the village near their property.

Dressed in our traveling attire, Amity and I entered the coach as we joined Elizabeth with the rest of the children. Leif secured the coach door on each side. He was cloaked, protected from the weather, and had adroitly hauled himself high above the coach onto the front bench when Finley finally came out of the stables with the horses and headed toward us. He led their two military horses, Mercury and Blaze, and hitched them to the back of the carriage.

Finley easily pulled himself over the bench onto the coach next to Leif. Shortly, the coach jolted into motion with four horses pulling us along. I gazed out the window as we swayed inside the carriage. We began winding along the road down a small gradient, and by this time, the trees had all lost their bright, colorful leaves. The trees now stood dormant in the forest, barren from life against the frigid gray sky. Winter loomed silently like a shadow.

~

THE JOURNEY WAS UNDULATING and topsy-turvy inside the coach as we wound through the Connecticut River Valley for a couple of days. There were times along the way that I felt an unwelcome tinge of motion sickness. I found the acupressure point inside my wrist and pressed on it for a bit as I rested my head against the back of the seat. It seemed to help after a few minutes. I anticipated, however, that once we cleared the Connecticut mountain range, the ride might become more tolerable.

We jostled about countless lakes, ponds, and streams throughout the enveloping desolate, naked forest. I supposed my current concern was the weather as we arrived over the final mountain pass. It looked continuously ominous with dark clouds, but there had been no precipitation for three days since our departure from Northampton.

The air was ice-cold as we entered a series of mist-filled fogbanks on the fourth day. Morning light illuminated the atmosphere like a hazy gray shroud. Trees emerged like distant skeleton ghosts among the mist. Their branches twisted like old bones glazed in crystalline ice against a frosty vaporous backdrop.

On the fifth day, we had finally arrived in Concord. It appeared to be a nice, quaint town that had been longer established with a slightly more abundant population, unlike the near frontier village we had left. There was a distant sense of urbanity to the town that felt remotely familiar to me, and I thought I rather liked it here.

At last, it felt really good to disembark at the end of our journey once we had arrived at the Buckingham dwelling belonging to Elizabeth's parents. They owned a large property that consisted of a New-England-style burnt-umber clapboard mansion with whitewashed window frames, and a similar but modest boardinghouse overlooking a large pond. There was a grass clearing that spread expansively behind the mansion, which was surrounded by mighty evergreen trees.

Elizabeth apparently originated from a family of considerable Massachusetts wealth. They were an industrious family, having established profit-making in the pelt trade. Still, her parents were unassuming and kind, like the rest of her family who had nicely received me.

FRESHLY FALLEN snow blanketed outside my windowsill when I awakened one morning. I could see at a distance across the snow-covered ground from my upstairs bedroom window. The evergreens surrounding the property before the pond were heavily dusted with snow, and their limbs sagged from the weight against an intensely bright cerulean sky.

The aroma of delicious cooking wafted upstairs into my room and encouraged the hunger pangs in my stomach. I hastened to dress myself, which always proved to be somewhat of a challenge for me. When I had finished, I joined the rest of the awakened household.

Like a vaporous hand tickling my nose, the scrumptious aroma led me to the kitchen. I entered the kitchen and discovered the main cook maid, Tess, along with two other cooks, Anne and Agnes, busily preparing food. Mrs. Buckingham and her two daughters, Elizabeth and Suzanna, also assisted in the kitchen.

It was evident that preparation for a significantly large meal was underway. I wondered what the occasion was as I recognized a couple of turkeys being gutted by Tess on a chopping block. Elizabeth was busy mashing diced pumpkin with a large fork for what appeared to be preparation for a kind of soup. There was also venison being prepared. Bread was baking deliciously in the Dutch oven, and Suzanna was currently working a wooden rolling pin over a mound of dough.

Mrs. Buckingham noticed me curiously observing and kindly acknowledged me. She offered for me to take my morning meal of buttered bread, blackberry preserves, and oat porridge with molasses in the dining room with a couple of other family members who were simply having tea with cranberry scones. I realized that I had slept in a little and missed most everyone else who had already eaten. But before I left the kitchen to have my breakfast, I commented on how lovely the cooking smelled while they were in the middle of preparing food.

"Why, thank you, deah," Mrs. Buckingham said kindly. "We hope it will be a blessed Thanksgiving feast."

"Is today Thanksgiving Day?" I asked, astounded.

"Why, indeed it is, deah," Mrs. Buckingham replied merrily.

"That's right—how could I forget?" I replied. I was shocked. It hit me like a ton of bricks just then as it occurred to me that I had been stranded living among these people for at least *two and a half—if not actually three—whole months!* A long time had already passed before I was conscious of it. An odd feeling came over me as I realized that I was going to spend my first Thanksgiving here long before it would have ever been declared a national holiday by President Abraham Lincoln.

As I sat at the table with a few other family guests in the dining room eating my bread with preserves, I remained in sheer disbelief, very much missing my family.

~

LATER THAT MORNING, I stepped out into the winter cold from the sunroom at the back of the house, and observed the children frolicking in the snow. Suzanna's boys, nine-year-old Henry and seven-year-old George, were busy leaping around chasing each other with their other boy cousins in a game of make-believe sword fighting. I supposed they were imagining themselves as pirates or soldiers with wood branches for swords. Snowballs hurled in the air like cannonballs struck each other while they ran around like moving targets and cavorted across the snow-covered ground. The girls simply ran around among the boys, trying to take part.

I noticed Mairie presently running toward me. She trotted over to the steps where I stood observing, appearing unhappy.

"What's wrong?" I asked concernedly.

"Henry won't let us play. He is being most unfair," Mairie explained crankily.

"Really?" I said curiously.

"Aye, he's a beast," she informed me dismayed.

"Is he?" I replied, holding back my amusement.

"Indeed!" Mairie said certainly.

"I see," I said.

"I think I shall no longer play with him," she said.

"Okay—that might be a good idea for now. Perhaps later he might like for you to play with him," I agreed.

"Mayhap not," she said, sulking.

I gazed out over the steps and located Henry's red stocking cap whizzing around across the snow-covered clearing with his brother, George, and their three other chasing cousins: ten-year-old Ethan, nine-year-old Timothy, and eight-year-old Daniel. They were completely involved in their own exciting, playful world and indifferent to their girl cousins.

"I have a better idea," I said, turning my attention back to Mairie.

"What is it?" she inquired with potential excitement on her ruddy face.

"Why don't we build a snowman?" I suggested instead.

"What a grand notion!" Mairie said excitedly. She quickly latched on to my mitten and eagerly tugged me down the steps into the snow. The snow was a bit deep—perhaps slightly under a foot. We trekked to gather Doireann, Amity, and their cousins Sarah and Anne, who were ages six and eight.

The girls and I had a fun time romping around as we constructed our snowman. It took us a while to build the three-foot snowman. But when we had finished, we were all so glad and impressed with ourselves—that is until the boys came sprinting around our work and took our poor snowman prisoner in their war game, then mercilessly decapitated him.

The girls were obviously annoyed about this occurrence, but seemed helpless to defend the rest of the disfigured snowman from their boy cousins' taunting play—until Doireann launched a nicely packed snowball into the air, which hit smack-dab Ethan's freckled face. Then, all of a sudden, all-out war broke out between the children as the boys frightened the girls by chasing and roaring at them like crazed conquerors with their raised stick-swords in hand.

I was not spared from the attack, however, as I felt several snowballs disintegrate against the lower portion of my velvet Jesuit. Without warning, Leif entered the playful scene from behind and swiftly swooped up Henry into his arms. He heaved Henry over his shoulder, as the boy had been chasing after a screaming Mairie, and spared her from further attack.

Responding to the smashing snowballs coming at my feet, I joined in the fun with a couple of defensive snowballs and blindly tossed them toward where I thought they were originating. Once the third snowball went airborne upon my release, I noticed it hit Leif's greatcoat smack in the middle of his back. He abruptly turned and put Henry back down on his feet. The boy playfully took off running when Leif noticed me standing nearby.

"Oops!" I said guiltily. He gazed at me with unexpected surprise. "Sorry," I said, noticing his expression.

"That wulnae do, lass," he said teasingly as a preposterous look came over his face.

"Well, you were in the way," I justified.

"An unacceptable excuse, I say," Leif replied. He started slowly pacing toward me. I perceived the mischievous expression in his eyes.

"C'mon, I said I was sorry," I said. I began stepping backward as he continued advancing.

"Ye best make haste, lass, lest I capture ye," he warned jokingly.

"Haven't you already done that?" I bantered back, further backing away from him.

"Are ye not fearful of me?"

"No."

"Humph! Weel, in that case, dinnae let me catch ye!" Leif suddenly sprinted toward me. I turned abruptly, taking off hastily running among the snowcapped pine trees.

He chased me well into the forest. I didn't think that I was going to be able to keep up my pace for much longer; he had long legs, was in breeches instead of skirts, had boots instead of slippers, and therefore would overtake me. But I could give him a bit of a run for his money—and I did.

I heard his feet crunching in the snow close behind me. He was gaining. Out of the blue, his arm wrapped around my waist from behind, seizing my gallop. He spun me around, making me closely face him with his hands holding my waist. Both of us were panting and laughing as our breath visibly escaped us like mist vanishing into thin air.

"I've caught ye. Now whit are ye going tae do?" he said playfully.

"I'm trapped. What can I do?" I laughed.

"It appears that ye cannae escape me." He chuckled, winded with lightheartedness. "Would ye care tae have a bit of cheer?"

"Yeah, sure," I replied breathlessly, simultaneously nodding my head.

"Let's go, then," he said agreeably.

He clasped his gloved hand over mine and started leading me through the woods. We came out of the trees on the other side of the property near the frozen pond not far from the boarding-house in view before us. Leif guided us to the coach house at the back of the dwelling and rummaged in the corner of the building for something. He briefly latched on to a sizable wooden-crafted structure and pulled it forth.

"Oh my gosh! A toboggan!" I said delightedly.

"Aye," he responded gladly. "I thought we micht go."

"Yes, how fun!" I replied eagerly.

"Very weel." Leif's expression was bright with pleasure and anticipation.

We left the coach house with lighthearted expectation. He pulled the heavy sled in the snow and led us to where we should go.

We eventually climbed a distance up a mild gradient until we reached the crest, where he situated the toboggan just so above the arch of the slope. Then, he intimated for me to sit first inside the sled and took my hand to help me. Once my cape and petti-coats were tucked suitably inside around my legs, Leif leaned close to the side of my head.

"Are ye ready?" he asked in a low tone. The warmth from his breath came around my bonnet and caressed my cheek.

"Yeah," I replied cheerfully.

"Haur we go," he uttered happily against my head, and started shoving off. His pace quickly increased as he pushed me in the toboggan. At the second I would have gone over the crest, Leif leaped inside, with his full weight easily slipping around me. He sat close behind me, further positioning himself snug against me with his knees raised, securely framing me inside the craft.

We whizzed down the slippery slope like mercury on ice. I couldn't help but scream, unbridled, as we swept downward in raw exhilaration, which felt identical to a roller-coaster ride. I shrieked wildly the entire way down.

In a moment that seemed all too fleeting, we arrived at the bottom of the slope, still sliding as we slowed to a halt. I was consumed with laughter and delight as we sat at the end of the run. I felt Leif's chest uncontrollably quivering with his own laughter. It took us a minute for us to collect ourselves.

"Was that jolly?" he inquired between his chuckling.

"That was tons of fun!" I laughed gleefully.

"Aye!" He laughed heartily some more. "Yer screaming has caught me with mirth!"

"Really?" I laughed, observing his ruddy, buoyant face when I turned to get a glimpse of him.

"Aye, quite!" He continued laughing.

After a moment, I sensed him wrench himself from behind me as he pulled himself out of the sled. His face was fuchsia with joy as he came around to help me plant my feet on the snow. I noticed tears in his eyes before he brought the cuff of his coat to his face and wiped his laughing face.

"Shall we do it again?" he asked, delighted.

"Absolutely!" I agreed.

"Alrecht!" he replied enthusiastically.

So, we trekked up the slope again. Just as before, we exhilaratingly zoomed along, coming down the hill like quicksilver. I screamed again. This time, however, I heard Leif shouting loudly behind me too, and I started laughing between my squealing. Both of us shrieked and laughed, free with sheer merriment the whole way down until we had reached the bottom of the slope. After a suspended moment filled with excited laughter, we were finally able to regain some sense of composure.

We decided to do several more runs down the slope, with each time ending up like the time before, filled to the brim with delight. After our last slide, Leif asked me if I wanted to do the big run, and I eagerly consented. Except once we had arrived at the top of the large slope, I suddenly changed my mind, given the sharp steepness of the dip and the tree obstacles in the way.

"Are ye afraid?" he inquired.

"I don't think this is such a good idea," I said reluctantly.

"Dinnae worry—'twill be cheerful. I promise that we shall arrive unscathed at the bottom," he guaranteed.

I wasn't so confident. The wooden sled was not modern and lightweight, ready to take quick turns. Leif gave me an encouraging look.

"Okay," I said, persuaded to go.

"Grand!" he said excitedly.

He proceeded to help me into the toboggan, and once again we were off on a run down the large snowcapped hill. We rushed along, whizzing by as before. Fear was instantly replaced with exhilarating glee and excitement. The run was fast and curvy, like a wild amusement park ride. I screamed thrillingly as Leif leaned the sled from side to side down the steep gradient, avoiding certain obstacles.

We began leveling out on the run toward the bottom of the gradient. Soon, we came to a nice glide at the end of the dodgy slope and slowed over a rough patch of ice. Leif quickly hopped out to bring the sled to a final stop. Once I had ceased moving, he assisted me out of the toboggan. My foot slipped from beneath me on the first step I took on the section of ice. He caught me around the waist, steadying me.

"See? I didnae let anything perilous happen tae ye," he said cheerfully as he still held me close.

"Yes, I see. I have to hand it to you—you did a good job steering. Thank you!" I replied happily, out of breath. He chuckled as I carefully brought my other foot over the ledge of the sled onto the ice.

Observing that I was now stable on my feet, he turned to push the sled off the ice. I started to follow him, but my undependable shoe slid far to the side. I automatically latched on to his greatcoat sleeve. He abruptly turned and swiftly clutched my elbow to keep me from losing my balance. But I had tilted too far over. I whipped out another grasping hand around his other sleeve and accidentally pulled him toward me, and he placed another rescuing hand around my back. The one foot I was using to stabilize myself slipped between his legs, and I plunged backward onto the ice.

"*Uhh!*" I gasped as I instantly hit the back of my head on the frozen slab with Leif's entire weight crushing me.

"Och! Guid heavens! Are ye injured?" he wheezed, suddenly concerned. He abruptly shifted some of his weight onto his elbows, allowing his full gaze to hover over mine.

"No, I'm okay," I panted, now that I could breathe again. Good thing my head was covered with my hard winter bonnet, I thought. Otherwise, I was sure that I would have bruised the back of my head.

"Are ye certain that yoo're not hurt?" he inquired worriedly.

"Yeah, I'm fine," I insisted.

"Guid, I apologize fur landing on ye."

"It's okay." I giggled. I smiled up at him as he hovered over me. "You know I'm usually a lot more graceful than this on ice," I joked.

"Is that reit?" he questioned captivatingly.

"Yes, actually," I said, reading his blithe, warm expression.

"I'd like tae see how that is so," he said.

"Maybe one day I'll show you," I replied.

"Then I shall bide with anticipation." He paused shortly and simply stared at me ever so close with fascination. I thought he was going to kiss me, but he didn't. "Come along, *àille dhubh*," he said momentarily. He shifted his weight off of me as he proceeded to stand. I stirred upward on the frigid sheet of ice when he stretched out a helpful hand. I slipped my gloved hand into his. "Let's go before we catch our death."

"All right," I agreed.

Leif assisted me safely back onto the snow-covered ground, then returned for the sled still out on the frozen pond. After retrieving the toboggan, we started our trek over the snow, headed for shelter and warmth.

CHAPTER 35

*L*eif set the sled against the side of the wall of the boardinghouse. We entered through the side door of the house, where he was lodging for the duration of our stay with Elizabeth's family, since quarters were limited inside the main mansion. Fortunately, he had the place all to himself, so he could come and go as he pleased without the interference of others.

I followed him through the kitchen and into the corridor until we came to the coatrack pegs beside the front door. I proceeded to untie the ribbons of my bonnet as he unbuttoned his greatcoat and put it on one of the pegs. I put my bonnet on the peg above and began removing my cape from my shoulders, hanging it on the peg next to his greatcoat. After he removed his second coat and hung it on the rack, Leif was now comfortably dressed in his shirt, velvet waistcoat, and breeches.

He led me into the sitting room, where he proceeded to rekindle the fire near the hearth. Shivering like a leaf in the wind, I stood there watching him, realizing how cold to the bone I had become. Leif glanced over his shoulder as he worked the flames and noticed me shaking.

"Come haur, lass," he said, gently taking my arm. I came to stand close to the fire as he pushed the sofa near the hearth. The fire was hot and felt good against my chilled face.

Swiftly, I began to warm, and I decided to sit on the sofa near the flames. He sat in the adjacent chair and started removing his boots. I thought about how good a nice cup of hot chocolate would be right about now, and I was remembering how the treat used to taste while I watched the leaping flames now before me.

"Whit are ye pondering?" he inquired thoughtfully. He gazed at me while kicking off his second boot.

"Um, just how I wished that I had some hot cocoa right now," I answered.

"Hot cocoa?" he echoed. His brow unexpectedly lifted with some surprise.

"Mm-hmm," I replied simply.

"Why, that's raither delectable," he remarked.

"Yes, it is," I agreed. "With whipped cream, it's even better."

"Whipped cream?" He grimaced, appearing a little uncertain.

"Um, I suppose the closest thing to it would be syllabub, I guess," I said.

"Och, that seems quite indulgent."

"It is. It's very good."

"Weel…" he started thoughtfully as he rose from his chair. He went to the cupboard and retrieved a couple of small wineglasses and a bottle of port. "This is raither not hot cocoa, but it micht suit ye better than rum," he said, slightly raising the glasses in his hand for me to see.

"Yes, I suppose so," I agreed.

"Alrecht." He placed the port bottle and wineglasses on the sideboard and began pouring us some wine. In a moment, the glasses were filled, and Leif strode across the room toward me. He passed a glass to me, and I took a sip. He took a sip also, and we watched each other drink a bit of wine.

I thought it tasted nice and was actually quite good. I took another sip from my glass, thinking that this wine was more than just *good*, it was smooth and flavorful—and really, *really* delicious! So, I kept sipping—and sipping—until the glass was empty. I think he was a little surprised that I had finished mine so soon, judging by the strange expression on his face. His glass appeared barely touched after only a couple of sips. He grinned quizzically at me.

"Would ye care fur a bit more?" he asked, somewhat amused.

"Sure, that would be nice," I said contentedly.

"As ye wish," Leif replied as he took my glass from me. He moved toward the sideboard and poured another glass, then handed the full glass to me.

I started sipping my port as he finished the last drop of his first glass. He stood from his chair and moved to place the empty glass on the stand. I was beginning to feel noticeably warm while sitting by the fire and sipping my wine. But the taste of the port was so delicious, I wasn't ready yet to have my glass placed back on the stand.

He returned in the direction of his chair, but strode past it toward me instead. I realized that I was beginning to feel a little different—not quite yet tipsy, but perhaps more relaxed as I pulled my glass from my lips. He knelt before me, and I felt his hand slip around my ankle as he proceeded to remove my pattens from my shoes. Then, he assisted me in slipping my foot from my damp shoe. Suddenly, I noticed myself feeling *really* relaxed. But I was simultaneously fully aware of my senses as I observed him carefully disengaging my second foot from my shoe and setting it aside with the other. I wiggled my freed toes and giggled slightly. Leif caught the tips of my playful toes in his grasp. My whole foot nearly fit inside his entire palm, I observed curiously.

"Yer feet are damp," he said, looking up at me again. His face was beet red, I could easily see.

"Yeah," I said, nodding my head a bit.

"It wouldnae be wise fur yer stockings tae remain, as they are too damp," he advised genuinely.

"No—I suppose not," I agreed. "I guess I could warm my feet by the fire."

"Aye, ye ought tae. However, yer stockings may not dry weel, and ye may git ill once ye return tae the cold," he said honestly.

"Oh, yeah, you're right," I replied thoughtfully. A quick thought suddenly occurred to me as I gazed back into his stellar blue eyes. I suddenly felt my temperature rise. "Well, I suppose I'll just have to remove them," I said. I didn't think Leif's face could get any more flushed, but it did. He cleared his throat, appearing slightly more in control.

"I was pondering that micht be reasonable," he said.

"Yeah," I responded. I carefully raised my petticoats to the bend of my knee and clasped the silk garter at the top of my stocking over my thigh beneath my skirts. I sensed his steady gaze on me as I untied my ribbon garters, fully conscious of what was starting to emerge between us. This was the first time we'd resumed spending time together alone since the misunderstanding we had several weeks ago.

I placed my garters beside me on the seat and started rolling the first stocking down my thigh and over my knee. I felt him gently move a helpful hand over my calf and take my stocking from me. He carefully removed it past my ankle and off my foot. The second stocking was removed in the same manner until he held the damp pair in his palm. He then leaned over to drape them over the arm of the chair close to the warm hearth.

When Leif returned his gaze to me, I could feel it happening again. The warmth and the yearning were apparent in his eyes. As I felt his admiring fingers discover my bare toes, I didn't think I had the strength within me to deny him this time if he asked me to do more than what we had already done.

"How is it that yer wee toes are so soft?" he commented, captivated.

"I don't know," I replied uncertainly, shrugging my shoulders a bit. His hands carefully clasped around my calves and warmly stroked upward over my knees. My skirts were being raised past my thighs, and I wondered about what was taking place.

"Whitever shall I do with ye, *àille dhubh*?" he said heatedly in a low tone. I shrugged again as he continued pushing my skirts high over my hips.

"What do you want to do?" I muttered cautiously. He simultaneously wedged my legs apart with his hips and fitted himself snugly between my thighs.

"I long tae kiss ye," he said with desire. I breathed unevenly, sensing him. He pulled me toward him decisively and firmly held me against his chest. "Do ye want tae?" he asked softly.

Of course I wanted to... but I was also slightly unsure.

"Yes," I admitted quietly, in spite of myself.

"Aye," he muttered as he lightly brushed his lips over mine and tenderly began kissing me.

"Mmm," I moaned as I kissed him back.

"Aye," he groaned. He slid his hand around mine and withdrew my wineglass from my grip. He set it on the oak-planked floor beside the sofa. I gently moved my wandering hands up over his sleeves, above his square shoulders, and around the back of his waistcoat, further drawing him into my accepting, full embrace. He pulled me tighter against him and locked me in his arms. His heated lips began moving more fervently over mine. I was helpless in my own desire and responsively kissed him back with the same intensity. At that point, the landslide had begun.

Leif's lips moved eagerly over mine and drifted passionately across my cheek and jaw, then down my neck. His slightly stubbled chin mildly scratched the side of my face as his lips trailed back up across my nose and lips. With one hand immersed in my hair at the back of my head and the other affixed unyieldingly around my back, he tugged me off the sofa and down onto his lap. My thighs straddled his hips. His hands gingerly moved upward over my bare legs, effectively raising my skirts scandalously high around my waist, completely exposing my lower half.

The touch of his caressing palms over my buttocks made my blood boil, and uncontrollably transformed my senses with expanding want and need for his closeness. I leaned into him even more, parting my lips, and allowed him to give me what he wanted to give as his tongue thrust sharply in a quenching kiss, causing me to gasp. He subsequently leaned to the side, coercing me to lie flat on my back on the black bearskin rug by the hot hearth, caging me beneath his formidable masculine frame.

"*Uhh!*" I uttered with bated breath when I abruptly sensed the familiar touch of his searching finger between my thighs.

"*Mmm,*" he heaved coarsely, close against my lips between his warm kisses. He began fondling me from within, quickly arousing my senses. At the rate he was going, I knew that I would not be able to hold on to myself much longer. Compounded by my own unbridled attraction to him, restraint was beginning to slip away from me like grains of sand through a sieve.

It was obvious that there was a real and raw carnal fascination between us, but there was also a nebulous magnetism that seemed more powerful, which inexplicably compelled us toward each other. I flung my palm down over his stimulating fingers between my legs, encouraging the rapturous sensation he was giving me and felt the breeching need to desperately climb toward the end.

"Aye, that's it, loove..." Leif mumbled in a hoarse voice over my lips. He leaned slightly back, still kissing me, and started untying the wide, pretty phthalo-blue silk ribbon lacing the front bodice of my velvet Jesuit. I sensed my bodice further loosening as his trembling fingers now worked to unfasten the front of my jacket.

In a moment, my bodice finally sprung free, exposing the top of my lace-trimmed shift beneath my stays. Leif abruptly released my desirous lips and shifted more upright. I felt his massive hand suddenly come gently over my right breast as his thumb discovered the stiffened nipple protruding beneath my sheer shift.

"*Och!*" he murmured breathlessly as his massaging hand found its way beneath my shift and over the warm skin of my naked breast. Suddenly, his mouth sealed over mine, instantly cutting off my breath as he shoved his hungry tongue between my lips once more. I sensed him trembling while he hovered over me and kissed me with deepening thirst.

The pace had swiftly gained momentum, and I thought he was going to consume me without so much as a mere thought when he vigorously inserted his finger as far as it could go between my thighs. I suddenly whined, longing to complete my disintegration.

"Do ye want me, *mo ghaol?*" I thought I heard him say when he whispered heavily against my lips. I was so intensely caught up in the escalating rapture happening to me that nothing else seemed to exist. Then, I felt Leif's hand unexpectedly stop over the little tuft between my legs, though his finger remained inside me. I opened my eyes and discovered him gazing concentratedly at me. His brow gleamed with tiny glinting beads of sweat. He was breathing heavily, and his body was shaking. "Do ye want me, Sylvie?" he asked tremulously. His face was ruddy as he gazed at me with sharp intensity.

"Yes," I gasped anxiously.

"Then, tell me so," he said coarsely. I supposed I felt a little surprised as he continued seizing my gaze with his. I hesitated. "Tell me—I need tae hear it from ye," he uttered thickly.

"I want you," I admitted breathlessly. Leif kept closely staring at me, enthralled, as if he didn't hear me. "I *want* you," I repeated with bated breath, feeling myself beginning to tremble beneath him.

"Aye…" he muttered, slightly nodding his golden head. "I've knoon fur some time now."

"You have?" I asked timidly.

"Aye," he replied softly. He carefully removed his hand from between my thighs and stroked my breast before he began gently stroking the arch of my eyebrow.

"Oh…" I whispered nervously.

"I must hear ye tell me so once more," he requested hoarsely.

"I *do* want you," I said to him again. The fire in his eyes suddenly billowed into an impassioned expression.

"Och, how I crave ye," he said hoarsely. I noticed just then that his accent had grown thicker. "If only ye merely kent hoo much I crave ye," he continued warmly. Leif leaned over, caging himself over me again, and returned to bestowing affectionate kisses on my lips as he inserted his finger inside me again. I moaned with yearning frustration between our kisses as I sensed his fingers withdraw from me.

"Will ye have me, Sylvie?" he heaved heatedly against my ear.

I knew at that moment, like a bolt of lightning striking me, that things had visibly manifested and taken on an uncontrollable life of their own. I knew what he wanted. I wanted the same thing.

"Yes—I'll have you," I panted longingly.

"*Och*," he uttered unevenly as if a tidal wave of unexpressed emotion had been allowed to course through the gates of a dam that would overcome him. He shifted slightly, and I sensed his hand move anxiously down below around his waist. He invisibly adjusted his breeches. Without warning, I felt him surge deep within me, coming up against the ceiling of my cervix.

"*Ughh!*" I gasped unexpectedly as he sheathed himself to the hilt.

"*Och!* Ye burn like searing honey," Leif moaned gruffly against my bare neck. His breath condensed warmly over my skin. He completely filled me from within with no margin for give. I thought he could surely hurt me if he unintentionally moved the wrong way. Except then he started slowly thrusting, and I felt him, completely. "Ye fit like a glove. So snug about me," he muttered above my lips. He started speaking softly to me in haunting scraping tones. He was saying gentle things in Scots that I couldn't understand. *"Tha gràdh agam ort... Ceisdein, mo ghaol... Ceisd mo chridhe..."*

Leif's voice came through so affectionately that I couldn't help but receive him, and I wrapped my legs securely around his waist, inviting him to do as he willed. He trembled, gently moving inside me and persuading my depths to ache for him. I felt unusually warm all over when my body began responding to each penetrating thrust of his shaft far inside me, and he felt like nothing I had ever felt before. I wanted him more than I'd imagined.

"Wait," I uttered suddenly, under my breath.

"Aye, *mo ghaol*?" Leif mumbled throatily in distant tones as he still tenderly propelled himself inside me.

"I might become pregnant," I gasped worriedly. Leif abruptly stopped moving. He didn't appear at all fazed.

"I ken the possibility," he said closely in a low voice. I stared up into his eyes, considerably surprised.

"Doesn't it bother you?" I inquired strangely.

"Nae," he responded surely.

"It doesn't?" I was amazed.

"The risk disnae trooble me," he whispered gently.

"Really?" I replied uncertainly.

"Aye." His response appeared genuine and affectionate.

"Oh," I responded, stumped for words.

"I dinnae mind ye bearing my bairn," he said.

"You don't?"

"Nae—the thought delights me."

Well... I didn't know what to say, except that I felt unpredictably comforted. So, instead, I smiled meekly at him, and he began tenderly kissing me once more. His lips soon grew feverish over mine again as his kisses started transforming from cautious inquiry into entitlement. Then, he began driving himself inside me again, this time with growing force as he asserted mindful power over me, and I ached badly for him.

Suddenly, without warning, a door opened unexpectedly somewhere in the house. Leif instantaneously froze over me. His enamored scarlet expression immediately changed into alerted alarm.

"Seamus! Whaur are ye, laddie?" Finley's unexpected voice echoed throughout one of the corridors as he unanticipatedly entered the house from the back door. Leif leaped off me like a cat pouncing out of water and sprang to his feet. At once, he gathered his breeches from around his ankles, tucked in his shirt, and buttoned his waistband. "I've come tae see ye, Seamus. Whaur micht ye be?" Finley obtrusively inquired as his tracking steps clucked determinedly over the hardwood floors, heading closer in our direction in the sitting room. He sounded impatient and purposeful. More footsteps were heard moving about the house, along with male laughter and chatter.

Leif immediately clasped my hand and brusquely whisked me up from the rug onto my toes.

"In haur, lass!" he whispered as he hastily pulled me across the room. He opened the door at the opposite end of the room and tucked me inside a small reading room. "Bide quietly in haur till I come fur ye," he said.

"Okay," I responded, shocked. I was aware of my heart racing in my chest. He swiftly closed the door, leaving me alone in the room. I could hear him promptly step away from the door.

"Och, haur ye are, brother," I heard Finley say from behind the closed door when he entered the sitting room. I silently stepped closer to the door and put my ear against it while I worked on fastening my bodice closed.

"Aye," Leif replied.

"Did ye not hear me calling efter ye?" Finley asked curiously.

"Aye—of coorse," Leif responded abstractedly.

"Then, whit kept ye?" Finley questioned with dissatisfaction in his voice.

"I was deterred," Leif replied.

"Deterred?" Finley asked.

"Aye," Leif replied simply.

"Humph! Weel—now that I have found ye," Finley started. I heard other people in the room with them also, but it was relatively difficult to distinguish through the solid wood door what was being said. So, I cracked the door open a little to listen better. "So, have ye yet spoken tae the lass?" Finley continued.

"Nae—not precisely yet," Leif responded uneasily.

"Whit does that mean?" Finley inquired.

"That I reckon I huvnae," Leif said.

"Ye reckon that ye huvnae?" Finley asked, sounding apparently disapproving.

"I huvnae had the proper opportunity," Leif responded.

"The proper opportunity?" Finley questioned doubtfully.

"'Tis difficult…" Leif hesitated.

"How difficult can it be, lad?" Finley seemed annoyed. Leif didn't answer.

"I believe that it is a delicate situation," Leif said finally.

"I dinnae perceive how it is a delicate situation," Finley said.

"Weel, it certainly is," Leif replied.

"In that case, we need tae simplify the matter, do we not?" Finley responded unpleasantly. Leif remained quiet on the other side of the door. I now started retying the fine silk ribbon at the front of my bodice and brought my jacket to a decent close. "I had the papers promptly drawn whilst in Boston. Thus, haur they are with me," Finley continued.

"I see—very weel," Leif said.

"So the matter is settled. The lads are haur tae witness," Finley said.

"Aye, I can see," Leif said.

"Aye," Finley said.

"Hullo thaur, lads," Leif greeted.

"Hullo thaur tae ye, Seamus," someone said.

"Aye, hullo tae ye, Seamus. How micht ye be?" someone else asked.

"Fair enough, thank ye. And yerselves, lads?" Leif inquired.

"We're grand," another man said.

"Och, guid," Leif replied.

"Now," Finley said.

"Aye, now," Leif responded. "I didnae realize ye lads waur going tae billet haur so soon."

"Aye, they are—certainly," Finley replied.

"Och—certainly," Leif echoed.

"We have run out of time now. Thaur is nae more use in dithering, as the matter has been settled. Ye do realize whit is tae take place tomorrow?" Finley inquired.

"Aye, of coorse," Leif replied.

"Weel, then, of coorse the lads are haur tae billet now. We must make certain that the Sacrament is done in an orderly manner that is correct before tomorrow," Finley said.

"Aye, of coorse, I am awaur of it," Leif said.

The brothers paused. I thought I heard feet shuffling around the room. Some low voices traveled unintelligibly through the thick door.

"We must get on with it," I heard Finley say in an exact, resolute tone.

"Yet the lass is ignorant tae the fact," Leif responded.

"Too much time has already lapsed. If thaur's aught that is going tae be done about it, then the time has come. The issue with Loudoun cannae wait," Finley said pointedly.

"I'm awaur of it," Leif replied.

"Very weel, then—she must sign these papers before the wedding," Finley said absolutely. Leif paused for a suspended moment. "Now, ye and Sylvina will wed, and it will be final," Finley said unquestionably.

"You ought to speak to the girl prior, lest she is disquieted," someone else said unexpectedly, who I did not immediately recognize.

"Nae more time weel suited than the present tae settle the matter, lad," Finley said firmly.

Well, by this juncture in the conversation, I was more than *disquieted*. I was stark raving livid! How *dare* they talk about me as if I had no say concerning the fate of my own life? And to top it off—to manipulate me into doing something I was dead set against!

I rudely barged through the door and entered the room. Suddenly, all eyes were on me—stunned with great surprise. I glared at all of their cousins standing there in the room, greatly astonished at what they were trying to coerce me into doing.

"Now you all just wait a *doggone* minute!" I charged excitedly. "I don't know what sort of crazy ideas have been running through your heads, but the buck stops here with me, and I'm getting off this wild train ride as of now! You listen to *me* now, because *boy*, do I have something to say! *News flash*—there is *no way* that I'm going to follow through with anything else that you say I have to do!

"I'm sick and tired of you guys pushing me around since day *one*! It's all you have ever done to me since you guys *shanghaied* me! You stole me and have held me hostage! *Un-believable!* You have bullied me into doing whatever the hell you've wanted me to do! *Telling* me what I can and can't do, where I can go—or can't! Running me like I'm some sort of *idiot* or naive kid! And now, you're continuing to manipulate me into marrying when I don't want to!

"And let me spell this out for you, since we're so *aptly* on the topic—I am an autonomous human being! I'm *beyond* tired of feeling like I can't *think* for myself and being treated like a second-class citizen! I have rights, you know?" I unloaded.

"Ye have nae reits! Ye will sign these papers and have done with it!" Finley interrupted abrasively.

"The hell I will! Yes, I *do* have rights! Inalienable rights endowed to me by my Creator! And I can choose to live my life the way I see fit—*not you*! You should be ashamed of yourselves for what you're doing to me! You are horrible, *horrible* men for scheming behind my back and *forcing* me into this situation! I don't like it—not one *bit*! And I don't like *you* for doing this to me!

"Now that you've heard from the peanut gallery, and have so *graciously* let me throw my two cents in, perhaps now I've got you dialed into my position on the matter!"

Once I had concluded my ranting tirade, I glanced around the room at the gawking, gaping mouths belonging to the utterly incredulous expressions surrounding me. Everyone was stunned categorically speechless as I recognized Angus, Cole, Derek, Fearghas, Lachlan, Liam, Bearnard, Derek, and Roy presently standing among the audience—victims of my wild harangue. My glance settled on Leif for a lapsing moment. He looked like a bomb had unexpectedly exploded in his face—completely shell-shocked and scarlet red—as he stood there near Finley, who also stared speechlessly at me with his jaw dropped.

"Who's he?" I asked abruptly when I suddenly noticed an unfamiliar man of lithe build and medium height.

"Claude Lefebvre," Finley informed me while clearing his throat from being bulldozed.

"*Bonjour, Monsieur Lefebvre*," I said calmly to him. I was surprised that I hadn't recognized the man. But I had only seen him a couple of times from afar on his property, and this was the first time we had met each other up close in person.

"*Bonjour, madamoiselle*," said the gaunt-looking fortysome-thing-year-old man in a kind, nonthreatening voice. Although, he appeared terribly shell-shocked too.

"Well, what's he doing here?" I asked freely, shifting my eyes back to Finley for an answer.

"He's a priest," Finley said stoutly.

"A *priest?*" My tone was more rhetorical than inquisitive.

"He's the only one who can rightly sanction the marriage," Finley informed me. Suddenly, a realization was dawning on me.

"So, uh, will you tell me, then, how soon you had intended for this wedding to take place?" I inquired.

"Promptly," Finley informed me.

"Like, *now?*" I questioned ironically.

"Aye," Finley said.

"Argh! Why don't you just club me over the head and *drag* me to your Neanderthal cave?" I retorted crossly, my angry gaze bouncing between Finley and Leif.

"*Alrecht!* That will be *enough,* lass! We have heard yer piece, now ye will *do* as *I* say and sign these papers reit now!" Finley exclaimed shortly.

"No! *I will not!* And you can't make me!" I said vexedly at him. "I quit! Do you hear me? I'm done! Finished with this! *Adios! Au revoir! Adieu! Auf Weidersehen! Arrivederci! Sayonara! Goodbye!* Get it?"

With that last verbal expulsion, I stormed out of the room through the hallway and stomped angrily up the staircase. I had not a clue where I was going in this unfamiliar house. But I was *going* somewhere—*anywhere,* just to get out of that room with those men!

When I arrived at the second story, I charged mindlessly through the corridor and automatically entered a random bedroom. I slammed the door behind me.

~

ABSOLUTELY CRAZY! I thought, as I paced angrily around the room. *I just cannot believe what they are trying to do to me!* Those men *never* considered my thoughts or feelings about anything—and I was just plain angry about it.

I realized that I was in deep *way* over my head. I plopped down, sitting on the edge of the strange bed, grumbling heatedly about all of this, and happened to notice a large Chippendale armoire in the corner of the room. The doors were ajar, and I could see that it was full of hanging clothes. There was a chaise lounge positioned not too far from it near the window with a pair of black breeches draped over the back. A pair of buckle shoes rested on the floor by the right front leg of the chair.

Oh, fantastic! I thought ironically—I had accidentally entered Leif's bedroom. How fitting… Of all the places to go, I ended up here.

It wasn't long after, while sitting alone and uninterrupted in my disgruntled state of mind inside Leif's bedroom, that I noticed the door handle began turning. The door opened and moved ajar, with Leif stepping forth inside the room. Our eyes met as he proceeded to close the door behind him.

"I don't want to talk to you right now," I said irritably as I heard the door click shut.

"Ye dinnae have tae speak tae me if ye dinnae wish," he said evenly. However, he still remained crimson, presumably from my hyper-spiel.

"Fine," I replied tightly.

"However, I *do* have something tae say tae ye, and I reckon 'tis yer turn tae listen tae me," Leif said resolutely as he moved across the room and sat on the cushion of the chaise. His imposing masculine stature seemed oversized for the moderate dimension of the chaise once he sat on it. He sat forward, slightly leaning his elbows on his spread knees with his hands clasped together. He had a perceivably grim and uncompromising look on his face. A sudden sense of apprehension silently came over me even as I stared determinedly back at him. "Now, I understand that ye may be feeling beside yerself," Leif started very seriously. "However, it was never our intention tae frighten ye or tae hurt ye... As ye have nae one tae claim ye, and perceiving that yoo're in peril with Laird Loudoun with nae one tae protect ye from him, or from anyone else fur that matter, it seemed fitting tae hold ye with us till we found a suitable situation fur ye... I apologize that yer feelings waur hurt. Nonetheless, ye must understand that Laird Loudoun seeks ye as we speak."

"What do you mean?" I asked abruptly.

"He has a warrant fur ye," Leif disclosed gravely.

"A *warrant?*" I echoed.

"Aye, he intends tae capture ye... and one disnae ken whit he will do if his hands seize ye," Leif explained, fatally serious.

"God! You've got to be kidding me. He's a corrupt megalomaniac, I'm sure of it," I said freely with some alarm. Leif's brows lifted high on his head.

"Whitever he is, he is knoon fur his certain determination and cruelty," Leif warned gravely.

"But what on earth could he possibly want with *me?*" I inquired. Leif faintly shrugged his shoulders, unwilling to respond. "I *swear* to you that I'm not a secret operative—I'm not a spy. I'm nobody," I assured him truthfully. Leif still just kept staring at me with a riveted, penetrating gaze without speaking a word for an extended minute.

"Weel... we are in a fix now, are we not?" he said finally.

"Yeah—it seems so," I replied, very troubled about this.

"Whitever the case, Laird Loudoun may also merely want ye fur himself," Leif said.

I sighed unbelievably. Leif also paused for a moment, letting his glance fall away from me down toward his folded hands. I gazed down at my own clasped hands in my lap, and vaguely began stroking my fingertips over the facets of my diamond ring.

"Yet," Leif started after a moment. I lifted my gaze toward him, and our eyes met again. "If ye waur tae wed..." His face softened a little from the sternness shrouding him. He seemed somewhat uncertain.

"Yeah?" I muttered.

"If ye waur tae wed, ye will be granted lawful rights and a measure of protection, as ye ken," he informed me.

"Oh—right," I uttered abstractedly. I noticed the expression on his face had changed. He suddenly seemed reticent and shy—maybe even a little embarrassed too.

"And ye may wed whom ye like. Ye dinnea have tae wed me if it isnae yer wish," he said as he appeared deflated.

"I see," I said simply.

"Thaur are plenty others who will have ye," he pointed out.

"You don't say?" I remarked with dissatisfaction.

"Aye, weel, Master Vinton, of coorse, is one who will certainly have ye fur his wife," Leif said.

"Yes, Mr. Vinton…" I commented unenthusiastically.

"Weel, he's quite smitten with ye."

"Yes, well… I'm not interested in him."

"Alrecht, then."

"Yeah, exactly."

"Fine. Then thaur is also young Master Hardy residing in Lexington, not too far away from haur. He will certainly rise tae the occasion and have ye fur a wife."

"Humph!"

"Whit about Angus?"

"*Angus?*" I responded ridiculously.

"Aye, he likes ye," Leif said.

"No way," I replied, shaking my head at the same time.

"Weel, Cole is also fond of ye," Leif offered.

"*Cole?* Are you kidding me? Absolutely not," I replied unequivocally. Cole was short, hairy, and bald, and a little on the tubby side. Also, he was crass with a vulgar mouth. He was definitely out of the question.

"Whit about Liam? He's charmed by ye," Leif suggested.

"No way," I said, rolling my eyes, unimpressed.

"Fearghus? He's fond of ye as weel."

"Nope. Not going to happen. He's just a kid anyway, and I'm not attracted to him."

"And—thaur is I," Leif suggested with disenchantment.

"Right…" I said.

"Ye will have tae promptly make yer decision—according tae the state of matters," he warned thoughtfully. "But—" He suddenly broke off.

"But what?" I urged.

"Weel… I presumed that—I thought ye waur fond of me," he said with disillusionment in his voice. The subdued expression on his face was clear disappointment.

"Well, I do like you. I *more* than like you, in fact," I admitted, feeling distressed.

"Then, I dinnae understand," he said.

"It's just that my life has been like a whirlwind since we've met. I mean, actually, you and I *just* met. We hardly know each other. We don't know what we're *really* like together. How do we know that we'll even get along eventually?" I said worriedly.

"I reckon that ye are correct. We have only met… However, my sentiment is that we may get on quite weel," Leif said.

"What makes you so sure?" I asked doubtfully. His expression suddenly went crimson. He seemed embarrassed.

"Weel… er… we have been close… Ye let me tooch ye. Why, merely a moment ago, we waur in the midst of—"

"I know, I know, *I know*," I interrupted nervously, suddenly feeling embarrassed too.

"In some respects, that already bonds us," Leif said.

"What are you saying?" I inquired.

"Mayhap ye may not consider the others due tae the fact that we ken one anither in a particular manner, and—" He stopped himself from continuing, appearing measured and pensive with a flushed expression.

"What are you telling me?" I asked.

"That I can presently assert my rights over ye, in which case ye will nae longer have tae trooble yer thoughts henceforth about this matter," Leif explained precisely in a careful way.

"You mean, because we fooled around, we consequentially could be considered married?" I inquired plainly.

"Aye," he said accordingly, nodding his head.

"But I didn't commit to you or anything like that," I responded anxiously. Leif's eyes suddenly became wide. He didn't at all appear indifferent, but instead certainly incensed.

"In a manner ye have committed tae me," he said overtly.

"But people have sex all the time, and it doesn't *mean* anything," I replied uneasily.

"Not according tae *my* principles," he responded, chafed, with obvious insult written all over his face.

"Well, I'm just saying people do. So—how do I know?" I said truthfully.

"And so, since we are discussing the matter, whit would ye do if we had finished our tryst, and ye discovered yerself with my bairn in yer belly without being wed tae me?" he asked earnestly.

"Well, I could manage—alone, I mean," I answered honestly.

"Alone, ye say?"

"Well, sure, I could."

"How? By whit means?"

"With my career. I have a career. Or at least I had one. But I could obtain one. I could support myself—and the baby—if it came to that," I said.

"Yer career?" Leif questioned doubtfully as he stared incredulously at me.

"That's right. I have a medical career that I could continue," I said. A light chuckle escaped his lips as he shook his head a bit.

"Aye, a medical profession—that only men acquire," he mocked.

"Hey, that's not fair," I responded, insulted.

"Mayhap it is not. But it is true. That is a man's profession."

"Well, I could manage it. Besides, there are plenty of women who rear their children by themselves."

"Do ye *truly* believe that I would bed ye without my consideration fur ye?" Leif asked sharply with a mixture of visible vexation and insult in his cutting crystal clear ultramarine eyes.

"I don't know," I responded unsurely, shrugging my shoulders a bit.

"I say!" he exclaimed, appearing very insulted. "I wouldnae have risked ye with possibly bearing my bairn if I had not intended tae wed ye—or keep ye."

"Keep me?" I frowned at him.

"Aye—fur my own—fur certain."

"Oh… hmm… well?"

"Weel?"

"Well, that might just be you, then. Other people could be of a different opinion and act accordingly. So, how am I supposed to actually know otherwise?"

"Is yer opinion of me so base?"

"No—it's not. I'm generally talking about others, not you specifically."

"I see. Weel, I believe a bairn needs a father and a mother tae be properly wed… Thaur are rules tae courtship, ye understand."

"Are there?"

"Aye, of coorse."

"Interesting."

"How so?"

"Well, for one thing, I'm guessing that you're actually not a virgin," I speculated. Leif's face quickly flushed.

"I am not—as it should be knoon," he acknowledged truthfully, gazing at me with an obvious, sober expression.

"So, you told me once that you had never been married," I recalled.

"That is true," Leif verified.

"Then, what happened to the last girl you were with?" I asked plainly.

"She was not mine tae wed," he disclosed.

"She wasn't?" I was significantly surprised to hear this.

"Nae." Leif's expression was open. He was being very candid with me right now.

"So, you had an illicit affair," I said, deducing.

"It was not quite like that," he said.

"Then what was it like?" I asked.

"She was a slave," he said.

"A slave?" I didn't think that I could have been more shocked.

"It was a long time ago—much longer than when I first arrived haur in America."

"I see… Well, go on—continue."

"She belonged tae a captain of a trading ship. She was his personal servant… On one occasion, I had been stricken with malaria when I was stationed in Guinea. She waited upon me, tended tae my health… She was nice tae me, and I tae her. That is the way it was," Leif revealed.

"I see," I responded thoughtfully. I paused momentarily, staring at him while I read his face. "So, you haven't had an intimate liaison since then?" I inquired finally.

"Aye, I have not," Leif said sincerely. I slightly nodded my head, pondering him. The fact that he claimed not to have had a sexual relationship with another woman for so long was substantially impressive, I considered. But a slave?

"So, was she the only one you had a sexual relationship with?" I continued.

"Nae," he replied, appearing honest.

"How many others?" I asked.

"Thaur waur three others," he admitted.

"I see. What happened to them?" I inquired.

"They waur courtesans," he said bluntly.

"Were they?" I replied with more surprise.

"Aye. I was a young, lonely soldier at the time whilst I was in France," he said.

"I see," I responded. Well, this tidbit of information was shocking and interesting. I wasn't sure how I felt about knowing this. I pondered him for a long minute. But I supposed I couldn't really judge him for it, because I understood in the time period where I was from how strangers became sexually intimate after as few as one date before they would have ever considered the idea of marriage. "But what about Constance?" I inquired doubtfully. I was compelled to ask. Leif sighed a tad, seeming weary of this particular subject.

"Once and fur all, we must lay this matter tae rest," he said resignedly.

"I agree," I said frankly.

"Thaur is entirely naught betwixt me and Miss Constance Pringle," Leif replied absolutely.

"But I saw you that day after church in the yard. You were holding hands," I said, remembering.

"Aye," he recalled, slightly nodding his head in agreement. "I was merely comforting her."

"Oh? How come?" I asked curiously.

"Pardon?"

"Why? I mean."

"She was weeping, since she had been dismayed," Leif explained.

"Why was she upset?" I inquired. Leif suddenly flushed slightly.

"Weel, er, she had conveyed her fondness fur me— " he was beginning to divulge.

"Uh-huh," I interrupted expectantly.

"Yet, as I've already told ye, I had expressed tae her, as weel as I could, that I wisnae suited fur her, since my feelings dinnae accordingly correspond with hers," Leif said.

"Right," I responded.

"I have nae feelings fur the lass whitsoever. I give ye my oath," Leif swore. He was convincing.

"Okay—I won't ever talk about it again," I agreed. He seemed relieved. The sincerity in his expression came through so unavoidably that I had no choice but to believe him. "Then tell me about Grete."

"Grete?"

"Yeah. Tell me about her."

"Thaur is naught tae tell."

"Well, the last time we were at the Rasmussens' house, I saw you two comfortably walking with each other," I recalled.

"Aye. Weel, she desired my company. But I am not fond of her either," he said.

"I see…" I replied contemplatively. "So, you're not interested in her?"

"Nae," Leif said, shaking his head a little. "The lass in whom I am interested is the one at whom I am presently staring and speaking tae."

"Oh…" I paused speaking for a moment, just thinking about him and the situation I was facing.

"Is thaur anything else trooblin' ye?" he inquired honestly.

"Yes, actually, there is," I admitted.

"Aye?"

"Well, I think you and I are two completely different people."

"Apparently," he acknowledged.

"Well, we *are*," I stressed seriously.

"I reckon I ken. Fur instance, ye are a bonnie lass, and I'm a man, evidently," he said.

"No, well, yeah, obviously," I responded unevenly. "But that's not what I mean."

"Then, whit do ye mean?"

"Well, you and I—I'm positive—come from diametrically opposing backgrounds."

"Quite possibly," he admitted.

"See?"

"Merely a wee bit—I dinnae suppose ye and I are *truly* opposing."

"But we have different ideas about things."

"Do ye suppose they are conflicting notions?" He gazed at me oddly with his brow slightly furrowed.

"Yes, I think so," I said.

"Weel, let me hear one of yer notions," he requested curiously.

"Okay, for example, and I'll probably shock you by saying this, but I have a much different perspective on a woman's place in society," I said.

"Is that so?" Leif replied.

"Yes, actually," I said undoubtedly.

"Will ye please be more specific?" he inquired quizzically.

"Sure. I think a woman should be able to freely speak her mind without consequence," I said. He paused, pensively pursing his lips with his brow knitted.

"Aye," he finally said.

"And women should be able to hold reputable professional positions without the approval of a man. You know—like have an honest career," I added.

"A profession? Like a man?" he replied with a novel expression on his face.

"Yeah." I detected one corner of his mouth tilting upward. It seemed he might have found me amusing. "I'm not being funny. I'm serious, you know?"

"Of coorse ye are—I plainly perceive yer earnestness," he said.

"Yes, well—that's what I think," I said.

"Do ye mean tae tell me, then, that ye seem tae reckon that a lass has the liberty tae earn a living as a man, although she may have a family or husband who will provide fur her welfare?"

"Why not?" I replied. A sudden chuckle escaped him. He was struck by the novel idea and appeared oddly entertained. "Lots of women work, you know?" I said with an insulted expression. Leif repressed his chuckling.

"Not by their own choosing. It is usually an occurrence forced upon women when thaur is nae other means fur survival," he replied.

"So? It still means a woman can honestly provide for herself," I said.

"Aye." The corners of his mouth curved upward as he silently gazed at me sitting across from him. I studied the amused look on his face.

"So, what do you think about a woman who can think and has opinions?" I asked.

"Weel, I reckon I raither fancy a wife tae be a thinker, and tae show her husband a bit of independent wisdom," he said thoughtfully.

"You do?" I replied doubtfully.

"Aye." Leif seemed genuine in his response.

"Oh…" I sat on the edge of the bed, thinking some more.

"Whit else?" he asked. I didn't know how to bring up this next topic, so I hesitated. Leif gave me an encouraging look.

"Well," I started, "I would really like to know what your view is on slavery."

"Och," he said as his brow lifted.

"Yeah, so tell me. What do you think of it?"

"Weel, slavery exists."

"Yeah?"

"Although, it is an abomination," he stated in an abhorrent tone.

"Mm-hmm."

"I dinnae entirely agree with the notion of slavery, and pray that one day all men may be free tae determine their own lives without punishment."

"I agree with you," I said.

"Aye," Leif responded.

A lull in our conversation ensued, and we sat silently together inside the bedroom. I pondered the situation before me. I didn't have much of an option, actually, as I thought about it. Being trapped in this time period with no means, or having the freedom to obtain any means, for my self-reliance, stuck with these men and being hunted by Lord Loudoun—what could I realistically do? I supposed marrying Leif wouldn't be such a bad idea. I mean, I was undeniably attracted to him, and we did share the same tender feelings for each other. Who really knew anything about what the future would hold for us anyway? Maybe it would work out nicely between us. He had never harmed me in any way, and had always shown fairness and kindness toward me. We seemed to have gotten along well so far. So, why would that change? I respected him, and he was a good, decent man. I supposed if I had to be forced into marrying anybody, it would likely be him.

"Micht thaur be anything else ye wish tae discuss?" Leif continued momentarily with a wondering gaze on me.

"Um—well, it might have helped if you had considered a more romantic proposal," I suggested.

"Pardon?" he asked.

"You know, getting down on one knee or taking a girl out on a romantic excursion to propose marriage," I informed him calmly.

"Och," he replied.

"Never mind," I said, dismissing the idea.

"Ye mean sledding wisnae enough?" Leif's expression subtly warmed with an encouraging little grin.

"No." I giggled faintly, a bit amused.

"Och. Weel, then, I apologize." The look on his face was warm and coaxing. I gave him a little nod.

"So…" I started thoughtfully.

"So…"

"You're really Catholic, then?"

"Aye, I am."

"But I thought you were Anglican."

"In appearance merely—I never swore my religious oath tae the Crown. Therefore, I remain true tae the Papist faith in my heart."

"Oh..."

"So, since ye and I are of the same faith, I reckon that we have that much more in common betwixt us."

"Hmm... I suppose so," I said, considering. Leif paused momentarily as it seemed another thought had crossed his mind.

"Do ye truly think me a terrible man?" he ventured after a second.

"No. I don't... I was just really angry," I admitted calmly.

"Och..." he said. He stopped speaking again. I could see that he was thinking. "I had wished tae speak tae ye about weddin' ye earlier, ye ken... except I wisnae certain if ye waur ready tae wed —or if ye wanted me fur a husband. The appropriate opportunity tae ask ye never seemed tae arise... I want tae wed ye, Sylvie. If ye will have me."

"Oh..." His words impaled me, and my heart expanded with admiration for him. I supposed he was right; the timing was always wrong to talk about anything serious between us. Also, I never thought that I would ever marry again until now. An easier silence fell between us now. I sat there before him, mulling it over in my head some more as I cast my gaze down to the luscious blue velvet skirts covering my knees. "Okay," I uttered under my breath after a lengthy period of contemplation, once again returning my gaze to him.

"Aye?" Leif lifted his eyes from his clasped hands and held my gaze.

"I'll marry you," I acquiesced.

"I beg yer pardon?" he inquired tentatively.

"I said, okay."

"Okay?"

"Yes. I'll marry you," I repeated gently. Suddenly, his face transformed. He cautiously stared at me with pending encouragement.

"Will ye?" he inquired uncertainly.

"Yes," I said sheepishly.

"Yoo're certain?"

"I am."

"Och! Ye greatly please me," he said happily. "Yoo're certain?"

"Yes. I am."

"Alrecht, then," he responded, looking abruptly pleased. All of a sudden, he straightened from his seat, beaming delightedly. "I shall let ye have a moment before ye return downstairs," he said.

"All right," I replied.

Leif swiftly moved toward the threshold and opened the door. He stepped out into the hallway, and in an instant, he had vanished.

CHAPTER 36

*A*fter a while, I finally gained the gumption to return downstairs and face my subjugators once again. The room was generally subdued with scant conversation among the men as I paced toward the sitting room. All eyes were on me yet again as Leif recognized me crossing the threshold, approaching him.

"Weel done. Come haur, lass," Finley said satisfactorily. Leif seized me with confidence by my elbow and reassuringly led me toward the letter desk where Finley was standing with the papers.

We arrived at the desk together and I noticed several large parchments sprawled over it. Finley dipped the quill into the inkwell.

"Sign haur," Finley instructed, holding the quill out for me to take as he pointed to the blank space at the bottom of the document. I quickly scanned the article and determined that it was a testimony certificate claiming the legal death of my late husband. My hand shook as I scribed my name in the empty space below. I was fully conscious of Finley's scrutinizing eyes hovering over me. Once I had finished signing it, he quickly shoved the next loose-leaf parchment in front of me.

"Ye have nae property, is that correct?" he inquired sharply.

"Yes, it is," I replied remotely.

"Sign it, then," he instructed. I signed it. The next one pushed in front of me was the marriage certificate. I watched my name emerge in black ink as I tremulously drew the quill across the parchment. Leif came around my side and gently withdrew the quill from my fingers. I watched surreally as he elegantly signed his name on the same parchment. "Guid," Finley said, satisfied, as Leif finished his signature. Leif submerged the tip of the quill back inside the inkwell. Finley swiftly collected the legal documents and rolled them into the leather tube once the ink soon dried. "Now, let's get on with it," he said, and gathered me by the arm. He led me around the front of the desk toward the center of the room.

Finley placed me next to Leif's right side as he was already standing before Father Lefebvre. I noticed Finley's hand lingering around my upper arm as I stood beside Leif. In fact, I sensed him hovering undeniably close to me with his broad chest at my back. I glanced to my left at Leif and noticed the concentration on his flushed face.

Father Lefebvre drew forth his missal. He cupped it in his hands, with his rosary entwined and dangling between his fingers. Leif proceeded to kneel, and at his indication, I followed suit. Father Lefebvre began in Latin as he opened with the familiar sign of the cross and blessings. Although I did not fully understand the spoken language of the Vatican, I instinctively knew through a lifetime of experience the procedures of a Catholic Liturgy.

I remained there, kneeling closely next to Leif, tremulous in utter disbelief. The idea of marriage in and of itself was enough to be nervous about, but to be married three centuries in the past was mind-boggling. I was essentially in the process of being forced to give up my hope of ever returning home, irreparably closing the door to my former existence, and ultimately sealing my fate in the past.

It hit me like a bolt of lightning; I had become fixed in time.

A hot flash unexpectedly came over me, quickly followed by sudden frigidness. Again, the hot flash returned, followed by a chill. It became a little hard for me to breathe. My head started feeling funny, and Father Lefebvre, standing in front of me, became slightly hazy. My body temperature rose and dropped alternately as I struggled to steady my breathing. But my breath only grew shallower, and the room strangely started to spin. Then, oddly, the room seemed to tilt.

"Nae, ye dinnae, lass," Finley muttered under his breath against the back of my head. Suddenly, the room straightened as I noticeably felt him buttressing me from behind.

Leif glanced anxiously at me as I sensed him taking my left hand in his. With my hand clutched determinedly in his, he stretched our palms out before the priest. Father Lefebvre draped a simple vestment cloth over our joined hands and continued sanctifying us in Latin. Subsequently, he reverently paused and gazed at Leif, affording him some allowance. Leif started to speak in Scots, and the words rolled from his tongue. He was pledging himself to me with stalwart conviction.

My ears seized on his name, *Leif Charles Seamus MacLeod Fitz-James Stewart,* and it echoed throughout my brain like a hammer as I stared at him, aghast. A sudden icy-cold chill shot down the middle of my spine like electricity, arresting my heart in the span of a beat. My blood ran frosty through my veins. My very breath was stolen from deep within me as I knelt there listening to and watching what was taking place.

My body buckled, but I was spared from collapsing onto the floor by Finley's quick grip on me. Leif glanced uneasily at me as Finley held me tightly. I observed Leif withdrawing the little red ruby ring he wore on his pinky finger. He reached for me and took my left hand in his. I watched Leif slip the ring on my ring finger above my wedding band that Matt had given to me.

My mouth had grown dry, and suddenly I was very parched.

"'Tis yer turn now, lass. Repeat efter the priest," Finley instructed close to my ear.

I took a couple of dry swallows. I found my faint breath and began to repeat after Father Lefebvre in English, "I, Sylvina Leilani Engel Cielo Esperanza, now take you, Leif Charles Seamus MacLeod FitzJames Stewart, to be my husband. In the presence of God and before these witnesses, I promise to be a loving, faithful, obedient, and loyal wife to you, until God shalt separate us by death."

After I had vowed myself to him, I caught the sight of something glinting being passed to him from his left side by Angus. The shining silver nine-inch officer's dirk was turned over in Leif's hand, and he sliced the inside of his right palm. I watched in horror as he brought the point of the blade above me and hovered the piercing tip merely five fatal inches away from my heart, all the while vocalizing coarsely in Scottish. Then, without warning, he caught my right wrist and tugged it affirmatively toward himself. The blade turned in the direction of my captured hand. He abruptly raised it above my wrist, poised for the plunge.

"What are you doing? Are you *crazy?*" I gasped, terror-stricken, successfully yanking my palm from him. Finley invisibly snatched my hand, suddenly recapturing it with certainty, and abruptly shoved it forth for Leif to take again.

"Quit yer wreathing, lass," Finley ordered unyieldingly. Making sure to assist Leif, he continued clutching my hand and locked it in his grip. "Finish it, lad," he told Leif.

"No! Don't!" I gasped, horrified.

All of a sudden, Leif raised the blade again. The look on his face was intense and filled with determined conviction. His eyes were wild. It was as if something else had taken him over, and he appeared bizarrely crazed while chanting in Scots. The words came from deep within him as he uttered them closely in guttural undertones. I had no idea what he was saying, but the hair on the back of my neck rose as if static electricity had crossed my skin. My blood chilled. He was appealing to something not remotely belonging to my world. His voice resonated, invoking something from an ancient past. The words expelling from him began taking on life and abruptly manifested as the sharp blade came down over the inside of my right palm, parting the flesh.

I flinched at the slicing pain as ruby-red blood swiftly emerged from the half inch incision on my palm. I thought my consciousness would leave me as I observed the stained blade drift into Angus's grasp. But I was further suspended as Leif continued fastening his left hand around my injured palm and lifted my wrist above my gaze toward his lips.

It took me a slight moment to realize that I was currently gazing at Leif's own bleeding palm held steadily before my eyes. Then, his bloodied right palm clasped over mine like a melding vise, and our blood mixed. The idea revolted me. It was medically ill-advised, and I didn't want to do this. Except there I was, kneeling before everyone closely watching me in clear anticipation. What else could I do?

He raised our hands, affixed in primal union. After, he concluded by summoning the last of his native words in a throaty resonance.

Presently facing each other before the priest and our witnesses, I sensed Finley release his unyielding grip on me as he moved to wrap a white linen handkerchief around our hands. When he had finished, he uttered something in Scots in a softer tone and then returned to kneeling beside me.

Subsequently, Father Lefebvre continued with the Offertory and we received Holy Communion. After the Eucharist, Father Lefebvre consecrated the holy sacrament of marriage with a final blessing and concluded, *"In nòmine Patris et Fîlii et Spîritus Sancti,"* in Latin with an aerial sign of the cross over our heads as we also crossed ourselves.

"Amen," Father Lefebvre said reverently in conclusion.

"Amen," Leif said deferentially.

"Amen," I repeated automatically.

Now that it was over, Finley gathered me to my feet from my kneeling position as Leif shifted and straightened upright. My knees felt like they had been frozen in an arthritic lock and ached as I stood.

"Weel done, lass," Finley said approvingly, and gave me a couple of supportive pats on my shoulder. The other men gladly followed suit with their votes of encouragement. They gave us enthusiastic congratulations as they heartily slapped Leif on the back and mussed his hair.

The house quickly erupted with echoing cheers as whiskey made a sudden appearance among the men. I was feeling queasy with an unsettled stomach as Leif unraveled the kerchief from around our joined hands. He began carefully rewinding it over my lone palm. My head felt floaty, and I thought Leif's affectionate grin looked a bit fuzzy to me.

Then, in an instant, everything disappeared.

I AWAKENED to the sensation of a damp cloth gently dabbing my brow and discovered Leif gazing attentively at me at close proximity. I could detect some concern on his face.

"What's wrong?" I asked dazedly.

"It seems that ye had a fit of the vapors," Leif informed me as I felt his fingertips gently stroking the side of my cheek.

"Oh," I said as I suddenly remembered everything.

"How do ye feel at present?" he inquired concernedly.

"I feel okay, I think," I replied.

"Ye ought tae quietly remain resting haur shortly before we

rejoin the household fur Thanksgiving dinner," he suggested thoughtfully.

"Okay," I agreed. It sounded like a really good idea. Aside from still feeling drained, I continued to remain significantly overwhelmed.

"Very weel, then," he said. I felt his hand spread over the side of my abdomen just around my waist. "Yoo're a brave lass, *mo ghaol*," he said proudly.

"Don't give me too much credit," I responded lightly.

"I'll give credit whaur credit is warranted," he said.

"Well, thank you for saying so," I said.

"Indeed. Now, ye must rest weel this evening. I dinnae wish fur ye tae undergo a similar bout tomorrow," Leif warned.

"Tomorrow?" I asked curiously.

"The rest of the wedding ceremony will take place fur all the family tae witness," he explained.

"What?" I asked, surprised.

"Aye, tomorrow is Friday and 'tis all prepared," he said.

"So quickly?"

"Aye, of coorse," he replied.

"But we already had a priest marry us—I don't understand," I said confusedly.

"In private is the only way it had tae be done betwixt us, fur ye ken it is against the Crown tae be Papists," Leif said.

"Oh, right, of course," I replied naively.

"Therefore, it must be done acceptably as weel fur all tae witness," Leif said.

"Right," I said, feeling floaty when I remembered the bandage wrapped around my hand. I sensed Leif moving his hand over my injured palm as I gazed up at him from the pillows. He affectionately enfolded his hand over my covered knuckles and lifted them close to view. Brightly colored, fresh blood seeped through the cloth, staining a large area at the center of my palm. He gently pressed my exposed fingertips to his lips and kissed them. Then, he drew my fingers away and gazed intently at me.

"Dinnae be troobled, *àille dhubh, mo ceisdein*, it is done. Ye wulnae have tae do it again," Leif said affectionately.

"Okay," I muttered, rather relieved.

"Yet I still await the king's formal blessing," he said.

"Oh. So, what does that mean?"

"It means we carry on as planned whilst we await word from His Majesty."

"Oh—okay… So, he has to sanction it?"

"In a manner."

"Oh… But what if he doesn't approve it?"

"The king cannot undo whit has been done by God."

"Yeah, but on paper he can null and void it, right?"

"Dinnae concern yerself, *mo ghaol*. I am quite optimistic about the king granting me permission, as there is little that will concern him in this regard."

"I don't understand."

"I dinnae belong tae the House of Hanover, and am not in line tae succeed the throne. It is out of mere courtesy that I seek the king's blessing."

"Oh, okay." I didn't understand his explanation and was still confused about why he needed the king's permission in the first place.

"Now, I shall leave ye tae rest more till I fetch ye fur dinner," he told me.

"Okay," I agreed. I felt depleted and could surely use what little rest I was afforded.

"Very weel," he concluded as his fingers gently remained cupping the side of my face, with his thumb placidly stroking the ridge of my jaw.

Leif leaned over and placed a couple of nice, soothing kisses on my lips. Then, he raised his affectionate gaze to me once more.

"I shall see ye later," he uttered softly.

"All right," I responded with the same affection.

I quietly watched him as he straightened from my bedside and strode across the room until he vanished behind the door. I heard his solid footsteps diminish on the hardwood floors in the corridor. Then, I closed my eyes.

CHAPTER 37

$\mathcal{L}$ ater, Leif returned to his room, and I was awakened from dreaming when my eyes focused on his warm face. He smiled as I suddenly gazed at him, a little startled.

"Oh, hi," I said softly.

"Hullo, lass," he said. I started shifting up from the pillows.

"Is it time to go already?" I asked, feeling a tinge disoriented.

"Aye, we must make haste. I wished fur ye tae rest as long as permitted. Yet presently we must take our leave," he informed me.

"Okay," I replied simply. He already had my dried stockings and shoes gathered between his fingers. He promptly assisted me in placing the stockings over my legs and initiated slipping my shoes over my toes.

With my feet suitably dressed again, I proceeded to follow him out of the bedroom back through the hallway down the staircase. I noticed the house was now significantly quieter as we came down the stairs. I wondered where the entire ruckus had gone. I happened to catch a glimpse out the window in the foyer and saw the animated crew had already started making their way across the snow.

When we promptly arrived near the front door where our outerwear had been placed hanging on the pegs, Leif swung my cape over my shoulders, and I buttoned it protectively around my neck. He then turned for his greatcoat. He proceeded to button it closed over his chest and wrapped a scarf around his neck. I quickly tied the ribbons of my winter bonnet beneath the back of my head as Leif had just finished covering his head with his tricorn hat.

We promptly stepped from the front door out into the twilight winter cold and began making our way across the snow. The sun rays streaked in illuminating cadmium red, yellow, and orange hues against the clouds, which appeared like ribbons suspended high in the atmosphere. The sky had been set aglow. The streaking clouds seemed like liquid gold veins floating in the air, superimposed on a dimming blue sky. The moon already hovered brilliantly like an incredibly massive white orb over the horizon through the dormant trees. The earth seemed ablaze, like after a volcanic eruption. The blanketing iridescent snow reflected the sky across the landscape, and it all appeared beautiful and primitive above our heads.

We trailed several yards behind the others for most of the journey back toward the mansion. It seemed Leif was in no hurry to catch up to his buddies and was comfortable walking at our own pace. I felt his palm steal over mine, and I smiled at him as we paced quietly together. His eyes twinkled as a warm grin curled his lips when he glanced down at me, and my body tingled as butterflies fluttered in my stomach. It took us a good fifteen minutes to clear our way through the snow and arrive just in time to join the rest of the family at the main house for Thanksgiving dinner.

The mood inside the house was pleasant and modest as Leif and I sat close next to each other, surrounded by family and friends at a large dining room table. Once Mr. Buckingham, the family patriarch, had said grace over the food, the meal began, and conversation flowed light and merry across the table. The dining table was bountiful with enticing Thanksgiving food. I recognized the roasted turkey and salted ham at the center of the table. There was also venison and an unfamiliar onion sauce prepared for the turkey. There was stewed pumpkin, recognizable skillet cranberries, unknown Marlborough Pie, and hasty pudding. While scanning the appetizing meal, I noticed that Mr. Claude Lefebvre was strangely not among our surrounding guests, and I wondered about his absence.

"I thought Mr. Lefebvre would have joined us," I said discreetly under my breath to Leif.

"Nae," Leif replied in the same subdued manner.

"Why not?" I inquired innocently.

"He has already taken his leave," Leif informed me.

"Oh… We should have thanked him though," I whispered regretfully.

"He received an acceptable donation fur his trooble," Leif murmured.

"Oh," I said faintly. I sensed Leif's hand steal carefully over my hand on my lap beneath the table. His hand stroked up my fitted sleeve around my wrist, and his fingers enfolded it. He gave me a tender squeeze of assuredness as he glanced admiringly at me.

"I shall like to send my best wishes to our betrothed couple sitting amongst us," Mr. Buckingham said unexpectedly as he gazed directly at us from the head of the table. Conversation around the table quieted, and attention was drawn our way.

"Thank ye, Master Buckingham," Leif responded kindly.

"We were quite pleased to have learnt of Your Grace's good news upon your brother's return from Boston," Mr. Buckingham said favorably.

I shot Leif a sidelong glance with internal surprise; evidently this wedding had already been planned well in advance without my knowing. *Your Grace...* What a strange thought; I had become the Duke of Monteith's wife.

"We have been most curious about your betrothed, and we can see she is quite lovely," Mr. Buckingham stated politely.

"Thank ye, Master Buckingham," Leif replied. Mr. Buckingham smiled plainly.

"Indeed, Your Grace," he said. "However, we have been surprised by Amity and are significantly impressed with ha unexpected enlightenment."

"Aye, Sylvina and Amity have developed a close understanding as a result of her tutelage. She has introduced tae her the technique of sign language," Leif explained.

"I see," Mr. Buckingham said curiously, while everyone else around the table appeared to be listening intently.

"Aye," Leif said.

"Tell me, what is sign language?" Mr. Buckingham inquired.

"'Tis whereby a system of hand signals are used tae communicate specific meaning," Leif further explained.

"Most curious," Mr. Buckingham said.

"It will be used with the intent tae permit her ability tae read and scribe," Leif informed him.

"I see. Well, that will be quite impressive," Mr. Buckingham said with amazement. He then shifted his interested eyes toward me and looked at me closely. "Might I inquire how you have come about such interesting and beneficial knowledge?" he asked.

"I once had the fortunate opportunity to learn from an instructor who specialized in the hearing impaired," I answered politely.

"Impressive," Mr. Buckingham said with marvelous approval.

"She appears lovely and useful at the same time," he observed. "My felicitations to Your Grace and to the good wife you will have."

"Thank ye, Master Buckingham," Leif replied.

"Well, we are indeed much anticipating the wedding celebration tomorrow," Mr. Buckingham said gladly.

"Aye, deah, you must not overexert yourself with excitement this evening, fah you will have much to contend with for tomorrow's celebration," Mrs. Buckingham added carefully.

"Yes, certainly," I agreed as I turned my gaze to meet Mrs. Buckingham's bright expression at the opposite end of the table.

"Elizabeth, you must see to it that she is not disturbed this evening. She must receive ha proper rest," Mrs. Buckingham instructed her daughter.

"Aye, Motha," Elizabeth said, consenting dutifully.

"Aye, we must see to it," Mr. Buckingham concurred. "We shall pray not to incur a similar occurrence of a bout with the vapors that took place auva Susie before we stepped foot inside the church on that splendid wedding day."

"Nay, Fatha. We shan't want that to occur," Suzanna agreed demurely as her cheeks turned pink. Leif and I exchanged surreptitious, knowing glances.

"Well, my best wishes to the happily betrothed couple. Let us not incur a hapless morrow and wish fah a swift nuptial exchange," Mr. Buckingham concluded as he merrily raised his port wineglass.

"Hear! Hear!" sounded out the male members around the table, and wineglasses promptly tilted upward to everyone's lips, supporting the toast.

THAT EVENING I lay in bed inside my bedroom upstairs, listening to the merry chatter from family and guests echoing from below. Leif was still downstairs enjoying himself with the rest of them. Sometimes I could hear his pleasant voice travel in muffled tones from behind my door as he moved below among the other rooms. I knew that I wouldn't be seeing him tonight.

I remembered the injury my palm had suffered earlier today. I slightly lifted my bandaged hand into view and saw that the bright red blood stain covering the lower half of the dressing had now turned brown and completely dried. It was a pretty dramatic and frightening thing that Leif had done to me, and I wondered why he did it.

I wasn't exactly sure how I felt about it. There was an unmistakable part of me that was immensely upset over the injury he had caused me, and yet, so strangely, there was an equal part of me that could not resent him at all for it.

I caught a glimpse of the ruby-red ring he had retrieved from his own hand and had placed upon my wedding finger. It was extremely beautiful, I thought. The perfect princess-cut faceted stone was set attractively in a solid gold band. The stone was encircled and fastened by an intricate engraving of an infinite ring of overlapping and interconnected looping lines that formed a never-ending circular Celtic knot. There was a series of three tiny individual amethyst stones attached at the base, forming a semicircle set on each side of the centered ruby stone.

I lightly stroked my fingers over the stones and noticed my other ring. I held them both above my eyes, and they both sparkled in the candlelight. The two-carat multifaceted pink cushion-cut diamond in its platinum Tiffany setting was set off like firelight against the subdued very lovely alizarin-crimson princess-cut ruby. The rings were individually mesmerizing, and each had adhered to my finger according to their own separate right. But Matt was gone. I would never see him again, no matter what, unless it was in Heaven, though he remained alive here in my heart. The feeling came to me now, and I thought it was time for me to let go of him, finally, after nearly four years of grieving —and so I removed the rings from my finger. I placed the ones Matt had given me on my right hand and replaced the one Leif had given me on my left ring finger again.

I continued to gaze at the rings on my fingers for a moment

longer, thinking how could all of this be? I let my rings fall from view, and I turned onto my side, completely consumed by the secret major event of the day. Discombobulated, abstracted, and incomprehensibly overwhelmed, I heard Leif's Gaelic tones run like a looped sound bite in my head.

Leif Charles Seamus MacLeod FitzJames Stewart…

How is this at all possible? How is it that, as I live and breathe, I can be here experiencing this? I'm not a widow anymore. I'm not married to Matt any longer; death and time have severed us, except for the memory and love that I still hold for him. And now, I'm married to Leif. And I hardly know him. But he's good, gentle, and kind to me. We're inextricably bound now in this ironic twist of fate. Our past, present, and future are entwined. I can't believe this is happening to me… I feel so out of control. Everything has turned upside down, and I can't tell which way is right side up. Leif… Is he for some reason for why I'm really here? I wonder if I can ever go back home? Am I ever going to see my family and friends again? What's going to happen to me now? It's hard to determine what the answers are when I am pulled between time, my past in the future and my future in the past. But what I do know for sure is that my tender feelings for Leif are real; I have fallen for him in spite of everything. If anything, that's something I can hold on to in this chaos that I'm in.

As thoughts swirled in my head while anticipating tomorrow, I finally submitted to the weight of my emotional exhaustion and tried to rest for the night, slipping into slumber. Taken.

THANK YOU FOR READING!

Curious to know more about Leif and Sylvie? There is more to come in the following novel *Hummingbirds Know Where to Fly* which continues their story.

Join the author's email list to receive newsletters for whenever E. C. Roderick publishes a new book, and more. Happy reading!

Scan QR code with phone to link to author's mailing list.

ENJOYED THE BOOK?

You can make a difference! If you enjoyed this book, it would be greatly appreciated if you would spend a few minutes to leave a review on the book's retailer page found on the website where you purchased the book. A simple written line or two for your review would be helpful in spreading the word. For ebooks, click the link below to find your retailer. For print books, scan QR code to find your retailer. Thank you so very much!

Scan QR code with phone for book retailer link.

ACKNOWLEDGMENTS

The story of Leif and Sylvie was a long time in the making between raising a family and writing, and I couldn't have produced this novel without the help of some very significant people who I would like to thank. First and foremost I thank my husband, Alan, who believes in everything that I do. Without your support this story would have never been written. I am immensely grateful that you encourage me in all of my creative endeavors and have inspired me to create them. I love you.

I also thank my editor, Tiffany Tyer, for all of her helpful notes and for her keen eye and attention to detail in making my manuscript read smoothly.

Thank you to Mary Ann Smith for creating such a perfect cover design for this story.

And last, but not least, to my readers. Thank you for taking a chance on my debut novel. Without you I would not be able to proceed with bringing you more stories to enjoy and to continue to do what I love while being with my family.

Thank you!

ABOUT THE AUTHOR

E. C. Roderick is an award winning, emerging author of romance fiction. TAKEN is her debut novel which begins the saga of Leif and Sylvie. As a classically trained fine artist who taught painting to adults and children for many years, she also spent time writing while raising her children.

When she isn't chasing after her children, or creating with a paintbrush, she is creating with her pen, developing strong characters in their environment for readers to enjoy.

Scan QR code with phone to connect with E. C. Roderick.

www.ingramcontent.com/pod-product-compliance
Lightning Source LLC
Chambersburg PA
CBHW061336190726
48288CB00005B/1478